Leagues
Aalholm
Komar
Isles
Ro'Arith
Orlis
Mocley
Velvithia
The
Endless
Ocean

1468/1500

# The Genesis of Oblivion Saga
by Maxwell Alexander Drake

## Book One
*Farmers and Mercenaries*

Maxwell Alexander Drake

# Farmers & Mercenaries

Book One of the
Genesis of Oblivion Saga

I.I.I.
fantasy

Imagined Interprises, Incorporated
Las Vegas

This is a work of fiction. All the Characters and events portrayed in this novel are either fictitious or are used fictitiously.

THIS BOOK IS PUBLISHED BY
IMAGINED INTERPRISES, INC.


Jacket art by Lars Grant-West

Illustrations by Maxwell Alexander Drake



Content Editor - Patrick LoBrutto
Line Editor - Jo Wilkins
Proof Editor - Loraine Stalians

Published in the United States by Imagined Interprises, Inc.,
6955 N. Durango Dr. Ste. 1115-717
Las Vegas, NV 89149
I.I.I. fantasy is a registered trademark of Imagined Interprises, Inc.
Genesis Of Oblivion is a registered trademark of Maxwell Alexander Drake

www.imaginedinterprises.com

ISBN: 978-0-9819548-1-3 (Collector's Edition)
First Edition: May 2009
Printed in the United States of America

*As this is my first novel, you have to suffer through a long-winded dedication page, so here it goes...*

*First and foremost, I want to thank all the professionals who helped, in large ways and small, for making this series a reality. Patrick LoBrutto for giving me courage, Jo Wilkins for giving me direction, David Compton for giving me confidence – though he may not even remember me, Lorraine Stalians for giving me encouragement, and the Henderson Writer's Group for giving me my first fans.*

*My heart also goes out to "The Group" – Paul, Jon, Ethan, Nick, and Kane. Without you having been in my life, I would not have had the imagination to create this. Always remember that a day does not pass without you being in my thoughts as well as my heart.*

*To those who gave me the spark for the love fantasy, Chuck, Shane, and Jonathon. I will always cherish our night-long gaming sessions. Though we have not seen each other in many a year, I hope that you have found all the adventure you sought as a children.*

*Finally, to my family. To my Grandparents and Mother for their continued support, both emotionally and financially. My lovely wife, who is the Joy of my Life. And my two boys, who are more than worth "paying what needs be paid."*

MAD

# Contents

# Farmers & Mercenaries

# PART ONE
# A Day in the Life

*Some say destiny is set, and you will do*
*what you were born to do.*

*Others say destiny is what you make of it.*

*I say, destiny is a word, in a vast dictionary,*
*with many different definitions.*

*All you have to do is choose the one*
*definition that fits into*
*the sentence that is your life.*

MAD

# Mocley

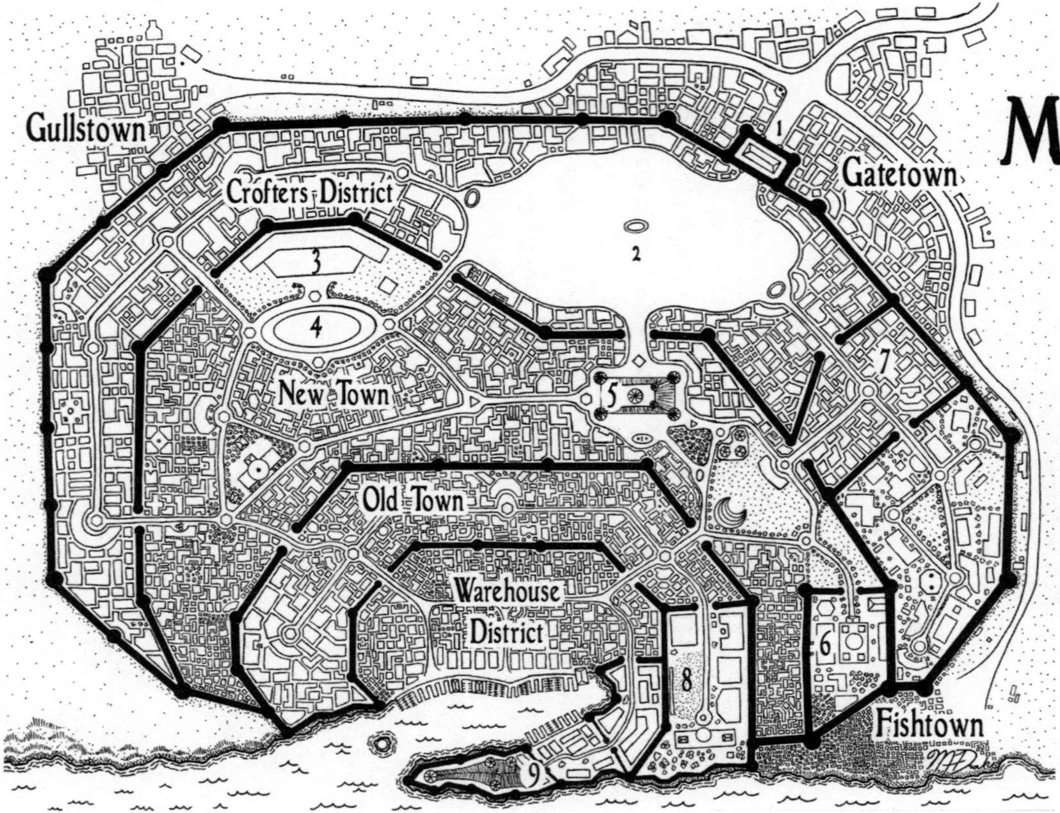


Legend
1 Main Gate
2 Bazaar
3 Gladiatorial Compound
4 Coliseum
5 Palintium
6 Chandril'elian
7 Merchantillian
8 Magistra
9 Proctor's Residence

# Chapter 1

Rolling onto his back, he laid back down on the hard stone slab that formed his bed and glared at the stone ceiling. Its wooden support beams stretched out like the fingers of a giant hand. Sleep had come little to him over the previous eve. Once more, he wondered how it would feel to have the ceiling come crashing down, ending his suffering, and releasing him from his burdens.

*I never rest well before a fight.*

Tilting his head, he squinted at the early morning light spilling through the bars of the tiny window set high in his cell wall. Dust motes danced above the dingy floor.

*Curse you, Lords of the Dark. Why must you retreat from dawn's light each morn?*

His muscles made their usual complaints. The pain in his right shoulder burned like a festering evil, nagging at him continuously. The wound causing this annoyance was a souvenir from a man whose body now fed the worms. Knots had formed during the eve as well. The combination of these irritated him and fueled his foul mood. Rolling to his side, he pushed himself off the rags that served as his bedding and swung his hindpaws to the straw-covered stone floor. The dank smell of urine wafted in through the small barred widow on his cell door, saturating everything.

*Filthy Humans!*

Reaching up, he massaged a kink from his upper back

and shoulder. While sleep eluded him, he had forced himself to endure an extra aurn of training. The dirt from the dingy cell mingled with his sweat, matting his fur in several places. Running his sharp claws through the tangles, he worked at combing them out.

*I need no matted fur beneath my armor this day. Provided the Julitans of the Games even allow me to wear armor.*

"Beast!" A bellow rang out from the hallway.

Focusing on the barred window set in the center of the ironbound-oaken door, he scowled with hatred as the bloated dark-skinned face of his Keeper popped into view. "My name is Klain, you hunk of pig dung!" Although Klain spoke no other tongue, his guttural growl made the Human words seem foreign even to *his* ears.

Baring his front fangs, Klain spat on the floor.

"Aye, mayhaps. Alas, the crowd will chant for the *beast* this day. They shall no sing your praises." The Keeper chuckled and leaned his forehead against the bars. "And they do care less than I of what your name be." Exposing a mouthful of rotted teeth, the man's dark black lips split into a wide grin. Chuckles turning into howling laughter, the Keeper withdrew from the window. "They do wish only to watch the Kith beast fight—and die."

A small slot at the bottom of the door opened and a tray of raw meat slid into the cell. Glancing at the Keeper who once again looked through the window, Klain knew his confusion was obvious by his opened-eyed expression.

"Aye, beastie, tis fresh. Twas slaughtered this morn. The Master did say to give his Kith beast a good, final meal. This day I do think you earn him back all the ta'narians he did spend on you these past few turns of the seasons." The black man turned, disappearing from Klain's view. The Keeper's laugh echoed along the stone corridor as he wandered down the hall smacking other cell doors in passing. The mumbled complaints from the occupants of those rooms increased the delight in his laughter.

Alone once more, Klain sat and stared at the dish resting on the dirty floor. His first impulse was to refuse the fresh meat.

His mouth watered over the rare delicacy he had enjoyed only once before during his short life.

*I will* not *give the Master pleasure thinking he has given his* pet *a treat.*

His heart boiled with rage. Within moments, however, he relented. He would need the extra energy it would give him for the tasks awaiting him this day.

*Besides, the fat pig could be correct. This may well* be *my final meal.*

With a grunt, he leaned over and snatched up one of the hindquarters by its protruding bone. He brought it close to his face, hoping to drive the stench of the dungeon from his nose, if even for a moment. His whiskers bristled.

*Lamb! Fresh, as the pig said.*

Klain sank his fangs into it, allowing the blood it still held to drip onto his chest fur. He fended off the urge to rush. Instead, he ate leisurely, savoring the flavor of the raw meat.

*The Julitans of the Games have planned my day. There is no need for me to hurry. My Keeper will come for me when the* Julitans *deem it right. I will be equipped with whatever pleases* them. *All for the amusement of* their *crowd.*



His Master, Estular Jerts, had delivered him into the hands of the Games.

*My life is forfeit.*

He heard the wild tales that accompanied his arrival to the city—knew the lies his Master told the people of his s*avage crimes.* How he had ruthlessly attacked a small farming stead, hunting and slaughtering its children for sport, feasting on the corpses of the dead. Stories of his fight against the Proctor's men spread as well, growing more outrageous with every telling. Of the small army of Humans it took to bring him down, bind him, and deliver him here to satisfy justice. At first, he had not understood why Estular had spread these lies.

*Now I know. The crowd hates me, and the Julitans will do everything in their power to please them. They have bought and paid for my death.*

A slam against the metal bands of the cell door snapped him

from his thoughts. Jerking into a half crouch, Klain growled with fangs bared, his long tail lashing out in a wild arc.

"Oh, you *are* in rare form." His Master smiled through the barred window. With his black hair combed flat, beard and mustache trimmed and waxed, and his olive-colored skin shining, the Human exuded perfection. Klain peered into the cold, green eyes he had grown to hate over the past two turns of the seasons and fought the urge to fling himself against the thick door that was the only thing separating him from his Master. Turning his back to Klain, Estular Jerts spoke to the hallway. "As I told you, Honored One, a frightfully uncivilized beast at the best of times. Please do not be shocked by what you see." Estular's accent was different from any other Human Klain had ever heard.

Rising, Klain hesitated as some *thing* replaced his Master in the window. Peering through the bars at him was a creature stranger than anything Klain had ever seen. The head of the being was the shape of an inverted teardrop. The smooth skin covering it, devoid of any facial hair, gave off a faint grayish-blue hue. Slim, deep-gray lips formed its mouth and a tiny set of slits created its recessed nose. Silky-white hair flowed up and over the top of the creature's head, accentuating the lack of any protruding ears. It gave the thing an eerie, alien appearance.



Having been exposed to many strange beings in his life, Klain did not understand why this creature would cause him to feel so uneasy. Yet his hackles rose and a low growl rumbled deep in his chest. He stood, locked in the being's gaze, unable to move. Large and black, like pools of liquid infinity, the creature's eyes held him. They lifted him up though his hindpaws never left the ground. They reached in and ripped out his very essence, paralyzing him. Never before had Klain felt naked, vulnerable. He wanted those eyes to embrace him forever, to hold him and let him weep. Though he had never wept before.

Klain searched his mind, or, more appropriately, watched as some other force searched his mind. He had no memories of freedom. Had never run anywhere nor hunted anything. All of his early memories were of chains and bars.

*I was a mere cub when they took me captive.*

Dreams stemming from the tales told to him in his youth still haunted him—stories of the Humans who slaughtered his family and sold him to his first owners. He hoped those were lies as well.

*The lies of a puny race.*

In his mind's eye, the vision of what he imagined his parents might have looked like took shape. His sire stood tall, even for a Kithian, head and shoulders above any Human. Golden-brown fur lay painted over his sire's muscular frame and a lush, dark-brown mane surrounded his head. The mane came to a point well below his chin and rested against a bulging chest. The image cast a striking likeness to what Klain thought he himself was growing into. The figure conjured of his sire both pleased and comforted him. Klain yearned to see the pride in his sire's eyes, longed to watch the older Kith's fangs creep from their sanctuary behind thin lips as his mouth formed into a smile.

*His roar must have put the fear of the Gods into anything that heard it!*



In times past, Klain had dreamed of his sire's claws brushing through his own developing mane, to scratch behind his round, tufted ears.

A second Kith also materialized in his mind. He had never before seen a female of his species, yet what he saw seemed correct to him. She did not have the large mane that he and his sire shared, yet was covered in the same golden-brown fur. She stood strong as well. It upset Klain to see that her face lay hidden by a shadowy shroud. The living image melted away as abruptly as it had appeared. A longing filled Klain once the image had fully fled from his thoughts and, once again, he grieved for the loss of a mother's embrace.

*I know in my heart she loved me, though we were not together long.*

Actual memories were drawn out and examined as well. Klain had spent his first turns of the seasons on display in a far-off land the Humans named Silaway. His first masters had kept him in a small cage raising him as a freak show attraction in their traveling ménagerie. He grew up in that tiny pen, or chained behind it while they pulled the cart along to the next town or village.

Two winters past, Klain had noticed many of the entertainers leaving as well as entire shows being canceled. The crowds of onlookers grew smaller and smaller. The ménagerie traveled to fewer towns, camping more and performing less.

Before that season's end, the owners of the ménagerie sold Klain to his current master, a vile and cruel little man named Estular Jerts. Estular had moved his new possession to a small villa on the coast and trained him in the art of combat. Spending the next full turn of the seasons with a dozen different trainers, each with their own style, they taught him how to use weapons, fangs, and claws. Showing him that anything could become a tool for dealing out death.

"Train hard, my beast, yet be well, for you *are* my future." This was a favorite saying of Estular's as he watched his pet's progress. The man watched little, however, instead choosing the comfort of his villa over the open air of the courtyard. Klain never understood how his skin held its permanent tanned appearance.



Then one day, without explanation, they packed Klain into a cage and set off.

Expecting to be put on display once more, the prospect appalled him. Even though his Keeper beat him often, and the trainers wore him down to the point of collapse, Klain relished this new life of fighting over that of a caged freak. The freedom to move about in a large, open courtyard seemed palatial compared to his past existence in that tiny cage. Though he fought with fake weapons and specially designed pads covered his claws, the elation that gripped him as he pitted himself against his trainers lifted his spirits to a height he had never believed possible.

Estular's agenda, however, had not involved the Kith serving as an exhibit. Once they reached their destination, they dropped Klain into a large, dirt pit surrounded by a throng of shrieking men. Klain's understanding grew as they tossed a large brown creature—all teeth and claws and fury—into the pit as well. The thing stank of something left to wallow in its own filth for moons. Any intelligence the creature may have possessed in the past had long since been beaten out of it. The hunger showing in its eyes had sent a shiver of uncertainty streaking through Klain's core.

*It had no fear of me until the very end, when it knew me as predator, not prey. Kill, or have death wrap you in its cold embrace. A pleasure I have come to know well these past few turns of the season.*

He still savored the memory of that first real struggle for life. Reliving it now did nothing to tarnish its glory. As he never had before, Klain knew what it meant to be alive.

Moons later, after many an opponent had made him feel life at the cost of their death, his Master booked passage for them on a sailing ship.

"We travel to Ro'Arith!" Estular stood watching as sailors lowered Klain's cage into the darkness of the vessel's hold. "The land of your birth."

*Ro'Arith! A place I thought I would never see.*

For near three tendays, Klain endured the rocking of the dank hold with the rest of the cargo. Other than his Keeper, who brought him food, the ship's rats became his sole companions. On the day the ship docked, Estular paraded Klain with much fanfare down the streets of Mocley. His Master rode the whole way, perched atop his pet's cage, announcing to all that a Kith beast would fight in the upcoming Games—something the man proclaimed had never before happened during the Game's long history. The trek through the massive city brought Klain to the cell he now occupied. During the past few tendays, he had resumed training to recapture the strength lost during the long voyage. Since they worked him in private, he seldom saw any faces other than those of his trainers or Keeper.

*And Estular, of course. I can never escape his smug face.*

The memories of his life ended here. He had heard that with every ending comes a new beginning. Spending the first part of his life as a caged beast—an exhibit—like some inanimate thing living life as a spectacle with no purpose. Worthless. Worthless, that was, until his current master had purchased him.

*I am now trained to fight, and I find myself here in my homeland.*

*Good the Gods must be. They have a purpose and all I must do is—*

The blue-gray creature stepped away from the small window of the cell door. As it did, its hold on Klain shattered. The sensation of dropping back into the reality of his existence washed over him. Losing himself within his own insignificant mind, Klain did not notice his visitors departing until he heard a scurry of footsteps following the strange being that had held him hostage within its eyes. He realized only then that several others had accompanied Estular and his honored guest.

The desire to step to the door for a better look at the gray creature as it walked away pulled at him.

*Alas, I do not think I would survive another encounter with those eyes.*

"Looks like a lion which walks upright, I do think." The Keeper's pock-marked, jet-black face filled the small window once more. Glancing over his shoulder toward the group, the man hurried to catch them up.



"And I guarantee you, Honored One." Estular's words dripped from his silky voice, drifting up the hall to Klain. "This day's Games will be the most exciting ever witnessed here in Mocley. Mayhaps the most exciting thing since your great-great grandfather landed on the shores of Ro'Arith. My Kith will be the first of its kind to compete in the Games. The Coliseum will be filled to the breaking."

Klain's ears perked as he heard the small group come to an abrupt stop.

"And the Julitans of the Games have no doubt paid you well for your...participation, yes?" The voice that spoke was as airy and soft as a spring breeze, yet so commanding it demanded attention. Klain knew the voice must belong to this Honored One. "How much to purchase the Kithian, hmm?"

A sudden chill shook Klain.

A great cacophony arose as people spoke over one another.

"What are you saying, Honored One?"

"Honored One, you cannot be serious!"

"It is a wild beast!"

"Silence." The command floated down the stone hallway

barely touching Klain's ears. Yet the group of men, and even the prisoners in the other cells, fell quiet. As the stillness stretched, Klain pictured the Honored One peering at Estular with those large black penetrating eyes.

When Estular answered at last, Klain heard the faint pitch of fear in his voice. "What would you do with it?" After a short pause, he added, "If—if I may ask, Honored One."

"My business is my own, yes? No doubt you have made hundreds of ta'narians from this one day alone, yes? I assume you expect the Kithian to live through the day allowing you to enter him into the Games again, hmm? How many times will he endure, hmm? Five, ten, hmm?"

Klain clenched and unclenched his paws while his mind raced to understand the conversation unfolding down the hall.

"If the Kithian does survive, you stand to become a very rich man, Estular, yes?" The Honored One's voice took on a mocking tone. "I think not. The Julitans will not allow this to last to long. Its novelty is its draw, yes? Besides, if the Kith does survive what the Julitans have planned for him this day, who will want to fight him on the morrow, hmm? No, I am afraid you will not be able to use this as a long-term venture, Estular. Now, I will ask again, how much to purchase the Kithian, hmm?"



"Um, Honored One, yes although—when your aide approached me...I, I thought you simply wished to see—um…"

Klain heard Estular clear his throat.

"The original purchase price was a large expense, not to mention the costs I have incurred since then. Pulling the beast from the Games now would destroy my reputation. Not to mention the wrath of the Julitans would be…" Despair trickled through Estular's voice as the last word faded from his lips.

"Your reputation." A tinkling sound, close to a laugh, echoed out. "Master Jerts, I ask a price out of curiosity, yes? Not necessarily as a buyer."

Klain sensed Estular relax. After a few moments pause, his Master continued in a stronger tone. "Honored One, I—I would not sell it." A false resolve covered Estular's words like a shroud. "I have invested too much!" The man almost sounded confident.

"A life's goal you might say."

The silence returned. Klain smiled as he imagined the sight of the Honored One's big eyes boring down on Estular.

"I—I do not think I could put a price on it, I mean for several thousand ta'narians—well—I guess I would...Yet to come up with—"

"My thanks for the information."

Klain recognized the dismissal in the Honored One's voice. The footsteps receded and the large door at the end of the hall banged shut. All noise in the cell area dissipated into silence.

A low growl rumbled deep in his chest. Noticing he still held a bare leg bone in his paw, he flung it across the room. It ricocheted off the far wall with a loud clack before skidding into a corner. Klain fell to his knees, pounding the floor with a clenched paw. The anger slipped from him with the same speed it had come. Staring aimlessly at the tangle of dirty straw on the ground before him, his head sagged and he closed his eyes.



*Somewhere I have kin that still live! Still walk free!*

Grabbing a second hunk of lamb from the tray, he stood. Returning to the edge of the bed, he took another bite of the succulent meat.

Most days, Klain kept his dreams and memories locked deep inside, not daring to look at them until long after a blanket of darkness covered the Plane. Having them drug from his mind and forced to face them, to take stock of his own miserable life, had him now turning them over in his mind.

*The mind of the condemned…*

Sitting on the edge of the stone slab, he gnawed absentmindedly on the meat. He was once again alone with his breakfast. A breakfast he stared at without seeing—hearing nothing save the whispering voice of the Honored One rolling over and over in his mind…

*If the Kith does survive what the Julitans have planned for him this day…*

# Chapter 2

A stream of sunlight poured through the glazed window striking Arderi Cor in the face. Opening his eyes, he blinked against the light of the early morn. Yawning and stretching, he made a half-hearted attempt to wipe the sleep from his eyes. Sitting up on his bed, he peered out at the blurry view the window offered through its wavy, semi-transparent glass. The Hild'alan stead was just starting to awaken for a new days work.

His eyes wandered up the fortification that protected the stead he called home. It towered over the public houses by a half-dozen paces. Like his parents, and theirs before them, Arderi had lived his entire life in one of the four-story public houses that were lined up in neat rows, rolling off into the distance. Their whitewashed exteriors stood out in sharp contrast to the grayish hues of the massive stone wall rising up behind them. He watched a guarder walking the battlements for a moment. Letting his gaze fall back to the public houses, his eyes slid on to the market area, with its wooden shops and tent-like pavilions. The area sat empty this early in the morn so Arderi leaned over to peer toward the center of town. Only the corner of the Palintium was visible from his bedroom window. The massive building's smooth marble walls and tall, intricately carved pillars were distorted by his window, yet recognizable. Other stone and marble buildings surrounded the Palintium, although none held his eye so well.

The cobblestone streets that sliced between the buildings appeared as nothing more than thin muddy rivers from where he sat. He traced the route he would walk to reach home from the Palintium, until the road disappeared from his view some ten paces below.

This is the view he had woken to every day for the past sixteen winters.

*However, this day I am a man.*

Sixteen winters past, he blessed the Plane with his birth.

*At least, that is what my Ma is always saying.*

Arderi reckoned he had grown into a fine young man. Working the fields everyday since age twelve, as was customary, had helped develop and strengthen his body. He held an inner drive, which pushed him to outperform the other fielders, most of which were men full grown. This drive became a private game known only to him and it gave him a sense of satisfaction at the end of each day. Even on Holiday, the one day of rest at the end of a tenday, he always exerted himself, striving for his best—to be the fastest runner, the cleverest hide-and-seeker, the most aggressive rillball player.



For the past four summers, during the Salintine Festival, he had taken first place in the tri-feat event against the other boys of the stead. This summer he would compete against the men, and looked forward to the added challenges it brought.

*I know I will rank well.*

Glancing around the tiny room, he stretched and yawned once more. Rotating around, he kicked the wooden frame of the bed resting next to his. "Rise and shine, brother. We have lots to do this fine day."

His older brother, Siln Cor, received the kick with a groan before rolling over and burying himself deeper under the covers.

Arderi stood and extended his arms toward the ceiling to loosen his sore muscles.

*I must find a moment to re-stuff my mattress if I ever intend to get any restful sleep again.*

"Come on, Siln, get up!" He kicked the bed frame once more. "Papa will break us if we miss the wagons for the ride out to the fields. I do not want to walk, *again.*"

"Alright, alright. I am awake!" Eyes still closed, Siln sat up in bed. The dense tangles of black hair upon his head gave him the look of a creature more than a brother.

Though Siln was a winter older, Arderi had felt responsible for him for as long as he could remember.

*If not for me, Siln would stay in bed all day, every day.*

Slapping him hard on the back of the head, Arderi jumped away.

"Oiy!" Covering the back of his head with a hand, Siln's eyes shot open. "Why, you!" Attempting to scramble out of bed, he only managed to tangle himself in his blankets.

Dashing out the door of their room, Arderi heard his brother's bed complain as Siln fought to release himself from the blankets. Bounding down the stairs laughing, Arderi knew his brother would get even somehow. However, the slap had served its purpose and forced Siln to rise and give chase.



As with most morns, Arderi took the long way to the dining hall by cutting through the kitchen. Wives, daughters, and grandmothers greeted him as he entered. They bustled to and fro, preparing firstmeal.

Chuckling to himself, Arderi marveled at the ordered chaos filling the room.

*Ma always says it is the womenfolk who are last to bed and first to rise.*

Eight extended families shared this public house, same as in each of the few score houses protected within the walls of the Hild'alan stead. Generations upon generations spent their entire lives here—work and play, love and marriage, from birth to death. Arderi did not know the exact age of the stead, yet he knew it was hundreds of winters old.

*Mayhaps over a thousand winters!*

The sight of all the women as they prepared firstmeal—the smells of fresh baked bread, the frying meat, and boiling vegetables—made Arderi's stomach rumble. "Well wishes, Ma, Mis'ams." Crossing to the center worktable, he reached for a slab of smoked pork resting on a clay tray at its center. Snatching his hand back, a wooden spoon thwacked the tabletop barely missing his fingertips.

"Arderi Cor! You know better!" A tall redheaded girl, around his own age, stood in front of him brandishing the large spoon as if she held a club.

"Mag'Oella!" Arderi rubbed the top of his hand as if the weapon had struck. "Lucky for you that spoon missed. I would hate for all these womenfolk to see you spanked."

The young redhead's feigned outrage was apparent to Arderi after their many seasons of flirting. She was thin for her height, yet, in his eyes, she had grown into one of the prettiest women in the stead. Fiery red hair, a rarity in these parts, added to her allure. She had stolen his heart many winters ago, along with most of the boys in the stead, although he knew she favored him.



Soon, now that he was officially a man, he would be expected to ask her father for her hand. They could then petition the Regent for an apartment of their own and start a family.

*At least Ma is pushing hard for that, now that my two older brothers have let her down with no grandbabies. Alas, I do not think it will play out that way.*

It was possible that Siln, the brother who shared his room, would not ever leave their parent's apartment, much less marry and have children.

*My two little sisters are her best hope for grandbabies I think. If not them, there is still little Rik, though it will be many a winter before he is even interested in girls.*

His eldest brother, Alant Cor—even though he brought a great deal of pride to the family—traveled a path that did not often lead to children. The Shaper's Order tested every child upon reaching adulthood to see if any possessed the natural talent to manipulate the Essence. The gift was rare. At best, one in several thousand may have it. Alant had scored higher than anyone in the recorded history of the Hild'alan stead. The local Grand Master Shaper, Grand Master Grintan, took it upon himself to lead the caravan that escorted his brother to the grand city of Mocley. Alant resided there now, being schooled at the famed Academy of Shapers.

*It makes Ma and Papa proud even though he may never give them grandchildren.*

Arderi dreamed of traveling to Mocley one day to see his brother—his favorite fantasy during the two winters since Alant's departure.

"All right, you two." His Ma carried over a pan of fried eggs, steam rose from its still sizzling contents. "Stop all this nonsense and get a move on, Arderi. The wagons will leave for the fields soon."

"Mag, will you be a dear and take this out to the dining hall for me?" Without waiting for an answer, she held out the hot pan for Mag'Oella to take.

"Yes, Mis'am Cor." The young girl placed her hands under the oven towels so as not to be burned. Taking the skillet, she turned and headed for the door.



Arderi admired how her blue frilled dress flurried out as she spun. She glanced over her shoulder and graced him with a coy smile before disappearing.

"Arderi, where is Siln? Still in bed?" Mis'am Cor wiped her hands off on her apron and squared her shoulders on her son, holding him within her stern gaze.

As if on cue, Siln strolled into the kitchen. "Here I am, Ma, and hungry as a prairie worm."

Mel'Ona Cor accepted a kiss from her second eldest son. "Well, off you two go then. Most of the men have finished firstmeal already. I would not want to be in your shoes when you have to deal with your Papa's wrath for missing the wagons again." With that said, she turned back to her work without a backward glance.

Siln glared at Arderi. "Watch yourself this day, *little* brother. I *will* have my revenge." He kept his voice low enough that their

Ma would not overhear.

Rolling his eyes, Arderi followed Siln toward the same door Mag'Oella had gone through. "Do not be so dramatic, Siln, I was only helping. You know—" Siln halted in his track causing Arderi to crash into him.

Spinning around, Siln pushed Arderi back a step. "Helping me? How is the knot on the back of my head supposed to help me?"

"Better than what you would have gotten from Papa, had you missed the wagons."

"Well...there is that." Siln wore that puzzled look that said he was thinking. "Nix, I still owe you one. And I *will* have my revenge!" He finished in a big booming voice, raising his hands over his head for effect.

Arderi shoved him in the chest and both young men laughed as they stumbled through the door.

The dining hall, a plain room used for all meals and gatherings, held several rows of tables and benches. Large enough for the hundred or so people residing in the building, it felt homey and well lived-in. A large fireplace rested at either end, while sconces and painted hangings hung scattered along the walls.



When they entered the hall, most of the benches sat empty. A few girls, his two little sisters included, scurried about cleaning off dirty dishes and wiping down tables. Tary'Ona, the younger of his female siblings, beamed at him without pausing in her work.

Two tables, however, still held food plates and clean place settings. Siln pointed to the one Mag'Oella leaned over as she set down the skillet of eggs their Ma had given her. The boys headed for it.

A large man sat on the bench opposite the spot they chose. "Morn, Siln, Arderi."

"Morn, Mir'am Toln." Both young men eyed each other for having said the same thing simultaneously, and then settled themselves onto the bench. "Where is Riln?" Arderi added this once they were seated.

"He ate at first-serving this morn, same as the last few days. I think he is taking being a man more to heart." Sorn Toln shoveled a spoonful of turnip mash into his mouth.

"Good for him." Arderi looked down at the food spread out on the table.

*Of course, when you find out what your son has really been up to...well, I would not want to be Riln at that moment. Which reminds me, I need to figure out what he has been up to, in case his harebrained scheme includes me somehow.*

Mir'am Toln pointed his spoon at Arderi. "You are less than a tenday behind him, are you not? When is your big day?"

Siln sat next to Arderi stuffing himself, as if he had not a care in his heart.

"Aye, Mir'am Toln, tis this day."

"Well, good for you! Everyone is excited about your Test! Just think, you might be even more gifted with the Essence than your older brother, Alant. You parents are so proud!" Mir'am Toln leaned forward with a serious look. "Now you watch out for whatever your Ma has planned for later this eve, hear?"



Arderi knew only too well that his Ma would not pass the day without some fanfare. He remembered what his two older brothers were forced to endure on their sixteenth naming days, and he was not relishing what this eve may bring. Pushing the unpleasant image from his mind, he turned his thoughts to filling his stomach.

In addition to the fresh pan of fried eggs Mag'Oella had just delivered, plates of smoked pork strips, turnip mash, rice pudding, and that wonderful-smelling fresh-baked bread lined the table. He loaded his plate with some of all of it, scooped out a glob of butter from the center dish, and forgot all about Riln Toln and whatever mischief he might or might not be up to. He pushed away thoughts of any impending ceremonies his Ma may be planning for him as well.

*I just hate being the center of attention.*

When the last man had left the table, Arderi buttered

one more piece of bread and stuffed it into his mouth. Most of it still stuck out from between his lips as he raced out of the dining hall and down the passage to the main entrance. Hurrying out the wooden doors, he stopped long enough to mumble morn to the elders who sat on the porch for their daily gathering, before sprinting down the cobblestone street toward the fielder's gate.

Rounding the bend, he was relieved to see the wagons still sat at the gate and slowed to a jog. The light morn breeze fluttered past, mussing his sandy brown hair, and he drank in the cool air. It reminded him how much he loved the early springtime of the Northron Plains.

*The air is always fresher here at a gate than deeper within the walls of the stead.*

"I see you finally decided to drag yourself down here." Siln, sitting in the back of a wagon next to their father, was grinning like a fool as Arderi ambled up.



Their father, Tanin Cor, leaned down and extended a hand to Arderi. "Well wishes, Son."

"Well wishes, Papa." Arderi took his father's hand and hopped into the back of the wagon.

Tanin was a good-sized man. He kept his face clean-shaven and the sandy brown hair on top of his head, now showing a sprinkling of gray, cut short. Not the tallest nor broadest man in the stead, he stood a bit over two paces. Wide shoulders and strong arms gave him a look many mistook for that of a guarder instead of a simple fielder. He did not even have the gut many fielders his age developed. Most agreed that Arderi, of all Tanin's sons, favored his father in looks and build and would soon be the tallest in their family.

"How do you feel this morn, Papa?" Arderi plopped himself onto the bench next to his friend, Riln Toln, who flashed him a sly look and that wait-till-you-hear-what-I-did grin of his.

*I must figure out what he has been up to these past few morns.*

"Fine, fine." Arderi knew his father would not have admitted it had he been dying of pain. "The Shapers delivered a Crystal from Alant this morn. He is to leave Mocley and be schooled now in Hath'oolan." Mir'am Cor raised a hand to forestall Arderi's questions. "He did not say the reason for this, yet says he is well, and sends his love."

"Hath'oolan!" Arderi blurted once he was sure his father had finished speaking. He could not believe his ears. Hath'oolan, the capital city of the fabled Isle of Elmorr'eth, was the birth home of the Elmorians, the most powerful Shapers on the entire Plane.

*Some say it is the birth home for the Essence itself, with all its power flowing from there!*

Arderi's mind raced. "Alant must be more powerful than even the Grand Master Shaper suspected! Do you have the Crystal with you, Papa? Can I draw upon it now? Please?" Unable to hide the plea in his voice, he chastised himself for sounding like a babe in swaddling clothes.

Tanin chuckled and a smile stretched above his strong chin. "Nix, Arderi, I would not bring a Crystal to the fields. It is safe at home. You may draw upon it this eve and hear for yourself what Alant has to say, and see what he has imbued on it." He patted Arderi on the shoulder. "Are you excited about being Tested?"



A lump formed in Arderi's throat and he made a sound he hoped his father would take for an affirmative answer.

Leaning against the back wall of the wagon bed, Tanin smiled at his son. "Aye, I know you are scared, son. Yet, keep in mind, everyone your age must be Tested. And we all survived. Besides, think of how wonderful it will be to follow Alant to Mocley and be trained as a Shaper."

"Move out!" The guarder captain, a grizzled looking man by the name of Flinnok Nime, shouted the command from his horse at the front of the small caravan.

One by one the wagons lurched as the teamsters urged their horses forward. Arderi rocked back with the motion of the wagon as it started down the road toward the fields.

They did not have far to travel. The field they were going

to work lay close to the stead, only one section past the animal pastures that surrounded the outer walls. Not wanting to think about the Test, Arderi gazed out over a herd of sheep grazing near the road, and to a group of herders who lounged beneath the shade of an old oak tree resting near the fence. He felt a pang of jealousy toward the men sitting around in a circle, talking.

As if Riln had read his mind, he leaned over close to Arderi. "Do not envy those lazy herders." His whisper had a conspiratorial edge to it. "They have a surprise in store for them."

Arderi shot him a quizzical look, yet Riln held his tongue for once.

Letting his eyes linger on the group, Arderi wondered once more what Riln had been up to. Herders occupied public houses on the opposite side of the stead from the fielders. They tended the many animals that lived within the walls of the stead. Even though Arderi did not envy them for how long their day was—having the job of taking all the animals from the protection of the stead walls and leading them to pasture day after day, as well as bringing them back inside eve after eve—he still saw their aurns in between as ill spent. "I do not think they work as hard during the day as we fielders do."

Arderi was speaking to no one in particular, although Riln chimed in. "Because they are lazy!"

"I would not be so fast to judge." Shaking his head, Tanin gave Riln a disapproving look. "Remember the saying, first to rise, last inside, a herders day is long."

"Mayhaps." Arderi glanced over at his Papa. "Yet they sure do sit a lot during that long day of theirs."

His father grinned back at him. "It is only what you see on the ride to and from the fields, my boy." Waving a hand, the older man indicated the vast pastures that hugged the stead's wall. "They also handle all of the slaughtering and skinning. I do believe you enjoy the meat they provide. And do not forget the wool and hides that you wear." A guarder, one of many accompanying the work detail, trotted by on a horse and Tanin nodded to him. "Aye, they may sit a lot during the day." Turning his attention back to the boys, Tanin raised one eyebrow. "Alas, remember we fielders let our fields run fallow during the winter season. Herders are still out there, day after day, season after season, regardless of the weather."

Arderi pulled his feet under him and sat up for more comfort on the hard, wooden bench. "It is not as if we fielders do not work during the winter moons."

"Aye." Tanin nodded sagely. "Alas, most of our day is spent on inside work, mending or making tools and the like. Not out in the cold wet weather."

"I never thought of it that way, Papa." Glancing back down the road, Arderi stared at the small group of herders as they faded from view.

"Nix!" Riln's whisper was sharp and he directed it into Arderi's ear so as not to be overheard. "I know it was some stinking herder who dumped the load of dung in my sleeping room. I still have to leave the window open for the smell. Yet, soon..." He sat back and smiled, bobbing his head like a fool in rhythm with the bounce of the wagon.



Leaning over toward his friend, Arderi kept his voice in the same conspiratorial whisper. "At halfmeal we shall steal away. You must tell what you have planned."

Riln nodded, his eyes twinkling.

Flopping back to enjoy the warm spring sun, Arderi followed the one stray cloud drifting high in the clear blue sky.

*What a perfect day. Not too hot, nice cooling breeze. A shame this day is not Holiday. At least the tenday is more than half-gone, and Holiday will be here soon.*

# Chapter 3

Reality appeared skewed—akin to peering through a kaleidoscope. A mish-mash of colored points of light floated in Alant Cor's field of vision, swirling and bouncing all around him.

*Like opening my eyes under water, yet instead of a wavy view, everything looks crisp and clear. I just cannot tell what anything is!*



"Now, Alant, focus. Bend your mind and see me." The voice of Sier Sarlimac, one of Alant's teachers here at the Chandril'elian of Mocley, came from somewhere in front of him. "Tell me what I am holding." Strain as he might, Alant could see no difference in the sparkle of colors spinning around him.

Focusing on the voice, Alant let his mind relax, allowing the floating swirls of colors to differentiate from one another on their own as he had been taught. Within moments, his eyes adapted, adjusting to the foreign sight they beheld. Nothing changed in the dots themselves, yet his Sier's face extracted itself from the surrounding background. It did not change colors, nor did it take on any real shape or form. Rather, Alant saw that the colored dots of Sarlimac's face connected, interacting in a way he did not quite understand, distinguishing themselves from the dots surrounding his teacher's face. Soon, patterns emerged and the contents of the room took shape before him in the eerie, multi-colored Sight of the Essence.

Finally, once Alant was certain he grasped what he saw, he was confident enough to answer. "You hold a book." Then more details became clear. "And you are not even looking at me!"

"Impressive." His instructor chuckled. "You outpace your classmates by at least two turns of the seasons."

Alant realized that Sier Sarlimac no longer stood in front of him, although he had not noticed the old man moving away. "You have moved."

"Yes, I now stand by the marble lab table." The voice came from his right. "Can you see me?"

As Alant twisted his head toward where he assumed his instructor stood, the suddenness of his movement caused the dots that created reality as he now saw it, to shift violently. He could no longer separate the colored dots into the patterns that made up his surroundings. Everything once again became a maddened mingling of indistinguishable points of color. Out of reflex, he whipped out a hand to steady himself on the stool.

*I am like a blind man. A dizzy blind man!*



"Do not lose the Sight, Alant. Here, I will take your arm."

A hand grasped Alant's elbow and helped him rise from his stool. He let the Sier guide him the few steps to the table. As they walked forward, the colored dots spun out of focus and everything blurred in a way that made his stomach queasy. If not for Sier Sarlimac holding his arm, Alant feared he would fall.

"Easy, easy now. There you are."

They stopped walking and the dots snapped back into sharp focus. One moment they were like a swarm of buzzing bees whizzing around him in an angry mass, the next frozen in midair about him.

"Now, the marble table sits right in front of you. I want you to focus on it if you can. You know what it looks like with your normal sight—now see it as it looks in the Sight of the Essence."

Alant let his eyes adjust once more, his mind fighting to make sense of the chaotic image before him. "Aye, Sier, large and flat." He studied what he saw. "Nothing is on it."

"I will add something now. Tell me what you see." A rustling sound permeated the room.

"A book." Alant was quick with his answer.

"Look closely."

"Aye, Sier, not a book, not enough there to be a book—" Alant paused. The pattern appeared the same as a book, yet also somehow different. "Some parchment then?"

"Yes, good." Sarlimac held the tone in his voice that made Alant feel like a happy puppy dog. "Now I will add a second piece to the right, do you see it?"

"Aye, Sier. At first, it too looks like a book. Then I see there is not enough interaction. It is like seeing water in a large puddle and thinking it is deep—only to realize later that it is shallow."

"A perfect analogy." Sarlimac chuckled. "Now, I will light one piece of parchment on fire."

A lantern shutter squeaked. Alant was silent as the colored dots moved about and shifted hues. "The parchment on the right has changed, Sier." He took another moment to better understand what he saw. "It does not seem any brighter, however, only altered."



"Yes, the Essence shows everything at the same luminosity. It is for you to see how the Essence of the parchment is changed by the fire."

"It is different, Sier, like the colored dots—"

"Spectals." Sarlimac voice had an exasperated edge to his correction and Alant chastised himself for the slip.

"Aye, Sier, the Spectals move slower now, and the parchment has more blue in it."

"Very well done." Off to Alant's left he heard the leather of one of the plush chairs in the room groan under the weight of his instructor. "And now what does it look like?"

Alant studied the two collective piles of colored dots.

*Not dots! Spectals.*

"They both still have the look of parchment, Sier. The one you burned, however, seems smaller, somewhat constricted now. Oh, and very blue. Its Spectals move even slower now, hardly at all."

"You may release the Sight now, Alant."

The Essence slipped from Alant's eyes like water passing over a sheet of glass. A grayish, shadowy chamber materialized around him, the strain of it forced him to rub his eyes. After a moment, the room became clear; in his normal vision, everything seemed dark compared to viewing it with the Sight of the Essence. He stood where he had assumed, a few paces from the large black-gray marble table. The only light in the room spilled from the few lanterns that hung in its corners. The piece of parchment Sier Sarlimac had burnt still lay on the table, crumpled and black.

*A useless pile of ash.*

The small lab, where Alant had spent more sessions in private tutors than he cared to remember, was lined with bookshelves stuffed with bound books, rolled parchment, and anything else that would fit upon them—dried and bleached skulls, as varied in size as in style, pieces of colored glass or crystal, small carved statues, and more that Alant had never been able to identify even up close. A set of four leather chairs, a half dozen stools, and the large granite table were the only other furniture in the room.



His instructor, Sier Sarlimac, was a plump old man with a shaggy white-gray beard that did not quite cover his chin. He sat, lounging in one chair, his dark blue robes stretched tight over his ample belly. Golden starbursts lined the cuffs and hem of the robe, marking Sarlimac as a Master Shaper. "You see, Alant." The teacher motioned for Alant to sit in the leather chair opposite him. "As you have learned, the Essence resides in all things. We see it as Spectals, this you know. It is a fact that can never change. What we can change is the item's potential here in the physical Plane." He pointed back to the table. "Could I burn the burnt parchment again?"

"Nix, Sier." Alant lowered himself into the plush chair. "It would not catch again."

"Why?"

"You cannot burn it twice, Sier, everyone knows this."

"Can you write on the burnt parchment?"

"Nix, Sier, it is now ash."

"Is that so? Did it change to the pattern of ash while you watched it using the Sight of the Essence?" Sarlimac put his hands in the form of a steeple and placed the point under his chin on a spot that had no hair, as he often did when lecturing. Several coarse bristles of his beard stuck out at odd angles.

"Nix, Sier. When I looked upon it with the Sight, it seemed to remain parchment. The Spectals simply changed color, most turning blue...And they moved more slowly."

Sarlimac nodded. "If you looked upon it with the Sight now, you would see the blue Spectals are motionless. This is because there is nothing left in the parchment that will burn. It has no stored energy—potential—left in it to create fire. As you learned from your studies, the color of the Spectals indicates their *potential.* Blue shows you an item having no more *potential* to burn."



"Alas, Sier, there are no blue Spectals within the lab table." Alant's interruption came close to being considered rude, yet in his excitement, he forged on. "Granite cannot burn so why would it not have blue Spectals in it as well."

"Ah, except the granite has never *had* the potential to burn. The blue Spectals indicate that an item does not have the potential to burn *currently.* However, the material holding the blue Spectals has the potential to burn in one of its *other* forms. Like the ash that used to be parchment sitting on the table, two distinctly different states of the same material. Now, as a Shaper, you will be able to reach out and manipulate the Essence within an item, to change the hues of the blue back to the greens of un-burnt parchment, speeding up the Spectals once more, so to speak. I am simplifying the process, of course. Plus, it would take several aurns, at least, for even a Master Shaper to return a single sheet back from ash to parchment. Much easier to simply get a new piece from market." He laughed to himself. "Remember, just because you can accomplish something by manipulating the Essence, does not mean it is the best way. Shaping the Essence is a painfully slow process, as you now know. Still, this is how a Shaper would manipulate the burnt and ruined parchment back into a crisp new piece."

"Sier, does this mean a Shaper would use the same method to manipulate the parchment and cause it to catch fire?" Alant loved probing questions. "By changing the Spectals blue and slowing them down?"

This caused Sarlimac to laugh aloud, something Alant had never before heard him do. "I am afraid not. A Shaper could manipulate it into ash, or rather parchment that no longer has the ability to burn, yet the act of catching it on fire would be too fast. We Shapers do not have the ability to instantly change the Essence. As I have said, it would take me the better part of several aurns to change the ash on that table back into what it was prior to me burning it. Even the Elmorr'Antiens do not possess the power to manipulate the Essence fast enough to make something burst into flames. Even though they are the strongest with the Essence, it is not as if they can look at a thing using the Sight and have it burst into flame."



"How are they stronger in the Essence than us Humans?" The young man yearned to learn about the Elmorian people.

*The most powerful Shapers on the Plane, and soon they will be teaching me!*

The Sier smiled and shook his head gently. "That is unknown to us. We are divided into two main schools of thought when it comes to the Elmorr'Antien's power over the Essence." Sarlimac leaned back against his chair. The leather creaking as only old leather could. "Some believe the Essence itself created their race. Others think they have a different physiology allowing them to interact with the Essence in a more natural way than other races. This would make them superior to us, whether it is by creation, or a chance of nature. Many Shapers, however, reject this. They cannot stomach to think they may be inferior." He scoffed. "They believe that the Elmorr'Antiens are privy to some great secret. Something they hide from the rest of the

Shapers on this Plane, and thereby keep themselves superior."

"Which do you believe, Sier?"

"It does not matter what I believe." Smiling, Sarlimac patted his student on one knee. Alant shot him a hurt look generating a small grunt from his teacher. "I have no knowledge to prove whether either of these theories are correct. I know only what I can do, and that is all that concerns me. Now, come." Standing, he made his way to the door. "You have packing to do, and I need you to run a few errands for me in town." He stopped at the door and turned.

"Alant?"

"Aye, Sier."

"I want you to know—the other Siers will not tell you this—you are the strongest student we have had here at the Chandril'elian in living memory. No one I know of has ever gained the ability to hold the Sight of the Essence and discern items, one from another, after only two turns of the seasons. Even gifted Initiates take four or five turns to advance that far."



"My thanks to you, Sier, I—"

His instructor interrupted him with a wave of the hand. "You have a long career as a Shaper ahead of you, son. I do not want to see you forfeit it." The old plump man bit his lower lip as if he was unsure of whether to continue. "I do not deny that it is a great honor to be invited to train in Hath'oolan by the Elmorr'Antiens. At best, only one Initiate every few turns of the seasons is invited. Yet be wary, a few who have gone before you have failed to return." It seemed to Alant that the Sier wanted to say more, yet the old man turned and hurried from the room leaving Alant standing in stunned silence.

*Some Initiates have failed to return?*

# CHAPTER 4

The noise of the crowd deafened Klain. When he had first stepped into the arena, he would not have believed so many Humans existed on the entire Plane, much less in one location.

*The number is meaningless to me, yet my Keeper said the Grand Coliseum held thousands upon thousands.*

The floor of the arena spanned hundreds of paces across, most of it covered by sand packed down by the multitudes that had fought here over the ages. The wall surrounding the fighting area stood well over ten paces high, its top half covered in a larger-than-life-sized fresco depicting combat of every conceivable type—man against man or beast or thing—all frozen in mortal struggle, paying no attention to the carnage strewn at their feet.



The throng packing the seats around the arena floor varied from one another as much as the stone carvings on the walls—a sea of bodies, wailing and screaming. A clash of color and movement.

*I fear they will crash down like a tidal wave of flesh onto the sands that surround me.*

A crystal-clear blue sky shone down as Klain surveyed the scene. The death dealt here this day before he had taken the field still in evidence all around. Bits of armor, steel, and flesh lay scattered near large bloody stains in the sand. The only bodies remaining, however, were the twenty or so he had killed since taking the field.

Fighting non-stop for near two aurns, Klain sensed his primal edge waning. The battles thus far had been comprised of single opponents or small groups of Humans. The Julitans of the Games had thrown them at him in succession, with only enough pause in between for slaves to rush out onto the field and clear away the weapons. The stench of death filled his nostrils. The slaves had left the corpses to bloat in the warm springtime sun to remind the crowd of what they had paid to see.

He found each opponent sent against him more skilled than the one before.

*Now they all lay dead in the sand.*

The taste of blood from one of the brothers he had just slain still filled his mouth.

*They never protect their throat well enough when they face my fangs. It is as if they see them for show. The* fools.

Sunlight glared off the battered shield in front of him, sending a bolt of pain through Klain's eyes ripping his mind back to the present. He knew a killing stroke would follow. Crouching low, Klain sprang toward the blinding light, his long tail lashing out to provide extra balance. Smashing against the shield, he drove the warrior protected behind it back and to the ground. Letting momentum carry him through, Klain hit the ground, tucked into a tight roll, and tumbled into a crouch. In one graceful, fluid motion, he turned and spun on one knee, facing the Human he now fought. Alas, instead of seeing a man floundering on his back, or at best struggling to rise, the warrior, who had cunningly used the glare of the sun to his advantage, crouched before Klain on one knee in a mirror image of Klain's own stance. The Human's sword and shield were back in play. The two stood together with deliberate slowness, each eyeing the other—weighing.

*This Human moves with a quickness and grace belying his size. He will not die as easy as the others. He has skills they lacked.*

Flexing his paws, feeling their sharp claws curl into the pads on his palms, Klain studied this new opponent. They circled each other. Still weighing, measuring. Klain smelled no fear from the man. The warrior seemed old. What little of his face that showed through the helm's visor looked withered and wrinkled. This stood in contrast to the strength and power evident in the man's arm as he gripped the hilt of his sword.

*Alas, the God of age has already begun to pull the skin down low under those strong arms of yours.*

The Human's armor bore none of the fine decorations most of Klain's earlier adversaries had fancied. It showed its age, mended here and there, yet looked well kept and in good repair, reinforced at all its points of weakness.

*I will find no chinks there.*

Klain had noticed how the crowd's mood changed when this Human took the field. They still created the dissonance of noise, although more reserved and sheltered, as if the crowd had become one large being, holding its breath in anticipation—or maybe awe.

*They see this one as the grand finale. The one meant to end this day's Games with the death of the beast. So be it.* 

A rumble emanated from Klain's chest and he let out a vicious roar hoping to unsettle the man. The warrior took this as an advantage and lunged, spinning his sword in a high, diagonal arc.

Jerking back to avoid the killing stroke, Klain saw the true danger too late. The edge of the warrior's shield smashed into the back of Klain's head like a hammer. His vision darkened as the ground rushed up and smashed him in the face. In blind panic, he scrambled across the ground, spitting out sand and blood. Trying to distance himself from the blade he knew would now be seeking a taste of his hide, Klain raced across the arena floor. His paws picked up the vibration of his opponent's footfalls as the Human gave chase. Even though Klain could not see him—stars filled his vision—the pads on his paws told him the direction and distance of the man with the sword. Klain knew when the warrior lost ground, and when he stopped his pursuit altogether.

Scuttling away a few more paces, Klain came to a stop to recover. The yells and screams of the crowd, which had risen in anticipation of the beast's defeat, had now degenerated. He shook his head to clear his vision, the thick mane of hair surrounding his neck swayed with the motion. Head throbbing, a lance of pain shot down Klain's spine in a wave of agony. Blood trickled from his scalp, ran down the side of his neck, staining the honey-gold fur of his shoulder a crimson red.

The pads on the bottom of Klain's paws picked up a slight vibration resonating through the ground and he knew the old warrior advanced once more. He turned to face the Human and noted that his flight had taken them to the opposite end of the arena. With a slow, deliberate movement, Klain brought a paw to the back of his head, probed the fresh wound, and again considered this adversary as the Human strode closer. He saw no fault in the warrior's guard—shield held for protection, sword poised to strike or defend. Klain could still smell no fear on the man.



As the distance shrank, Klain's sharp ears picked up a wheeze coming from within the man's helm. Watching, he noted the warrior's thick chest rise and fall as the Human gulped down air.

*You have revealed your weakness* old *man. You need me to die quickly before you are spent.*

Withdrawing a blood drenched paw from the back of his head, Klain's knees buckled. Stumbling forward, he barely kept his footing.

At this show of weakness, the warrior picked up his pace.

Staggering backward, it was all Klain could do to keep the two of them far enough apart so that neither could attack. The man bellowed and charged with a fresh burst of speed. Klain quickened his retreat, then turned and ran. Awkwardly, he weaved off in different directions, searching for an escape. The beast let the pads of his hindpaws keep track of his pursuer.

Once the Human broke from the chase, Klain slowed his blind flee, yet he continued for another fifty paces. A hindpaw snagged a dip in the sand flinging him forward hard onto the ground. Flopping over, Klain glared at the Human and let out a low growl, baring his long fangs. Scrambling back on all fours, he sought to add distance between them. His strong arms gave out as he reached the body of a little man he had killed in an earlier bout. The man's weapon was gone.

*Alas, I do not seek his weapon, just* a *weapon.*

Using the dead man for support, Klain turned his back on the Human and fought to rise. Before he could fully stand, his hindleg gave way dropping him to one knee. Grabbing the back of his head, a jolt of pain shot through him. Peering over his shoulder, he saw what he already knew—the old warrior advanced, about fifty paces away now, walking at a steady gait toward him. It was satisfying to see the man's sword and shield both hung heavily to his sides. Placing his paws on the chest of the dead body, Klain leaned on it and struggled to rise once more. With his entire being, he concentrated on the information emanating from the ground. The vibrations picked up when the Human began to run.



Waiting, Klain ignored his ears—the noise of the crowd overpowered the sounds he needed to hear anyway—and relied on the pads of his hindpaws to judge the distance between them.

Thrum, thrum, thrum, the warrior's feet hit the ground.

*I can see you in my minds eye. Twenty, ten, five.*

Klain rose, spun, and launched the dead man's body in one fluid motion. Blood sprayed as the force of the spin tore away strings of flesh that still clung to the corpse's face.

The warrior thrust his shield forward to fend off the sudden attack. With tremendous force, the body struck the Human's defense like a ballista bolt shattering the man's arm. Corpse and shield slammed into the man's chest. His feet flew out from under him as they continued on their path. The back of his head hit the ground first after the two bodies collided onto the arena floor. A tangle of arms and legs skidded across the blood-soaked sand.

Without hesitation, Klain pounced. He crashed down on the old fighter before the two bodies could slide to a stop. Grabbing the warrior's helm by its face guard, Klain jabbed his sharp claws through the eye slit, digging them into the unseen flesh within. The sound of the man's scream bit at his ears as he pushed his claws as deep as they would go. Hooking his thumb under the chinstrap that held the piece of armor in place, it became wrapped in a spongy, warm embrace as it penetrated the soft fleshy underside of the Human's jaw. His arm muscles bulged under the strain of closing his fist over the front of the face armor. A crackling of bones rang out from the helmet and the screams emanating from it became a gurgle. Klain listened with satisfaction to his foe choking on his own blood. Ripping the helm up and off, the beast tore away whatever part of the warrior's face he still held in his grasp.

Klain had planned to use the piece of armor as a weapon to bash the man's head in, yet what he saw gave him pause. He knelt there, straddling his downed opponent, arm raised high in the air, fixed.



Although the Human still lived, his face was horrifying to behold. Klain's razor claws had penetrated the flesh below the eye sockets on either side of the man's nose, his thumb had hooked deep under the chin. Everything in between—nose, mouth, cheeks and jaw—had ripped away with the helm leaving a gory, gaping hole where the old warrior's face should have been. Tattered flesh and juts of broken bone formed a gruesome bowl-like shape now rapidly filling with blood. The shredded remains of a windpipe twitched, spraying out a fine mist of red fluid. The blood splattered Klain's fur-covered chest as the last of the Human's breath escaped his lungs. The man's left eye slipped from what remained of its broken socket and tumbled into the destroyed fissure of his face. The right eye, still surrounded by most of its boney socket, focused on the sky, never to see its blueness again.

Standing, Klain dropped his arm to his side, and stared down at the corpse. His hackles rose. The icy hand of terror gripped his core. He whipped around searching for the source of his unease. Then he knew.

*Silence!*

Surveying the stands, Klain tensed his muscles in anticipation of the next test to be thrown at him. The crowd stood, leaning over the rails, all sound fled from them. Fear burned deep in Klain's veins.

*How can I survive a host that will not rest until I bleed out my life for them? It is not me against those they send to kill me. It is me against them! I cannot win.*

The full weight of the arena crushed down then, forcing his shoulders to slump with dejection. The fights of this day fled his mind. Never before had Klain known defeat.

*And with defeat, comes death…*

Then, as if someone flipped a switch, the crowd exploded into a cacophony of voices. Sound hit him from every side. He discerned nothing specific. The mass of noise sounded like a mountain collapsing into the sea. A rumble of jeers, shouts, and yells.



Still, one word became clear. Starting on his left, in a small group at first, it caught like wildfire until the entire crowd picked up the call.

"Kith! Kith! Kith!"

It rumbled on and on until every voice in the arena took up the call. They chanted so loud Klain reeled toward unconsciousness. Wave after wave struck him. He turned in a slow circle, truly seeing the crowd as never before. They chanted not for his failure, his destruction, nor his death…

*They chant for my VICTORY!*

"KITH! KITH! KITH!"

Raising the gore-filled helm he still clutched in his paw high above his head—bits of flesh and bone dangling from the neck hole and blood oozing down his arm—caused the crowd to go mad. He would not have believed it could grow louder, yet he was wrong. The very air screamed out in agony. Clamor fell from the stands like torrential rain.

The creature who had been raised in a cage and had never tasted a moment's freedom, felt something he had never experienced before…

Klain felt pride.

# Chapter 5

Clytus Rillion stood on his seat, screaming with the rest of the three hundred thousand spectators packed into the Grand Coliseum. In all his seasons of attending the Games, never had he witnessed such a spectacle.

When the Kith beast first appeared from the under-tunnels, it shocked Clytus. He had heard the tales of how big these creatures grew, yet the one down on the arena floor stood nearly three paces tall. He had never met a blacksmith with shoulders as wide as the ones this creature possessed. The man who sat next to him made a jest that the beast's chest was so large it looked like the rump of a mighty bull. Clytus sat too far away to see the creature's face, yet he made out the full mane surrounding its head clearly enough, it was the color of creamed chocolate. Honeymilk-colored fur, covered with darker spots, glistened over the rest of its body. When the beast had emerged, it let out a roar so loud that the stadium fell silent.

How he envied the first man to face such a creature.

*To have the glory of slaying such a ferocious beast in front of a crowd the size of which the Coliseum has not seen for generations!*

Alas, the first fight was short lived. The beast had charged the poor man and, in passing, had ripped off his arm as easily as if it was made from straw. The crowd had sat stunned as Ginnius Mulma'Asion, champion of at least a dozen Games, laid writhing and screaming on the arena floor. Ginnius' life force spurt from his shoulder like a fountain. All his triumphs ending as a red stain in the sands he had ruled this past turn of the seasons—a stain that would soon be washed away and forgotten.

The creature had let out another roar and flung Ginnius' severed arm into the stands. Ginnius was dead long before any Shaper could tend to his wounds.

*Not that I noticed any Shaper rushing to Ginnius' aid with that demon of death lurking down there.*

The fights that followed took much the same course. Whether singly, or in small groups, Clytus watched man after man die by the claws and fangs of the ferocious Kith creature.

When the twin brothers, Baylain and Gaylain, took to the field, Clytus knew he would see an end to the monster. He still remembered the Games of last spring when the brothers had defeated a horde of O'Arkins—a barbarous pig-faced race—outnumbered five to one. The brothers' mastery of combat had become legendary, each having been raised from birth to fight in the Games.



Baylain died first. When the beast ripped into his throat, the crowd had gasped in unison as if rehearsed. Then the creature turned to face the brother, shoving Baylain's body away, shredding half the boy's neck off with the motion. Blood spurt from the gaping hole. The boy's head dangled down between his shoulder blades like some street urchins floppy playdoll.

His brother soon joined him in the aftermore. The Kith scooped up Baylain's dropped sword and launched itself in a furious attack.

*It hacked Gaylain to pieces with his own brother's blade.*

While watching the action, Clytus noticed that the beast possessed little skill with the weapon.

*It chopped at Gaylain like a young boy smacking a tree with a stick. Each strike sending a chunk of bloody flesh flying into the air.*

The remains were not even recognizable as Human once the creature had stopped its attack.

Now, Clytus stood, caught up in the excitement of the crowd.

*Like so much the drooling idiot.*

"KITH! KITH! KITH!" His voice strained. He knew he looked like a fool as he added his calls to the rest of the cattle in the seats around him.

*Yet, my Gods, what a sight!*

The Kith beast stood over the limp bodies of Harnith, a net warrior from the coastal Isles of Komar, and poor old Salmik. A legend in his own lifetime, Salmik had seen more Games than any other in living memory. He had been much loved by the crowd.

*Live in the Games—Die in the Games, as the saying goes. The crowd will not mourn his passing long.*

Lowering its arm, the beast dropped the helm with what remained of Salmik's face. It fell to the ground like so much trash. The Kith headed for the arches that lead to the under-tunnels below the Coliseum. The crowd still stood, screaming and wailing. Clytus pushed through the throng of bodies along his row of seats toward the exit.



*The day wears on and I have much to prepare.*

As he headed out, he heard the Game's Master Julitan's voice echo out of the center box. "Now *that* folks is something you will tell your grandchildren of! Alas, WAIT! This day is yet half-done! If you will fix your eyes now upon the southron tunnel, you will see one of the O'Arkin beasts from the Morlis Mountains just emerging.

"You witness the return of Orm, King of the O'Arkin horde! Followed closely by his elite guards. This day, they have challenged our very own Tomathya, captain of the Mocley Royal Patrol and his Black Outriders!"

The roar of the crowd faded behind Clytus as he ducked through a side tunnel that led down to the main streets surrounding the Coliseum. The booming drums heralding the Black Outrider troop rumbled deep in his ears.

Clytus chuckled.

*Ha! Another band of O'Arkins lured to the Games by the promise of riches for Tomathya to slaughter.*

Exiting the Coliseum by a small side archway, he stepped onto the wide, cobblestone street. Mingling with the people wandering by, he let the throng sweep him deeper into the city.

# Chapter 6

The wagons rolled to a stop near the field they would work this day. Standing and hopping off the back of the last wagon, Arderi Cor fell in with the rest of the forty or so fielders heading for the supply shed. The half score of guarders in escort trotted off toward a copse of trees to make their rounds, scouting the area for safety.



The morning chill had dissipated under the clear blue sky spreading out across the horizon. Arderi smiled at a squirrel chattering in defiance at the guarders who penetrated its domain.

*I love springtime! Even though it means the plow, and seeding, and a day spent bent over the hoe.*

This field, like every planted section surrounding the Hild'alan stead, spread out and away from the protective wall like some giant spider's web. This one consisted of a large, flat dirt area, squarish in form. On the far side from where he stood the ground rose to create a small, steep hilly area where the land had been allowed to grow as it willed—hardwood trees and undergrowth, for the most part.

Arderi's group had spent the entire tenday so far working this one section, planting wheat. This particular field had lain fallow for several turns of the seasons and the number of small stones that had collected here during that period amazed him.

*Where do all the stones come from? This field has been planted over and again for hundreds of turns of the seasons! Surely, some fielder before me should have removed them.*

He was glad they had finished more than half the field already. They should have no problems completing the rest by Holiday.

When they reached the tool shed, Tinim Wilk, a rotund man who served as equipment keeper, handed Arderi a hoe. Continuing across the field to where they had left off the prior day, Arderi bent to his labors, letting his mind drift off to Alant's Crystal that waited at home. Near two winters had passed since the last communication from his brother.

In the first Memory Crystal, Alant was newly arrived in Mocley. He had not seen much of the city, yet the sights and sounds he had imbued for his family to experience were wonderful. It had been Arderi's first experience with a Thought Crystal—they were expensive and not for simple folk like fielders. Alant had explained that all new Initiates of the Academy were allowed the use of one Crystal when they arrived at the school. The Crystal had allowed Arderi and his family to see and hear Alant. However, the most wondrous part was that it allowed them to experience the city as if they had actually been there themselves.



*What a fantastic device! Yet, Alant has been in Mocley long enough to know the city much better. I wonder what he will show us with this one.*

Alant had imbued the memory of his approach to Mocley on that first Crystal. He sat on the front bench of a wagon, Grand Master Grintan sitting proudly by his side, in the caravan that had taken him to the city. The Thought Crystal made the user drawing from it feel as though they were the one on the bench, sitting next to the old Sier. Arderi remembered feeling the strong breeze they rode into, how it felt as it blew across his exposed arms and tussled his long hair about. It carried the smell of salt in it, something Arderi had never smelled before. While the caravan drove down the road, Arderi was amazed to see houses and barns and planted fields sitting out in the open, exposed, with no protective walls. When he commented on them—in his brother, Alant's, voice and not his own—the driver said they were called farms, each housing a single family who tended their own set of fields. Arderi could not imagine the feeling of sleeping so open and vulnerable. There was much on this Plane that could end the life of a fielder tending his crops.

*I suppose not everyone can afford the protection of a stead.*

When the wagon crested the last hill, the city of Mocley spread out before them like a wondrous blanket. He could not believe how large it was. The outer walls of the city snaked off into the horizon and he saw no end to them. A vast, blue-green ocean rolled off the left side of the city. The sheer size of what he beheld terrified him.

*Alant said the city itself held over a thousand thousand people, yet I never dreamed...*

Rows of houses and shops, tens of buildings deep, clung to the front of the massive city wall like moss on the side of a tree. There were more buildings and people, wagons and animals, on the outside of this place, than were contained within all of Hild'alan! The walls rose high, three or four times the height of his own stead's walls, and Arderi marveled at how they could even stand at all. Over the tops of those walls, great buildings climbed even higher—reaching for the heavens themselves—as if each tried to outgrow the other.



The caravan approached the main gates to the city of Mocley by winding its way through the town outside—the wagon driver named it Gatetown. The sights and sounds overwhelmed Arderi. He found himself dizzy with the commotion. They came to a stop in a large cobblestone-paved area in front of the entrance to the city proper. The gate looked wide enough to accommodate four or five wagons abreast with ease, and tall enough to admit a giant.

He gaped with awe at all the guarders, both afoot and ahorse, who milled about the area. Their tailored uniforms—yellow and blue tabards adorned with a talon clutching a wheat stalk, worn over a mail hauberk—glistened with bits of plate at strategic points around their bodies. All of them wore long swords and dirks about their waists. Some even carried long poleaxes—these being decorated with yellow and blue streamers to match their tabards. Their splendor put the guarders of his home—with their bland brown leather armor and plain shortswords—to shame. After a few moments pause, while those in charge of the caravan spoke with the guarders of the gate, they continued into the gaping jaws of the city of Mocley. So thick were the walls they passed through, everything around them plunged into darkness. Torches burning along the interior created the only light in the passage. In the middle of the tunnel, they rode under two huge iron portcullises.

*Like the teeth of the Great Beast, swallowing us whole, wagons and all.*

He could not fathom the power it would take to lift such an immense gate. The crossbars alone measured several paces deep and at least one pace thick. Each of the upright bars looked as broad around as any tree. Archer slits lined the entire passageway at two levels, halfway up the arch—some three heights of a man off the ground—and again near the apex. As he passed these death-dealing nooks, he felt the horrifying effect they would have on an enemy who tried to enter uninvited. Holding his breath, he did not release it until the tunnel spit them out into the light of day, thrusting them into the bowels of the city. Sighing with relief, he blinked at the glare of the sun after the darkness of the entry tunnel.



That was the only memory view of the city Alant had imbued on the Thought Crystal. He claimed that upon reaching the Chandril'elian his instructors immediately pressed him into his studies, never allowing him to leave the school grounds.

*Alant called the school the Chandril'elian, as it is named in the Old tongue, yet I had never heard it referred to as anything other than the Academy.*

He did describe the city for his family, however. "The city of Mocley, founded by Artimus Mocley, is well over two thousand winters old," Alant spoke in an intonation like that of a schoolmaster's. He faced the person who drew upon the Crystal as though standing right in front of them in the same room. "Artimus was a lesser Prince of the Elmorian people from the Isle of Hath'oolan. The original town makes up the center of the city we find now, encompassing the harbor and dock areas. The common folk refer to it as the Warehouse District, yet shops and homes, hotels and brothels, gambling dens and fish markets all litter the area as well as the warehouses. It is this place that keeps the Mocley Royal Patrol most occupied."

Arderi continued to till the dirt of the field, smiling as he recalled how much Alant had sounded like a local, not one describing a city he had arrived in a mere tenday before.

"The Warehouse District also contains the great Millitinia, which houses the might of the Mocley naval strength. The original wall still surrounds this district, as it did when the city called it the outer wall."

"Several hundred turns of the seasons later, as the city grew, a second outer wall was added. At first, this newly enclosed area consisted of a mishmash of more shops and houses. Over the turns of the seasons, however, the wealthier townsfolk—merchants, clergymen, officials and the like—purchased the properties. Most of this area now contains large mansions and villas. It is referred to as Old Town, which is odd as it is hundreds of winters younger than the Warehouse District."



"As the winters passed, Mocley became a center for trade. With the added income, the magistrates commissioned some truly magnificent buildings. During this period, the Grand Coliseum, the Great Palintium, and even this Chandril'elian were all constructed. The wide, paved roads, the large fountains, and the interconnected sewer system were all added or upgraded as well. A new, third outer wall was erected to encompass this new construction and is referred to as New Town, though much of it, such as the Grand Coliseum, is well over a thousand winters old."

"The final outer wall we have currently was added a few hundred winters ago. This newest addition to the city was designed to promote trade and commerce. It contains the Bazaar, the large area set aside for the buying and selling of products and produce brought in from the surrounding farms and steads. The Gem District is where everything dug up in the mines of the Morlis Mountains ends up. The Crafters District houses most of the blacksmiths, carpenters, dyers and clothiers, cordwainers and coopers. This is also the area that holds the prominent Merchantillian, which contains the most prosperous merchant shops in the entire Plane."

"Over the last few hundred winters, the city has continued to grow outside the boundaries of the outer walls. Gatetown, a group of a hundred or so buildings, surrounds the main gates to the city. On the bay side, you will find Fishtown and Gullstown. The poor, as always, build their hovels and shacks against the walls wherever they find room. At the council meeting this morn I recommended that a new fifth wall be considered for—"

Alant abruptly stopped talking. "Well, I did say I do little outside of my studies." A sheepish tone crept into his voice and a thick, leather-bound book came into view. "I am reading from one of my lesson books, *Mocley – A History* by Minroehe Granger. Sier Granger was a teacher here until not long ago."



Standing in the middle of the dirt field, hoe in hand, Arderi's thoughts shattered when a man yelled, calling an alarm. Someone grabbed his arm and he almost lost his footing.

"Pay attention, son!" Arderi looked into the worried gaze of his father. Releasing the boy's arm, Tanin jogged off toward the wagons on the far side of the field.

Glancing around, Arderi realized that most of the men from the work crew had already made it to the safety of the wagons. He jumped when a scream of pain sounded from his right. Spinning around, he looked at the tree line some twenty paces distant. Horses bayed and men shouted within the dense foliage. The sharp snap of breaking branches emanated over the field and Arderi caught a glimpse of movement through the foliage.

"Come on, boy!" Even though Tanin was yelling for him,

Arderi paused.

Stealing a glance over his shoulder, Arderi saw his father sprinting away. Turning his attention back to the trees, he stood rooted. A crash made him leap back and raise the hoe he carried for protection. Smashing through the underbrush, a horse and rider tumbled sideways, then danced backwards down the small rise that separated the copse of trees from the plowed field. The steed reared up and slipped on the mud of the steep slope. The guarder in the saddle grasped a large fur bundle tightly to his chest. Letting out a cry of pain, the man toppled over the horse's rump. Horse, rider, and furry bundle all smashed to the ground. The man's shriek ripped across the field as they went down. The horse landed on top of him cutting his scream short. The horse thrashed about, trying to regain its footing. Fear evident in its wide, rolling eyes.

That is when Arderi saw it. The furry bundle extracted itself from the tangle of man and horse. It looked like a cat—a huge, bushy thing with large gray spots across its brown fur. It must have been two paces long in the body, easily half the height of a man at its shoulders. Two large fangs jutted down from either side of a blood covered muzzle. Crouching down, it arched its back. It seemed to look for an opening to pounce on the fallen horse and rider.



A second guarder, still on horseback, burst through the trees a few paces away. Arderi recognized the man as the guarder captain, Flinnok. He held a long hunting spear at the ready. Like an arrow, he spurred his destrier on toward the beast. The big cat lunged for the trees. Dropping flat to the ground when a second guarder on horseback smashed through the underbrush into the field right in front of the beast, the creature growled and spun. It squared itself on Flinnok as the man spurned his mount to charge.

The guarder captain raised the spear, drew back, and let it fly. When he released, the beast darted to the side, deeper into the tilled field and toward Arderi. The spear kicked up dirt as it struck the ground where the beast had been a hare's breath before.

Turning, Arderi ran. A jolt of terror shot through him as he tripped on a mound of tilled earth and went down hard. Wind forced from his lungs, the boy looked back toward the tree line. The cat-thing charged directly at him. Flinnok rode hot on its tail yet losing ground every moment. Scrambling back on hands and feet like a wounded crab, Arderi's heart seemed to stop as he watched the creature draw near where he lay. Letting out a scream, he curled into a tight ball, covering his head with both hands.

The beast kicked up dirt, launching itself over the boy. It landed some three or four paces beyond, toward the road. Scurrying around the wagons, panicked fielders scattering in an attempt to get out of the way, the creature raced across the gravel road. It tore through an adjacent field faster than any horse could possibly run and vanished into a copse of trees on the far side. Staring after it in stunned silence, Arderi did not hear the horse trot up behind him nor the man dismount.



"Are you alright, boy?" Arderi turned a blank stare up at Flinnok Nime who held down a helping hand. Three large rips traced their way across the guarder captain's leather jerkin.

Arderi took his hand, allowing the guarder to pull him to his feet. "What was that?" His voice quivered with the fear that was still pulsing through his veins.

"That, my boy, was a Krugour. And a might big one at that." Flinnok turned, took hold of his horse's reins, and started back toward the group of guarders who had gathered around their fallen companion.

Arderi tensed when a hand grabbed him by the shoulders and spun him roughly around. "What in all the Planes of Hell were you thinking, boy?" A look that Arderi had never before seen plastered his father's face. The man was obviously mad, yet he looked frightened as well.

"Papa, I—" Tanin crushed him in an embrace. Upon his release, Arderi saw the seed of a tear welling in his father's eye.

Tanin quickly turned his face and his anger to Flinnok. Mir'am Cor trotted a few paces to catch up with the guarder captain. "How did a Krugour get this close to the stead, Nime?" The anger in his voice shocked Arderi. He had never known his father to lose his temper.

Flinnok Nime came to a stop and turned to face the fielder. "Not sure." He rubbed his chin in frustration. "We missed the bugger on our first patrol. Truth be told, it found us—or at least me." He fumbled with his ruined chest armor. Blood visibly stained its torn edges. "Came out of nowhere, it did. Knocked me off my horse before I knew what was happening. If not for Ralin over there, I would not be talking to you now." He looked back to his men and let his eyes linger. "If you will pardon me, Tanin, I have my own to be looking after." Flinnok crossed the field and joined his men.

Tanin strode back to his son. Snagging Arderi by the arm, he led the boy in the opposite direction to where the rest of the fielders stood gathered. All of the men gathered in a tight knot around the wagons.



"Do you think that guarder will be alright, Papa?"

"We shall find out in due time, son. They are Militants. They will tend to their own. For now, let us see to ours shall we?"

He watched his father, who again had become the same easy-going man he had known all his life. Arderi tried to stop the shaking that filled him. Unable to calm down, he let Tanin guide him as they walked.

Masstin Wilt, a worn, thin man broke from the group of fielders. "The boy alright?"

Tanin glanced over his shoulder at Arderi. "Fine, I think. A little shaken." He made a motion with his arm to the far side of the field. "Anyone know who the fallen guarder is?"

"Nix, not as yet." Mir'am Toln's answer was accompanied by a scowl. "What say we break for halfmeal, huh Tanin?"

Tanin reached over and planted a hand on his son's shoulder. "Arderi was just talking about being eaten—I mean...eating." He made no attempt to hide his grin.

Several of the men gave out laughs and muttered agreement. Mir'am Wilt pulled out the food baskets and passed them around. Basket in hand, Riln caught Arderi's attention and motioned for him to follow. Gathering up his own food, Arderi fell in step behind his friend.

"Oiy!"

Arderi froze. He knew that tone in his father's voice all too well.

"And where might you be going, lads?" His father's voice had his do-not-mess-with-me tone.

Both boys looked back at the group of fielders. "Just a walk, Papa." Though Arderi still shook inside, he hoped it did not show in his voice.

"I do not be thinking so, lad. I allow the beasties only one chance a day to eat one of my young." Chuckles resounded through the group. He pointed off to the other wagons. "You boys can stay near us if you need to talk."



"Yes, Mir'am Cor." Riln chimed in with a quickness that Arderi found discouraging. Pointing toward the furthest of the wagons, he drug Arderi to it by the elbow.

Hopping on the back of the wagon, Riln unwrapped his meal. "That was wicked!" He kept a low voice so no one except Arderi could hear. "What were you thinking when that thing charged you?"

Arderi looked at him as if he were an idiot. "What in all the Planes of Hell do you think I was thinking?" Keeping his retort low, it came out more as a harsh whisper. "I thought I was going to die!"

Riln bit into the piece of flatbread he pulled from his basket. "You did look rather silly flinging dirt all around." His giggle barely made it around his mouth full of food. A large piece of dried beef came to Arderi's rescue and followed the bread into Riln's mouth, forcing him to chew instead of talk.

Tearing off a piece of his own flatbread, Arderi placed it in his mouth. It tasted of ash.

*There is no way I can eat anything just now.*

He wrapped up the rest of his meal and set the food bundle in the wagon behind Riln. "We got a Crystal from Alant this morn. Came in with that caravan yesterday I suppose." Arderi stared off toward the woods into which the Krugour had disappeared.

"You all right, Arderi?"

Arderi glanced at his friend and noted the concern on his face. He nodded his head. "Why?"

"I was with you this morn when your Papa told you about the Crystal, remember."

"Aye, right. I meant about the caravan." Arderi let his eyes drift back to the tree line.

"Aye...and?" Riln continued to eat.

"You remember when we were younger, how we used to always say that one day we would leave on one of them caravans? Just hide in one of the wagons and go wherever it took us?"

"Aye, yet Arderi, that was just boy's talk. Why bring it up now? What are you getting at?"



"It is just—" Arderi let out a sigh. "I do not know any more, Riln." He hopped onto the wagon and sat down hard next to his friend. "I have thought a few times of doing that here recently. Jumping on one, you know. Going wherever it takes me."

"You got a lot of nerve, Arderi Cor!" Riln threatened him with a half-eaten piece of dried beef as if it were a knife. "I ought to sock you one right here and now." He turned and gestured toward the trees. "It is a shame that cat did not whack you a good one!"

The anger in Riln's voice took Arderi by surprise. Arderi did not try to keep the heat from his own. "What is that supposed to mean?"

"You! That is what it means." Riln slammed the remainder of his flatbread down into his food bundle. "Look, I may not know much about things, due to me being a *fielder* and all, yet you!" He poked Arderi's chest with the knife-of-beef for added punctuation. "You are special! We all know it. We knew it about Alant and we know it about you. This is just you being scared of being Tested soon, huh?"

Arderi rubbed his chest where Riln had jabbed him. "Mayhaps, I am a man grown now. I should be Tested soon. Yet, so what?"

"So what?" Riln looked as though his head was about to explode. "Alant has been taken to Hath'oolan! By the Twelve, Arderi, Hath'oolan!" He flung his arms into the air. "That is incredible! I do not think our stead has ever produced a Shaper who has been taken there. Ever! And you are next, Arderi! I only wish I had that opportunity."

Shaking his head, Arderi ran a hand through his brown hair. "You act as if I have already been Tested, Riln. Remember Siln Tested and was found to have nothing. No ability with the Essence. There is no guarantee that I will be any different."

"Siln!" Riln snorted to show what he thought of that. "You think you are like your brother? No one expected anything different of him." He cocked his head and gave an inquisitive look. "Did you?"



Arderi hated thinking negatively about his brother. Despite all of Siln's faults, Arderi loved him. Of all his siblings, they were the closest in age as well as spirit. He paused before answering, guilt welling inside. "Well, no, not really." He was only being honest. Looking over at the other fielders eating a few wagons away, he eyed his brother, shame at feeling the way he did getting the better of him. "Alas, it does not work that way, Riln. The Essence owns its will, as the saying goes. You cannot possibly believe I will have any ability with the Essence just because Alant is my brother."

"Why not? You do." Accusation filled Riln's words. Arderi shook his head in protest as Riln continued. "Really? You have always believed. You have always known!"

"Nix! That is the problem. I have always wanted to be different, to get away from this stead. I am terrified of growing to be nothing more than a fielder—like my Papa before me, and his before him. I lay awake sometimes and ache. Ache with the desire to run. Escape what I am going to become. What I am becoming." Letting his head droop to his chest, Arderi stared at the tilled dirt around him.

"You think we all have not dreamed those dreams—dreamt of the adventure, the excitement? Aye! I have! Yet you, you are going to do it, Arderi. We all have known that, not just from what happened to Alant, either. I have known since we became house mates. You *are* special, Arderi, and once they Test you, the whole Plane will know it."

"What if I do not pass? What if I am not special? I do not think I can live life knowing I will never be more than a fielder."

Arderi flew from the wagon and found himself lying in the dirt for the second time this day. He looked up at Riln who stood over him staring down with fists clenched.

"And what is wrong with being a fielder, Arderi?" Riln looked as angry as Arderi had ever seen. "You love to sit there and feel sorry for yourself, even though we all think you are bound for something more. Yet what do I have to look forward to, huh? I do not have a famous brother gallivanting around the Plane! I did not pass the Test when I took it! Remember! I am a fielder, plain and simple. Do not try and…" Kicking dirt at Arderi, Riln stormed off toward the other fielders. "Nix, forget it."



Arderi watched Riln stride toward the other men, the remainder of his food held tight in hand. "It is not that…" He spoke under his breath then raised his voice. "Riln, I am sorry!"

Riln simply waved a dismissive hand over his shoulder and hopped into a wagon with a few other men.

Rolling over on his back, Arderi stared up into the clear-blue sky.

*It is not that! It is this…gnawing in the back of my mind that something is not right. And it scares me. I do not understand why, yet by the Twelve, I am scared!*

# Chapter 7

The day had turned out to be a good one for Clytus Rillion. He had spent much of the morning in the bazaar procuring items needed for the trip—filling some five or six wagonloads of supplies for himself and his men. Very little else needed to be done. All stood in readiness.

"I will give you three Pynes per pound, Grilmire, and I will take all you have." Clytus waited for the fat merchant sitting in front of him, sweating even in the cool breeze of spring, to mull over the offer.



"Three Pynes is a bit shy. Still, if you take the full two hundred stones worth…" Grilmire whipped a multicolored cloth across his brow. A grunt escaped his lips causing his multiple chins to jiggle. "I do not even know why I bother haggling with you, Master Rillion! You come to me knowing what you will pay. Fine, all will be ready come morn. Everything we have agreed on will be loaded and waiting for you outside my warehouse in Gatetown."

Shaking the merchant's ringed hand, Clytus pulled out a small sack containing coins and bounced it in the palm of his hand. "Aye, mayhaps you lose the ability to haggle. Still, you know where you stand with me." He tossed the bag onto the wooden counter between them. "And I always come to you first for my supplies."

The merchant, Grilmire, eyed the list of items he had written down. The sleeve of his tent-like silken robe—red covered in green and yellow embroidery in swirling patterns—billowed in the slight breeze of the Bazaar. "I think it will all fit on two wagons. You say you also need dayhires to drive them?"

"Aye. I have four wagons already loaded at my villa. I have men that can drive them to Gatetown, yet only one of those will be accompanying me on my journey north, so I will need five men to drive up to the Wartin'alan stead. I will pay for their lodging there and they can return home on the morrow."

"Who will drive them on the morrow after that?" The merchant squinted at Clytus.

"My merc troop is camped near Wartin'alan. I will pull men from their ranks to drive the rest of the way."

"Two hundred stones of dried beef, half hundred of salt, a veritable wagon load of dried fruit, and the list goes on. All this will last even your troop of hungry men for a quite some time. I have never known you to travel out so far." Grilmire did not bother counting the coin and simply moved the bag from the counter to a lockbox on the floor.



"Aye, this one is personal. We will be heading off into the Nektine." At the puzzled look from his old friend, Clytus sighed. "The Nektine Mountains. North, past the Artoc River."

"What? Up near Stillwater way?" Grilmire looked shocked.

"Aye, we will be crossing the Artoc at Stillwater."

"What in the name of the Eternals would drag you up there? Are not those the lands of the wild O'Arkins?"

"Aye, yet it is not O'Arkin we hunt, it is something much, much worse. And more precious to me than you will ever know, my old friend."

The fat merchant grunted. "I hear the ruckus in the coliseum has finally subsided."

"You should have seen it! The Kith beast was a terror!" Clytus could not help except grin. "It slew Ginnius Mulma'Asion before he could even make his first attack!"

"Ginnius?" Grilmire hrumphed. "I never liked that pompous fool. Twas about time someone put him down." He again wiped the sweat cascading down his brow. "Who killed it then? The

Twins?"

Clytus leaned back in his chair. "The Twins did not fair any better." He raised a hand to forestall the merchant's interruption. "Oh, they lasted longer. Alas, both now have met the Twelve in the aftermore."

"Nix! Keep me in suspense no longer! Who felled the beast?"

Shaking his head, Clytus answered after a moment's pause and a grin at the merchant's boyish excitement. "No one. It came down to old Salmik, yet by that point I did not envy him his task. He made a good showing—wounding the thing and almost ending it—only the beast's strength remained too great. He also dwells with the Twelve now."

"Live in the Games, Die in the Games." Grilmire made the sign of the Twelve in front of his chest. "What of the beast? What of it now?"

Pushing his seat back, Clytus stood. "Who knows? The Julitans will think of something I am certain. They will have to recoup some of the losses from this day. The amount they spent in death tax alone must have been substantial." He turned and mingled with the stream of people passing through the Bazaar.



"Be careful up north, Clytus!" He heard Grilmire shout. "I would hate to lose one of my best customers!"

Clytus chuckled.

*Aye, old friend, I would hate to short your bank account as well.*

The main thruway of the Bazaar led in the direction he needed to go so he let the current of people sweep him along. The Bazaar in Mocley, much like any market area of the major cities he had seen in his day, sat near the main entrance gates. Permanent stone and mortar shops surrounding temporary wooden stalls intermixed with tents sitting next to farmers on wagons where people criss-crossed harking the wares they carried on trays or bags or boxes. They sold a variety of items from every corner of the known Plane. A mixing of colors and sights and sounds and smells that never failed to impress

Clytus.

He considered leaving the Bazaar by way of Main, past the Great Palintium—the Temple of the Twelve Gods of Man was the first sight one saw when coming from the Bazaar through the gates of New Town. It was a huge building, some thirty stories high with many spires and steeples. Its large, grandiose staircases led past massive statues of the Twelve Gods of Man to spill onto wide patios bedecked with finely crafted columns and frescos. Unfortunately, it was nearing midday, which meant priests standing along Main, with incense braziers burning, holding the artifact of their God, taking in offerings and doling out prayers for the midday worship session.

*It never ceases to amaze me how much people need to believe in something.*

This inevitably slowed traffic to a crawl as it crept past the Great Palintium, and Clytus had no time for such.

Instead he continued east through the Bazaar coming out at Narian Way.



*Narian, ha! As if this street was paved with gold.*

He passed by the Boulevard of the Gods at an intersection where a large center fountain stood. One of many fountains located throughout the city. Water flowed over statues of Mermidian at this one, depicting the sea folk who lived in the waters of the Glonlore Bay. Each one appeared frozen in time as if caught while playing and splashing in the fountain's water. Their nakedness, spackled with scales and fins at strategic locations, accentuated the allure of the water creatures.

*Though I would wager that only a handful of people in this city have ever laid eyes on one of the creatures that live in the waters at their very doorstep.*

Continuing down Narian Way, and closer to the gates of the Merchantillian, he found the crowd thinning. With a grin he noticed that not only did the dress of the people around him improve, so did their smell. Reaching the small gates, he stepped around two people whom the city watch had stopped. The guards questioned the dingy clad men as to what possible business they had with any merchant of the caliber housed within this particular section of the city. A few of the guards glanced Clytus' way, though none made any motion to hinder his progress. Passing under the main portcullis, which protected the Merchantillian and separated it from the rest of Mocley, the captain of the merchant guard, Faztilmin, nodded at Clytus from his perch on a tall stool sitting next to a gatehouse door. It still astonished Clytus that the merchants in this section had their own guard separate from the city watch.

*The merchant's guard—or merkswords, as the locals refer to them—are better trained, that is for sure.*

Inclining his head toward the man, Clytus continued on his path. Since many of the men who employed him owned shops in the Merchantillian, his was a face the merkswords had seen many a time.

In this section of the city, one could find the more expensive items that might be on one's shopping list. As he walked its broad, tree-lined and flower edged, cobblestone streets, he was greeted here and there by passers-by and shopkeeps he had come to know over the past decade. He waved or nodded to each politely, not pausing in his stride. It pleased him that his reputation was of someone who got the job done, and one that could be trusted as well.



Passing through the rear gates of the Merchantillian, nodding to the merkswords stationed there, Clytus entered the Sept district. At the next intersection, again with a large ornate fountain—this one depicting the Twelve Gods of Man in various poses atop a mountain, the water cascading down between them like miniature streams to form a lake in the basin—he picked up the tail end of the Boulevard of the Gods. Glancing down the road toward the Palintium, he shook his head at the mass of people who milled about the street. With midday prayers in full swing, he knew he had made the correct decision. That area of the street moved like chilled molasses. Making his way down this road and away from the Palintium, he found himself at the main gates to the Academy.

The front gates, always closed and locked, sat at the very end of the Boulevard of the Gods. He had never seen its portcullis raised on any occasion. He was not even sure if they could open. Turning southwards, through the small alleys that wound between the homes of workers and servants who made their living off the Academy, he skirted the school's outer wall. Halting outside the small postern gate used by those who wished to enter the grounds, Clytus reached over and pulled a cord dangling from the right of the gate. Patiently, he stood waiting the arrival of an Academy Guard.

*Unlike the merkswords, these hobbswords who work for the Shapers are merely errand boys and doormen, all prim and proper. The children of wealth found to have no ability with the Essence, yet whose parents wish them to be close to it anyway. Although, the elite guard here is a cut above.*

After a fashion—a suitable enough time to show whoever waited they were not as important as those within—a hobbsword walked out from the gatehouse and strode up to Clytus. This one was a young man, no older than twenty winters. Like all hobbswords, he was smartly dressed. His red and gold stripped tabard with a large yellow starburst on the breast—the symbol of the Shaper's Order—was spotless, pressed, and fit smooth and snug over his chainmail shirt. Matching breeches, tucked neatly into polished black calf-boots, completed his ensemble. Tall and fair of hair, the hobbswords showed good muscle for his age.



*With long sword worn on the right hip, makes this one a lefty.*

Without thinking, Clytus adjusted his stance to better defend against the off-handed fellow.

The guard came to a stop just inside the gate. "State your purpose, sir."

"I have an appointment with the Council of Elders. My name is Clytus Rillion." He always hated coming to the Academy.

*With all its layers of formality, it is a wonder the Shapers control anything.*

The guard turned and spoke into a small door off to the

side of the gate. "Mir'am Clytus Rillion here to see the Council of Elders by appointment."

A youngster around the age of twelve winters walked into view, nodded, and took off at a swift jog along a crushed-gravel path. The boy disappeared into the lush foliage, which covered the outer area of the Academy grounds.

"If you would please clear the gate area, Mir'am Rillion." The hobbsword gestured to a bench that sat against the outer wall along the street. "You may have a seat over there while you wait." He took up his post again, ignoring Clytus.

Stepping away from the gate, Clytus walked to the bench the young man had indicated, sat on one end, and waited—his mind a whirlwind torrent of what he was about to do. Within a few moments, the young boy who had run off with the message hovered in front of him. Clytus cut his eyes to the gate and noticed that it stood open.

*I did not even hear it. I* am *getting old.*

Clytus raised an eyebrow and inclined his head.



"The Council of Elders will see you, Mir'am Rillion." The boy had a country accent that Clytus pegged for one of the northron steads. "If you will permit, sir, I will lead you." He stretched out a hand showing the gate that stood a pace away.

*I know the way inside better than you, young one.*

Standing, Clytus gave an over-acted motion for the boy to lead on. They stepped through the gate and proceeded down the main path leading to one of the larger buildings. The grounds themselves boasted some of the lushest plant life within the city. Never had Clytus walked these paths and not seen flowers in full bloom, trees dangling plump fruits, and the bushes decked out in brilliant green leaves.

*They put the richest villa gardens to shame. Alas, being able to bend the Essence to your will should afford the Shapers some privileges.*

Tall trees bathed the area in a cooling blanket of shade. Deep green grass covered any location not meticulously planted with shrubbery or flowering plants. The crushed white stone paths laid out for foot traffic were wide and smooth, easy to walk.

*It always strikes me how clean the air is here, so unlike the stench of the rest of the city.*

The building the boy led him to—called the Ques'lian, meaning great hall in the Old tongue—stood three stories high with a mass of ivy growing up its northron face. Grand, lead-lined stained-glassed windows ran the length of every level giving the building a feeling of elegance that escaped other stone buildings of its type. They entered through a set of large wooden double-doors then went up a small flight of steps to the entrance hall area. Several doors pierced each wall and two staircases emptied into the room. Tapestries, most depicting nature scenes in various seasons, hung between the doors. Of the furnishings there were little. A few benches lined the walls. Lit braziers stood in strategic places, casting light around the room. A small desk and chair took up one corner. As with every time Clytus had been here, an attendant sat at the desk. This day a young man in a gray robe sat behind it. The gray robe with a small yellow starburst on the breast he wore marked him as an Initiate of the Academy. The guide-boy walked up to the desk and waited.



The Initiate did not pause in his reading at first. Finally, he looked up and eyed the young boy in front of him. "Yes?"

"Mir'am Rillion to see the Council of Elders by marked appointment as confirmed by Initiate Wirlane." The boy did not relax from his formal stance.

"My thanks, you may return to your post." At a wave of the Initiate's hand, the guide-boy bowed with a nod, turned, and marched out of the reception area. "Mir'am Rillion, please have a seat, the Council of Elders knows of your arrival and sends word they will see you shortly." The Initiate smiled then buried his nose back in the book, effectively dismissing Clytus.

*Arrogant, even before they learn to control their gift.*

Clytus walked across the room toward the row of benches. Before he sat, a familiar voice called out from behind him. "Master Rillion, how nice to see you again."

Turning, he faced the elderly man descending the staircase.

A warmth sprang in Clytus that his face reflected. Sier Felstar Lysentoc approached him dressed in his usual deep-blue silk robe. Fringed with golden starbursts around the cuffs and hem, the robe marked the man as a Master Shaper. His long white hair raced down his back in a vain attempt to catch up to the even longer gray-white beard flowing down his chest. Clytus had no idea how old the Sier was, yet his wrinkled age-spotted hands and face betrayed the straight back and walk of a younger man.

Sier Lysentoc crossed the chamber with purposeful strides and clasped Clytus' outstretched hand. "I feared you had already left before I could bid you well on your journey." The old Sier held his hand with a fatherly grace.

"Nix, Sier Lysentoc. I was going to come see you after I met with the Council. How is your health this fine spring day?"

"Better, my thanks to you." Felstar motioned toward the benches. "Please, let an old man sit with you while you wait."

"I would be honored." Both men took a seat. "Why do I sense this meeting of ours is no accident?" Clytus glanced around the room to insure no other could overhear their conversation.



"How cleaver you are, for a simple *Tat'Sujen.*" The title, though the Sier barely whispered it, made Clytus flinch and glance around the room once more. Just the mere mention of Tat'Sujen could be deadly if spoken in the wrong ear. Felstar's smile took any sting from his words, however. "I wanted to speak with you before you went inside." The old Sier lowered his voice and leaned closer. "Those fool Elders will ask you for something, something you are forbidden to accept by your *Order.*" He stressed the last word and Clytus knew the Sier would not repeat the Tat'Sujen title even if they could not be overheard.

"My son—" Clytus stopped speaking when the old man raised a hand and pressed his fingers to Clytus' lips.

"We have little time, friend. You will understand when you hear the Council's offer. It appalls me that they would even ask this of you. And I did protest. Alas, those old fools on the Council never bother to heed my words. They, like most Shapers, do not believe in the Foretelling. I do not blame them for this. So many charlatans have proclaimed to have it. Know this, Clytus, my good friend, the men in that room are the most dangerous ever appointed to the Council. Alas, that is no concern of yours. You must forgive an old man's rants.

"What I have come to say is this—you must accept their terms. You have my word that you will not have to fulfill them." Felstar sat back.

Clytus' insides tightened and bile rose in his throat. "Sier, as you say, I am…" He could not help himself and glanced around the room once more to insure their privacy remained secure. "Tat'Sujen. You may be the only person in all of Mocley who knows my Order even exists. Just you knowing could end your life. Yet, you know some of the truth to our Order. You know I cannot break a vow once given. If they ask a service forbidden to me—if I accept, I must keep to my word. If I cannot…"



The Sier simply smiled and patted Clytus' hand once more. "My old friend, I know your Order better than you think. And yes, I know what you must do. You know I have always been true to my word as well, although I have never thought you truly believed in my Foretelling." He raised a hand to forestall Clytus' rebuttal once more. "Hear me, there is even less time now, they are about to call you in. The Council will offer something they think will tie you to them. Something they will not understand that you cannot agree to. To this thing, you *must* agree! If you do, you have my word you will not have to fulfill this vow, and your son, Sindian, will live. If you deny them, Sindian will die. These two paths I have seen clearly."

Sier Lysentoc was correct, Clytus was unsure if he truly believed in Foretellings. Yet, hearing his old friend speak of Sindian's death sent a wave of agony through Clytus' very core.

"Mir'am Rillion?" the Initiate at the desk called out. "The Council of Elders is ready for you now."

Clytus nodded to the boy before returning his attention to

Felstar. "Sier, as always you have given me much to think on. I will take your words to heart." Rising to his feet, he helped the old man stand.

"I have cherished your friendship, I will miss it most of all." Sadness coated Felstar's voice.

This made Clytus chuckle. "I shall only be gone for a few moons—" He meant to say more. The look of sadness in the old Siers eyes stopped him. A wave of resolve rippled through him. Adopting a more formal tone, he inclined his head. "I am grateful, Sier Lysentoc. For your council as well as your friendship. I shall miss these as well. Alas, I will pay what needs be paid, if it means my son shall live."

The two men shook hands once more, this time with great intention. Clytus turned and stalked to the door leading to the audience chamber he had visited so many times before as if the Headsman himself waited within. He did not look back at his friend.

*I will pay what needs be paid!*



The audience chamber was not a large room. On a center dais at its far end rested a curved lacquered redwood table, beautiful in its simplicity. Behind this sat seven high-backed chairs, each made to match the table and each holding one member of the Council of Elders of the Shaper's Order. No other furniture occupied the room. Crossing the chamber, Clytus came to a stop a pace short of the table and eyed the men who sat across from him. The seven men occupying the chairs were all old. Each he knew by name, most he thought were good men. All wore the same deep-blue silken robes trimmed in the golden starbursts of their Order that Sier Lysentoc wore.

*Master Shapers all.*

Yet each also wore a large, golden sun medallion hanging from a gold chain around their neck.

*Leaders of an Order that stretches to almost every corner of the Plane.*

Some wore beards, others clean-shaven. All were men of great power here within Mocley.

*The Proctors of Mocley may have power, command of the guards and fleet. Yet it is these seven men who truly rule this city, if not the Plane.*

"Mir'am Rillion." Arthimius Blanch, the Grand Elder, sat in the centermost chair looking at Clytus with withered, baggy eyes. "You have made your preparations I may assume?"

"I have, Grand Elder." Clytus found that proper etiquette with this group worked better than not.

"And when do you plan to leave?"

"On the morrow, if you have the device I need."

"We have it."

None of the men made a summons, yet a side door opened. A boy dressed in an Initiate robe entered carrying a leather pack, which he offered to Clytus. The Initiate left by the same door while Clytus opened the pouch.

"The apparatus is quite simple to use. Insert it into the beast and it will extract the blood automatically. It will also keep the blood fresh for your journey home. Once the blood of the Drakon is in our possession, we will then be able to save your son from his illness."



Closing the pack, he returned his attention back to the Shapers. "My thanks to you, Grand Elder." He pivoted to exit through the door he had entered by.

"Mir'am Rillion, we have not yet agreed to a price."

His heart sank and his mind reeled.

*What is the price going to be that I cannot agree to?*

Turning back, he faced the Council. "My apologies, I am anxious to set upon my task."

"Your son has Dispaxion, with less than one season to live I understand." Clytus forced his jaw to relax—it tensed at the mention of his son. "To cure the boy we need a very rare component, the blood of a Drakon which is Essence infused." The Grand Elder recited this as if reading it from a script.

*Again with the formalities, you say this every time we meet old man. As if I need the reminder that my son has little life left to live!*

"You are to provide this blood as we have no means to

retrieve it ourselves. Even with this ingredient, the risk to those who will heal your son is great. A Shaper himself may die from the feedback the Essence could unleash during the Melding that is required to cure this illness. Not to mention, it will take over a tenday to Meld the Essence in the boy and rid him of the sickness. This risk will be shared by the eight Shapers it will require to accomplish the Meld." Arthimius leaned forward in his chair. "For this we require an equally valuable payment."

*He is like a wolf standing over a cornered hare.*

"I have already told you, Grand Elder, however much narian it takes, I will pay." Clytus knew, by the feeling inside him, he was not going to like the next few moments of his life. It was a feeling that he had had many times before. A feeling that usually ended with something sharp piercing a part of his body that he would rather not have pierced.

"Gold? You think the Shaper's Order has need of more gold?" Arthimius shook his head. "No, Mir'am Rillion. This council has a different sort of payment in mind." He sat back. "Your reputation as a swordsman is well known. Some even drop the name of Tat'Sujen when speaking of you. Common folk have always loved their mythical tales." The old Sier hacked into a white linen cloth. "However, you are good to your word, and the merc troop you command seems well trained and disciplined. Fanciful tales aside, sir, the Shapers can use a man like you from time to time. We shall save your son, provided you bring us the blood we need. As payment, we require five turns of the seasons worth of service from you and your mercenary band. You shall be paid your normal wages during this time, of course, yet you will do as this council bids." He waved his arm around the room to indicate the other six men. "Without question, without hesitation."



A stabbing agony shot through Clytus' heart. Head spinning, his knees weakened.

*I need to sit down. No! I need to get drunk!*

Clytus stared at the old man behind the desk as if he had never seen him before. "You know…" He bore his gaze into

Arthimius'. "You are taking a grave risk, Grand Elder?"

"And how is this so?" A bit of uncertainty laced the old man's words.

"You say you do not believe in the tales of the Tat'Sujen, yet like all men you have heard them. If the Order truly exists, and if I were one—for as you say, it has been dropped from time to time—you know that I would be forced to decline your offer. The vows of that Order would never let me agree to such terms."

"Why would that be, sir?"

"Well, in the stories, a Tat'Sujen can never go against their core principles. To agree to serve someone unconditionally, someone who is not bound by those principles, could make things...complicated."

"So? If you were one of these farcical Tat'Sujen, what grave risk have I taken then? You would simply decline our offer." Arthimius waved a negating hand. "Your son would die for some stupid principles of some preposterous Order."



"Ah, yet Elder, remember the stories. A Tat'Sujen will resort to killing if it means keeping his Order secret. Every street urchin knows this. If I decline, it would prove that I am Tat'Sujen and that this farcical Order truly exists. I would then have to kill everyone on this council to conceal myself and my Order, would I not?" Clytus let his left hand come to rest on the hilt of his sword.

When Arthimius' eyes opened wide, Clytus enjoyed watching them dance from his face to his sword and back again. And not just the Grand Elder, each of the old Siers sitting at the table were eyeing him with growing trepidation. Clytus' laugh resounded through the room. In fact, he had to restrain it from becoming a hysterical outcry. "Siers, Siers." Holding up his hands, he waved them not to stand. "I am astounded that men of such learning could believe, in the smallest way, a myth like the Tat'Sujen Order." He bowed low to hide the horror he knew must be spreading across his face. "My apologies, Siers, for the jest. It has been long since I was able to see humor in anything." He let out a laugh again as he held up both hands in submission. "Of course, I will accept your terms. Five winters of loyal service from myself and my troop in payment for the life of my son is nothing." Clytus' insides wove into knots and then twisted upon themselves.

*What am I doing? How can I allow myself to be bound to men who may use me for ill gain? And with a smile on my face no less!*

Clytus, in such turmoil, failed to realize the Grand Elder had come to his feet. "How dare you! How *dare* you!" Spittle flew from the old Sier's mouth. "Get out, you abomination!" The Grand Elder's voice screeched through the small chamber. "You have accepted the terms! I do not want to see you in my presence unless I summon you! Do you hear me? Get out!"

Clytus did not remember leaving the audience chamber, nor the grounds for that matter. The only thing he remembered was retching in a side ally somewhere outside the Academy. He then put his head in his hands and wept. Wept for his son. Wept for his very soul. Lying crumpled in that ally, tears rolling unabated down his face, time vanished for him and soon the shades of day deepened into the shadows of darkness.



Looking up past the edge of the slate that overhung the roof above him, his eyes followed the tiny, yellow moon, Traynor, as it crept from one side of the thin alleyway to the other.

*Felstar, I am lost and following the only light you have given me. I hope it is not a will-the-wisp.*

# Chapter 8

The chanting and yelling of the crowd still rang loud and clear in Klain's ears, even as dusk fell upon the land. He had finally stopped pacing the small cell. The excitement and adrenalin he had felt earlier had been subdued by sheer physical exhaustion. Resting stretched out now on his rag-covered stone bed, he mused at the wooden fingers above him keeping the ceiling at bay.



*You did not crush me this day, nor did anything the Games threw at me. Mayhaps on the morrow you will have more luck.*

A grin parted his lips and his eyelids dropped, fatigue slowly winning the battle over the elation he had been drunk on since returning to his cell.

The small trap door used to feed him swung open and Klain noticed his Master, Estular Jerts, had come personally to pass him lastmeal, something the Human had never before done. Freshly slaughtered lamb rested on the large platter once more. Rising quickly, Klain whipped up a leg of meat. Listening as Estular paced outside his door, Klain attacked the food with fervor.

"What a magnificent sight!" Stopping his pacing, Estular peered through the bars of the tiny window. "I never dreamed you would survive this day." Klain heard the man rubbing his hands together in his excitement. "The Julitans are furious! The money they lost in death tax alone must have been—" He stopped. Grasping the bars, he peered directly at Klain, watching him eat. "They say they will not fight you again, you know?" A wicked grin crossed his face. "Well, not against any Human opponents anyway. You have ruined the Games for any future Kith who might want to play." Estular resumed his pacing. "They offered to buy your death. Can you imagine! They will pay me just to see you tortured and dispatched for the crowd. Glorious!"

The more Estular spoke, the further Klain's lips rose to bare his blood-drenched fangs. A deep growl erupted at the Human's last words and Klain flung the half-eaten hind leg he held at the door. The force of the blow sent Estular fleeing to the far side of the hall. Klain would love to have laughed at the pathetic Human, yet he was too furious for such pettiness. "And what of me, you cur! Have I not done what you wanted of me? Am I now to lay down and die for your amusement?" Paws gripping the bars of the cell door window, Klain glared at his Master who stood pressed against the far wall.



Klain watched as Estular regained his composure when the man realized the ironbound door stood intact. "You? You are a beast!" Shoving himself off the stone wall, Estular closed in on the small window, staying far enough away to be out of Klain's reach. "I purchased you to make me rich!" Contempt dripped heavy in his tone. "You did that this day, yet you did it too well! You are worthless to me now! An expense!" The man's raised voice echoed in the enclosed space. "Living, you now cost me money. This leaves me with only one option where you are concerned." Holding up one finger, he pointed it to the ceiling, then jabbing it to the ground. "Death." With exaggerated effort, he brushed his lavish red coat with his hands and straightened his collar. "Are you such a stupid thing that you cannot see this?" Estular laughed and walked down the hall to the exit.

Madness overcame Klain. Throwing himself savagely at the cell door, he clawed and bashed at it. His roar shook the dust-filled air of the cellblock, shattering the normal silence of the place. His Keeper and several jailers appeared, yelling and screaming at him, though in his enraged state, Klain heard none of their words.

"I will rip Jerts' head from his shoulders with my bare claws!" His screams were almost an unintelligible roar. "I will feed on his flesh. I will drink—" Reality crashed down on him as if the hand holding the ceiling above him finally had given way. He found himself on his knees, stars shooting through his eyes. He looked up to see a pain staff sticking through the bars of the window. The stick was nothing new to him, having been beaten by it many times in the past, yet this had been different—much more intense.

The cell door swung open and his fat, black-skinned Keeper strode in. "That be max foci, beastie, want more?" The puffy face of the Keeper floated at the far end of the black onyx staff.

Fast as his body would allow, Klain whipped out a paw and grabbed the end of the stick. His brain screamed as pain laced through his hand. The very marrow of his bones scorched with agony. It ripped up his arm with such ferocity that the force flung him backward. His legs folded under him and his head slammed against the stone wall behind him. Vomit filled his mouth and dripped from his face onto his chest. Trying to howl in rage, only a meager whimper came out. Laughter rang in his ears like a bell heard from far away. "It be too bad the Master wants you whole."

Klain rolled over onto his side to clear his mouth. Cell door banging shut, he listened to the footsteps receding down the hall. He wanted to sit up and knew he was far from that. Laying there, breathing in the stench of his own puke, he lost focus and had no memory of the cell any longer.

# Chapter 9

The rest of the day continued normally for Arderi Cor. Raking and hoeing, removing stones and rocks, planting seeds. Riln avoided him, which suited Arderi fine just now.

*No one understands. I cannot live life as a fielder—locked away in this stead. I want to see things. Travel. Like my Brother.*



The ride back to the stead was not much different from the rest of the day. Sorn Toln tried a few ribs about Arderi and the Krugour. These got a few chuckles from the others, yet for the most part, the men rode in silence.

The guarder, a man by the name of Ralin, would have died even if his mount had not crushed him to the ground. Ralin's body now occupied its own wagon. The fielders who had ridden out in it found seats amongst the other wagons. Arderi had caught a glimpse of the corpse as the rest of the guarders carried it across the field. One side of his neck was torn away and bits of flesh and tendon jutted out at odd angles. One man held Ralin's head while they carried it. If he had not, the head would have ripped off under its own weight.

After halfmeal, the fielders had returned to work as if nothing had happened. Reaching the spot in the ground where the guarder had died caused a pang of guilt mixed with remorse to envelope Arderi as he stared down at the large spot of dirt drenched with the man's blood.

*I did not know a man carried that much blood in his body.*

It sent a shiver down his spine thinking of it even now, on the journey home.

The wagons rolled to a stop just outside the fielder's gate. The men dismounted silently from the wagons and dispersed, going to their own apartments. Jumping down behind his father, Arderi followed Tanin who approached the guarder captain. "The men and I will be by to pay our respects after lastmeal. I am truly sorry for your loss."

Flinnok took Tanin's outstretched hand and shook it. "Tis our life Tanin. We, each of us, have our jobs to do. Ralin's job was to protect the people of this stead, or die trying. He was a good lad. He shall be missed."

The sincerity in Flinnok's voice touched Arderi.

His father nodded once and turned toward home.

There was much fuss during lastmeal over Arderi's near-death experience. His mother would not leave him alone and made sure he ate a second helping of everything.

*As if she feels guilty for having almost missed the chance to feed me my final meal.*



Mag'Oella hounded him as much as his Ma did. Never before had he been annoyed with the redheaded girl. Yet for the first time he saw her as just that—a girl. Arderi did not like being the center of attention and hated more the fact that he was unable to break away.

*I simply want to draw upon the Crystal from Alant, then go to sleep.*

When the buzz of Arderi's brush with death subsided and the dishes had been cleared, Arderi finally caught his father's attention. "May I go to my room and draw upon the Crystal from Alant now, Papa. Please?"

"Nix, lad." With a heavy sigh, Tanin rose from his bench at the table nodding to several other men who did the same. "Not until we return from paying our respects." Tanin's face became somber. "A man died this day protecting you, son. It is only right we go bid him well on his journey to the aftermore."

"Yes, Papa." Arderi was not sure he wanted to see the dead man again.

*He is right, though. Ralin had been there to protect us.*

# Chapter 10

Torches shone brightly, casting dancing shadows around the courtyard when Clytus Rillion rode up to his villa in Old Town. The shoes of his brown destrier, Starborn, echoed off the small walls enclosing the entrance courtyard. The warhorse had spent the day at the ferrier getting new shoes. It may be a long while before the horse would have the change again. He had had Starborn now for three turns of the seasons. A gift from his wife, Lilaith, the horse always made him think of her.



*Mayhaps the reason she gave it to me. Women are usually wiser than men.*

When he dismounted, his master of arms, Ragnor De'haln—a large armed, black-skinned Silawaian—came trotting up to take the reins from him.

"Good Eve, Master, I do hope you found your day productive." His thick accent marked him from the southron lands of Silaway as much as the man's jet-black skin—skin with a sheen of sweat covering it as if the man had been working hard, even this late in the eve.

"As productive as it needed to be, Ragnor. Where is the lady of the manor?" Clytus pulled his saddlebags from the rump of Starborn and flung them over a shoulder.

The large brown warhorse nuzzled its nose against Ragnor's familiar palm. "After lastmeal she did retire with the Young Master. Shall I have the cook prepare you something to eat, Master?"

A rumble in Clytus' stomach reminded him he had not eaten since firstmeal. "Aye. Something quick would be agreeable, if you do not mind, Ragnor. It has been a long day." He bounded up the stairs and into his home.

From the entrance hall, his wife's silhouette was visible out on the patio. She bent to tend her plants. Moonlight washed over her silky-black hair giving it the appearance of a silver river cascading down her back. He watched her for a moment before quietly heading up the marble staircase on his right.

Reaching the doorway to his son's dark room, he peered in. The shutters stood open to allow the cool spring breeze to enter. In the dim light, he made out his son's sleeping form lying on the bed. Waiting for his eyes to adjust to the dimness, he crept like the breath of a mouse into the room. Standing beside the bed, he gazed down at the boy, drinking in the sight. The sandy blond hair covering the child's head, which matched his own, lay slightly tussled from sleep. The boyishly round appearance of his face, so prevalent in children his age—the essence of youth—peeked out just above the silk covers. Clytus knelt down and cupped the boy's face gently in his hands.



Sindian Rillion's eyes fluttered open. "Father? I wanted to wait up for you. Mother said I needed my rest." The boy blurted the words out, though Clytus knew the boy was not fully awake.

"Shhh." Smiling down at his son, he kept his tone to a whisper. "I would not have you sleep this eve without telling you farewell."

His son sat up in bed. "Will you be gone long, Father?" The young boy wiped his eyes with the back of a hand.

*It amazes me how fast a child wakes from sleep.*

Leaning over, Clytus kissed Sindian gently on the forehead. "I am afraid I will, Little Bit." He stroked his son's hair. "This will be my longest journey yet." A pang of guilt crept into his heart at the half-truth.

*If Sier Lysentoc's Foretelling comes to pass.*

A gentle cough racked Sindian's small frame and Clytus enveloped the boy in his embrace. Once the coughing subsided, the boy pushed from Clytus' chest and stared up into his eyes. "I will miss you, Father."

"And I you, Little Bit." Clytus placed his hands on each of the boy's shoulders and looked into his eyes. "Alas, you must be brave for me. You must take care of your Mother and the villa here. For you will soon be rid of your cough, and you will grow to be a strong man."

"When you return can you teach me the sword?"

*I will not let the last sight of his father be one with tears in his eyes!*

"Hush, now, my Little Bit. It is time you are back to sleep. You are not done with your illness yet. Your Mother speaks true, you need your rest." Clytus carefully laid his son's head onto the pillow and pulled the silken sheets up, tucking them under the boy's chin.

"Will I see you in the morn, Father?" Sindian's tiny hand rose to stifle a yawn.

"Nix, my Little Bit, I will set out long before you rise. Now, close your eyes and return to sleep." Clytus moved his fingers over the boy's eyes to close them. He stayed, kneeling next to the bed, lightly stroking his son's brow—etching every smooth curve of the boy's face into memory. He remained long after the boy's breathing became deep and regular.



*I will miss you most of all, Little Bit.*

Lost in thought, he nearly missed hearing the soft steps approaching from behind.

"Ragnor has left a tray of meats and fruits for you in our chamber." The soft flutter of Lilaith Rillion's voice caressed the inside of his ears. Her hands did the same to his shoulders. "I fear he babies you far too much." She loved to tease him about his closest friend.

"We have seen much, my love, him and I. He is the best leftenant a leader could wish for." He snorted. "As fierce in battle as he is in keeping me happy."

"A wife could get jealous." Lilaith's chide was soft and warm. "Let us retire, my love."

Clytus reached up to hold her hand on his shoulder. When she started toward the door, he let it slip from his grasp. Turning, he watched her tall, slender form sway under her gown as she left their son's room. Returning his attention to the boy, he stayed for a few more moments, etching the scene to memory. Reluctantly, he rose and followed his wife.

Entering their private chambers, he went straight to the side table where a large silver platter waited piled high with food.

*Too much for one man's meal.*

He poured himself a glass of honeywine and sat on the edge of the bed. Lilaith wrapped her arms around him. Reaching over him, she plucked a grape from his plate and popped it into her mouth. Biting it in half, she let its juices dribble past her lips to land on his shoulder. She slid his shirt from this spot, bent down, and licked the juice from his bare skin. Clytus closed his eyes and let the sensation of her warm mouth fill him. He felt her shift and found her lips pressed to his. He returned her kiss like a drowning man tasting his last gulp of air. They embraced and soon the hunger in his stomach was forgotten, replaced by the hunger of his desire.



After their lovemaking, they lay in each other's arms, staring at the dark ceiling, content in each other's embrace. Time passed without meaning.

*However, all things must end, and time will not wait for the likes of me.*

"I am leaving Ragnor behind this time." He kept a casual tone trying to make it sound normal. Lilaith's body stiffened and he knew he should not have spoken at all.

She rose onto her elbows and gazed deep into his eyes. The look of pain and fear in her eyes sent a jagged agony ripping through his very being. Finally, she lay back down, burying her head in his chest. Her body tensed and pulsed as she silently wept. Embracing her tight, as if by sheer strength alone he could save her from the future, he fought for any words that might release her from her burdens. In time, her body relaxed and her breathing fell into a rhythmic pace. He held her long into the eve, gently stroking her dark hair and enjoying the smell of fragrance it held.

*You, I will miss as well, my love.*

# Chapter 11

The body rested on the alter of Hezmire, the God of Fallen Warriors, in the temple of the Twelve Gods of Man, called the Palintium, which stood in the center of the stead. A statue of Hezmire loomed overhead. Some four paces tall, carved from a stone with a reddish hue, the statue portrayed the God as a powerful looking warrior, with a strong face and body. Hezmire wore no armor, just a simple cloth robe that left half of his chest exposed. A scabbard, belted around his waist, sat empty. It was said that Hezmire waited at the gates of the aftermore to pass each warrior on a new path of training. A path of peace and ease. A path of rest.



Arderi Cor had been inside the Palintium only a few times in his entire life. Rarely would a common fielder have a reason to come here. When a fielder or herder passed into the aftermore, their bodies were cremated. The service was usually held out in the fields where they had spent so much of their lives. The only ceremony common folk observed requiring homage be paid to the Twelve was Talintithe, the festival of creation. Like most families, however, they held this ceremony in the large dining hall of their public house with the rest of the residents of the apartment. "The Gods have time only for great men, not the likes of us." Arderi's father had told him this once when he was younger.

When Arderi entered the chamber, a sticky-sweet smoke greeted his senses. It bellowed from several braziers that lined the walls. The chapel itself was a small, simple room. One of the dozen nestled inside the Palintium, each designated to a different God of the Twelve. There were no benches or chairs to be seen, only the alter standing alone against the far wall. Tapestries covered the walls depicting fields of wheat or barley all bent to their side by a slight breeze blowing over them—the Plane of fallen warriors.

His father walked next to him in a line of others who came to bid well the man who passed this day. The room remained hushed although not silent. The two men in front of Arderi peeled off to the side and he found himself looking at the body of Ralin Sard. The neck had been wrapped in a deep gray cloth to match the robe now covering his body. He lay with his eyes closed, hands placed on his stomach, fingertips touching. On the man's feet, he wore the simple brown leather sandals you might see on any common man.

*He seems more asleep than dead, if you can escape noticing that his chest does not move with breath.*



It struck Arderi how peaceful the man's face seemed. Remembering the gory-horrid look on it when they loaded the body into the wagon, he wondered how it could have changed so much in such a short time. Tanin nudged him and pointed off to the side, toward a woman standing at the head of the alter. She was a pretty woman even if well past her prime and a little on the heavy side. She wore her long brown hair pulled back in a tight braid—as was common in the Hild'alan stead. Her braid fell down the back of the gray robe she wore, one identical to the dead man's.

Stepping up to the woman, Tanin took her hands in his. "I am sorry for your loss and grateful to your husband for saving my boy."

The woman turned to look at Arderi, tears welling in her eyes. She pulled her hands from Tanin and embraced the boy. Arderi hesitated for a moment, unsure of what to do. Finally, he draped his arms around the woman. She sobbed into his chest. After a time—what seemed like an eternity to Arderi—the woman released him yet kept her hands on his shoulders. "We never had any children of our own. The Gods never felt it right for us. You must not let me down boy! Ralin has paid for your way with his life. Make it a good purchase."

"I will, Mis'am Sard." Arderi shifted his weight from one foot to the other.

His father took him by the elbow and escorted him out of the sanctuary, through the outer hall, and onto the cobblestone street. When they were well away from the Palintium, Arderi looked over at his father. "What did she mean, Papa?"

"Son,"—Tanin stopped and faced him to look deep into his eyes—"a woman like that has not except her man. No children to call her own, do you understand?"

Arderi nodded even though he did not.

Tanin grasped the back of his son's neck with his right hand. "It is like this, when someone loses all they have, they are left with nothing other than memories. Seems to me that someone must have given her a good memory about her husband's death—a heroic one."



Looking back down the road to the Palintium, Arderi sighed. "You mean they told her Ralin saved my life somehow?" He looked back at his father.

"Aye, son. Let her feel something good from her loss." Tanin ruffled his hair and they walked again.

"Alas, Papa? Now she feels I owe her something. She said as much."

Tanin chuckled. "You owe her no more than you owe your Ma and I."

Arderi glanced sideways at him. "What do you mean?"

"Well, we expect you to grow well, work hard, and achieve all you were born to."

*Aye, Papa, and if I fail the Test? I will let you and Ma down. I will let everyone down.*

They walked on, each man deep in his own thoughts. Soon home loomed before them.

"Sleep well, Papa. I am off to bed, I think." Reaching for the door, Arderi stopped when his father grabbed his arm.

"Are you alright, son?" Concern filled Tanin's voice.

"Aye, just tired." Arderi gave a halfhearted smile. "Hard day I guess."

"Must have been, since it seems you have forgotten about Alant's Crystal."

The boy's eyes flew open. "Ahh! May I draw upon it now?"

"Aye, come." Tanin chuckled. "We will fetch it together." Clapping Arderi on the shoulder, the two entered their public house.

# Chapter 12

A cool, fresh breeze washed over Klain and with it came the sensation of floating on a soft billowy cloud. Consciousness crept upon him with a gentle caress. He half opened one eye, content to drift in the realm of semi-sleep. Something soft and silky covered him. His sluggish, lazy mind conjured up an image of a spider web.

*Spiders! I hate spiders!*

Jerking upright, he flung off the filthy mess, and watched in befuddlement as a thin silk blanket drifted to a pristine marble-tiled floor.

His eyes darted around as he took in his surroundings. He found himself in a spacious room. Ornately carved stone pillars, each with colorful silken curtains dangling from them, reached up to support a high vaulted ceiling. An intricate designed painting stretched across its expanse, depicting winged creatures frolicking amongst clouds. Wide chairs, covered in plush pillows, lay scattered about the room. These matched the huge, bed-like bench Klain occupied. The blanket, a light blue wisp of fine silk, thrown away in his moment of repulsion, now lay crumpled on the floor. An airy, open balcony led out into a vast darkness. A fresh breeze blew through the opening causing the curtains flanking it to billow into the room. Opposite the balcony, a set of massive wooden doors stood closed.

*Yet they seem puny. Not even re-enforced with iron bands.*

The fresh scent of meat took hold of his nose and drew

his eyes to a wondrously carved table, upon which sat trays piled high with food. Sitting up, he felt something tight around his midsection. Looking down, he noticed that a pair of loose fitting breaches covered him from waist to ankle.

*Much like a Human would wear.*

Even though the pants felt odd, he let them be and stood, scanning the foreign chamber with a wary eye. Stalking to the table, the claws of his hindpaws sinking into the plush rug that covered the center of the marble floor, he kept sharp for any signs of danger. Marveling at the assortment of food sitting before him, he wondered whom it was all for.

*Surely, this must be meant to feed many.*

"Actually,"—Klain recognized the wispy voice instantly—"it is all for you, Klain, yes?"

A shiver cascaded down Klain's spine as he spun toward the balcony and the direction of the voice. His muscles clenched in anticipation for fight or flight. He glared at the Honored One as the strange gray creature stepped from the balcony and into the room. A low growl rumbled in Klain's chest. Displayed in all its grandeur—not simply a face through grimy cell bars—the sight of the being gave him pause. It stood almost as tall as Klain. Blue-gray skin covered its entire body, matching the color of its face. It wore a thin red-silken robe draped over its right shoulder that hung to about mid-thigh, accentuating the thinness of the creature's arms and legs. So thin were its appendages, Klain remained at a loss to understand how they could even hold up its weight.



*My thigh is thicker than its chest!*

With trepidation, Klain peered into its eyes, waiting for the same feeling to wash over him as it had done in his cell—taking control of his mind. That first encounter with the Honored One seemed like an age ago. Nothing happened. Klain blinked and waited.

"Please." The creature extended a bony arm and waved it over the food table. "Serve yourself what you wish and let us sit and talk, yes?" The Honored One pointed one long, slender finger toward the seating area. Klain noticed the finger had only two other digits joining it on the hand.

*I see none missing. It simply has only three naturally.*

A compulsion to eat overcame Klain and he grabbed a plate—made from a type of metal, shining like the surface of a puddle of water—from the end of the table. It seemed a shame to mar its beauty by putting food on it, yet he grabbed some meat from the nearest platter and slapped it over the engraving of a bird covering the plate's center. Joining the Honored One, who had already taken a seat, Klain chose a chair opposite the being so he could keep his eye on it.

"To ease your mind of some of its burdens, please, allow me a moment to talk, hmm?" The being waited as if on an answer. When none came, it spoke again. "I will start by assuring you that you are safe, the food is safe, and you may now eat."

Even though the Honored One's voice did not change, a sensation much like he had felt within his cell, only not so intense, fell upon him and he relaxed. He looked down at his plate, picked up a sliver of meat, and put it into his mouth. Never had he tasted its like before.



*The sheer flavor of it is intoxicating.*

"My name is Sarshia'Mian Mocley and I am an Elmorian." The Honored One continued as if it was normal to talk over a meal with a savage beast. "I have purchased you from your old master, Estular Jerts. I am not your new master though. You are now free, yes?"

Klain continued to chew. "You are female?" He asked through the food filling his mouth. She nodded once, her black eyes never breaking contact with his.

*I do not understand what this creature wants of me.*

"I do not want anything of you, Klain, yes?" Sarshia's thin, deep-gray lips curled into a smile.

Klain paused in mid-chew and stared once more into the fathomless black pools of her eyes. She sat calmly before him, her hands resting in her lap. He again expected the paralyzing feeling he had experienced during their first encounter to envelop him.

*It does not come, as it was before. I might simply run.*

He turned and studied the doors.

*There is no way those doors will keep me in.*

"They are unlocked, Klain, yes? You need not run nor damage my beautiful doors. You may walk up to them and open them if you wish, yes?"

Klain turned back to the Elmorian. Without breaking eye contact, he set his plate on the floor. Rising, he kept her in his sight and backpedaled to the door. Reaching a paw behind him, he found the lever and lifted it. The door swung open. He risked a quick glance over his shoulder. What he saw forced him to turn around and take in all that lay before him. The doors opened onto a grand entrance hall. Marble floors, with lush carpets covering their centers, flowed away in all directions. Statues lined the sidewalls between large, open archways, which led off to other areas lost from his vantage point. Huge columns rose to support a ceiling high overhead. At the far end of the hall, opposite from where Klain stood, two massive wooden doors stood propped open. A lush garden lay beyond. Elaborate stained-glassed windows towered up either side of the doors. Moonlight filtered through the colored glass and played gently on the floors.



"You may leave now, yes?" The voice of the Elmorian rang from behind him. "Or you may wish to hear what I have to say first, hmm?"

Turning back to the Elmorian, Klain thrust a thumb over his shoulder. "I can leave?"

"Of course."

"I can walk out? Where are the guards?" Klain let his hackles rise.

"There are no guards."

"I can...stay and eat?" Klain pointed to the table of food.

"If that is your wish. I have already told you, the food is for you, yes?" Sarshia extended a thin gray arm again to the table.

Long moments dragged on. Klain felt trapped, frightened.

He had never known fear to rage this deep inside of him. He had no direction, nothing to fling himself against.

*I am like a mouse in the middle of a field looking into a sky full of Owls!*

"Come, sit. Eat and listen. You may then make a choice as to what you will do, hmm?"

Klain took hold of the command as a wounded man clings to life. "Aye, I will sit. And eat." He tried to make the statement his own and knew it for foolishness. Returning to his chair, he picked up the plate of meat once more, yet did not eat. Instead, he stared at the being sitting a pace from him.

*She has no expression. Like looking at the face of a corpse.*

All at once, the eyes on the thin gray creature brightened. "You are correct, yes? We Elmorians do not show emotions the same as the other races of Talic'Nauth. However, I assure you, I am much like you."

"Why did Jerts call you the Honored One? What are you?" Klain felt somewhat braver having said this and plucked another piece of meat from his plate, popping it into his mouth.



"I have already told you enough about me. Let me now tell you something about you, hmm?"

"About me? I know me well enough." He set the plate of food down on a nearby pillow. "Why have you brought me here? What is this place, another holding area?"

Sarshia cocked her head to one side and for the first time Klain saw thin, semi-transparent sheets slide down and up her huge globe-like eyes as the creature blinked. "You are in my home. A small villa in what the locals call Old Town, within the City of Mocley."

"Where I fought in the Great Coliseum."

She nodded once and glanced to the patio and out into the darkness beyond. "You can see the Coliseum from my balcony if you choose to, hmm?"

Klain cut his eyes toward the open doors then shook his head. When he did this, his mane swayed in a way that caught his attention. Lifting a paw, he ran his claws through the coarse hair. Instead of being dirty and matted, as it had been his entire life, it felt soft and full—the torchlight of the room made its golden highlights glisten.

"While you slept, I had you bathed and groomed, yes? I hope you do not mind, hmm?"

It struck Klain, that for the first time in his entire life, his body felt magnificent. Nothing itched. No parasites used him for their daily sustenance. He rotated his right shoulder.

*Even the old wound is healed.*

"They bathed me and I did not wake?"

A smile crept over Sarshia. "When I went to retrieve you, you had been injured. I...took certain steps to insure that you would remain asleep while you were transported here. I felt it best to leave these in place while my servants prepared you. For their safety, yes? I also took the liberty to heal your wounds, both past and present."

This brought his attention back to the pants he wore. "I am to be paraded around as an attraction again then?"



"No, Klain. You should be dressed if you are to go out into the city, yes? This makes Humans feel...more comfortable—less likely to see you as an animal, yes? You will need to learn these things if you are to fit in, hmm?"

Klain snarled. "Why would I wish to fit in with *Humans*? They are vile little things."

"Not all Humans are vile, Klain, yes? This you will come to learn in time. You will come to learn many things in time, yes? Did you know you are the only Kithian to be successfully raised in captivity, hmm?"

Klain bared his fangs. "Do you now wish to taunt me?" The words came out in a growl.

The Elmorian's expression did not change. "Do not be angered by your past, Klain. Your past makes you who you are now, yes?" Sarshia said nothing more, as if waiting until Klain calmed a bit before she continued. "It is almost impossible to take a Kithian as a captive. The Slaver's Order claims it is a waste of their funds. They never seek out your kind as their...

product, yes?" Reaching over the arm of her chair, she retrieved a golden goblet from a side table and took a sip. "You see, if you take a Kithian captive, they will fight you relentlessly until they have no strength left with which to fight, yes? When their mind is broken, as all slaves' minds are, they realize they cannot win through force, and they simply stop living, yes? They do not eat or sleep, instead wasting away to death."

"What lies are these? I am not dead! I have been a slave, as you say, my entire life! Yet my mind is my own!" Klain growled.

"That is the trick, yes? To make a Kithian a slave, they must be taken very young. The age of eye opening happens to a Kith cub around two weeks after birth. If they can be taken prior to this time, as you were, there is a chance they will accept their captive surroundings, yes? Once the age of eye opening has passed...well, let us say this is why Kithians do not make good slaves, hmm?"

"So the stories told to me were true, my family was murdered?" A small piece of hope—the one that had nestled in the back of Klain's skull for so long, the one he would pull out late in the eve—broke away and fell to the ground like a dead leaf in autumn.



"I am afraid they probably were. Nevertheless, Klain, it is those truths which give you your strength, yes? You are still very young—you have not yet reached your tenth winter, hmm? Still you have an inner fire that burns brighter than most I have seen—it is so bright that your future is hidden from me by its radiance. This is why I purchased you and set you free, yes?" The Elmorian took another drink from her cup.

With her last words, fear crept back into Klain's heart. He looked around the room seeing nothing in particular.

"I realize this will take some time for you to understand." Sarshia words regained Klain's attention. "We will take it slow, yes? For now, let us say that you are confined to my villa grounds, hmm?"

"So I am a captive!" Klain's blood heated again and he

welcomed the familiar feeling.

"Once more, I will tell you that you are not a captive, yes? I am not your master and there are no guards. I will say to you, however, that you will not leave these grounds. Nor will you hurt anyone who is on this property."

Her last words washed over Klain like a bucket of cold water—a sensation, once again akin to the first time he had met the Elmorian, spread through him. It filled his core and confusion crept into his mind as his desire to fight or flee melted away. It lasted only a moment and Klain felt calm once more. Looking around the room, it seemed like any other cage or cell. Without thought, he reached down and picked up a piece of meat, shoving it into his mouth.

*It is nice enough, yet I will not be broken by it. I will find my escape, eventually.*

# Chapter 13

A breeze from the window washed over him, the smell of the sea heavy in it. The flavors in the wind varied—at once the rich texture of honey, next the putrid tang of something unwashed and unwanted.

He leaned out the window for a better look.

The side of a building dominated his view, separated from him by a narrow alley, litter lining the ground near its base. He inched further over the sill and saw a bustling street where people traveled amidst the jumbled sounds of tinks and thuds. 

"This is the only window in the school with any type of view." He heard himself say. His voice sounded a little deeper than it should be. "Not that I have time for sightseeing." His voice told him this without him saying the words.

Something pulled him from the window, and the small room he found himself in looked to be some sort of library. Several plush chairs stood between the bookshelves lining each wall. "This is one of the rooms of study. I do not have any classes here, yet most Initiates know of this window and I try to come here when I can."

He felt himself sit down on one of the chairs. Alant Cor could *feel* the soft leather covering the armrest beneath his palm. When the room spun, a moment of uncertainty gripped him and he struggled to understand how he could now be looking down at himself, sitting on the plush chair.

*Only it is not Alant! He is my brother. I am Arderi Cor!*

The realization tickled the back of his mind.

*That is right! I am drawing upon the Thought Crystal from my brother!*

"I wanted to let all of you know that I have been called to attend class for the next few turns of the seasons in Hath'oolan." Alant spoke the words yet Arderi still felt as if he was speaking them. This was made even stranger by the fact that, to Arderi, it felt as if he stood facing his brother who now sat before him in the chair. "This is the reason I was allowed to send you a second Silrith'tar—sorry, Thought Crystal. We are encouraged to call items and places by their proper, Old tongue names. Anyway, it is a great honor to be chosen. I am not sure I am up to it. As always, I will do my best. I hope to make you proud."

"Ma, I know you will want to make the trip to Mocley and see me before I go. Alas, I am told that by the time this Silrith'tar reaches you, I should have already set sail for the Island. I know this is longer than you hoped to have me away, yet I am learning much and excelling in my studies. I have already passed all of my classmates who started with me. I suppose this is why the Elmorians chose me."



Gazing around the room at all of the books, Arderi felt a weird sense of pride and care for them as if he had actually held them, studied them. "I am really enjoying my studies." Alant's words began again and once more Arderi felt as if he spoke the words. "The work is hard and they give us little time for anything else. It is great to succeed in something I failed at yesterday. I have always remembered your advice, Papa, 'When you fail at something it simply means you have not tried hard enough.' I have kept that to heart."

"Well, I hope everyone at home is doing fine. I am sure the rest will be drawing upon this also, so I will say a few words to them, I suppose."

"Siln, I miss our games of—"

Arderi felt his throat tighten and the room jerked violently. If not for the fact that he had no control of his movements, he was sure he would have fallen. The bookshelves blurred and the whole room melted before his eyes. He gagged, tried to wretch, yet his body would not comply. Attempting to yell for help, to scream out with agony, he found his voice had failed him, causing fear to course through his veins. Then it was done. He found himself standing in a small room, bare of any furnishings save a small cot with a footlocker pushed against its end. The room was so tiny he could have reached out and touched either wall at the same time.

"Hello, brother." Arderi heard himself address himself with Alant's voice. "I have gotten a little wiser in the use of these Silrith'tars since my first. This part of the message you alone will be able to draw out."

Arderi's head spun, it took a moment to realize he still drew upon the Crystal. He yearned to sit on the cot, to collect himself after what had happened. Again his body would not obey his commands.

*Not that it is my body, it is Alant's. I am still just a spectator.*

"I wanted to let you know how much I believe in you. You cannot possibly hope to understand how wonderful shaping the Essence can be. However, you will know soon. If you have not already taken the Test, I know your sixteenth winter has passed so it should not be long until you do. You have it in you no matter if you believe it or not. I did not understand things when we lived together, yet oh brother, the things I have learned over these last few winters. The *power* the Essence lets you wield! I wish I could be here in Mocley to receive you when you come to the Chandril'elian. The Cor brothers!" He felt himself chuckle. "We shall be remembered in the history books, you and I."



"I remember how much you wished to leave home. I still remember you clutching my arm and making me promise to come back for you once my training was complete. I did not have the knowledge to tell you then what I can now. Do not fear the Test! You have an inner strength exactly like mine. I have felt it. You shall be fine."

"I cannot tell you how, brother, except we will be able to talk once you arrive at the Chandril'elian. I will speak with you then."

Reality spun again, though without the force that had yanked him into his own, private message. Arderi found himself back in his own room, sitting cross-legged on his bed—the dim light of the yellow moon, Traynor, barely visible through his glazed window. He reached up and plucked the Crystal from his forehead. His queasy stomach twisted in upon itself and his head ached as if someone had hit him. Arderi had drawn upon the last Crystal Alant had sent dozens of times without any bad reactions.

*I do not think I will draw upon this one ever again!*

# Chapter 14

When Clytus Rillion awoke, he had no idea how long he had slept while lying there holding his wife. Her head rested on his chest and her arms remained draped around him. Sensing that dawn would be upon the land soon, he extracted himself gently, leaving Lilaith asleep on their bed.



The house lay dark and quiet as he made his way downstairs to the kitchen. His stomach was so empty it felt as if a hole ran through him. To his ever-constant admiration, he found the cook—a plump, middle-aged woman by the name of Darma Di'Anty—busy kneading dough. "Do you ever sleep, woman?"

Darma looked up from her baking and smiled. "And a good morn to you, sir." She transferred the dough she kneaded into a baking pan and slid it inside one of the ovens. "It seems some person entered my pantry late last eve." She wiped her hands on her white apron.

"Aye, I was late in coming and needed to eat. I did not want to wake you for such a trivial matter." Clytus opened the coldbox and retrieved a chilled pitcher of milk. He poured himself a goblet full.

Darma pointed to the large wooden box from which he had taken the pitcher. "The coldbox is not as cold as it once was. Need I remind you again to get a Shaper to come and re-Meld it?"

"Nix, woman!" Clytus had not meant to growl and

immediately regretted it. "Tell Ragnor of this later and he shall have it done." Raising the mug to his lips, he took a swig. The chilled milk tasted good as it slipped down his throat.

"Ragnor? I thought you were heading out before the sun rose this morn."

"Aye, I am. Alas, Ragnor will be staying behind this trip." He slid his gaze across the kitchen looking for anything to fill his empty belly.

"By all Twelve Gods!" The terror in her voice made Clytus abandon his hunt for food. "Is he ill? Have you summoned a Shaper? Do you not have some Oolant drought to give him?" She made a bolt for the door.

Clytus snagged her arm as she passed to prevent her from leaving. "Darma, Ragnor is well." He took her with both hands and shook her slightly when she tried to break free and continue on her way. "Ragnor is well!" He tried to sound reassuring.

"Yet he has never been away from your side. This trip will be one of the most dangerous you have ever been on. Should you not—"



Cutting her off, Clytus grabbed her attention with his eyes. "He will be staying behind to look after things for me. Things more precious to me than all else on this Plane." When she made no further attempt to leave, he released her.

Darma turned and fiddled with some pans. Before she could hide her face, Clytus saw the tears welling in her eyes. "Fine then, go busy yourself elsewhere and I will have firstmeal ready soon." Her words were almost as cold as the milk in his mug. Almost.

Clytus did not begrudge her the cold shoulder and did not want to watch her grieve. "Aye, I will go to the yard and ensure all is well for leaving. I shall be eating firstmeal on the road, however." He left the kitchen.

When he arrived in the yard, as he had suspected, all was ready. Four traveling wagons, loaded to bursting with the supplies he had purchased over the past tenday, sat waiting. He would pick up the final two from the merchant, Grilmire, on the way out of the city. Wagon drivers milled about making last moment adjustments. Men checked the cargo straps, insuring nothing would shift during the journey.

"Morn, Master." Ragnor's deep voice called from the other side of the courtyard. Clytus noted that the man had braided his thick black hair into a ponytail as he did when they journeyed away from home. The leftenant headed over to meet Clytus.

Reaching for the leftenant's outstretched hand, Clytus slid past the man's guard, and embraced him. Ragnor returned the hug with a bemused chuckle. When he attempted to pull away, Clytus held him tight, mouth pressed to the black man's ear. "You will not be going with me this time, Ragnor." Trying to keep his voice in a low whisper, it came out more of a croak.

At this, Ragnor pushed away to arms length yet kept his hands on his commander's elbows. "I do no understand, Master. Be there something you do want me to see to first? Shall I catch you up later?"

"Nix, old friend. I want you here." Clytus stared into the man's chocolate eyes for a long moment. From his pocket, Clytus withdrew a piece of parchment—folded and sealed with his mark—and held it out to his leftenant. "You are a good man, Ragnor, and have been a better friend to me than any man could hope for. This letter grants you full power as regent over my lands and estates. My wish is for you to care for things until Sindian is of age. I hope you will serve him as you have me all these winters."



Ragnor looked from the letter to his Master. "You Ro'Arthians and your Foretellings. I do think you have been with Felstar again, have you not?" A big grin parted his dark lips and he chuckled. "Master, the future has no been written. You speak as if you do know for a certainty that you will no return."

At his friend's mirth, a smile forced its way onto Clytus' lips. "Mayhaps, my old friend. Alas, I want to be sure this time. I have things in my life now that matter more to me than my future, and I am leaving them all here. Besides, I have Alimia now to do my fighting for me. You know she has had an eye on your job for the last turn of the seasons."

"That psychotic wench?" The leftenant snatched the folded parchment away from Clytus' hand and shoved it into a side pocket as if it had no value. "No man do have the ability to keep up with her. She be more apt to kill the entire troop by driving them too hard. Still, she will keep you safe, while she do still hold breath anyway." The smile dropped from his mouth and he nodded gravely. Clytus had seen that look in his dark-brown eyes a hundred times prior—each time they entered a battle together. "I will do as you ask, Master, without hesitation nor complaint. That be something you should know by now." Turning, the large black man headed back toward the wagons. After a few steps he stopped, glancing back. "Still, you will feel foolish when you do ride back through them gates in a few moons time. I will laugh at you then, just as I do now." With a loud cackle, he turned and trotted off to help with preparations.



Clytus had to laugh as well.

*Aye old friend, yet I must know everything at home is taken care of so I can bend my full attention to my task. And there is no man on this Plane I trust more than you!*

Within moments, his warhorse, Starborn, was saddled and brought out. The drivers that had been milling about the courtyard making last moment preparations mounted up. He heard the soft patter of his wife's bare feet wisp across the cobblestone courtyard. She glided up to him and he leaned into her as she embraced him from behind. When she relaxed her hold, he turned and picked her up. Letting his mouth find hers, he held her tightly, allowing their bodies and essence to mix. Breaking from her kiss, he set her down onto her feet. "You will tell Sindian I wished him well before I left?"

"Aye, Husband, although he knows. He is near six now and smarter than most." The resolve in her eyes told him all he needed to know. *If I could make you promise to return, I would,* her eyes said to him.

"All will be well." Trying to make it sound like a promise,

Clytus slipped from her grasp. Turning, he walked to Starborn and swung into the saddle. Once he sat astride the large brown destrier, his eyes wandered back to his wife. She still stood where he left her. The light from the torches burning in the yard played off her silk sleeping gown. She crossed the courtyard and held up her hand. Clytus reached down and she pressed a small wooden bauble into his palm.

"I know you do not follow the Twelve." Her eyes shined with tears that he knew would not fall until he left. "I want you to wear this for me. It will make me happy."

In the dim light, he could not make out which God the trinket represented. He looped the leather cord over his head and let it dangle down onto his chest. "Goodbye, my love."

She looked up at him and he felt his very core rip out as one lone tear traced its way down her cheek. Still, her voice was hard as steel. "You do what must be done to save our son. I will not survive if I must grieve the loss of both my men." With resolve, she turned and walked, stiff backed, into the villa.



Clytus watched her go until he lost her form within the shadows of the house. He looked over at Ragnor who stood by his own spotted steed, watching him. His leftenant had his saddle half removed from his own mount and stood there holding it in his strong arms, yet had not noticed that his water skin had fallen to the ground, its contents draining out onto the cobblestones around the man's boots. The two men stared at each other for a long moment. Finally, Clytus inclined his head and Ragnor nodded without the mirth from earlier in his dark brown eyes.

*Take care of them my old friend.*

Nudging Starborn gently with his knees, Clytus led his small caravan out of the villa toward the main gates of the city.

# PART TWO

## The Road Less Traveled

*They say that you are what you make of yourself. That you can take hold of any situation and mold it to your will.*

*I say that until you allow a situation to take hold of you, to fill you to the brim, you will never be successful in anything you do.* MAD

# Chapter 15

Arderi Cor awoke to a pounding headache and bile floating in the back of his throat. Covering his eyes with his hand to block out the morning light, he rolled over with a groan and forced himself to sit on the edge of his bed. "Siln, time to get up." His voice, thick with sleep, came out as a rasp. When no response came, he struggled to open one eye and took in his surroundings.



Other than rumpled covers lying upon his brother's bed, it lay vacant. Fearful of the time, he snapped his head around to look out the window and see where the sun stood. The sudden movement caused pain to slice from his temple to the back of his skull. Once the ache subsided to a tolerable level, he focused on the light of the sun, trying to discern its location in the sky.

*It is late! I have overslept!*

Arderi flinched when the bedroom door burst open, releasing a grimace as his mother rushed to his side, a worried expression on her face.

Sitting on the bed beside him, Mis'am Cor threw a hand to his forehead. She then moved it to the side of his neck. "Are you all right? You do not feel warm. Siln said he tried to wake you, yet you would not stir!" She cupped his cheeks in her palms and peered into each of his eyes one at a time.

"I am fine, Ma." He made a weak attempt to remove her hands and succeeded only because she let him. "I just did not sleep well last eve."

"Well, after your ordeal the day prior, no one will begrudge it if you do not feel like working the fields this day."

Dreading the thought of staying home under the over protective care of his Ma, he struggled to stand, leaning heavily on her for support. Once on his feet, he felt better. Extracting his arm from hers, he walked on unstable legs toward the door. Turning, he smiled at his Ma, she smiled in return. The look of concern never left her eyes.

Upon reaching the bottom of the stairs, other than a throb still hammering away in his head, Arderi felt normal. Skipping the noise of the kitchen, he opted to go directly to the dining hall. Entering the large room, his heart sank further at the realization that even the dishes had been cleared from the tables. Forcing himself not to stop in the doorway, he reached the first bench and sat down with a thump. He sank his face into his hands and tried to keep his head from bursting.



*This is no illness. I wonder if it is a reaction from using Alant's Crystal last eve. I will not deny it was a strange and bad experience. What was my brother thinking doing this to me?*

He heard the door to the kitchen swing open and the swishing of skirted legs making fast progress across the room. Looking up, Arderi was glad to see that his mother had entered carrying a plate and mug. "You should not go to the fields this day. You do not look well." She set her burdens down in front of him.

A batch of cheesed eggs, grits, and a thick slice of ham covered the plate. The mug was full of cool water. He picked up the cup and took a long drink. "I am not ill, Ma. Simply tired, like I said." He put on what he hoped was a brave face.

*I have no desire to spend the day cooped up in my room with Ma hounding me.*

"Well, be that as it may, you have already missed the wagons." She ran a hand through his short, sandy brown hair in a motherly attempt to comb it flat.

"That is all right, Ma. The field we are working is not far.

It will do me good to walk a little this morn." Turning his attention to the meal, he picked up a fork and dove into the eggs with zeal. He had not realized how famished he was until he took the first bite.

"Hump. Well, you are a man grown now. If you feel you are up to the task, far be it for a mere mother to stand in your way." She leaned down and kissed him on the top of his head before heading back to the kitchen. "Just leave your plate when you are done. I will have one of the girls fetch it later." This she called out over her shoulder before disappearing through the door.

By the time Arderi finished firstmeal, the throbbing in his head had receded to a minor pulse. Pushing his empty plate to the center of the table, he stood and left the dining hall. The usual group of elders sat gathered on the porch and he took a moment to pass pleasantries with them before picking up a brisk walk toward the fielder's gate.

A bright blue sky covered the horizon and a nice cooling breeze snaked its way through the streets of the stead. Arderi, in as high of spirits as he could muster, considered the horrendous start to his morn. He did not enjoy the effects the Thought Crystal had had on him, yet he certainly loved his brother's message.



*Alant could feel the power in me! I am going to be a Shaper and join him in Mocley!*

The fielder's gate came into view once he rounded the final bend in the road. A couple of guarders milled about the area looking bored. Arderi did not envy the thick leather armor they wore now with the weather growing warm. As he drew nearer the gate, one of the guarders waved to a Hobbsword who leaned against one wall. When the guarder pointed at Arderi and said something to the Shaper's guard, Arderi's heart skipped a beat, yet he continued toward them without pause.

The Hobbsword held up a hand. He appeared only a few winters older than Arderi, although a little taller and fuller in the shoulders. The large yellow starburst on the breast of his red and gold stripped tabard looked as if it had just been stitched into place. "Hold, fielder. Are you Arderi Cor?"

"Aye, sir." Arderi felt his face flush and his pulse quicken.

"You are to accompany me. I am to deliver you to the Shapers for Testing." Without waiting for a reply, the young man pivoted on his heel and marched away. The sword and scabbard hanging at his side slung away from his hip and returned with a slap against his thigh. He angled in the direction of the market area and the center of the stead, striding away at a brisk pace.

"Go on, boy." The guarder pitched his head in the direction the Hobbsword was going. "It is never wise to keep a Shaper waiting."

Jogging to catch up, Arderi fell in a step or so behind the man and followed him as they wound their way through town. He could not help except stare at the chainmail shirt that seeped out from under the striped tabard of his escort. The guards of the Shapers were the only ones in all of Hild'alan who wore armor of a grade better than plain brown leather. He noted more than one passer-by stopping to gape as they passed.



Sweat licked Arderi's palms as the Magistra came into view. The building that housed all authority within the Hild'alan stead was a large, two-story stone building. Even though it sat in the shadow of the Palintium, it held its own beauty. Grooved columns, holding aloft its arched ceiling, lined the stairs ascending to the main entrance. The Regent, along with his clerks, scribes, and anyone else needed to run an efficient stead, worked inside. The top two floors, however, were reserved for the stead's Shaper Order. Other than to be Tested, the only reason a commoner would have in coming here would be for healing.

*I remember when I broke my arm while playing with my house mates. I was only five or six, and I do not recall much of the visit. I have never had a need to return since.*

Yet now, as he approached, Arderi found his trepidation far exceeded his desire to take the Test. The fear growing inside him over the past few weeks bubbled up and lashed out as strong as anything he had experienced while facing the Krugour. His head whipped from side to side as he thought of ways to avoid his fate.

*Get a hold of yourself! Where does this fear come from?*

Taking long, deep breaths, he forced himself to relax and followed the Hobbsword past the main stairway and into a side alley that separated the Magistra from the Palintium. "Why are we going this way?" Stopping, he eyed the deep shadows between the buildings.

"I am not told reasons. The Shapers tell me what to do and I obey. I was told to deliver you to the side kitchen entrance." The young man never looked back nor broke from his stride.

A small wooden door set in a recess of the wall stood partly open. The Hobbsword took a step past it and stopped. Turning, he raised an arm indicating that Arderi should enter.

Stepping into the dimly lit room—a single lantern set on a small wall hanger the only source of light—Arderi found himself in a large storage area. Stacks of boxes lined one wall. The other was home to various sacks, bags, and barrels arranged in an orderly fashion on a row of wooden shelves. Sitting on a stool, under the lantern and next to the only other door in the room, sat a boy several winters younger than Arderi. The boy was dressed much like the man who had escorted him here, save that the boy wore no armor nor carried any weapons. When the two entered the room, the boy jumped up, made a bowing gesture to the Hobbsword, and dashed from the room.



"You may take a seat on that stool. Someone will fetch you shortly." The young man stepped back into the alleyway, closing the door behind him.

Arderi sat down in nervous anticipation of what was about to happen, putting his hands in his lap. To keep his mind occupied, he looked around the room. The task proved to be short lived as the place held no secrets.

*Just a plain old storage room.*

Luckily, before his fear had time to manifest itself once more, the door opened and a Shaper stepped into the room. The man seemed about the same age as Arderi's father. He had brown eyes, which sat exceedingly close to a beak-like nose, giving him a shrewd, bird-like appearance. With his short brown hair cropped in the local style, he could have been mistaken for any commoner. That is, if he were not wearing the dark blue robes with the golden starburst of the Shaper's Order embroidered over the breast. The sickly smile he wore did little to relieve any of Arderi's discomfort.

The man gave a short nod. "Good morn and well met. I am Sier Witlan Singe, Hon'nar to Grand Master Grintan of Hild'alan."

Popping to his feet, Arderi was unsure if he should bow or not. "Morn, sir...Sier! And well met. I am Arderi Cor, sir." His face burned.

The Sier smiled yet Arderi could not tell if the man was being polite, or amused. Sier Singe raised an arm and indicated the door that led into the interior of the Magistra. "Please, the Master Shaper is awaiting you in his study."



Trying to imitate the boy who was in the room when he arrived, Arderi made a small, awkward bow and stepped into a kitchen. Women busied themselves about the room, though only one looked their way as they crossed and took a side door. Arderi followed the Shaper down a small hall. About halfway down this hall, the Sier slipped up a narrow stairway. Ascending the stairs behind his guide for several levels, Arderi found himself in an area with more grandeur and riches than he had ever before seen. Lush, red carpet covered the center of a wide hallway. Rich tapestries hung between the massive oak doors that lined the hall. Pristine wooden pedestals, some with fine vases resting on them, others with intricately carved statues, rested in front of each tapestry. The shear wealth presented here overwhelmed the young fielder.

*Not even if I combined the entire worth of every family in the stead could I come up with so much!*

"Are you all right?" The smug voice of the Shaper jolted Arderi and the boy realized he had stopped walking and now gawked like a fool. "You look pale, boy. Do not fear. I assure you the Test is painless. Ignore what your friends have told you. It is common knowledge that the older kids love to tell tales of the horrors of being Tested. They do so simply to torment children who have not yet been Tested." The Shaper gave his unsettling smile once more. Like a bird would give to a worm it was about to snatch in its beak.

"It is not that, Sier, sir." Arderi paused to build up the nerve to continue. "I was just wondering...if I may?"

With a nod and wave of the hand, Sier Singe bade him to continue.

"Well, Sier, sir. I was just wondering why the Master Shaper will be Testing me?"

A look of understanding fell on Witlan Singe and he quietly chuckled. "I see, well...You have your brother to thank for that, I am afraid. Did Siln not tell you that he was Tested by the Master Shaper as well?"

Arderi shook his head. "Nix, Sier, sir."

"Well, there you go then." Sier Singe cocked an eyebrow. "Shall we?"



"Aye, Sier, sir." Except that Arderi did not move. Instead, he turned and indicated the small stairway they had just ascended. "Why was I brought in the back way, Sier, sir?"

Singe's face remained calm. Like a bird that had just eaten a worm. "When your brother, Siln, was brought in for Testing—Well, let us just say that this time the Master Shaper decided to have some privacy from the Regent and his staff during your Test, shall we?" The Sier turned and started down the corridor. "Now, it is not polite to keep such an important man waiting."

Of their own volition, Arderi's feet dragged the carpeted floor as he followed the Sier. Before he knew it, they arrived at a gilded door, carved with an array of symbols and runes that Arderi found beguiling. When they passed through the door, he found himself in a large, round room devoid of any windows. A plush, exquisitely decorated circular rug covered most of the floor—blue and red patterns danced and traced their way throughout it in a complex design. Several bookshelves, designed so they would rest flush against the curved walls of the room, encircled the chamber. Books stuffed every shelf and in front of these sat trinkets and artifacts, which Arderi could not begin to identify. He was again struck by the amount of wealth presented here. In the center of the rug sat a large oval table.

*An artisan's hands must have labored a lifetime to create the intricately carved and decorated patterns covering that table.*

Six equally beautiful chairs surrounded it. In one sat a wizened old man, dressed in a deep blue silken robe much like Sier Singe's, except gold starbursts lined the edges of his sleeves and hem marking the old man a Master Shaper.

*Not just a Master Shaper, Grand Master Grintan. Head Shaper here in Hild'alan!*

Upon the table rested an object that drew Arderi's eye like a moth to a flame. It was a large, light-blue Crystal device, about the size of his chest. It looked like a giant mushroom that someone had turned upside down and placed on its cap. It pulsed with a steady rhythm. As Arderi approached, the pulsing grew in intensity.



The old man sitting at the table smiled when he saw this and struggled to his feet. "Good, good. Welcome, young Mir'am Cor. I have been expecting you." He gave the steady, wheezy laugh only the very old can give and not sound maniacal.

Arderi bowed his head. "Well wishes and well met, Master Shaper, sir...Sier!"

"Oh, aye. I am sure you are dually humbled and impressed to meet me." Master Shaper Grintan shuffled over and patted the boy on the arm. He waved a hand toward Sier Singe. The bird faced man bowed and withdrew from the room, closing the door as he left. "Now, if we can dispense with the formalities, I am most anxious to get started." The Shaper turned back to his chair. "Help an old man back to his seat, will you, lad?"

"Aye, Sier...sir." Grasping the old man's arm, Arderi walked beside the Grand Master as he hobbled to his chair.

"Hmp. Sier will do fine, lad, Sier will do fine." The old man grunted as Arderi helped him to sit back down. Once settled, Grintan gestured to one of the remaining seats. "Please, move a chair closer and sit in front of me."

Arderi did as instructed. Pulse racing, a sheen of sweat covered his palms. Looking over at the large Crystal sitting on the table, he noticed that it now pulsed in time with his heartbeat. With growing fascination, he watched as it beat in a steady rhythm.

"Now, my boy, do you know why you are here?"

Ripping his eyes from the strange device, Arderi returned his attention to the Master Shaper. "Aye, Sier. I have come to be Tested. To see if I have the ability to manipulate the Essence." Arderi could not help the trepidation that corroded his voice.

The old Shaper smiled. "Aye, tis true. Let me ease some of your fears now, shall I?" He settled back into his chair. "You have no doubt heard many stories of what will happen to you. When I was a boy, I remember well the wild tales that my older siblings tortured me with—the pain and horror that would befall me when I took the Test." His eyes focused on some far off place as he spoke. Taking a deep breath, he looked back at Arderi. "Rest assured, my boy, these are all tall tales. I will begin by preparing you for the Test. During this time, you will feel some tingling, yet nothing unpleasant. Once you are ready, we shall use this device,"—he gestured to the Crystal—"called a Ka'ilyth, which literally translates from the Old tongue as test of power." Leaning forward, he took Arderi's hands into his in a kind, grandfatherly way. "Using this device, I will attempt to Meld the Essence through you. If successful, you will feel the power I am wielding pass through you to me. Do not be frightened by this, it will not harm you."



"Sier?" Arderi waited until the old Shaper inclined his head. "What will happen if it is not successful?" Bile rose in his throat even as he said the words.

The old man smiled warmly, his eyes twinkling. "Son, very very few on this Plane are blessed with the ability to manipulate the Essence." He patted the top of Arderi's hand. "There is no shame in not possessing the gift. If I am unable to manipulate the Essence through you, you will feel nothing."

"Yet, you do not usually give the Test yourself, do you, Sier?"

"Nix. I will not lie and say that we are not hopeful in you. Your brother, Alant, may turn out to be one of the strongest of our Order yet to live. That is a great honor for us here in Hild'alan. A second would be an even bigger blessing for us. Alas, as you saw in your other brother, Siln, the gift does not necessarily run in families." The smile slipped from him and he leaned back, letting go of Arderi's hands. "Now, if we are done with the questions, I would like to begin."

Not trusting himself to speak, fear and panic once again threatening to overwhelm him, Arderi nodded.

The Master Shaper sat and stared at Arderi for several moments. Arderi soon realized the old man was not looking at him. Rather, he was looking through him. A wave of nervous anticipation swept through Arderi. He felt odd looking into the old man's vacant eyes. Shifting his gaze back to the Crystal, the boy was soon lost in thought, drawn in by the device's rhythmic pulsating. For almost half an aurn, he stared into the facets of the Crystal. Imagining that it was some type of deep, bluish colored water, he dove through it with his mind, each layer taking him deeper and deeper into its folds. He jerked away when he felt himself physically falling into the device, as if something reached out to pull his body into its depths. Sitting up straighter, he returned his attention to the Master Shaper who looked as if he had not moved at all.

*He seems as if he has fallen asleep!*

A tingling sensation cascaded through Arderi's body. It started with his hair—each strand feeling as if it stood on end—rippled through his scalp and down his neck, spread out to his shoulders, then cascaded all the way down to the tips of his fingers and toes.

The old man's eyes once again focused on Arderi. "We are now ready." Grintan moved to the Crystal device. Reaching out, he placed both his hands, palms down, inside its bowl-like base. "Please place your hands in the Ka'ilyth as I am doing now."

Arderi did as the Master Shaper instructed. The device was ice cold to his touch and he fought the urge to jerk away.

"Now, relax. I am in control. Some find it easier when they close their eyes."

Shutting his eyes, Arderi sat back and forced himself to calm down. He could feel the Ka'ilyth pulsing against his hands. Each pulse sent a radiation of cold shooting up his arms.

Within moments, it felt as if he had buried both his hands deep into a snow bank. Pain seeped into his mind, lacing through fingers, wrists, and forearms. Instinct took over and he tried to snatch his hands from the device yet found he could not. A gasp escaped his lips and his eyes flung open. The coldness became so biting it felt as if his flesh had caught fire. His face contorted into a grimace of agony.

Arderi almost forgot his own suffering once he saw the horrified look plastered on the old man's face seated before him. Jagged bolts of red slashed through the blueness of the Crystal. Gritting his teeth, Arderi was appalled by the wail of despair that emanated from the lips of the Master Shaper.



The door crashed open and Sier Witlan Singe rushed in. "By all Twelve Gods!" The Shaper stood, seemingly frozen by the sight laid out in front of him.

Arderi had never felt pain like this before, it was as if his arms were being ground away, crushed into a pulpy mash. His sight dimmed and he knew he was losing consciousness. A bright red flash stabbed him in the eyes and he was hurled backwards, crashing onto the floor as he toppled over the chair. Pain racked his whole body forcing him to curl up into a tight ball.

All thought disappeared and blackness enveloped him.

# Chapter 16

The Bazaar was bereft of any inhabitants as the train of wagons rolled through. The echoing sound of iron-shod hooves on cobblestone street rang out loudly in the chill of the pre-dawn morn. A feral, slat-ribbed dog, some forty paces ahead, looked up at Clytus Rillion on his mount from a treasure of filth it pined over. Raising its hackles, the dog growled, baring its teeth in a vain attempt to protect its hard won food. Once it came to the realization that this was not going to deter the group of beasts heading its way, it dashed off into a side alley, disappearing into the dark shadows with its tail tucked between its legs.



The air was crisp and clear.

*The air here is cleaner without the stench of all the people and animals that shall be packing the place within the aurn.*

The permanent shops of the Bazaar, those built of stone or wood, stood silent and locked for the eve. Open area stalls, their canvas roofs rippling slightly in the waif of a breeze that managed to rise inside the great walls of Mocley, stood in dark silence. Clytus knew he was early and would have to wait on the supplies that Grilmire would have ready for him at his warehouse in Gatetown. Still, this was fine. The anguish he felt back at his villa had spurned him to get the day going.

*I do not grieve for myself. I grieve for the pain I cause those I love.*

"Halt!" An old guard, a captain by the golden tassel with

a large knot perched upon his right shoulder, limped out into Clytus' path, though the wagons were still several paces away from the main gates. His uniform, the standard yellow and blue of the Mocley Guard, had the appearance of having been slept in for much of the eve. His poleaxe—which looked more as if it carried him instead of him carrying it—made a clacking sound on the cobblestone street as he hobbled to the approaching wagons.

"Rilmoth?" Drawing rein a few paces short of the man, Clytus was surprised to see the old captain still wearing a city guard uniform. "I thought they would have retired you by now." He dismounted and strode over with his hand out.

"Nix! Those old fools who run this city are never going to let me have any peace." Rilmoth took the offered hand and shook it. "What brings the famed Clytus Rillion out at this Gods-forsaken aurn?"

"Heading out. I am on business for the Shaper's Order. How is the Mis'am?" Clytus handed the old guard a flat, square Crystal object.



"Old and cranky, same as when she was twenty." The old man gave a bark of a laugh causing Clytus to grin and shake his head. "You know, it is still an aurn till the gates open?" He looked apologetic as he took the Crystal and placed it to his temple.

The old captain's eyes lost focus for a moment and Clytus waited until he removed the Crystal from his head before speaking. "Aye, I figured I was a bit early. However,"—Clytus took the captains other hand and pressed a ta'narian into the old man's palm—"I was hoping whoever was in charge might see fit to let me squeeze out early."

The gold coin disappeared into a side pocket as Rilmoth turned and glanced at the guard shack. "Aye, I have one young whipper-snapper leftenant on duty who does like to follow the rules,"—he held up the Crystal object Clytus had given him—"yet your license here proves you are on Shaper's duties. I think I can convince him it is in his best interest to let you pass."

He looked past Clytus toward the wagons. "You have enough supplies?"

"Nix, I have two more wagons waiting on me in Gatetown."

Rilmoth grunted. "So much? You heading to Velvithia or some such?"

"Nix, old friend." Clytus grasped the reins of Starborn and put a foot in the stirrup. Swinging into the saddle, he adjusted himself and looked down at the old man who had not moved and instead simply stared up at him.

*All I need is to sit here all morn and entertain some old soldier.*

"I am heading up into the Nektine. Be gone for a few moons. The Shapers have me going after something they need." He hoped his words would start the old captain to his task.

Taking the hint, or not wishing to talk up to a man ahorse, Rilmoth grunted and hobbled back to the shack.

Clytus shot a glance at his lead teamster, Trilim Grith, who grinned back at him. Shaking his head and laughing silently, Clytus raised a hand and motioned for the group to start moving. He maneuvered his brown destrier alongside the guard shack and watched as the four wagons drove past him and into the tunnel leading out of Mocley.



A younger guard, the golden tassel hanging from his right shoulder marking him the rank of leftenant, came out of the shack and scowled up at Clytus. He then dashed across the yard and into a door at the base of the barbican.

Captain Rilmoth stepped out of the guard shack next and held up Clytus' Crystal license along with a wide grin. "He will not be any trouble. The gates will only be raised enough for you and yours to pass under, however, so be quick about it."

"Aye, my thanks to you, Rilmoth." Clytus reached down to the man and took his Crystal. "Give the Mis'am my best."

"Aye, I will. And safe travels to you as well." The old man stood watching as Clytus spurred Starborn into a trot and disappeared into the mouth of the tunnel.

A loud clank echoed through the darkness as Clytus entered.

A squealing of metal on stone pierced his ears as the large center portcullis rose. In the dim light cast by the smattering of torches that remained lit even at this late aurn, he watched the massive bars of the gate slipping into the recess of a huge slot that cut across the top of the arched tunnel.

The wagons moved as soon as the grate gave them the clearance they needed. Before he exited the tunnel, Clytus heard the wail of the bars making their decent to return to their closed position. Gatetown materialized out of the gloom in front of him as he trotted out of the dim passageway. Looking down the road, he saw the faint glow of dawn spreading over the eastron horizon. Spurring his mount into a canter, he headed for the front of his small caravan.

Dawn was fully upon the land, and many of Gatetown's residents roamed about by the time Clytus added the additional two wagons, each loaded with supplies, to his caravan. Clytus found himself pacing outside of Grilmire's Gatetown warehouse, impatience getting the better of him.



"I have never seen you so, Master. If I may be so bold."

Turning, Clytus was shocked to see Trilim Grith standing behind him.

*I really have lost my edge if I cannot hear an old man sneak up on me!*

Reaching up, Clytus rubbed the back of his neck. "Aye, Trilim. I made it no secret that I wish to be on the road early. Where are those damnable dayhires Grilmire said would be here?"

"I sent a boy out to fetch them when we arrived. It is still an aurn till we were meant to arrive. I cannot see how you can hold them accountable. It should not be long now." Trilim patted his Master on the back and returned to the wagons.

*Aye, in my current mood I would not want to be around me either, old friend.*

Trilim Girth *was* getting old Clytus realized. The man had been in his employ for well over two decades. Trilim served as stable master when they were home in Mocley, driver and camp cook while on the road. The man had been instrumental in teaching young Sindian how to ride, although during the last turn of the seasons the Young Master had not the strength for such activities.

The sight of a Shaper running up the road interrupted Clytus' thoughts. A large pack smacking against his back, his deep blue silken robe flapping away as his feet made their hasty progress. No golden embroidery adorned the trim of his robe marking him of lowly rank within the Order. A grin crept upon Clytus as he watched the Shaper.

*It seems this one is new to the Order. Yet still, it is very undignified for a Shaper to hurry so.*

The smile dropped from his lips when the Shaper came to a stop next to Trilim and the lead wagon. The young man stood there, bent over, sucking in air and waving franticly, trying to convey something to the driver. Shaking his head, Clytus walked over to them.

"Nix, Sier. Please, catch your breath. I am not understanding you." Trilim reached out a hand to steady the young Shaper. He was rewarded for his offer with the pack from the Shaper's back. Grunting when the unexpected weight was added to his outstretched hand, the old man's arm was pulled down by the extra burden of the bag, crashing to the ground.



"Here now!" The young Shaper glared at the old man even though he still sucked in air. "Careful with that, man!" The boy was slim and his robes did nothing to hide that fact. Sandy brown hair and a plain face did little in the way of making him memorable. Clytus did not think the boy could have seen more than twenty-two winters.

"I do not think anyone in my employ needs to be hauling your bag, boy, Shaper though you may be." Clytus reached over, snatched the satchel's carrying strap from Trilim' hand, and held it out for the young Shaper to take.

"They do if you are Clytus Rillion!" A sharp tone laced the words the Shaper shot back.

Clytus let the bag fall from his grasp to thud back to the

ground. He cocked his head and smiled at the look of outrage that sprang to the young Sier's face. "That I am. And you are?" Clytus asked the question without a trace of his smile in his voice.

"Jintrill Deln. I am a Shaper!" Jintrill drew himself up.

"Really? I just thought frilly blue robes were all the rage these days." Clytus spun and stalked back to his horse. Footsteps staggered behind him as the young man tried to keep up with his brisk pace.

"Sir! Sir?" The boy's voice lost some of its edge as Clytus walked away.

"I have had enough of the Council." Clytus spoke over his shoulder. He refused to give this young man an inch. "Whatever advice you may have, or message from those dusty old goats who run your Order, I am not interested."

"I have no message, sir. Rather, I am the message."

This forced Clytus to stop mid-stride and turn on his pursuer. "What?"



Jintrill pulled up at the sudden halt of Clytus and took a step back to add some distance between them. "I have been ordered by the Council of Elders to accompany you."

*Great! Just great!*

"Why you?" Clytus was happy that the growl in his tone caused Jintrill to flinch.

"Sir?"

Keeping the growl, Clytus enunciated each word as if he were speaking with a child. "Why did the Council send you?"

"I am afraid I do not have an answer for that." By the way the young man wrung his hands together, Clytus knew the boy was sufficiently cowed.

Clytus rubbed his chin and sighed. A pang of guilt slouched in the back of his mind. "Did the wise and mighty Council even tell you where I am headed?"

"Aye, to the Nektine. Hunting a Drakon, I was told." Jintrill glanced back over his shoulder. "Which I am not sure why anyone would—"

"Aye, hunting a Drakon. So I will ask again—Why you?" Noting the boy's concern for his bag did nothing to save the fact that Clytus had lost all patience with this conversation.

"I am unaware of the reasons I was chosen, sir."

"Go back to the Council and tell them I respectfully decline their offer of help." Clytus turned and continued the trek to his horse.

"I was told you would not agree with having me along. Grand Elder Blanch wished me to remind you of your vow to do as the Council bids."

A lump hardened inside Clytus' chest as he stopped once more. He stood a long moment, clenching and unclenching his jaws. When his anger abated, he returned his stare to the young man in blue.

*Felstar, I am regretting your council more and more!*

"I am skilled in healing, if that helps." The young Shaper seemed eager.

Clytus dropped his head and shook it. "So be it!" He looked  up and pointed to the wagons. "The man at the first wagon is Mir'am Grith. Ask him where you can stow your bag. You can ride with him for now." The young Sier nodded and left to see to his things. "Oiy! I do mean for you to stow your own gear. No one will cater to you on this journey, *Shaper*."

Striding to Starborn, Clytus mounted and trotted over to the wagons. "Trilim."

"Aye, Master."

"I have had enough of this waiting around. I will ride out and check the road." Clytus cast a glare at the Shaper who struggled to find a location for his pack in the back of the loaded wagon. "As soon as the dayhires arrive, get these wagons moving. I will meet you within the aurn."

"Aye, Master. The message boy has already returned. All of the drivers should be here within moments. I will handle everything till we meet on the road." The old man nodded once.

Nudging the sides of his large brown warhorse, Starborn

trotted forward carrying Clytus east down the road that headed out of Gatetown and away from Mocley.

# Chapter 17

The patter of bare feet whispered off to Klain's right. Crouching low, he scuttled on all fours down a row of hedges. He smelled the sweat off the small Human girl-cub on the wind, yet could not pinpoint her exact location from the vibrations she made through the ground. His stomach rumbled with hunger.

A flash of golden hair dashed out from a tree and into a cluster of rocks. The girl-cub was trapped, he would have her. Dashing out of his hiding spot he pounced on top of the boulder and growled, teeth bared. The small child let out a shriek and fell backwards onto her backside in the soft dirt. Jumping down, Klain landed with his lower paws on either side of her slim frame and snatched her from the ground and into the air, his sharp claws just penetrating the fabric of her dirty robe.

Giggling, the young girl clung to Klain's paws as he spun in a circle. "You found me again!" The squeak in her voice reminded Klain of a mouse.

"You are easy prey, girl-cub! It is better for you that you live behind tall walls." Klain set the girl down onto her feet. "Now, Yerina, it is well past halfmeal and I have the hunger to devour even you. Let us go find something to eat, shall we?"

Yerina hid her mouth with her small hand and giggled. "Silly, you can't eat me. I would eat you first!" Slipping her tiny hand into his paw, she led Klain through the garden area toward the back entrance of the villa.

The time Klain had spent at the Elmorian's villa had been the most enjoyable of his short life. It had taken Klain only a few tendays to understand the full implications of the word *free.* He was forbidden to leave the grounds, yes, yet he understood now that he was not ready to leave them—that his upbringing inside a tiny cage had not prepared him for interactions with others.

*I am learning, however.*

He spent all his time with the servants of the villa, although he had developed a fondness for the girl-cub, Yerina, the cub of one of the cooks. Without understanding why, he enjoyed her company and even though he saw her as a cub, he sometimes felt she was his older. They explored the grounds together for aurns without end. Rolling and climbing, leaping and running, everything that had been denied him in his youth now filled him with elation. It was as if he had been reborn into a new existence—an existence of peace and love.



As the pair walked hand in paw down the crushed-gravel paths, Klain marveled at the variety of fauna that surrounded him. How lush and green. Manicured shrubs, their foliage groomed to take on the shapes of low walls, or sculpted into marvelous designs and even wondrous creatures. Massive trees, their canopy bathing the area in cool shadows, littered the gardens—offering up delectable fruit hanging for the taking by any passerby.

*Even though high walls surround all, I know they are not there to hold me. I may leave if I so choose.*

Just outside the door to the kitchen sat a large stone table and benches surrounded by lush green bushes displaying a wide array of multicolored flowers. Yerina let go of Klain's paw and motioned him to the sitting area. "You wait here and I will fetch us something for halfmeal."

Klain stared after her as the little girl skipped into the villa. Sitting down upon a bench, he closed his eyes and breathed in deeply, allowing the fragrances of the air to invade every corner of his senses.

*It is intoxicating out here, under the sun. I may never want to leave.*

"It is lovely, at that, yes?" Sarshia came strolling out of some deeper part of the garden. "Alas, I am afraid the time draws near when you must depart."

It always shocked Klain that he could neither hear nor smell nor feel the vibrations of the Elmorian's approach.

*I feel vulnerable when in her presence.*

A look that Klain had grown to suspect as being one of mirth passed over the Elmorian's cold, gray features. He watched her stroll over the gravel path—her impossibly thin legs moving gracefully despite their odd appearance—until she sat on the stone bench opposite him.

"I see you have been enjoying your time with Yerina, hmm?"

"Aye." Klain did not know why her words made him feel uncomfortable, yet his eyes drew to his paws and he ground one sharp toeclaw into the crushed stone below the table.



"You need not be embarrassed, Klain, you are still merely a cub yourself. If you had grown up amongst your own kind, you would be doing much the same with other Kithians your age, yes?"

"Mayhaps, yet I did not grow up that way!" Anger filled him and he clinched his jaw.

Sarshia cocked her tear-dropped shaped head to one side and her long, flowing white hair slid to cover her shoulder. "Why does your upbringing still anger you so, hmm? I have told you, your past is what will give you the strength to achieve what you must in the future, yes?"

Raising his head, Klain looked the blue-gray being in her black, liquid-pool eyes. For a moment, he thought of the feelings he experienced on their first encounter. "This is not the first time you have mentioned my future. How can someone know what will take place on the morrow?"

Again, the look of amusement passed over Sarshia's features and she gazed at Klain for a long moment. Finally, she nodded her head. "You have improved much during your stay here. You feel more at ease with your freedom, yes?"

"I understand what you have given me, aye. As well as the debt I owe you, if that is what you mean."

"You owe me nothing, Klain." She raised her three-fingered hand to forestall Klain's rebuttal. "It is I who owe you."

Letting out a snort, Klain waved a paw in dismissal. "What could you possibly owe to me? If not for you, I would be long dead."

"Of that I have no doubt. Yet, I also have no doubt that that was never to become your fate. You remember our first meeting in the dungeons of the Coliseum and the feelings you felt, hmm?"

Klain nodded, his golden mane bouncing with the motion of his head.

"It was at that time when I preformed the Chi'tar upon you."



"Chi'tar?"

"I hope you are hungry—oh!" Yerina voice squeaked as she came bounding out the backdoor of the villa. Stopping abruptly, the little girl curtsied while balancing a large, silver tray of meats and cheeses. "My apologies, Honored One."

"Nonsense, child. Please, bring the food to the table, yes?"

Keeping her gaze averted to the ground, the blond girl hurried to the table, set the tray down, and took a step back standing with her hands clasped behind her back.

"My thanks, Yerina. Alas, I must ask you to eat halfmeal elsewhere, yes?" Sarshia raised a hand indicating the kitchen area. "I have some things to discuss with Klain before I depart." Her thin black lips parted into a semblance of a smile. "You will have him back soon enough, hmm?"

"Aye, Honored One. As you say." Yerina bowed once more then spun around so fast her golden locks of hair twirled into the air. Casting a shy grin over her shoulder, she disappeared back inside the villa.

Watching the dark doorway for a moment longer, Klain

returned his attention to the Elmorian. "What do you mean before you depart?"

Picking up a slim, silver eating prong, Sarshia stabbed a small cube of cheese and held it up between them. "I must return to my home in Hath'oolan. There are—*things* there I must attend to. Yet that is no concern of yours, yes?" She put the cheese to her lips and slipped it into her mouth.

"It is, if I am to somehow repay you for what you have done!" Reaching out a paw, Klain stabbed a thin cut of meat with one claw and shoveled it into his maw.

"I think that can be arranged before I leave the shores of Ro'Arith, yes?" She set down her eating prong. "I am in debt to a Human in much the same way you feel you are in debt to me."

"And this Human, he saved your life?" Klain was astonished at the thought.

A small snort emanated from the Elmorian. "No. I owe him a debt of a different kind, yes? Suffice it to say that he is in need of an additional bodyguard for himself and his family. I think this would be a fine profession for you to consider, hmm?"



Klain let this roll over in his mind. "So, this Human, he would be my Master?" It surprised him that the term did not leave a bad taste in his mouth.

"Not Master in the way you have come to know, Klain. You are a free being. The man would be your employer. You would be able to leave his services any time you wish, if you become dissatisfied with the arrangement." Sarshia reached out and idly moved a second piece of cheese with her eating prong. "He is a good man and I feel you will learn much under his guidance—many things that could help you in the tasks you will encounter on the path which you now walk, yes?"

Swallowing a bit of meat, Klain leaned forward, resting his elbows on the table. "Again you speak of my future as if you know something. Tell me of this Chi'tar that you spoke of earlier."

Nodding, the semi-transparent sheets that were Sarshia's

eyelids slid down and remained closed. Klain had never seen her keep her eyes shut and the sight disturbed him. He could still see the Elmorian's dark black eyes through the semi-transparent lids, yet now the normally deep-black eyes held a hazy film over them. It was unsettling to realize that even with their eyes closed, an Elmorian would still be able to see everything around them.

Shaith took in a deep breath. Releasing it slowly, she opened her eyes. "It is considered taboo for one of my race to speak of the Chi'tar to another. It is a gift that almost all Elmorr'Antiens possess. And a few from the other species as well. Kithians, however, are different. Your race was not born from the Essence like the others—yours was created by the Essence." Klain did not understand where she was leading him. Her look of amusement returned. "It does not matter, yes? You knowing what the Chi'tar is will not affect the balance."

"Whether you believe it or not, each of us has a role to play during our life. Some might call it destiny, others fate, yes? The Essence that is within all things—within you and I—contains a shadowy glimpse—an image, if you will, yes?—of the possible outcomes that may happen based on the path one is heading."



"I do not understand."

Reaching down, Sarshia plucked a small stone from beneath her bench. "Take this rock." She held it out and Klain took it into his paw. "If you were to throw the rock at the villa wall, what do you think the outcome would be, hmm?"

"It would not damage the wall, no matter how hard I threw it. It is too small."

"No, it would not damage the wall, in that you are correct. Alas, that is not what I meant. I mean would the rock hit the wall, hmm?"

Klain looked from the wall to the stone. "It is only a few paces. I could hit it with my eyes shut if I wished."

"Possibly. You see, that is the obvious outcome. Yet, what if a bird swooped down just as you threw it and intersected it. The rock would then fall to the ground without hitting the wall. Or, what if a mighty gust of wind blew the stone from its course, or one of a thousand other outcomes, hmm?"

Eyeing the sky, Klain searched for anything that may impede his throw. "I see none of these."

The Elmorian smiled. "No. None of those are likely to happen. I am just using the stone as an example, yes? To show that what you perceive—a stone about to be thrown against a wall—is all you know for certain. The Chi'tar is something that we Elmorians have been able to do for millennia. It allows us to glimpse a few of the possible outcomes of what may or may not come to pass. Specifically, it allows us to see the possible outcomes of a beings life based on the paths they have traveled and are about to walk. The choices they have made and could make in the future."

"You can see the future?"

Sarshia tilted her blue-gray, tear-dropped shaped head to the side. "No. Not the future exactly, more of possible futures, yes?"



"And you have seen mine? That is what I felt in my cell the first time we met?"

Nodding her head, her semi-transparent eyelids slid down and up her pool-like eyes. "That is what you felt. However, I could not discern anything of your future."

"Why? I do not understand." Klain's confusion threatened to morph into anger. Feeling his hackles rise, he forced himself to calm down as he had learned to do over the past few moons.

*I know very little of this new life I find myself in. Yet I know anger will not solve these issues.*

A smile crept over the thin dark-gray lips of the Elmorian. "You have gained much wisdom in your short stay here at my villa. There are beings on this Plane who have the potential to do great things during their lifespan. When performing the Chi'tar upon these individuals it is like looking into a blinding light, as if one looked directly at the sun. This is what I saw when I performed the Chi'tar upon you, Klain, and it intrigued me."

"I am destined for greatness?" Klain sat up straighter on his bench, a feeling of euphoria passing through him.

"No, there is no such thing as destiny, yes? We—all the sentient beings upon the Plane of Talic'Nauth—are shaped either by the decisions and actions we ourselves make or those that others make for or against us. There are no set paths, no guaranteed outcomes, nor futures. Yet, based on where a person has been, what they have experienced, and the road upon which they currently walk, the Chi'tar can give a glimpse of possible outcomes. When I preformed it upon you, I saw potential, that is all. Potential so great, it could rock the very foundations of everything, to be sure. Yet, it is all dust on the wind depending on what you choose in life, yes?"

"I have never chosen anything in my life. Even the freedom I have now, I had no say in. You are the one who chose this for me."



"In this you are correct. Yet, I think it is time that you take the reins of your life now, yes?" The Elmorian rose from her bench. "Duty calls to me and I must leave Mocley and return to my home in Hath'oolan."

The statement hit Klain in the chest like a hammer. "What is to become of me?"

"I have some suggestions, yet as to where you go from here, that is for you to decide, yes?"

Klain felt an unnatural sense of fear creep into him.

*No!*

Clinching his paws he forced the feeling away.

*I am* not *a slave anymore! I will* not f*ear the decisions I must make! I am my* own *master now!*

Standing, paws clinched so tight his claws dug into his pads, he nodded to the Elmorian who had helped him overcome so much. "I welcome your council, Sarshia, yet you are correct. I must face any challenges head on. I will *not* fear my future!"

Smiling, Sarshia bowed her head toward him. "The Human whom I owe the debt to is named Rohann Vimith. He is a merchant in the trade of Diamonds and wished to speak with you about protecting his son. If you were to take employment with this man, you would relieve me of my obligation to him. Also, by doing me this favor, your debt to me will be considered paid in full."

"And in doing this, I would not be obligated to stay with this Human?"

Nodding, Sarshia indicated that he was correct.

"Then I will meet with this Rohann. If his manner is to my liking, I will let him employ me."

Bowing low, the Elmorian smiled. "That is all that one being can ask of another. I will arrange a meeting on the morrow, yes?" With that, Sarshia turned and glided into the backdoor of the villa.

Watching her go, Klain once again tried in vein to pick up any vibrations that her steps made upon the ground and found he could detect nothing through the pads of his hindpaws.

*I do not think I will ever be at ease around one of their kind.*

# CHAPTER 18

Arderi Cor woke with a start. He lay on something soft. A cool wet cloth covered his forehead. Sitting up and removing the rag from his head, he found that he occupied a small sleeping chamber. A tiny writing desk sat against the wall opposite the bed. A little stand with a washbasin on top took up the entire wall adjacent from the only door to the room. It reminded him of the place Alant had been during the private message he had shared with Arderi in the last Thought Crystal.



The door opened and Sier Witlan Singe entered carrying a large bowl. "Ah, you are up. How do you feel?"

Taking a moment's pause, Arderi realized he did not feel anything out of sorts. Even his headache from earlier this morn was gone. "I feel fine, Sier, sir. What happened? Why am I here?"

Singe set the bowl on the desk—steam rose from the water inside as it sloshed about. "The Master Shaper is also well. A nasty bump on his head. Sier Quilart is tending to the wound."

"The Master Shaper was hurt?" Arderi did not understand. "How?"

Pulling out the small stool from under the desk, the Shaper sat motionless for a long while, boring his eyes into Arderi's before speaking. "Do you know what happened? Did you do something to interfere with the Test? Keep a true tongue with me, boy."

"Nix, Sier! I do not know what you mean." Arderi retreated further onto the bed, putting some distance between the two of them.

"Tell me what happened." Witlan Singe's tone was harsh and commanding. "I will know if you lie!"

Swallowing hard, stories of a Shaper's power bubbled up inside Arderi's head. He searched his memory—his fuzzy mind, stuffed with what felt like cotton, would not bring up the actual turn of events that had led him here. He shrugged his shoulders and shook his head weakly. "Aye, Sier, sir. You sent me in to see the Master Shaper. We talked for a time. He told me what the Test would be like. He stared at me for about half an aurn until I felt a tingling. We put our hands on the large Crystal thing and then…"

*Then what?*

He racked his brain and could find no answers. "Then...then I woke up here." He gestured feebly at the bed.



Sier Singe sat in silence. Finally he stood. "Come. The Master Shaper wished to see you when you felt up to it. I think that time has arrived." He strode out of the room.

Arderi followed the Shaper through the halls once more, this time taking no notice of all the grandiose paraphernalia that lined them. His mind raced as he struggled to remember what had happened. They ascended a long flight of steps that ended in a large waiting area. Plush chairs and small ornate tables lined the walls. Rich tapestries, elegant statues, and magnificent vases were scattered about to please the eye. Arderi saw none of it.

Witlan Singe turned and gestured to a couch. "Be seated. I will see if the Master Shaper is ready to see you." Turning, he disappeared through a set of double doors.

Walking to the indicated seat, Arderi stood, arms crossed over his chest, fear and doubt threatening to overwhelm him. He stared at a tapestry without seeing what it held. He turned when he heard the doors again open. Sier Singe waved him over and shuffled him inside the room.

Light spilled into the study from two tall windows set on either wall flanking the doors. More finery—statues, portraits, carvings and other artifacts—littered the place. A monstrous desk filled much of the center of the area, the top of it neatly organized with quills, parchment, and stacks of books and scrolls.

A single door behind the desk opened and Master Shaper Grintan stepped through. Arderi could not say that he was happy to see the old man. His blue robes, trimmed with their golden starbursts, trailed out behind him. A Shaper, whom Arderi had never before seen, helped the old Sier to a chair sitting behind the desk. Once situated, the Master Shaper waved the man away with a flip of his hand and turned his gaze upon Arderi. "Come, boy. Sit. We have much to discuss."

Arderi glanced over at Sier Singe and did as he was told.

With a second wave of the hand, the Grand Master eyed Witlan Singe. "You may leave us as well Hon'nar." Sier Singe bowed and retreated from the room, closing the doors as he left. The old man contemplated Arderi with such intensity that the boy was forced to avert his eyes. "I am told you are well after our...ordeal."



"Aye, Sier, sir."

"That is good. Tell me what you saw once we Melded with the Ka'ilyth."

"Melded with it, Sier? I do not understand." The image of the blue Crystal sucking Arderi into its folds sprang to his mind and gave him a queasy feeling in his gut.

The Grand Master smiled sagely. "Once you put your hands on the Ka'ilyth, what happened? Do you remember touching it?"

"Aye, Sier. I do remember putting my hands on…the Crystal device. It was cold, yet…" Squinting, Arderi shook his head and tried in vain to remember what happened next. "Yet that is all. I only remember waking a few moments ago, in a bedroom somewhere below."

Master Grintan sat silently for a time. When he spoke, he

sounded tired and old. "Cold, you say? That should not have been." He combed his age spotted fingers through his scruffy white beard and mumbled to himself for a time, a puzzled look on his face. Finally, he returned his attention to Arderi. "I am also unable to recall any events past the start of the Melding."

When it was apparent that the old man was not going to continue, Arderi cleared his throat. "If I may ask, Sier. What happened?"

The Sier slowly shook his head. "I am unsure. It seems that the Ka'ilyth somehow...backlashed. Sier Singe described to me a scene that I do not wholly understand."

"What will happen now? Will I be Tested again, Sier?" Arderi did not like the thought of repeating the ordeal, yet knew it must be done.

"That is unnecessary." The old Sier said the words absently. He seemed more interested in staring out the window than talking with Arderi.



"Unnecessary, Sier? I do not understand."

"Hmm?" The old man sat up and looked at Arderi, seeming as if he suddenly remembered that the boy was there. "Suffice it to say, it seems that you have failed the Test."

"Failed?" Arderi felt his heart tear in half. "Sier. You said the device, the Ka'ilyth, did not work. Mayhaps…"

"Nix, son. I was able to use it to Meld with you first, prior to the..." He waved a hand weakly about. "I am sorry, son. You do not have the gift. Only after I had seen this did the Ka'ilyth error in its operation. Now go. I am tired from the experience and need to retire."

A numbness fell over Arderi. Without a word, he rose and turned for the door. He was aware of someone taking him by the arm and leading him, yet he took no notice of whom. Once outside the Magistra building, he had no direction to follow and simply wandered the streets.

When he found himself at the fielder's gate, he took the opportunity to leave the stead. The weight of the surrounding buildings crushed what little sensibility he clung to. He felt dead. Empty. A hollow spot had welled inside his chest while he sat at the desk of the Master Shaper. It had grown ever since and now threatened to fill him completely.

Once clear of the gates, he took off at a full run. He fled down the road past the animal pastures. Once clear of the fences, he veered from the path and into a freshly planted field. His feet sunk into the tilled earth as he ran. Field after field sped below him. He raced blindly to nowhere. Hot tears streamed freely down his cheeks. His limbs burned and his chest pounded, yet he kept up his frantic pace. Finally, his legs gave way and he slammed hard into the ground. He lay there panting, muscles burning. Long after his stamina returned the tears still fell. Feeling drained and empty, he rolled over onto his back and stared up at the sky.

*Alant told me he* felt *the power in me! How could I have failed!*

With a loud animalistic roar, he screamed at the sky. "Why!" Nothing answered him. He rolled to his side as sobs racked his body once more. "Why?" The dirt soaked up his whimper.

*Why?*

# Chapter 19

Alant Cor sat on the large canvas bag which held all of his worldly belongings—books and clothes for the most part—and rested his head on a wooden piling. The predawn light shined just enough to allow him to see the swarm of sailors loading goods and supplies onto a large, four-mast barquentine floating before him. A few of the men had the sun-tanned look that fielders and herders from his home stead had. Yet the majority of the sailors had dark black skin that Alant found exotic looking. The vessel they worked was bound for the Isle of Elmorr'eth and he hoped he would be leaving with it on the morning tide.



Alant stared out the narrow harbor mouth directly east of where he sat. The sun broke over the horizon, the distant ripples of the ocean caused the edges of the big yellow ball to shimmer and dance as it clawed its way into the sky. Small jagged dark spots—the masts of fishing boats that had left earlier that morn—were scattered about like grains of pepper. Sea waves lapped against the sides of the ships and boats tied up to the docks of Mocley's harbor. Together they created a cacophony of blurp-blup noises barely audible under the pounding of feet, groaning of rope, and yelling of men.

"It always fascinates me when I come down here." Sier Sarlimac rested a hand upon his student's shoulder. "It is so chaotic; one wonders how they get anything at all done." He chuckled.

"Aye, Sier." Standing, Alant faced his teacher. "You were able to book passage with the Captain, Sier?"

"Yes. The ship is named the *Mistbreeze Trader* and you shall be sharing a room with its young cabin boy." Sarlimac looked over his shoulder. "Ah, here comes Captain Garson now."

"Sier, sir." The Captain was a big, burly black-skinned man—well over two paces tall—with broad shoulders and well-muscled arms. He was naked save for some loose fitting trousers that hung from his waist held in place by a thin rope that served as a belt. Large, gaudy necklaces covered much of his hairy chest and lighter black scars laced their way out from under these. More than a few of the scars extended down his stomach to disappear under the waistband of his pants. Apart from a cutlass strapped to his left side, the sandals he wore completed his outfit. Even though the air was chilly this early in the morn, sweat rolled down the man's face and chest. "Do say your farewells, if you please, Sier. I needs be getting the lad aboard now. We do cast off with the tide." His thick accent was odd to Alant. Reaching down, the big man plucked up Alant's bag from the dock, flung it effortlessly over a shoulder, and headed back to the plank that connected his ship to the dock.



"Yes, it is time at that." Sarlimac smiled warmly at Alant. "You take care, my boy."

"Aye, Sier, I shall make you proud." When the old teacher made no move or any additional comment, Alant lowered his gaze and strode past him to follow the Captain.

"Alant, wait." Sarlimac's words came as Alant was reaching the plank. He turned and watched the old man approach. A mask of determination covered the Shaper's visage. His teacher stood in front of him for long moments, his wrinkled face showing signs of a war raging behind his sharp blue eyes.

*He is worried.*

"Aye, Sier?" Alant kept any sign of impatience from his voice.

Sarlimac's hand disappeared into the folds of his robe and a wave of resolve settled over him. Taking the boy by the arm, he pulled Alant away from the hustle and bustle of the crew, and down an offshoot pier where smaller fishing crafts sat moored in a neat row. Looking around the dock area, the Sier pulled his hand from beneath the folds of his dark blue robe. In his palm, he cradled a small, golden medallion. It was in the shape of a fiery sun—masterfully crafted—in the center of which rested a large red Crystal that held the flicker of a flame nestled deep within it. A thin silvery cord ran from a loop in its top and pooled over the Sier's fingers. "You must not reveal anything I am about to tell you." The old man's eyes bore into Alant's. "Do you understand?"

"Aye, Sier." Alant's heart raced almost as fast as his mind.

"What I am revealing to you has been told to very few Shapers—and only once they held the title of Master Shaper. The Council forbade me from sharing this with you, yet I feel it is time something was done." Sarlimac gnawed on his lower lip and once again scanned the area. "The Elmorr'Antiens are not to be trusted...I think."

Alant's mouth dropped open as the shock of what the Sier said hit him full in the chest. "Sier, I do not—"



"Be quite now, I have much to say." The fatherly smile on the Sier's face took all sting from the command. "I know it has been engrained in you to revere the Elmorr'Antiens, and it is so that they are the most powerful with the Essence of any race here on the Plane of Talic'Nauth. Alas, heed me in my words."

"Many a promising student has been invited to study on their Island. One every few turns of the seasons since before I became a teacher here, some forty winters past. Few have returned from the training unscathed. Some have even perished."

"How do they explain the deaths, Sier?" Alant did not like the direction this conversation was taking.

"Some few from accidents. We are led to believe that most are due to weakness—that their training methods can prove too strenuous for us mere Humans. I have no doubt their training is tough, and even here in Mocley we have had a few expire during our training. The Essence is no toy, as you well know. Yet, even those who do return seem no better trained than our students." Sarlimac waved a hand in dismissal.

"What do those who return say of their stay, Sier?"

"That is the oddest point. I have questioned many, and they all tell strangely similar tales, as if they all experienced the exact same thing." The old man looked down at his hand and ran a thumb over the amulet. "Which brings me to this. We call this amulet a Tarsith. It is from a time long past and although we have used them for over a thousand turns of the seasons, we know little about them."

The sunlight glinted off the red stone and drew Alant's eyes back to the piece of jewelry. "Is it Essence enhanced, Sier?"

"Yes, that it is. Yet, of a method even our brightest Shapers are unable to fathom. I am afraid much knowledge has been lost from the past."

"Sier, if they were not made by Shapers, where did they come from?"

"Oh, they were made by Shapers, of that I am certain. It is just more powerful than anything any Shaper alive here and now can create."



Excitement rushing through him, Alant stared at the gold medallion. "So the Shapers who created that knew more than we know now?"

"No, it is not lack of knowledge that prevents us from creating items such as this. It is as if whoever created the Tarsith had access to a more powerful Essence than exists now." Turning the Tarsith in his hand, the Sier allowed the sunlight to glint through the center stone. "Alas, the Tarsiths were made many thousands of winters before recorded history as we know it. A few score were recovered during an expedition to Sar'Xanthia by our Order long ago."

"Sar'Xanthia? I have never heard of such a place, Sier."

Sarlimac chuckled. "That is not surprising. Sar'Xanthia was destroyed eons ago and lies buried deep in some swamplands far to the south. We know little of this city, even less of the time it hails from. No one knows who built it nor of the people who lived there save they were Humans much like us. When Mocley was young, some fifteen hundred winters past, an expedition was sent to explore the lands of the south. Sar'Xanthia was discovered and many ancient and powerful artifacts were recovered. Among these treasures were the Tarsiths. Centuries passed before their use was uncovered." The old man reached out, grasping Alant's hand, he pressed the medallion into it, closing the boy's fingers around the amulet.

"This is mine own personal Tarsith, and it will be the first time I have not had it around my neck since I was given it some twenty winters past. As I said, I was forbidden to give you one of your own."

Alant stared at it in wonder. "What does it do?"

"It will protect you from some of the powers the Elmorr'Antiens possess." Sarlimac shook his head when the boy tried to respond. "Listen, you must depart soon." Again, the Sier glanced about the dock area. "The Elmorr'Antiens have a few powers they use for their own ends. They have a knack for knowing what someone is thinking, as well as the ability to control others by forcing an idea into their minds and making that person think it was their's all along. With these abilities, the Elmorr'Antiens have caused us no end of trouble, albeit they use them subtlety and only sparingly." He lifted Alant's closed fist and held it between the two of them. "Yet, we know the Tarsith protects its wearer from both."



Opening his fingers, Alant gazed upon the amulet. "Sier, how do the Elmorr'Antiens come by such power over the Essence that we Shapers cannot?"

"This is unknown to us. I am of the opinion that these powers are not Essence related, rather more of a natural ability of their race. There is an uneasy tension between Shapers and Elmorr'Antiens—friendly at the best of times." Sarlimac smiled. "Alas, the answers to these questions are for men far wiser than you or I. All I wish for you is safety and prosperity. You have been a great student and have given this old man new hope." Releasing Alant's arm he flicked a finger from the necklace to the boy's neck. "Put that on now, and do not remove it for any reason, not even when you bathe."

Alant let the golden amulet drop from his hand to dangle from his fingers on its thread-thin silver chain and held it up to eye level. He admired the way the sunlight glinted through the flames inside the large red gem for a moment before he looped the necklace over his head.

"Tuck it inside your shirt, quickly." The old Sier's face grew somber. "Neither show nor tell anyone of it! Never let any of the Elmorr'Antiens know of its existence. Do you understand? Yours is not the only life that could be forfeit if that fell into the wrong hands."

The teacher placed both his hands upon Alant's shoulders, a look of pride fought with sadness for dominance over his face. "You have been the finest boy I have had the opportunity to instruct in all my days. Keep your wits about you and come back safe." Releasing Alant, the old man glided past. The old Sier did not look back as he stepped onto the main dock. Soon he was lost from the boy's vision, disappearing into the crowds that had materialized with the sun.

"Oiy!"



Alant jumped and jerked his head toward the foot of the small dock he stood on. The Captain stood at its base, hands on hips, glaring at him.

"Am I to carry you aboard as I did your bag?" He flung an arm over his shoulder. "The day be afoot and the tide...she be a leaving! Stay dockside if you do wish, we cast off now!" The big man spun around and headed for the gangplank.

Alant glanced once more in the direction his Sier had gone yet could gain no sight of the old man. He placed his hand to his breast and covered the Tarsith that hung beneath his shirt.

*Maja'Kasta, I know I do not pray to you as often as I should. Still, watch after me for my path leads to that which is unknown and I am frightened.*

Taking a deep breath, Alant exhaled. His eyes roved over the large ship in front of him. Nodding to himself, he started after the Captain.

# Chapter 20

The shadows falling from the nearby trees had stretched long once Arderi Cor finally stopped crying. He sat up and brushed away the dirt crusted to his face.

*The sun has almost dipped below the horizon. I must go before I am locked out of the stead for the eve.*

Forcing himself to stand, it took him only moments to take in his surroundings and get his bearings. At a brisk stride, he headed toward home—his mind a blank slate. No thoughts wandered its halls. He felt lifeless inside. By the time he reached the fielder's gate, dusk had fallen. A guarder made a comment to him as he entered, yet Arderi paid the man no mind.



Once inside the walls, he found no desire to return home. Instead, he meandered into the market. Most of the shops had closed for the day, the rest were in various states of closing.

His feet led him to the Palintium. He thought he would never want to set foot in the place again after last eve's funeral, yet he felt compelled to enter.

*Has it just been one day? It seems like a lifetime ago!*

A group of priests gave him quizzical looks—it was not forbidden for common folk to enter the temple, just uncustomary when there was no ceremony to attend—still, no one made to stop him.

The main hall was a massive, marble-floored chamber. It was round like the inside of a grain silo and capped with a domed ceiling high overhead. Twelve archways lined the walls, radiating out like the spokes of a wagon wheel. Each led to the inner sanctum of one of the Twelve Gods of man. Even this room, void of any finery save the beautiful stone of the floor, walls, and ceiling, humbled Arderi. Peering down one of the arched halls, Arderi caught a glimpse of the statue of Hezmire.

A young priest walked up. His white, silk robes indicating that he was a servant of Saltus, God of Healing. "May the enlightenment of the enlightened Twelve be with you, young one. How may I guide?"

Arderi felt foolish. "I am unsure. I have never been here on my own before." He turned to leave.

"A troubled mind, or one that despairs, can usually find solace in wisdom. Mayhaps you should seek out Saphanthia and see what mysteries she may unravel in your life?"

Arderi paused. Looking over his shoulder, he saw that the priest pointed to an archway leading off to the right. Arderi nodded. Taking the hallway indicated, the scent of fresh cut flowers greeted his nose. The short hall led to a sanctuary with a deep green carpet running down its center. Tapestries hung from the walls depicted everything from forests and meadow scenes to the crowded streets of some unknown city.



The sanctuary itself was a small, comfortable room. Several cushioned benches sat layered before a simple statue of an elderly woman, who stood looking down at them. Not knowing what to do, Arderi walked into the chamber and sat on the back row. Time passed without meaning as he contemplated all that had taken place this day. On more than a few occasions, he would tilt his head up to stare into the face of the Goddess. He searched for answers in the chiseled features of her wise old face and found none. He sat there in silence for well over and aurn. When he started to leave, a voice from behind him made him jump.

"May the enlightenment of the enlightened Twelve be with you, my son."

He turned and saw an elderly woman standing next to the

statue. Her long white hair flowed past her shoulders, cascading down either side of her neck to rest on the front of her dark green robe. A warm, grandmotherly smile graced her lips as she glided over to him.

Arderi was sure that she had not been in the small chapel before he turned to leave, and he could see no other doors in the room. “Well met, Mis’am.” He could not help his stammer.

“Well met to you as well. How may I guide?” Her young, strong voice belied her older visage.

“Begging pardon, Mis’am, I am just a simple fielder and not sure how all this works.” His face reddened and he cursed himself for being a country lout.

“I think you will find that all men are more than just the job or title they hold.” Her smile grew even larger and Arderi thought she was amused at his expense. “How can any mere mortal know how to approach a God? Please, sit and we shall converse.” Taking his hand, she sat with the grace of a queen upon the bench, pulling him down next to her. “There, that is better. You seem so young to have such worry in your heart.”



Arderi looked sheepishly into his lap. “I am a fool.”

She placed a finger under his chin, raised his head up, and looked deep into his eyes. “It is the wise man who has the hard road to travel to reach enlightenment. For the foolish man, however, that same path is wide and easily navigated.” At his puzzled look, she giggled. Taking his hand into hers, she continued to gaze into his eyes. “We are all fools in life, for none of us know the direction we will be taken. We could choose a path, knowing it to be true and just in our hearts, only to have it lead us to ruin. Whereas, an uncontrollable event—one caused through no action on our part—could lead us to greatness. True wisdom can only be gained when one looks back on one’s life, for the future is the fool’s playground.” Standing, she glided to the exit. The old lady glanced over her shoulder, a wicked grin on her face. “And you have a lot of playground yet to explore.” Passing through the arch, she disappeared from Arderi’s sight.

Sitting there, Arderi rolled her words over in his mind.

None of them made any sense to him, yet he had to admit he felt better. Time stretched on as he sat there in silence. Finally, he pushed himself off the bench and headed out of the small sanctuary. As he left, he paused and looked back to the statue.

*I never even learned that woman's name.*

# Chapter 21

The jingle of tackle and equipment, the stomp of shod hoof, the crunch of iron-reinforced felloes of the wagon wheels as they rolled over crushed stone, all combined to make a sound not wholly unpleasant to the ear. The sun shone down on Clytus Rillion and his caravan as they meandered up the wide state road that ran between lush, hilly grasslands sparsely peppered here and there with dense copses of hardwood trees.



*Say what you may about taxes, traveling well-maintained roadways across country is a luxury I do so enjoy.*

They had passed the last of the inner villages over an aurn ago. There was still an aurn's ride ahead of them before they would see the first of the true walled steads that lay on the fringes of Mocley's protective influence. His stomach grumbled informing him that halfmeal would be due soon. Letting his destrier, Starborn, slow its pace, he dropped back to ride even with the lead wagon. Ignoring the young Shaper who sat with a gloomy expression plastered on his face, Clytus nodded to Trilim and adjusted his saddle pack into a more comfortable position. "About time for halfmeal?" Clytus asked the driver.

"Aye, we—"

Clytus cut him off with a raised hand, his other dropping to the hilt of his sword. Scanning the distance, he searched for the origin of the sounds that had penetrated his senses. Two riders crested a small hill from the eastern side of the road at a full gallop. He let his thumb flick off the leather thong that locked his sword into its scabbard while motioning for the wagons to come to a stop. Out of the corner of his eye, he noticed Trilim reaching for the crossbow that rested on the floorboard of the wagon. The ratchet made a steady clank-clunk-clank sound as the Trilim bent the prod to load the weapon. Soon, similar sounds joined in from the other wagons as their drivers did the same.

*I have not heard of any bandits this close to Mocley. Still, one can never be too cautious when traveling.*

At a quarter of a league distance the two riders slowed to a canter and then to a steady trot as they approached the group. "It is Alimia, stand down." He smiled to himself as he saw Jintrill visibly relax. Clytus turned Starborn off the road and into the meadow. He spurned the dustier into a canter, riding out to meet his people.

"Stand down!" He heard Trilim yell out to the others. Clytus thumbed the thong back over his sword hilt so he would not have to worry with it as he rode. Enjoying the ride in the warm spring afternoon, he kept this pace through the field of tall grass. As the two riders approached, he slowed to a trot and the three horses came together.



"Hail, sir." Alimia Felts was a tall, lean woman. Arms strong as hemp from the sword work she had done in her life. Her long, dirty blond hair was pulled back into a braid that left her hawk-like face and penetrating green eyes exposed. She wore light armor—a thin chain byrnies under a thick studded leather jerkin covered her upper half, steel splinted greaves strapped over the leather breeches of her lower legs—as was her companion, a man unfamiliar to Clytus.

"Hail, report." Clytus eyed the other rider. He was a small man, a good half head shorter than his female leftenant. The man was equipped as a scout, light leather armor, short bow, and shortsword, which looked more like a long dirk.

"We made camp some ten miles off road. Jam'ees here,"—she waved a hand at the other rider—"was stationed as lookout and fetched me when you were still some leagues down road."

"Everyone show?" Clytus asked.

"All out of Orlis except Hindar's elite group. They sent word they would meet us in Stillwater. None out of Komar, I am afraid. No word from them either."

"Aye, tis to be expected. When I sent Mallin and his men up that way, I warned him the Priests of Fatint are a shifty lot. Alas, he feared for his uncle's safety so he took the job posting. Might be he is just locked into something he cannot break from." He gave her his best hopeful grin and nodded sagely.

*Of course, if that were so, he would still have sent a messenger.*

Alimia seemed satisfied, however. "Aye, tis probably so. Not counting Hindar and his, we have thirty-seven. Hindar has about six in his 'elite' employ. Them, and the crew from Mocley should put us over the fifty you requested, sir." She glanced over his shoulder at the wagon train. "I see old man Grith in the lead, yet the rest have the look of commoners. Where are the Mocley men, if I may ask, sir?"



"In Mocley. I left them with Ragnor to look after things there."

"Ragnor is not with you?" She looked stunned, a sight Clytus had never seen on her.

"Nix, you will be handling leftenant duties on this one, if you feel you are up to it that is." He grinned as the other man lowered his head slightly, looking as if he had eaten something that disagreed with him.

*He may be new, yet he has been with the troop long enough to have formed an opinion of Alimia Felts it would seem.*

"Aye, sir. I feel I am up to it." Alimia sat straighter in her saddle. Her large black mare cocked her head as the beast sensed her master's excitement.

"Aye, and I as well feel you are ready. Besides, Ragnor is getting too old to be wandering about in the mountains. What were your orders before you left the men?"

Alimia beamed at this first test of her leadership. "They will have broken camp by this point, sir. I told them to meet up with us at Wartin'alan stead. I estimate we should arrive at the same time as them, sir."

"Well done." Clytus reined his horse around and the trio headed back to the wagons.

"I see you have procured us a Shaper, sir. I am surprised that any of those soft bellies would consent to going into the Nektine."

Clytus shot her a disgusted look. "*Procured* is not the word I would use." When he did not respond to her questioning look, she let the subject drop. He turned to the other man. "Who are you under?"

"Under Master Hindar o de scouts, Master Rillion, sir." The man's thick accent and olive skin meant he was one of the Komar Islander folk. "Been wit him in Orlis mos de turn o de season, sir."

"Ah, scouting bandits for the Prince. How does Orlis fair against the Komar Isles of your birth?"



"I do be missin de sea n all, tho life do tend ta be longer, the further one do drift from de Isles. If ya get me meanin, sir?"

"Aye, I have been to Komar a few times now. Not the best working conditions with every new pirate lord trying to lay claim to the place. Not to mention the Priests." Clytus reined Starborn in next to Trilim's wagon. "Since we are stopped, pass out halfmeal to the dayhires. We can eat while we travel."

Once the food was handed out—fresh flatbread and dried meat—Clytus motioned for Trilim to follow as the three rode down the crushed stone of the road.

"Onward!" the old man yelled. Flicking the reins, his wagon lurched down the roadway. The young Shaper rocked in the seat next to him.

"Jam'ees, fall back and take rear guard." Alimia never had to repeat an order. She then fell in beside Clytus and the two rode in silence as the grassland slipped passed.

A gentle breeze had followed them from the coast of the Glonlore Bay and the city of Mocley, the ting of salt still evident in it even a league away. The tall wild grasses covering much of the rolling hills around them swayed as the wind brushed over the land. A stray cloud raced along high overhead. Lost in thought, Clytus was startled when Alimia finally spoke. "Following Maja'Kasta now, I see?"

He glanced over at her with a questioning look. To this, she pointed at his chest. Looking down he saw the small wooden trinket dangling from its leather cord and pain laced through his heart. Reaching up, he tucked the amulet his wife, Lilaith, had given him inside his jerkin. "It is a woman thing." He grinned over at her. "You would not understand."

She barked out a laugh. "Are you saying I do not understand women, or that I do not understand why you would be acting like one?" When Clytus did not return her mirth she cleared her throat. "Sir." Nervousness laced the honorific.

Clytus softened his face. "I mean only that I wear this for a woman." He turned his head to the sky. "And that you cannot possibly understand why men do the things we do for them."

"I always assumed it was to get into our pants, sir." The uncertainness still in her tone pleased Clytus.



*She may one day become a good friend. Still, she will have to learn how informal with me she can be on her own.*

"Aye, for some men tis true." Clytus let the silence stretch on until it felt uncomfortable. Finally, he smiled over at his new leftenant. "Maja'Kasta, he would be the God of…?"

"I do not follow the Twelve myself all that well, yet Maja'Kasta grants protection, and peace it is said."

If wearing a trinket of wood could grant me peace, I would strap an entire tree to my back and never once complain!

Clytus squinted up at the sun to estimate the time they had traveled since Alimia's arrival. "We should be less than a quarter aurn from Wartin'alan. Ride on ahead. If the troop is there, I do not wish to waste any time. Have them ready to move when the wagons arrive. I need only enough time to water the horses and release the dayhires."

"And if they have not yet arrived, sir?"

"Then you will wait and catch me up when they do and

the dayhires will ride with me a bit further. We have some five aurns of daylight left and I plan to make the most of it."

"Aye, sir." She dug her heals into the mare's sides and it burst into a gallop. Clytus admired the way the animal's muscles rippled as it tore into the distance. He had always had an eye for good horseflesh, and she had picked hers well.

"Trouble?" Jintrill called out nervously from behind.

Clytus turned in his saddle, noting that Trilim shook his head, a big grin on his face. "Believe me, boy, when trouble comes to find us, you will have no need to ask."

# Chapter 22

Two sailors, their skin as dark as tar, pulled the gangplank from the dock once Alant Cor had both feet upon the deck of the *Mistbreeze Trader.* The hustle and bustle of the crew—those without the dark skin were deeply tanned, all were barefoot and most shirtless—exploded around him. People yelled, pulled, lifted, climbed, and ran in every direction. The big black Captain stood upon a raised platform at the back of the ship. His muscular arms waved or pointed to punctuate the orders he shouted at the men scurrying about. Everyone seemed to ignore Alant standing amongst the chaos of the ship. Striding to the front, stumbling slightly when the ship lurched forward, he leaned out over the railing and peered down into the water some ten paces below. Directly under him, attached to the front of the ship, a wooden beam jutted out away from the boat. An assortment of pulleys littered the beam and four heavy, hemp ropes jutted out from the inside of the boat at an angle to disappear into the murky, blue-green water of the harbor. All of a sudden, the ropes stretched taunt. The boat slid forward several paces then all four ropes turned to his right in unison, as if they were fishing lines attached to some monstrous fish that was trying to get free. The deck tilted sharply in their direction forcing Alant to grip the handrail as the ship slipped away from the dock and out into the center of the harbor, being pulled by whatever was on the other end of the ropes.

"Mermidians." Alant jumped at the squeaky voice that sounded next to him. Standing just behind him was a young black boy of about thirteen. His long, dark hair—a tangle of curls that looked like it would be more at home on a mop head—billowed in the breeze that blew in from the bay. The boy looked much like any of the rest of the crew in his loose fitting pants and nothing else. Save for the fact of his young age, and the broad, bright smile that spread across his face. "There be Mermidians at the ends of the guide ropes." Placing his right hand against his stomach, he bowed his head. "Krin Garson, cabin boy here on the *Mistbreeze Trader*. I be at your service, Sier."

A pang jolted Alant. "Nix!" His voice rang out louder than he had intended. "I am no Sier, just an Initiate. I am heading to Hath'oolan to finish my training." It was the first time anyone had addressed Alant as Sier, and it made him feel odd.

The boy's smile grew larger. "Aye, mayhaps. Still, to us common folk, an Initiate be more than we shall ever be, Sier. I do think you will find it be the same with the rest of the crew as well." Krin put both hands on the railing, closed his eyes, and drew a deep breath. "I do love the sea air. It be much better than that stink of the crowd on dock. Do you no agree, Sier?"



In spite of himself, Alant smiled. The boy spoke in the same thick accent as Captain Garson. Although he could not tell from what region, he knew the boy was from Silaway—and not just due to the color of his skin—far across the Great Ocean. Returning his attention to the ropes pulling the ship, Alant wagged a finger at them. "You say there are Mermidians at the ends of those ropes?"

"Aye, Sier, that there be. Four or five to a line, I should expect." The young boy pointed toward the mouth of the harbor. "They will pull us out into the Glonlore Bay a piece before they do let us go."

"I have never seen a Mermidian before. Will they come to the surface?"

"Nay, Sier, it no be likely. They stay to the depths they do. I did see one of the beasties myself, once. When I did be dockside with the Captain."

Alant peered in vein at the murky-green waters, eager to catch a glimpse of movement. "What do they look like?"

The boy laughed aloud. "Like a man who did eat one too many fish!" He shook his head causing a curly lock of black hair to fall across his face. He flicked it aside with a finger. His natural smile slipped from his face as he looked up into Alant's eyes. "Actually, they do look much like you or I, Sier. Their skin be greenish and thick as that of the great whales who do live out in the deep oceans. And their hands and feet be more suited for swimming than walking. Still, the strangest thing about them be the slits on their necks. The Captain did say it be how they do breathe, yet they did look ghastly to me. All gaping wide, like someone did take a knife to their throats." The boy gave a shudder. Then his big smile returned as if it had never left.



Leaning back on the railings, the two young men stood in silence as the city of Mocley slipped by. The *Mistbreeze Trader* had been moored deep inside the harbor and Alant enjoyed the view of the city as it silently slipped past as Mermidians pulled them out to sea.

To his right, pier after massive pier—each some ten or twelve paces wide—pressed against the stone wall that made up the bulk of the city-side shore. At each sat ships of every size and make, most large enough for long, oceanic voyages. Smaller docks jutted out from the larger ones like branches of a mighty tree. These held the myriad of smaller fishing boats that reaped the bounty of the sea for the inhabitants of Mocley. Swarms of people now covered the docks and piers. Several small crafts, either ahead of them or pulling away from their resting spots, joined the *Mistbreeze Trader* in the harbor.

To his left side sat the Millitinia that housed the mighty Mocley Royal Navy. Over the high wall that skirted the shore in front of it, Alant could see its ornate towers jutting up into the clear-blue morning sky. He assumed these spires must be part of the Proctors Residence, nestled inside the protective fort within the walls of the city. Guarders patrolled the battlements and it conjured up an image of his home in Hild'alan. A spasm of longing ripped through him.

*It will be many long turns of the seasons before I see the shores of my homeland again.*

More fishing boats joined the large barquentine in the middle of the harbor. As they neared the mouth, Alant feared for the safety of the smaller crafts. "They are darting in every direction, are those fishermen crazy? Why are they getting so close to us?"

"They no have control, Sier. No boats can navigate Mocley's harbor without a Mermidian guide. The bottom of the harbor be filled with underwater barriers that can rip the hull off any ship." Krin pointed to a boat streaming alongside of them. "Do you see the rope that be tied to that one's bow-stem, Sier? She do also be led, just as we."



"Watch the windfall as we do enter the bay and be prepared to back and fill!" Captain Garson perched at the rear of the ship, yet his shouts rang clear even where Arderi and Krin stood at the front. "When we do raise sail, I no want to be taken aback!" Alant wondered what the man meant.

*It is like they speak a completely different tongue!*

As they neared the mouth of the harbor, Alant turned to ask the young cabin boy the meaning of the Captain's words, yet his breath escaped him as the full expanse of the open sea filled his vision. "Never before have I seen so much openness! It goes on forever!"

"Aye, tis be as beautiful a sight as a man did ever see." Krin motioned ahead of them. "Do you see the tower that juts out of the water in the middle of the mouth, Sier?" Krin waited until Alant nodded. "That be Gatekeep. If you do look closely at the waterline, you can just see where the chaingate slips into the water below."

"What is the chaingate?" Alant had never heard the term used before.

Krin gawked at him in genuine befuddlement. "They really do keep you locked up in that Academy, huh, Sier?" He shook his head. "I can no imagine living so...confined." The boy gazed back toward the open sea. Pointing off to the Millitinia side of the harbor exit, to the last tower that stood on a small strip of land, he wagged a finger at it until Alant looked that way. "Inside that last tower be a massive chain—links the size of a man—it extends down into the water and then crosses to Gatekeep in the center there." He traced the path with a finger, continuing past the center tower. "A second one—you can see a few of the links just there—extend on to that tower on the city side of the mouth. To block the harbor, they raise the chaingate and no boat can get in or out of Mocley."

"I have never heard of it." Alant words came out hushed.

"As far as the Captain do know, it has no been raised in living memory. Most of the crew do think it be an old woman's tale. Still, you will get a good view of the few visible links when we do pass out into the bay, Sier."



Turning around, Alant leaned against the railing and stared back into the heart of the city. "I have been in Mocley for nearly two turns of the seasons now. Yet I have seen almost nothing of it. The Coliseum, Great Palintium, the Bazaar...all as foreign to me now as they were before I arrived." He shook his head and looked down at the boy standing next to him. "And you, at barely half my age. You have seen what?"

A sheepish smile sprang to Krin's dark face and he averted his chocolate eyes. "I did sail with the Captain since he did take me in as a babe, Sier. My home be somewhere near Nithshilo. At least, that be what the Captain did tell me."

Alant cocked his head to one side and gave the boy a quizzical look. "Nithshilo? Where is that?"

"It do lie on the coast of Silaway on the other side of the Great Ocean, Sier. I did cross the Great Ocean many a time now. I have gone as far north as Katsujai and south down to Aktita covering the breadth of the Silawaian coastline. Circled the Isle of Elmorr'eth, stopping at all three of its great cities, and have seen most ports here on Ro'Arith, from Aalholm to Velvithia."

*This boy has seen so much, and I still have a farm boy's understanding of things. What kind of Shaper will I make?*

The smile slipped from Krin's face and reaching out, he put his hand over Alant's. "Did I say something that upset you, Sier?" There was genuine concern in his voice.

"Nix. I simply lost myself in thought." Alant smiled at the boy before he leaned onto the rail and watched the *Mistbreeze Trader* slip past the last towers standing their stoic watch on the harbor. He saw the two visible chaingate links jutting out of the side of the tower and slipping into the waters below—each link easily big enough for a man to walk through. The land peeled away to either side and the full expanse of the Glonlore Bay opened before him revealing nothing except white-capped waves extending off into the horizon. Alant's stomach lurched. He forced himself to turn back to the city for reassurance that land still existed and they had not, in fact, fallen off the Plane and into emptiness.



The cabin boy giggled and Alant realized his mouth hung open. Shutting it with a click, he mentally kicked himself for acting like a fool, yet he could not bring himself to turn back to the vacuous sight that lay in the path of the ship. "Could you show me to my quarters? I need to lie down for a while."

"Aye, Sier." Krin took him by the elbow. "Let me help you. The deck do shift when the sails be set."

Alant let himself be led. The cacophony of sights and sounds swirling around him dissolved and numbness overtook him.

# Chapter 23

Dusk had settled across the land before the walls of the stead came in view. Clytus Rillion nudged his dustier, Starborn, into a canter and noted with satisfaction that Alimia matched his pace without hesitation. This far out from Mocley he had no wish to camp outdoors when a fortified place lay so close at hand.

*Things will be rough enough once we cross the Artoc.*

Approaching the main gate to the small stead with Alimia by his side, Clytus' heart gave a flutter when he saw the gates were already down for the eve.

"Do you have any contacts here?" Alimia called out over the pounding of the horses' hooves.

"Nix! I am not even sure what stead this is." He hoped the Crystal from the Shaper's Order would carry some extra weight out here in the sticks.

*If it does not, I will wave that annoying Jintrill in their face. At least the boy will be good for something!*

They reined in their mounts at the gate and Clytus dismounted. The sally-port, a small, man-sized door set within the larger, main gate opened and a guard stepped out. He looked to be a stout man about two paces tall. Short-cropped black hair peppered with gray gave his age to be well over thirty winters. He stood there, dressed in a thick, brown leather jerkin and pants, with a shortsword belted on his left hip. The fact that several archers looked out from slits set nearly ten paces off the ground was not lost on Clytus.

The guard approached with a weary look in his eye. "Well met."

"Well met. I am Clytus Rillion. I command a merc troop out of Mocley." Reaching into a belt pouch, he withdrew a Crystal and offered it to the man. "Here is my license."

The guard held it to his brow, his eyes losing focus for a moment. "Attached to the Shaper's Order, huh?" The man returned the Crystal, his stance visibly relaxing. "I am Dartin Sim, Guarder Captain of the Third Watch here at Hild'alan. What might I do for you, Commander?"

"My host and I are traveling north and were hoping to take refuge inside your stead for the eve."

Dartin looked over Clytus' shoulder. "How many in your troop, Commander?"

"Thirty three ahorse, seven wagons with drivers, a dozen or so spare mounts, and a Shaper, Guarder Captain." Clytus hated to note that, to this country lout, the Shaper had more impact than the rest combined.



"Aye, we have a spot that can accommodate you, Commander. Alas, I will warn you. We have no accommodations for entertainment—no taverns or such. We are a working stead, not one meant to entertain. Keep your men in camp if you please."

"Aye. I had no intention of letting my troop have any leave time this eve, so that will not be an issue. And I am grateful for the hospitality, Guarder Captain Sim."

The guard turned and let out a loud, shrill whistle, waving his arm in a circle above his head. The gates groaned as they broke from the ground. The loud clickety-clack of a hoist and ratchet sounded through the cool, early-eve air. Clytus remounted and stared down the road at the approaching wagons.

Once inside the stead walls, a wide-eyed young guard escorted them to a section of dirt covered by a sparse layer of grass between two in-stead animal pens full of bleating sheep. "This is our only camp area, Commander. We use it for fairs and festivals."

Nodding, Clytus dismounted. "This will do nicely." He flicked a silver pent to the young man.

Snatching it from the air, the boy grinned openly and nodded to Clytus. "My thanks to you, Commander, sir. I will be by in an aurn or so to see if you need anything else."

*Probably a full moons wage for the lad.*

As soon as the wagons came to a stop, Jintrill jumped from his perch and bustled over. He snagged the young guard by the arm as the man was leaving. "Take me to the Ques'lian." At the baffled look of the young man, he sighed. "The Hall of Shapers."

The young guarder's eyes bulged. "Sier, sir…My apologies..." He stared around in panic. "Hall of Shapers?"

Clytus shook his head. "Jintrill! This is a farming stead. You will find no Ques'lian here."

"Aye, I mean nix, Sier…sir." The young guarder tried in vein to extract his arm from Jintrill's grasp without making it appear impolite.



The Shaper released the guarder. "You do have Shapers here, do you not?"

The guarder rubbed his arm as if he had been burned. "Aye, Sier. There are several." His eyes lit up. "I could take you to the Master Shaper! His apartments are in the Magistra." Clytus chuckled at how proud the young man seemed at his revelation.

"That would be acceptable." Jintrill waved a hand. "Lead on then."

"Oiy!" Clytus yelled and was rewarded by a jump from both young men. "I suppose then, you will not be in need of a tent this eve?"

A horrified look sprang to the young Shaper's face. "I should hope not. Civilization should at least extend this far from Mocley, should it not?"

"Aye, mayhaps. Just do not get used to this. It will be the last time you sleep in a bed for several moons." Clytus started to turn, then paused. "Oh, and if you are not with the troop when we move out in the morning, it was nice traveling with you, young Sier."

Jintrill's jaw dropped open. "The Council…You would not leave me here, surely!"

"Oh, aye, lad, I would indeed. Keep in mind that *you* have been ordered by the Council to accompany me. I was only ordered to let you. I am under no obligation to help you keep up nor to make your journey comfortable." Clytus shifted his smile into a vicious grin. "Or even insure that you return home alive."

He watched with amusement while the implication of his statement settled into the young Shaper. Jintrill shrank away in terror, stumbling as he turned to flee into the buildings that made up the center of the stead.

Clytus chuckled and nodded to the young guarder. "Go get him and make sure he makes it to the other Shapers."

The man grinned and trotted off after Jintrill.



Watching his troop dismount and start their chaotically organized camp setup—complete with Alimia spouting off orders where needed—Clytus spied some young boys who had taken note of them and stood on the fringes, staring.

Trilim walked by carrying an armload of cooking pots. "The smell of the animals should add to the taste of this eve's stew nicely, Master."

Clytus snorted. "Mayhaps. Still, tis better than *becoming* something else's stew."

"There is that." Hefting his load, Trilim continued to the spot he had chosen for the camps cook fire.

Glancing once more toward the country boys on the fringes of the camp, he took a moment to study them.

*I have always wondered how the Proctors of Mocley keep these labor steads operating. One step above slavery, and the fools who live here do not even realize it. Yet, when you are born into it, with no knowledge of what the rest of the Plane holds, how are you to know that you have less than you should?*

Shaking his head, he set off to see to his own tent.

# Chapter 24

A bitter wind raked Arderi Cor's skin. Despite a nagging voice in the back of his head telling him to go home, he continued to wander aimlessly through the stead. Goose-pimples sprang up on his uncovered arms. When he left the house this morn, he had not expected to be out after dark and had not dressed for the chill of the late eve. Early spring eves could still get nippy, and this one turned out to be no exception.



The desire to avoid bumping into anyone who might know him forced him to wander away from the fielder public housing district and into areas he had rarely been. The tall, whitewashed buildings cast the alleys between them into total darkness causing his imagination to wonder at what lay hidden inside. Even the dimness of the main streets, lit only by a smattering of oil lamps, hung an ominous gloom over his spirit.

Tracing the southron wall, losing himself in the simple sounds and smells of the animals as he wound through in-stead pens and the odd barn or feed silo, he was shocked to find a large group of men making camp on the fairgrounds. Curious, he snuck closer, crouching down in the shadows of a corner fence.

Across from him, standing in opened-eyed wonder, stood a group of young herders gawking at all the goings on. Hidden, he watched the camp take shape. Many tents had been raised and a cooking fire blazed away in the center of the area. A large pot dangled over it and the aroma of a stew drifted out. Scores of horses stood picketed on a rope line that stretched between the fencing. A cluster of wagons rested on the far edge of the grounds nearest the main road.

*They look to be fighting men. Still, they wear no uniforms so they cannot be soldiers. Mayhaps they are mercenaries!*

Arderi's mind raced remembering the tales he had heard—in this very field—from bards who came during festival times. They told of the free ranging fighting men who would sell their swords to those who could pay. He turned and sat, leaning his back against the fencepost, and pulled his knees to his chest. Imagination took the better of him and he dreamed himself living the adventure of a bard's tale.

*They* must *be heading to Mocley! Those wagons look stuffed full of the treasure they acquired on their journey!*

For well over an aurn he sat huddled up in his shadow, listening to the bustle of the camp, daydreaming.



Arderi awoke with a start. He did not remember falling asleep, yet knew he had. Looking around the camp, he saw that all was quiet. The fire had burned low, snores and snorts emanated from the dark mounds that littered the area closest to him. All the tents sat dark and silent.

As Arderi stood, pain shot down the back of his neck. Remaining in the position he had drifted off in caused his muscles to stiffen and tighten. With no moon visible in the sky, and since he had never learned how to use the stars as guides, he had no idea how late it was. A pang of guilt ripped through him. His parents would be upset since he failed to come home this eve.

*They must be worried sick!*

Even with this realization, he could not bring himself to start the journey home.

*I am a failure. Better that I never return than to see the look of shame in their eyes.*

Casting his gaze over the sleeping camp, with its tents and men, horses and wagons, his heart hardened with resolve. Melting into the shadows of the southron wall, he stalked like a cat, skirting the animal pens so as not to disturb their occupants. He made his way around to the far side of the camp—and more importantly, to the wagons.

Breaking from the dark cover, he crept across the last bit of ground that separated him from his goal. His breath caught in his throat when a small stone shot out of the darkness to his right and skidded across the ground, coming to rest directly in front of him. Dropping flat to the ground, he strained his ears, listening for any sound. Footsteps followed the stone from the direction it had come.

*Someone draws near!*

Glancing back, Arderi knew he could not make it back to the safety of the wall before whoever approached discovered him. Hardly a wisp of air escaped him. He lay prone in the chilly darkness, listening to the footsteps draw near. The shape of a man materialized out of the darkness some twenty paces away. The guarder used a spear as a walking stick and bore a line that would take him directly across the spot where Arderi lay. Pressing hands to dirt, Arderi prepared to rise and bolt.



"A bit of crock I say!" A loud whisper came out of the dark from off to the left.

The man with the spear stopped and turned, scanning the area. He nodded and a second man's form came into view. "Aye." The first man nodded his head. "I see no reason for a third watch inside these walls either, yet we do as we are told. Master Rillion is in charge and it was by his order. Even Alimia voiced against it."

"Aye, I saw the exchange. Better her than me in dealing with that man, I say. I have yet to meet a man such as him." The new man gave a grunt of a laugh. "He walks among us like a lion surrounded by sheep."

"Aye, tis true. Alas, I have seen the man fight. We are all sheep compared to his skill with the blade. I am not so sure I believe all the bard's tales about some mystical Tat'Sujen Order, yet if they are true, Master Rillion is not far from the telling."

"Mayhaps, you will—" A quick wave of the hand silenced the man. Whipping his head around, he looked directly at the spot Arderi lay. Panning his gaze off toward the animal pens, he turned back to the other guarder. "You will have to tell me what you have seen over lastmeal one eve. For now, keep to your rounds. That demon of a woman seems to know when to show up and I will not risk her wicked tongue if I can help it." He slapped the other on the shoulder and broke away, disappearing into the darkness.

Arderi watched the first man stand for a short time, then head off as well, toward the main cobblestone street that ran along the northron side of the fairgrounds. Not realizing he was holding his breath, he let it out in a slow, quiet quivering stream. When he was sure he was once again alone, he let his muscles relax as well.

*That was close!*

Rising up on all fours, he scrambled across the field and slipped underneath one of the wagons. Trying to regain control of his breath, Arderi listened to the sounds surrounding him. He forced himself to wait a half an aurn to insure he had gone undetected. The guards made two more passes by his hiding spot during that time, yet raised no alarm.



After the guards had passed him for the third time, he slipped to the side of the wagon and studied the jumble of gear and supplies that filled its interior. Working quick and quiet, he adjusted the crates and barrels, sacks and bags, until he created a small tunnel into the interior of the pile. Twice during his excavation, he was forced to take cover beneath the wagon for fear of discovery by the roving men with spears. When satisfied that all was ready, he took one long panning view of the only place he had ever lived, steeled himself, then slid feet first into the small compartment he had created. He sealed off the entrance with a large sack of grain put aside for that purpose.

Unsure of how long he laid there—his mind chasing stray thoughts like a cat dropped into a room full of mice—exhaustion overcame him and he fell into a deep sleep.

*Alant, I will be with you soon, brother.*

# Chapter 25

The morning started out normally. Klain awoke just after sunrise and immediately made his way to the kitchen area to break his fast. Grabbing the plate of raw meat that always awaited him, he strode out of the villa and into the garden area. Sitting at the bench and table, eating his food from a serving fork as opposed to off the dish directly—or off the floor as he had done until recently—still made him feel odd, as if this new life were merely a dream that he would wake from at any moment. As always, the food tasted incredible.

*Everything in this new life is incredible.*

The warmth of the morn spilled over him. Spring had fallen full upon the city of Mocley and Klain enjoyed the sun's rays penetrating his lush, spotted fur. Distant smells of fruit and fauna filled his nostrils with their fragrances. After devouring all that lay on his plate, and about to return the dish to the kitchen, he noticed Sarshia step out the backdoor.

"Ah, Klain, I trust you slept well, hmm?" The Elmorian glided across the crushed gravel and sat down opposite Klain. A serving girl followed her out of the villa and placed a silver tray of fruit and cheese upon the table. "My thanks, Friaya, this will do nicely." The dark-haired girl curtsied and withdrew back inside.

Eyeing the pittance upon her tray, Klain waited until Sarshia settled on the bench before answering. "Aye, Honored One. I slept well. I was unaware you were in the villa. I thought I heard your carriage leaving early this morn."

"Yes, I had things to attend to for my journey home, yes?" Skewering a cube of cheese, she lifted it to her dark gray lips. "I was also able to meet with Rohann Vimith, the merchant I spoke of."

An uneasiness fell over Klain. "Aye."

"He is in town and would very much like to meet with you and discuss your employment."

A blue bird flitted out of a nearby tree and landed on the gravel path that led deeper into the garden. Klain took a moment to gaze at it. It pecked around in the crushed stone looking for its firstmeal and he thought back on his own life. Himself no more than scratching in the dirt for his food. All that had led him here. At his hesitation in seeing it come to an end.

*I knew I could never stay here. The thought of losing my freedom however…*

"Employment is not slavery, Klain, yes?" The Elmorian set her eating prong down on the table. "You have come along well and are not the beast you were when you arrived. You see how things fit together, yes? I think this is your greatest ability. Under the employ of this merchant, you will gain much, I think."



Casting his gaze across the villa grounds, the loss Klain felt grew. "Gain? What is there that I need?"

A smile touched Shaith's lips. "Again, I will state that employment is not slavery, yes? You will do as the merchant says, yet in return for your loyalty and hard work, the merchant must give to you as well, yes?"

A snort escaped Klain's nostrils. "So he will feed me. Even my old Master did that."

The odd look of amusement took hold of Sarshia's features for a moment. "Yes, he will feed you. He will also have a room for you to stay in and pay you a wage. You would like to have coin of your own, hmm?"

"Aye. Yerina's mother has taken me shopping in the markets. I understand the use of coin well enough." Klain still found the practice of trading something as worthless as a pretty coin for something you could use such as food to be absurd.

Letting a moment pass, her penetrating stare held Klain silent. The Elmorian reached out and placed a three-fingered hand on Klain's arm. Her touch, something Klain had never felt before, was ice cold. It penetrated the thick fur of his paw instantly, yet he did not pull away for fear of offending her. "He will also be there to teach you."

Using the excuse of showing her his strength, he pulled his paw out from under her hand and flexed it. He always admired the way his claws extended and retracted.

*It gives me power over the weaker races that surround me.*

"I have been taught. I proved that in the Games."

"Oh, yes. You did at that. I am not doubting your physical skills, hmm? Yet, would you not now like to learn to read, hmm? Or to write?"

Waving into the air, Klain shook his head. "Why would I have need of such things? I have the claw, the fang, the sword if I am given one."



Bowing her head, Sarshia blinked. "This may be so, and those things will serve you well, yes? I think, however, that you are clever enough to know that if you are going to have a future, you will have to know more than just brute force." Pushing herself up, her thin arms flexing, she stood. "Come. We need to meet Rohann. And I have one final gift for you before we leave."

Following her into the villa, they passed through the kitchens. Little Yerina peeked out from behind the doorway that led to the servants' quarters at Klain, yet would not come out into the open with Sarshia in the room. Cutting through the main dining hall, its marble floors enhancing the sounds of Klain's claws as he padded along behind his host, they entered the entrance hall. The tall main doors stood open to allow a cooling spring breeze to flow throughout the residence. Fresh flowers, arranged in vases, lined the walls adding to the allure of the place.

A deep, redwood box rested on the center table. Sarshia glided up to it and opened its lid. Stepping back, she indicated for Klain to come forward and look inside. Lying in the box, nestled in soft folds of red cloth, lay a sword. Jets of black streaked through its length. At first, other than the color, Klain saw nothing unusual about the weapon. Upon further inspection, he realized that its hilt was unlike any he had ever seen.

The hilt was split in twain, as if someone had driven a wedge through it, bowing out one side.

"This was not something easy to come by, yes?" Sarshia's voice snapped Klain from the almost trance-like state he had fallen into. "These weapons, a Mi'nathe blade, have not been made for millennia. Not since your race was more abundant upon Talic'Nauth and had more influence in civilized matters, yes?"

A cold shiver slammed through Klain as if he had been struck. "My race? I thought the Kithians were scattered out amongst the northron wastes. It is said they are more rare than diamonds."



The Elmorian tilted her head slightly into a nod. "That is true, now. Yet in times past the Kithian race was a force, helping to carve the future of many races. Mayhaps now is not the time for history to be told, yes?" Holding out a hand, she indicated the box. "The hilt is designed to fit around a Kithian's paw. Try it, hmm?"

Klain reached out and scooped the sword from the box. It was heavier than he had expected, easily twice as heavy as any normal sword of this length he had wielded. The black streaks he assumed were part of the blade's structure, shifted as he lifted the blade.

*As if the blade absorbed the light.*

Hefting the weapon, Klain ran a paw down its length.

*It is the length of a long sword, yet twice as thick. A slashing weapon then.*

Slipping his fingers into the gap in the hilt, he found that the bowed portion rested comfortably around the back of his paw.

His thick fingers wrapped around the triangle-shaped grip, the ridged portions slipping between his fat knuckles.

*It fits my hand like a second skin!*

Taking a few practice strokes, it amazed him at how well it complimented the attacks he had learned with the sword.

*Except, with a sword made for Humans, I always felt as if I would lose my grip. This…*

"As I said, it was made for the paw of a Kithian." A twinkle lit Sarshia's liquid-black eyes.

Not wanting to offend his host, Klain returned the sword back to its box. "It is masterfully made. I am sure you are happy to have one."

A thin smile split Sarshia's dark lips. She reached out a bony arm and plucked the sword from the box as easily as a child picking up a dry stick. Holding it before her, she bowed slightly. "The Mi'nathe is meant for you, yes?"

Klain was speechless. Reaching out, he cupped the sword in his paws. His vision blurred, irritating him because it took the weapon out of focus. He could not understand what would cause that until a drop of water fell onto the blade. He looked up. "Is the roof leaking?" Something had caught in his throat as well, causing his words to come out in a croak.



Smiling, Sarshia reached out a hand and wiped a tear from the side of his cheek. "No. You are."

Dragging the back of a paw over his eyes, Klain was shocked to see it come away wet. Embarrassment filled him at his show of weakness and he fought to control this new and foreign emotion. Returning his attention to the sword, he slid a paw into the split, V-shaped hilt, marveling once more at how snug it felt. He glanced back into the Elmorian's black eyes and tried to speak finding that no words would escape his lips.

Sarshia bowed her blue-gray, teardrop shaped head, her strange look of amusement enhanced beyond any Klain had seen before. "It is my pleasure to have given this to you. No words are needed, yes?"

Clinching his jaw, Klain remained at a loss as to what to

do. He bobbed his head in quick succession, reached back into the box and withdrew the belt and scabbard that sat next to where the blade had rested. Slipping the sword into place in the sheath, he belted it around his hips.

*Even the belt fits me well. This will not rub me as one made for a Human does.*

Stretching to his full height, Klain had never felt so proud. "Sarshia, Honored One, I am grateful for your gift." Hot tears rolled down the fur covering his cheeks as he said the words. He felt no shame in them now. The knot that had lived in Klain's core his entire life seemed to loosen.

Smiling, the Elmorian tilted her head slightly. "Come, it is time for you to leave and start the next chapter in your life, yes?" Raising a thin, gray-blue arm, she pointed back toward the kitchen door. "Say your goodbyes."

Turning around, Klain caught sight of Yerina hovering in the doorway. Tears streamed down the little girls face and she stood with her arms wrapped around her thin waist rocking on the balls of her feet. Klain took a step toward her and the little girl ran to him. Falling on one knee, he wrapped her in his strong, furry arms as she slammed into him crying harder than before.



"I will miss you, my little Human prey."

Nuzzling her face deep into his spotted fur, she hung on as if for life. "You will come back and see me, will you not, Klain?"

Glancing up at Sarshia, his eyes asking the question he did not trust his voice to speak aloud. At the Elmorian's nod he pulled Yerina out to arm's length and looked into her eyes. "Aye, my little cub. You shall see me again."

Giving him one more long hug, the girl slipped from his grasp and ran deeper into the villa. Klain stayed in his kneeling position watching her go. Then stared at the empty doorway she had disappeared through until the Elmorian laid an icy cold hand upon his shoulder.

"Come, my carriage waits outside."

It was the first time Klain had ever ridden in the carriage. He had not ventured out of the villa except a few times during his stay there—those being simple trips to the market down the street. Yet, every time he ventured outside, people gawked and stared at him. At first, this had upset him since it reminded him of his days with the ménagerie. Sarshia had calmed him with the explanation that there had never been a Kithian in Mocley before, so of course they would stare. They stared at her all the time since Elmorians were rare walking amongst Humans as well.

*Now I understand why she travels in this carriage!*

This small box on wheels was not unlike the cage he had grown up inside.

Yet this has no bars and the doors are not locked.

Thick, blood-red curtains covered the windows so if anyone stared at the carriage as it passed, Klain was unaware of them. The two sat in silence, and for this Klain was glad. Inside his mind a war raged.



*Who is this Rohann Vimith? What could he have done to earn the Honored One's debt? How will I fit in with the Humans who have done nothing for me except give me grief, pain, and agony?*

This and much more raced through Klain's head while the carriage rolled through the streets of Mocley. It took well over an aurn for them to reach their destination, yet finally, the carriage came to a stop and Sarshia slipped out and into the bright light of the early midday sun.

Joining her, Klain found himself in a wide, open courtyard at the foot of a massive set of stairs. The stairs ascended to a patio lining the front of a villa. A villa so large, it put Sarshia's to shame. It was a three-story monstrosity of stone with stained-glass windows covering most of the second and third stories. At intervals between the windows, large evergreen trees, twisted into spirals, shot up to just below the clay-shingled roof. A fountain, its water streaming high into the air, sat in the center of the cobble-paved courtyard the carriage had stopped in.

Gazing around, it dawned on Klain that he could not see the

massive walls of Mocley. "We are no longer inside the city?" Lush farmland, small copses of trees scattered throughout, spread as far as he could see.

Sarshia threaded a bony gray arm behind Klain's elbow, the unnatural cold of her touch sent a jolt down his spine, and they walked up the stairs together. "No, we are a ways from the city. This is the countryside, yes?"

The air intoxicated him. He had always enjoyed the smell of Sarshia's villa. Compared to anything he had lived in in his past life, it was wonderful.

*As sweet as the air is at the Honored One's villa, it is more so here!*

At the top of the stairs stood a Human dressed in a green tunic. A broad smile, partially hidden by a thick, graying beard, split his lips. Reaching out his arms, the man descended the stairs to meet them on a wide landing at the midway point. "Welcome to my home once more, Honored One." He made a gracious, sweeping bow.



Tilting her head in return, she did not release Klain's arm. "As always, Rohann, the pleasure is mine, yes?"

Shifting his attention to Klain, the man nodded. "And I have heard much of you! The mighty Kith who became a hero of the Games."

Not wishing to appear rude, and thereby dishonoring Sarshia, Klain remained still as a statue, simply looking at the man. For some reason, this caused the man to fidget.

A strange, high-pitched laugh emanated from Sarshia. "You must forgive Klain, Rohann, hmm? Though he has spent his entire life with Humans, he was not included in your race's social edicts." Uncoiling her arm from Klain's, she turned to him. "This is where we part, yes? I am booked on a ship that departs this very day for my homeland."

Klain felt heart-stricken. "What do you mean, Honored One?" The ferociousness of his tone forced the man to take a step back. Klain ignored him.

"I mean what I have said. You are not the animal you were

when you first arrived at my villa. You have grown over the last few moons, yes? This,"—she extended an arm toward Rohann—"is the next part of your life's journey."

Forcing himself to relax, Klain regained control of his tone. "I understand. I will submit to this Human."

The Elmorian's semi-transparent eyelids slid down and she tipped her head to the side. "You are not being asked to submit, Klain, yes? I only asked that you meet with Rohann. If you do not like that which he has to offer, you are free to choose another path."

Waving a paw to the surroundings, Klain felt his temper flair once more. "Yet you are abandoning me here."

"No. If you wish, I will wait for you to speak with Rohann. Once you have decided, I will then depart."

Shooting a glance at Rohann, Klain decided he did not like the smell of the man. He rested a paw upon the hilt of his sword.

*Yet I have given my word to employ with him.*



"Nix, Honored One. You have done more for me than anyone alive." Closing his eyes, he tilted his head in a bow. "I will stay with this Human."

"Very well. I wish you good tidings and long life, Klain. I only wish I could see where the path you are on leads."

"Surely we shall meet again?"

Sarshia shook her head. "I am afraid not."

"I thought you said no one could predict the future."

Her normal look of amusement passed over her features. "It is easy to predict that which you know will or will not happen. My time in Ro'Arith is at an end, yes? Once I arrive home, I shall not be leaving Elmorr'eth again." With that, she turned and glided down the stairs to her carriage. When she slipped inside, the footman closed the door and hopped onto his perch at the rear. The driver flicked the reins and the two horses lurched forward.

Klain watched the carriage turn around in the cobblestone courtyard. He watched it pass between the low stone walls that surrounded the villa and onto the dirt road. Watched the dust from the road spew high into the air behind the carriage. Sarshia's horse drawn carriage trundled down the country road and Klain was still watching long after it disappeared around a copse of fruit trees.

"Father!" The shout of a young boy broke the ominous silence that had fallen causing Klain to whip his head around toward the villa. A Human boy-cub came running down the stairs. Small and thin with long blond hair, the boy wore a light, cream shirt that billowed as he ran and a pair of brown pants. He had the clean smell of having just been washed with soap. Skidding to a stop next to Rohann, the boy-cub wrapped an arm around him and peeked out from below the man's elbow. "Is that the Kith?"

The man smiled a weak smile, turned and went down to one knee before the boy. "Char, it is not polite to address someone by their race." Rohann looked back up to Klain. "This is Master Klain. He is our guest and hopefully he will agree to become your new friend."



The young boy, Char, scrunched up one side of his mouth. "Oh, aye. So it is to be my new body guard, is it?"

"Master Klain is *not* to be referred to as *it*!" The man's rough tone caused the boy to flinch. "Do I make myself understood?"

Nodding, the boy glanced at Klain. Pulling from his sire, the boy stood, a defiant air about him. "Well met, Master Klain."

"Good, now, go and tell the cook we will have a guest for halfmeal and to have us served in the garden." Char nodded and raced up the stairs. Standing, Rohann looked apologetically at Klain. "I am sorry, Master Klain. Charver can be a bit rude at times."

Grunting, Klain watched the boy disappear into the villa. "Do not apologize. He is a boy-cub."

Rohann laughed, ascending the stairs after his son. "That sounds like the voice of experience. How many children do you have?"

The growl that poured forth from Klain made the man recoil

in terror, slumping down on a step. "I was a slave to you *Humans* my entire life." Realizing that he had spoken rough, upsetting the Human and causing the man to fall, Klain chastised himself.

*If you let your anger rise, you are beaten you fool!*

Imitating Sarshia, Klain inclined his head to one side, closing his eyes briefly. "I have never seen another of my kin." He reached out a paw, holding it down to Rohann. "I apologize if my tone has *offended* you."

The man reached out with trepidation, yet griped Klain's furry wrist and let him pull him back to his feet. "Not at all, Master Klain. I have never met one of your kind either. It is I who should ask forgiveness for my statement...As well as my reaction."

Releasing his hand, Klain walked up the steps, his claws clicking as he went. "It seems we both have much to learn, then."

The layout of this villa, at least from the entranceway, looked much the same as what Klain was used to from his time spent with Sarshia. Two large double-doors opened into a wide, marble-floored chamber. Instead of a big, round table in its center, like the one in Sarshia's home, this room's floor was patterned into an ornate design that radiated out into points like a star. Planters lined the area and archways led off deeper into the building. A curved stairway hugged the walls on either side leading to a balcony, and presumably more rooms.



Following Rohann under the balcony, they emerged on the other side of the villa onto a patio area. More shrubs and small trees grew scattered throughout, and in the center, resting in the cool shade cast by the villa itself, sat a large stone table surrounded by comfortable looking chairs.

Behind the chairs, half hidden behind foliage stood a group of burly men.

*Their hands do not stray far from their weapons, yet the stink of fear fills them!*

Without realizing it, Klain let out a low warning rumble and glared at the men in turn.

Stepping into his line of sight, Rohann put up his hands. The smell of fear wafting from him as well. "You are a guest here, Master Klain. These men are my personal guard. They are no threat to you." He indicated a chair. "Please, join me for breakfast."

Nodding, Klain took the chair Rohann offered. Once seated, Rohann sat opposite him and motioned to a doorway. Klain had noticed the aroma of raw meat when he smelled the fear of the bodyguards, yet now it gained his full attention.

Two women, one thin one plump, both older than Rohann, stepped out from a side door carrying trays of food and approached the table. "The Honored One informed me as to your taste in foods. I hope it is acceptable." The man waited as the skinny woman placed a dish of fried eggs and an assortment of cooked meats in front of him.

"Aye, I do have a weakness for fresh lamb." The aroma of the raw meat on the tray the plump woman carried filled Klain's nostrils and his mouth salivated. Without waiting for the woman who hovered beside him to place his plate fully in front of him—she seemed unwilling to move closer to the table—Klain reached out and picked up a leg. Sinking his fangs into it, he closed his eyes and relished the taste of the blood that remained in the flesh.



"That will be all, ladies." The two women did a quick curtsy and withdrew to where they had come. They did not go far, for Klain sensed they hid to watch. He could still smell them.

The young boy, Charver, joined the two at the table. He sat nibbling on a muffin of some sort. Rohann turned to the boy. "Master Klain here was the star of the Games a few moons back."

The boy looked up. "You competed in the Games?" His words came out in a whisper.

At first Klain felt his hackles rise at mention of his time with the Games. Yet, at the look of wonder and admiration upon the boy's face, he settled down.

*It is as if he sees having been in the Games as good.*

"Aye, I did."

"Master Klain is being modest! He fought near a score of men, one after the other, for well over two aurns." Rohann leaned toward the boy. "Master Klain is the one who put down the Twins you held is such high esteem."

The boy's mouth fell open. "You fought the Twins...at the same time?" Charver set his muffin on the table. "Father will not let me go to the Games! He says I am too young still!"

"You are barely into your tenth winter, Char. You know I will not take you before your fourteenth."

Klain knew death. Knew what it looked like, smelled like… felt like.

*Yet these Humans seem to think it glorious! A thing to entertain them. I will never fully understand their race.*

Not wishing for this conversation to continue, Klain set the leg of lamb back on his tray and stood—not missing the fact that several of the men who still hovered in the shadows reached for their weapons. "It is my understanding that I am to be employed with you."



Klain's abruptness caused Rohann to lose his air of ease. For some reason this pleased Klain.

*They are unsure of me. I think this is good. I gives me the advantage.*

Wiping his mouth with a cloth from his lap, Rohann stood. "Aye, I would like to employ you. These are dangerous times and I have people who would do me and my family harm." Waving a hand, he indicated the other men. "I feel adequately protected. Most of my men have been with me for many winters. Char, here, seems to have a way of discouraging loyalty with anyone I assign to protect him. It is my hope that you will take up this post and insure his safety. You will be paid—"

"I will take your employ." Looking down at the boy, smelling his anxiety, Klain raised his upper lip exposing his front fangs. It pleased him to see the Human boy-cub's eyes grow wide and white with fear. Looking back to Rohann, Klain nodded. "I will allow no harm to come to your boy-cub. And I doubt there is anything he can do to discourage me. If he does, I will simply eat him." A small smile crept out of the corners of Klain's mouth that Charver did not seem to appreciate.

Klain saw a twinkle in Master Rohann's eye. However, a look of nervous apprehension quickly replaced it as the man eyed Klain's fang bared grin.

*Aye! A great advantage to have them unsure of me.*

# Chapter 26

Arderi Cor jerked awake with a start as pain laced up his back. He whipped his hand behind him, his elbow striking something hard and wooden. His hand went numb as the sensation of hundreds of needles sticking into him all at once shot up his arm. Squirming around, he took hold of the object stabbing him in the back—what felt like the handle of a skillet—and twisted it aside.



The sounds of wheels churning through crushed stone, the jingle of tackle, and the steady clop-clop of horse's hooves resounded all around him. Stray beams of sunlight filtered through the wall of items entombing him, yet he had no direct line of sight from which to see by. His stomach grumbled and the urge of the days first need to relieve himself were at the forefront of his thoughts.

*Mayhaps I could have planned this a bit more thoroughly.*

"Hail, Master Rillion." The voice came to Arderi muffled from somewhere front of the wagon, yet he easily made out the words.

"Aye, Trilim, what is on your mind." The rough reply came from somewhere off to the side.

"Stillwater should be close now, Master. I thought we might break for halfmeal before we get there."

*Stillwater! That is well over a days walk from Hild'alan! How could I have slept so long?*

"Nix, old friend. It will take some time to ferry this large a group across the Artoc. I want you to go with the first crossing. You can then start passing out halfmeal once everyone arrives on the other side."

"Aye, Master."

"Still, keep it quick. I plan to get in a few aurns travel before sundown once we are across. Mayhaps even get into the foothills by this eve."

"Aye, Master." The sounds of a horse galloping away answered the first man's reply.

Alone in the gloom of his hiding spot, Arderi at once felt the full weight of what he had done. Sorrow swelled in him like water filling a bucket. Even though he had longed to leave his stead, to explore the Plane, the actuality of doing so now threatened to overwhelm him. Never before had he been so far from home. The thought of his mother worrying where he had gone and fretting for his safety sickened him. He could not create a viable solution so he continued to sulk as the wagon plodded on.



*Alas, Stillwater is not even on the* way *to Mocley! I have no idea where I am heading.*

Less than half an aurn had passed when the wagon came to an abrupt stop. Again, something hard shifted, this time jabbing Arderi in the ribs. He slithered an arm down and shoved whatever it was aside just enough to curtail the pain. So far, the wagon ride had been mostly comfortable, save for the odd poke here or there. The supplies he had buried himself in had concealed him well as far as he could tell.

*At least, no one has raised the alarm nor dragged me out by my boots.*

The grumble of his stomach and growing pressure in his bladder gave him serious concerns as they continued on their journey. He pushed these issues aside hoping for the chance to ghost away and resolve them both eventually. Although he did not have any idea how this would to be accomplished.

"Hail, Ferrier." The cry came from the man Arderi now recognized as the leader of the group, the one the driver called

Master Rillion.

"Aye." The reply came from a rough, deep-throated man.

"We have wagons and men that needs be ferried across. What is the fee?"

"Wagons? There be no roads north of the Artoc, my friend. You be wanting to head on into Stillwater proper so as to book passage on a barge if you be heading up Orlis way."

"Nix. We have needs across the river, not in Orlis. Now name your fee man." Arderi could tell by the tone in the leader's voice that he meant to have an answer without any further questions.

"Well then, sir, no need to fuss. Man and horse are three pynes each. Never had no wagon cross before, so I am unsure as to their price." A pause stretched and Arderi wished for a better vantage point with which to watch. "Let us say a pent for each wagon and driver?"

"Aye, done is done. I have seven wagons with an additional forty-six men on mounts. How long till we may cross?"



"Well, that is a hefty fee. Lets see that is…" Another pause rambled on and Arderi mentally added up the sum to two ta'narians and eight pynes.

*Two ta'narians! That is more gold than I have ever seen! How can anyone expect to pay so much just to cross a river?*

"Two ta'narian, four pents." Arderi silently shook his head in protest at the Ferrier's conclusion.

"Nix, man. That would be two and eight pynes by my counting." The leader, Master Rillion, was obviously a much better counter. "And, if you have my company and supplies ferried over before two aurns have passed, I will pay you three ta'narians total."

"Boys!" Excitement was not hard to spot in the Ferrier's yell. "Get out here and get that barge a-hopping!" Arderi heard the man trot away.

"You spend coin as if you have no care." This came from a female voice. "In two aurns time we will have little daylight left. Can I re-state my—"

"Nix!" The growl from Master Rillion made even Arderi flinch. "You may not! I am not much on having my leftenant question me once a decision has been reached."

"Aye, sir." Arderi could tell that the woman was not happy yet heard the sounds of someone dismounting. The woman started yelling out orders. "All right you dogs! We have two aurns to cross this little trickle of water! Drivers, get those beasts lined up down to the dock there! As many men as can pack in on each trip shall do so! Arminton! Where in the Nine Hells do you think you are off to! We need no scouts on this side! I want you and the other scouts on first crossing with me! I expect a full report and a path chosen by the time the last wagon crosses! Now move and look alive you son's of goat farmers! Or I swear by all that is holy, not a single man on this little expedition will enjoy themselves!"

The wagon lurched and Arderi jostled back and forth with the rest of the cargo. The sounds of the horse's hooves

pounding on the ground turned hollow when they landed on the wooden planks of the dock. A sickening, swaying motion washed over Arderi and he knew the wagon had rolled onto a floating barge.

*The sound of the river flowing below is doing nothing for my need to relieve myself.*

# Chapter 27

Clytus Rillion watched in amusement as Alimia dismounted to spout off orders. Her thin, wiry frame stood out against the larger build of most of the men. Still, she carried herself well. Having spared with her several times, he also know that she could take most men in a sword fight, despite any size advantage they held.

*She may need more handling than Ragnor, yet she should learn in time. At least the men seem to follow her. Or fear her. Not a bad rapport to have from the men in this line of work, especially considering her sex.*



He sat back in his saddle and caught sight of his scoutmaster, Hindar, huddled with a group of his scouts who accompanied him from Orlis. He was relieved when he found the man and his group waiting on them when they arrived at the barge dock.

*I will need his tracking skills if I am to succeed in this venture.*

Grinning, he watched his troop scramble ahead of the shouting leftenant. With the day starting to warm, he reached up to loosen the top lashes of his leather jerkin. The Ferrier, a short, rotund man in his late forties, herded a group of four young men out of a house sitting next to the dock and hurried them onto the barge.

*Four* big *young men. With the right motivation—and gold is always a good motivation—they should have us across fast enough to please even Alimia.*

The Ferrier waved the second wagon onto the boat and then conversed with Alimia. Clytus grinned seeing the two argue.

It was obvious the leftenant wanted to pack on more men than the Ferrier thought wise. Still, they reached a compromise soon enough. She pulled the reins of her mount and motioned for the ten scouts clustered at the foot of the dock to join her. Clytus did like her spirit.

*She will pack them butt cheek to nose if she can.*

With the barge filled for this trip, the four men on the pull rope gave a tug and the barge slid from the dock. The current flowed strong on the Artoc and soon the barge sagged down river on its line. The Ferrier hobbled up wringing his hands, a nervous glint in his eyes.

Dismounting, Clytus eyed the man. "You look worried. Will the rope hold?"

"Oh, aye. She will hold. Essence enhanced that one is. Both docks as well." The man turned and gazed out over the expanse of the water. "The current of the Artoc is too strong otherwise. Just means more work for my boys is all."

"Aye, they look like they can handle it. Your sons?" Clytus reached into a side pouch dangling from his saddle. Starborn's large head turned at the sound of his owner's hand plunging for grain. Clytus' fist came out full of barley and the destrier nuzzled his fingers, nipping at them with its lips until he opened up and allowed the horse its treat.



"Aye, the Gods have blessed me. Good lads all. Though they eat their weight daily!"

The two men stood watching the water flow by. Sunlight glinted off the occasional ripple on its surface. Following the rope that stretched out past the barge, Clytus could just make out the landing dock on the far bank some league distant. The barge had drifted about a hundred paces downstream by the time it reached halfway across. The strong current pulled the guide rope into the form of a giant smile.

*Or frown, depending on which way you view it.*

"Does the ferry always sag that far downriver?" Clytus was not concerned, if it was Essence enhanced, it would hold well past the time a normal rope would snap.

"Nix, I told that wench—" The Ferrier's mouth snapped shut

with a click and he cut his eyes at Clytus. Clearing his throat, he rubbed his chubby hands together. "Begging pardon, sir. I told that *woman* not to pack on so many. My boys will have a time pulling her upriver with such a load, against the current and all. Alas, she said her men would help pull if needed."

*Aye, they will do that...with Alimia on their hides. I am sure the extra money I offered up did nothing to hinder her argument either.*

Motion out of the corner of Clytus' eye caught his attention and he turned to look upriver. A large boat, the type used to carry cargo and passengers up and down the length of the Artoc, floated lazily toward them. Clytus thought it odd that she had all of her ores in, yet at this distance, he could make out little detail. He had taken a few trips upriver to Orlis for business over the seasons and had always been impressed by how fast those ships maneuvered against the strong current of the Artoc. The large craft was still some distance away when he noticed it was listing to its starboard side, her stern slowly spinning the ship around backward.

Pointing upriver, Clytus tried to keep his voice calm and level. "Do the river ships come this far south?"



"What?" The Ferrier's head whipped northeast to the walled town of Stillwater that sat at the edge of sight upriver. "By all Twelve Gods!" The man's screech tore from his throat even as he launched himself down the small hill toward his home.

The other men in Clytus' troop milling about the area halted their tasks and flooded forward to the riverbank in the wake of the Ferrier's screams. Clytus glanced from riverboat to ferry and back again. The runaway boat made good time.

*Little chance of them making it to the far dock before it strikes.*

Clytus headed after the ferryman who now stood on his porch with a spyglass pressed to his eye. The man whirled around when Clytus' boots thudded onto the wooden stairs leading up to the house.

"She is derelict. I can see that her mooring ropes have been slashed. They are dangling over her side." The old man glanced downriver. "My ferry is in the middle, they have no hope to make either bank now." He brushed past Clytus who turned and followed the man down to the dock.

"What will happen to the ferry when the guide rope breaks?" Running a hand through his hair, Clytus walked along in the Ferrier's shadow.

"I told you, the line will not break." The man spoke to Clytus over his shoulder without breaking his stride, yet fear tinged the corners of his words.

"Then why the fuss? Surely they will not be struck. The river is too large. The odds of that happening are small indeed."

"Nix, mayhaps not. Still, I would not wish to be on board the ferry when the guide rope is struck either. Especially with all that is packed onto her." As they reached the landing, the Ferryman waved his arms above his head and whistled in a loud, shrill tone that cut across the top of the water like a knife. Several of the men on the barge turned to look their way and the Ferrier avidly pointed upriver.

Even at this distance, Clytus knew when the people on the boat understood their situation. All at once it looked like an anthill had just been kicked—men raced this way and that with no actual place to go.



Clytus laid a hand on the Ferrier's shoulder and spun him around. "What can we do?"

"Do?" The man snorted. "We can watch. My lads are good swimmers. I hope yours are as well—if worse comes to worse."

Looking up river, Clytus had a good view of the ship as the current swept it toward him. From this angle, however, it seemed that the boat hardly moved forward at all. It crept along. For what seemed a time that stretched on too long for the distance it had to traverse, the boat oscillated down the river—switching from bow to the flat of its port side leading the way downriver. When the craft neared, his angle of view changed, and it seemed to all at once shoot forward at an incredible speed. Looking back to the ferry, he noted it was more than two thirds across now, coming close to the far dock, and safety.

*Yet not quite.*

The river barge plowed into the guide rope—gasps and exclamations from the others who stood watching resounded around him. First, the rope pulled taunt, then stretched well past what should have been the breaking point. The small ferry launched violently upriver. Men slammed to the deck, whatever they held onto wrenched from their grasp. Horses bucked and reared up in panic. One, at the back of the craft, made a huge splash as it slipped into the chilly waters of the Artoc.

The derelict ship spun sideways, smashing its port side fully against the rope that now stretched twice further downriver than it had with the ferry alone. It listed hard to starboard as the strong current tried in vain to force it past the barrier.

The rope held, and the ferry appeared none the worse for wear after the initial hit. Clytus watched the overboard horse swim to the far bank. Most of the men returned to pulling at the guide rope, heading for the safety of the far shore. The ferry had slid back, closer to the center of the river, when the large craft struck. The collision increased the distance his people needed to travel to reach the other side. The angle of the rope meant they must pull the craft almost directly upriver. More and more men joined the task and the ferry made its way at an agonizingly slow pace. Shouts from the spectators on the bank around him bounced over the water as his men on the shore added their encouragement to their comrades laboring on the barge.



"Aye, not as bad as all that." Bobbing his head, the Ferrier turned to Clytus. A loud crack ripped over the water and the man whipped his head back to the scene.

The port side of the derelict barge caved when the guide rope sliced through it, sending huge shards of timber flinging into the air. The remaining piece of hull did a barrel roll and spun into the water, plunging down and under the rope. The speed at which the ship broke up was staggering, the rope cut through it like a sharp blade through warm bread.

Free of the added weight, the guide rope snapped back upriver like a bowstring. The ferry jerked violently upriver. One of the horses attached to the front wagon went mad, rearing and bucking. Clytus saw a figure dash forward only to be thrown back, body limp. The man tumbled in the air, plunging into the river beyond. The sound of the panicked horse ripped over the waters surface and bit into Clytus' ears. The noise cut off abruptly once the beast slipped into the water. The horse harnessed to it screamed as it was jerked into the river as well. The wagon placidly followed the pair of animals, water from its entry splashing up to drench much of the ferry.

*Only the second damnable day, and already a wagonload of supplies lost!*

Clytus watched a slim form run to the edge of the ferry and dive into the churning water. His men gathered at the edge of the craft staring helplessly into the murky depths as long moments past. When Clytus had lost all hope, one of the team horses broke the surface in a cacophony of noise. The shrieking wail the panicked beast emitted was nothing Clytus could have imagined from a horse's maw. In its panic, it fought to climb back aboard the ferry and, for a moment, Clytus thought it might cause a second catastrophe. Finally, after much persistence from the men on the craft, the animal turned and headed for the far bank.

Returning his attention to the surface of the river, Clytus saw nothing of the person who dove in after the wagon.



"What kind of madman would dive in after a wagon?" The Ferrier failed to keep any scorn from his voice.

"I am unsure, yet I have my suspicions. Damn them for a fool, whoever they were!" Clytus flung a hand to his brow to shade his eyes from the sun, trying to gain some fraction of advantage with which to see. "Do you see them anywhere, have they surfaced?"

"Nix, the horse came up, yet—" The Ferrier pointed off downriver. "There! I see someone!"

Focusing on the spot where the man pointed, Clytus was stunned to see a small form making its way to the far shore. The river had carried them much further than he expected. Tension melted from him now that they had made it back to the surface.

Clytus did not enjoy standing on this side of the river, helpless to do anything. He watched the last pieces of the destroyed river barge float around a far bend to vanish from sight. Eventually, the ferry made land on the far dock. Men and horses made their way to shore. Before long, the four sons of the Ferrier were again pulling the guide rope, returning to this side of the river.

The thunderous sound of horse hooves pounded the ground long before their riders came into view. Clytus glanced at the Ferrier. "Expecting visitors?"

"Nix. Still, I would be shocked if someone had not come to see what happened to the riverboat." He gave a nod out to the river, toward his boys. "If I am not back when they arrive, please tell them I wish to see them before they leave with the second load of your men."

"Second load? You feel it is safe then?"

"I did tell you the rope is Essence enhanced. I doubt a second derelict boat will be soon in coming, unless all law has fled Stillwater. Mayhaps these riders will tell me if it has."

Clytus watched as the Ferrier waddled off to meet the small group of men riding up.

By the time the Ferrier returned, Clytus could clearly make out the form of Alimia standing on the front of the ferry making its way back to this side of the Artoc. "What did the men say happened to the boat?" Clytus asked the man.

"As I said, the moorings were cut. They have not as yet figured out who or why, though odds say it was deliberate." He looked to his ferry making its final approach. "Seems it was that woman of yours who dove in." He gave a bark of a laugh. "She looks like a drowned rat."



Clytus did not respond. He waited to hear her side first. Before the ferry touched the dock, Alimia leaped the last pace of water and jogged up the small bank to where Clytus stood, her clothing wet, and her boots squelching as she approached him. "Report."

She paused—Clytus wondered if she feared being blamed for the misdeed or if it was something else entirely. She stole a glance over her shoulder. "I set the scouts out. Nothing for leagues north other than rolling hills that I could see. They should all return by the time we are ready to leave. Trilim made sure they all had halfmeal to travel with, says he will have something for the rest as they arrive on the far side. One of Master Hindar's scouts, Tylin, took a nasty hit from a horse. He is injured—broke ribs I think—yet he will survive. The Shaper is tending to him now."

Clytus took in the news and nodded, yet continued to stare at her without responding. He enjoyed watching her shift nervously under his gaze.

"We also lost one wagon and draft horse, sir." Her voice quivered as she continued. "And a man was lost. Another scout under Master Hindar, Wilim, out of Orlis. He was thrown overboard and we never saw him again. I did not see him go over. If I had, I would not have gone after the wagon. I did manage to cut one of the animals loose, yet when I did, the wagon sank with a quickness I did not expect. Nearly took me to the bottom."

In his line of work, lives were lost. That was a simple fact of the trade. He always hated to lose lives, however, and was glad that he had never grown accustomed to the feeling the loss brought. Wagons and horses could be replaced.

*Well, in this business, so can lives. Yet, men are not a currency I enjoy spending. I never even met the Wilim boy.*

Pushing thoughts of the dead to the back of his mind—Wilim would be dealt with later—Clytus steeled himself for what he had to do. "A damn fool thing you did, woman."



She glared at him, wet hair sticking to her forehead. "The horse went over so fast, I thought—"

"That horse cannot lead, Alimia! You had no hope of salvaging the wagon nor the supplies. Freeing one animal was not worth the risk." He let all his anger and frustration seep into his tone.

"Sir, I could see both animals struggling under the water, I thought the wagon to be on shallow ground. I could not simply watch them drown!" Bowing her head, she kept her eyes averted as she finished.

"Aye, tis probably so." Clytus reached out a hand and rested it on her shoulders. "It was a tough situation and you did what you could." She smiled up at him and he almost regretted giving the encouragement. "Now, daylight is wasting. The Ferrier said it should be safe to continue the crossing. I still expect to put some distance between us and the Artoc before we break camp this eve."

"Aye, sir." She immediately turned and barked out orders to get the next group loaded.

*A little more work mayhaps, though I do like her spirit.*

# Chapter 28

Klain sat on the edge of a large, feather-stuffed bed looking around his new sleeping quarters. Rohann had shown him to the room once Klain finished firstmeal, stating that mayhaps Klain needed to settle in after his journey and rest.

*As if riding around in a box on wheels for half the morn is taxing!*



Upon entering the room, Rohann had shown Klain the large chest of drawers. "There is plenty of storage here. The Honored One said she would send your items by day's end. If this is not enough room, I can have trunks brought in."

Glancing down, Klain took in his pants and the scabbard holding his new sword. "I have little more than I wear now."

"Well, anything you need, you have only to ask." With a nod of his head, Rohann withdrew from the room, closing the door and leaving Klain alone.

Now he sat.

Muscles tense, rippling below his spotted fur. He clicked his sharp toeclaws onto the granite tiles of the floor.

*If this is not a cage, why do I feel imprisoned so!*

The handle of the door turned. Snapping into a crouch and preparing to launch himself at whatever menace was about to enter, Klain stared into the white eyes of Charver. Rising to his full height, he glared down at the Human boy-cub. "I was just—" Cutting himself off, Klain stood in silence as Charver entered the room and shut the door.

The little boy walked past him and jumped up on the bed, bouncing slightly. "You do not frighten me, you know."

Taken aback, Klain let out a grunt of a laugh. "Aye? It that so?"

"Oh, aye! I know you are here to keep me out of trouble. You cannot do that if you eat me."

Crossing the room, Klain pulled a small, wooden chair closer to the bedside and sat. "Nix, you are probably correct. I may lose my employ if I eat you." Cocking his head to one side, Klain smiled, baring his fangs. "Besides, Humans do not taste good."

Eyes wide, the boy whistled. "You have eaten a Human?"

Klain stuck out his tongue and grimaced. "With the way you creatures smell? I do not think I could."

Waving a hand through the air, the little boy giggled. "I do not smell. Mis'am Frinly forces me to bath each morn. She says it is proper. I say it is a waste of time." He hopped off the edge of the bed and slipped his hand inside Klain's paw. "Wow!" Grasping the paw with both hands, Charver turned it over to examine it. "It is rough. What are these puffy things?"



"The pads protect my paws." Exposing the bottoms of his hindpaws, he pointed at them. "They are on my hindpaws as well."

"So you do not have to wear shoes!"

"Nix, my pads are thick. They also speak to me."

Letting out a snort, the boy looked up into Klain's eyes. "Feet cannot talk!"

"Ah, yet mine do. They hear the little patter of steps and let me know that you did not come to my room alone." Klain pointed to the door.

Looking over his shoulder, Charver wiggled his head. "Nix, my father said I could not come and see you unless I was accompanied by someone."

"Two someone's. They are both still outside the door."

A look of awe swept over Charver. "Your feet told you

that?"

"Aye, little boy-cub."

"Well," Charver tugged on the paw he still held and Klain allowed himself to be pulled up from the chair. "I thought you would rather be outside than stuck inside on such a nice day."

"Is that so?"

"Aye." Letting go of his paw, Charver padded to the door. "Would you like to play with me outside?"

Uncertainty washed over Klain and he glanced around the room.

Putting a tiny fist on his hip, Charver let out a gasp. "If it makes you feel better, I could get hurt outside playing on my own. If you are there, you can protect me. That *is* your job you know?"

"Very well." Klain headed for the door, then paused. Returning to the bed, he scooped up his sword in its scabbard and strapped it around his waist. Turing back, he noticed the look of mirth upon the boy-child's face. "In case you need protecting!" Even though he spat out the words in a deep growl, the boy-cub giggled.



The two stepped into the hall and Klain saw that two Humans flanked the door. They smelled of fear, though not the pungent odor they had had upon his arrival. Following Charver's example, Klain walked between them without acknowledging their presence. The two Humans fell in behind them as they walked the halls that led to the back of the villa in silence.

They left the building through the same double doors that led out onto the patio where they ate firstmeal. Threading their way through the wall of plants that enclosed the area, Klain was amazed to see how open the space beyond was. A large, dirt area covered the immediate ground flanked by a stable and a few other, low-roofed buildings. Past this, open fields stretched off as far as Klain could see, broken only by the occasional copse of trees. A slight, warm breeze ruffled the hair of his mane bringing with it the smell of life. Clean and fresh, the smells that invaded his nostrils invigorated him. He picked out wheat, barley, and a host of other grain smells. Pine and birch, flowers of many flavors…

*And the stench of Human sweat.*

The clang of metal on metal rang out in the early morn air. Grabbing Klain's paw, Charver dragged the Kithian toward one of the buildings. "The men are practicing, let us go and watch!"

Followed by their two guards, They rounded what looked like a workshop—tools and anvils littered the area inside a large open door—to find a small circle of men. Most of the men had stripped their shirts and stood watching two men sparing in the center.

The two men—sweat running off in driblets and the blunted edges of their practice swords marred and nicked from use—attacked each other with fervor.

The larger of the two men, an older Human with a bald head, feigned a low stroke that became a high attack. The blow would have landed if he had not stopped it short. "Keep that guard up, Narn, or I will put a lump on that fowl looking head of yours!" The two guards who followed Klain and the boy laughed aloud and went to join the circle of men. "Come on then, are you going to try and hit me with that stick, or just stand there and wet yourself?"



The smaller man, Narn, lowered his blade to the ground and the older one pointed his sword at him. "You call yourself a bodyguard, yet—" A loud clang resounded as Narn batted the other's sword away and lunged in for an attack, jabbing violently. Narn was caught off guard as the older man let his practice blade fly from his hand, sidestepped, and looped his free arm over and around Narn's sword arm. A loud snap sounded when the older man spun, forcing the younger man's arm to bend back on itself. The practice sword fell from his numb fingers and Narn joined it on the ground howling in pain and clutching his broken arm.

The older man spat upon him. Looking up, he pointed to one of the spectators. "Poltin! You and Brin take this pathetic heap of dung into town and have a Shaper see to his arm." Bending down, the old fighter scooped up his dropped practice blade from the dirt. "Lith, you are up!"

Poltin and Brin shuffled forward and, not too gently, plucked the still whimpering Narn from the ground. Half helping—half dragging the man, they headed for the villa. A burly, well-tanned Human with short-cropped black hair stepped forward and retrieved the discarded practice sword from the ground where Narn had lost it. He gave a salute to the older man, then dropped into an attack stance.

Just then the older man caught sight of Klain standing next to the workshop and raised a hand for the other to hold. "Well, well, if it is not our famed Kith! I wondered when you would crawl out of hiding and take a sniff around." The few laughs that joined the older man's jib came out strained at best. Klain could smell the fear level rise even over the stench of their sweat.

"He did not come out of hiding. He came out to play with me!" The laughing increased and Klain did not feel his situation had improved from Charver's aid.



Kneeling down, he put a paw on the boy's shoulder. "Mayhaps we could find somewhere less crowded?"

"Nix, I want to watch the men practice. Hey!" His eyes lit up. "Mayhaps you could spar with them?"

"Oh, that is a wonderful idea!" The older man's voice dripped with sarcasm. "How about it Kith? A little early morn exercise to get the blood pumping?"

Holding his tongue, Klain stood and headed back toward the villa.

"Uh oh! It looks as if our kitty has decided to go back inside!" The rest of the men laughed louder. "Come on, kitty, kitty. We just want to see if the stories we heard of your skill were true, or are they tall tales like so much that goes on inside the Coliseum!"

Klain felt the small vibrations of the boy-cub running up behind him. Charver grabbed his paw just as Klain rounded the corner of the building. "Where are you going?"

At the boy's touch, Klain stopped yet did not look down. "This is not wise. I am not here to fight for anyone's amusement!"

Whipping around to face Klain, the boy stood defiantly. "Nix! You are supposed to protect me. How are you going to do that if you run from a fight?"

A rumbled growl rattled Klain's chest and he glanced down to glare into Charver's eyes. "These are your father's men." Spitting the words out in a whisper, he did not even part his fangs. "I will run from nothing that is a danger to you."

"You are a coward!" Charver stomped his feet onto the dusty ground receiving a loud round of laughter from the men standing in witness.

The Human who won the fight with Narn stepped forward. "Go on, I will not spar with some *thing* that is frightened of its own shadow."

Blood trickled from Klain's paws and splattered to the ground from his sharp claws digging into them.



*"An angry fighter is a dead fighter." Master Flayt, my old trainer, your words still ring true. Still, I hope your bones are rotting in the ground!*

Forcing himself to relax, Klain walked back to the men amidst a chorus of heckles. "I misunderstood. If it is only sparing you are looking for, I could use some exercise this morn."

A wicked grin slid over the old man's mouth. "Good, I was hoping you would say that." He flicked his head at one of the men who jogged to the workshop. Returning with two thick, cowhide mittens, the man tossed them to Klain.

Looking down at them in his paws, Klain snarled. "What are these?"

Still smiling his wicked smile, the first man chuckled. "Well, we would not want any *accidents* to happen, now would we?"

"I will not even be able to hold my sword wearing these!" Flinging the gloves into the dirt, Klain crossed his arms defiantly.

Tisking, the Human bent down and retrieved the mittens. "Well, any excuse huh? Do not hide behind gloves if you will not face me, beast!"

The dam holding back his anger burst. Rage boiled up inside Klain. Without word, he thrust out his paws to the man and held them there. Taking a step closer, the Human pushed first one, then the next glove over his paws, tying each securely in place with leather thongs. The man then handed Klain one of the blunt practice swords. Grasping the hilt, the bulky leather gloves bending only reluctantly, Klain took a practice stroke. The sword slid from his grip and slammed onto the ground, kicking up dirt. A chorus of laughter resonated through the area as one of the men bent down to get the weapon. Taking the sword once again, Klain forced his claws to extend as far as they could in their cramped prisons and griped the sword with all his strength.

*If I must grip this tightly, I will not have long before my paw cramps.*



Again he gave a practice stroke, this time retaining grip on the sword.

"You ready then, beast?"

Facing the Human, Klain crouched into the fighting pose he had learned to use when wielding a sword without a shield. The two circled each other. Too late the overpowering odor of Human alerted Klain that someone had stepped close behind him. Stars filled his vision and pain lanced through the back of his skull. Slamming to the ground, a multitude of blows assaulted him from all directions. Scrambling, working on instinct alone, he pulled his paws under his body. Digging his hindclaws into the dirt, he launched himself forward and slammed into whoever stood in front of him, continuing through. Landing once more on the ground, he tucked into a tight roll, twisted his body, and came up standing on his hindpaws. On shaky legs, he took in the blurry scene before him.

Half a dozen Humans rushed him, blunt practice swords at the ready. Sidestepping the first to reach him, Klain used the man's momentum to fling him beyond and to the ground. A second stopped short and swung his weapon in a vicious downward attack. Pouncing back, the sword tip narrowly missed Klain's face and instead struck the ground throwing the man off balance. Whipping his right paw in a wide arc, Klain caught the man in the neck and was disappointed not to see blood flinging into the air.

*Damnable gloves!*

Yet the force of the blow spun the man around and drove him into the dirt. Before Klain could recover from this attack, a third man, this one wielding a wooden stick, cracked it across Klain's outer thigh. Howling in pain and rage, he went down on that knee.

The man with the stick attacked once more, this time aiming for Klain's head. Klain threw up his forearm, allowing it to absorb the full brunt of the blow. Snatching the stick, he yanked it to him. Man followed stick, and Klain abandoned his end of the weapon in favor of grabbing the man with both paws. He locked one paw around the man's neck, the other on his groin. The man gurgled out a scream as Klain stood and lifted him high in the air. Stepping forward on his uninjured leg, he launched the man toward the remaining two Humans. Caught by surprise at their comrade hurtling toward them, the flung man slammed into them and all three landed in a tangled heap upon the ground.



A guttural laughter echoed through the yard. "Well, well." The older man stood spinning a sword.

*And not a practice blade either. This one holds an edge!*

"Seems as if some of the stories about the kitty are true. You have got some skill." Grinning, the man advanced. "Let us see how you fair against a real opponent, beastie!"

"Satner Timms! I will have an explanation for this!" Rohann came storming around the workshop.

Klain's head still rang. Glancing around, he tried to locate Charver to insure the boy was unharmed. He saw the boy leaning around the far side of the workshop, eyes wide with fear and guilt. When he saw Klain looking at him, the boy bowed his head and fled. Reaching up, Klain cupped the large lump on the back of his head that had sprung up from the first blow.

*This whole thing was a setup! And that little whelp was a part of it.*

The older man, Satner Timms, lowered his blade and gave a baleful look at Klain. "This beast of yours attacked my men! I told you this was not a wise idea, sir!"

Rohann stopped between the two, looking at each in turn. "And before Klain here decided to attack a group of armed men—for no reason—he chose to put on mittens?"

Stuttering, Satner looked around searching for something. "Well, he...Look at my men!" He pointed with the tip of his sword to the group still tangled with each other.

"Aye! Look at your men! Six of you against one! And Master Klain without a weapon! Seems like I should look for a better class of protection for my personal bodyguard!" Rohann flicked a hand toward the man. "Clean this up and get out of my sight!"



Satner reached down to help the man nearest him to his feet.

"And if there is so much as another shouting match with Master Klain here, you will all be looking for new employment!"

Trying not to put his full weight on his injured leg, Klain stood and watched as the Humans gathered themselves and headed off.

When the last man vanished from sight, Rohann turned to Klain. "Master Klain, I apologize. It seems that some men are less tolerant than others. I will understand if you turn down my offer of employ."

"It was not your fault, Rohann. I have found that I understand little of Humans." Klain limped forward a step. "It will take more than this to shake me."

Rohann smiled. "Come, then. I have some Oolant drought in the villa. Let us attend to your wounds, eh?" The man turned and headed toward the villa.

Suppressing a wince, Klain followed.

*Besides, I have nowhere else to go.*

# Chapter 29

Dusk settled over the foothills of the great Nektine mountain range like a scorned woman. Clytus Rillion stood gazing off at the distant snow-covered peaks. The mountains stretched both west and northeast, grazing the very sky until they disappeared into the horizon. A chilly breeze had stalked the troop since the day prior and with the coming of dusk, it had become ferocious in its tenacity. Clytus feared a storm approached and knew it would be cold this eve.



The way thus far had been relatively uneventful, and for that, he was glad. The land, albeit hilly, held few large rock outcrops or rivers to traverse. There were a few copses of hardwood and pine, though these grew separated by the vast brownish-green oceans of grass and the wagon train easily circumvented them. The troop had made good time and Clytus was more than satisfied with their progress.

*If things hold like this, we should be into the Nektine on the morrow's eve.*

Footsteps from behind alerted him to someone's approach. Turning, he watched Alimia ascend the hill to his vantage point.

She stopped next to him, content to look off at the distant mountain range for a time. "How far do you make them, sir?"

"We should see their base on the morrow's eve, I should think. Mayhaps the next eve will see us deep into the foothills."

Crossing his arms over his chest, Clytus returned his gaze back to the distant mountains.

"What is your plan for the wagons, sir? Surely we will not find passage for them within the jagged peaks of the Nektine."

Looking over his shoulder, Clytus cast his gaze over the small camp nestled at the base of the hill. "My plan is to set up a basecamp as deep into the mountains as the wagons will go. From there, I will take a small team and hunt for a Drakon. I expect the scouts to search as well, yet they are not to engage the beast if they find one. If, after half a tenday or so, that area turns out to be fruitless, we will relocate the basecamp a few days further east along the range and start the process once again."

"How long do you think the hunt will last, sir?"

"Could take moons." He gestured down at the wagons. "Thus the reason for so many supplies." He squared his shoulders on the leftenant and took a stern, hard look at her. "I should not have to state the fact that *that* area,"—he jabbed a finger toward the distant mountains—"is infested with O'Arkin. And I speak not of the Morlis Mountain creatures that often frequent Mocley. The O'Arkin found here are much larger. A wild and barbaric race unaccustomed to outsiders. They will not be kind to strangers in their domain. I expect everyone on guard at all times. The scouts are to travel in groups of no less than four. I want a double watch set around the basecamp at all times. You will be responsible for things while I hunt. The supplies are critical to my success. I have not the luxury of returning to civilization for more."



Crossing her arms below her breasts, Alimia nodded her head and her expression serious. "How do you plan on felling the creature, sir?"

A sly grin crossed Clytus' face. "I spent a near fortune procuring a toxin that should do the trick. I hope to kill it with a single bolt—if I am lucky. A Drakon is not a thing to toy with."

"Have you ever seen one, sir?" He took note of the queer

tone in her voice. Many tales of woe and doom accompanied the word Drakon.

"In art, aye, and story. Never known anyone to actually see one of the creatures. I am not sure I believe all the tales said of them." He smiled broadly. "We shall soon see if the legends are true, huh?"

Without returning his mirth, Alimia dipped her head and walked back to the camp.

They traveled north the following day and the gentle rolling hills gave way to steeper, rockier terrain. This slowed the caravan down and caused, on one occasion, an aurn's delay when a broken wagon wheel needed to be changed. Still, that eve saw them camped deep in the foothills of the Nektine Mountains. Ominous, snow-covered peaks towered overhead, causing even the heartiest of the troop to stand in awe of their mighty visage.

Alimia gave orders to park the wagons in a tight clump under a massive natural outcrop of rock. Clytus hoped this would give some semblance of protection from the storm that hung overhead preparing to unleash its fury upon the land. The men drug out more tents than they had on the previous eve. They set them up, taking advantage of any natural cover they could find. Several barrels were also placed around the camp to collect fresh rainwater.



*The mood of the men is as dark as the clouds in the sky. Many of the superstitious fools will see this storm as a bad omen to start a hunt. Not that the trip has not already been plagued with problems!*

Thinking of the lost wagon of supplies the Artoc had claimed, he walked over to Trilim. The man was busy raising a tent for him. Bending over, he picked up a few wooden support rods. "I will worry with mine own, Trilim. You get busy with yours. It shall not be a pleasant eve."

Trilim handed over a pole he held. "Aye, Master." He glanced up to the sky and pinched his lips tight. "That it will not."

Bending his mind to his task, Clytus set about pitching his tent and arranging his sleeping area in a manner to his liking.

Once done, and not wishing to allow his mind occasion to drift and linger on thoughts he knew it would, he pulled out a Silrith'tar and sat down. Rolling the semi-translucent, bluish Thought Crystal in his fingers, he stared off to the south, and all he had left behind. Placing the stone to his forehead, he let the Essence of it Meld with his mind.

He stood in a field of wildflowers. A gentle breeze blew and a myriad of colorful butterflies raced around in their frantic search for food. No sun was evident in the bright blue expanse overhead nor did any shadows fall onto the ground. Sky and field swept off into the distance to merge at some infinite point. The surroundings set his spirit at ease. He had created this place with his mind many times and used it when he composed messages for his wife or son.



Conjuring up an image of Sindian standing before him, joy spread through his core. Though, on this occasion, the presence of his son filled his heart and body with longing and grief. Smiling, Clytus bent down on one knee. Pausing, he forced the pain away and gained full control of his voice before he spoke.

"Sindian, my son. I am not sure what to tell you." He gave a shallow laugh and shook his head. "I am not even sure if you will ever draw upon this message, yet I felt I needed to create it." He reached out and brushed his son's cheek, the cheek that would be there if ever his son drew upon this Silrith'tar. "You will not appreciate a father's love until such time as you hold your own child in your arms. Mayhaps not until then will you be able to forgive me for what I have done to you and your mother. My only hope in making this is that you will understand why I did what I did." He sat down cross-legged amongst the flowers and rested his arms on his raised knees. "I always thought I was a strong man, stronger than anything that could be thrown at me. I never expected that your birth, holding your small body in my hands, could change me so. Yet it did. I simply wanted you to know that…" Clytus trailed off, staring off into the distance.

*To know what? What could I possibly say that will make him understand?*

"I want you to never forget how much I love you."

Dark clouds, the sounds of men milling about, the smell of horses and unwashed bodies all ripped back into view as he yanked the Crystal from his head.

*Damn you for a fool, Clytus Rillion!*

He shoved the stone into a pouch that hung from his waist. Standing, he headed for the cook fires.

His mood grew darker when the young Shaper, Jintrill, came strolling up to him. The boy had not said word one to Clytus since his threat back at the stead two eves past. He did not feel he missed neither the boy's wisdom nor his council.

*Yet, I must admit, the boy did well in healing Tylin. And having a Shaper along has raised the men's moral.* 

"Mir'am Rillion, sir?" Jintrill wrung his hands as he approached. "Might I have a word please?"

"Aye. What is on your mind Sier?" Clytus had not meant it to come out as a growl, and felt a pang of guilt when the boy flinched.

"Well, sir. Um, the Order did not equip me with the items it seems that I need."

"And?"

"I do not have a tent, sir. I was told I would need nothing other than a bedroll and warm clothing." Jintrill waved a hand at the sky. "I am not prepared for this type of weather."

Wiping his hand across his mouth and chin, Clytus took a moment to feel the growth of a few days facial hair. It felt good.

*The one thing I do enjoy about traveling away from home is being able to grow a manly beard without Lilaith hounding me to shave!*

He almost laughed aloud watching Jintrill's nerves get the

better of him. "Come with me." He led the young Shaper over to the cluster of wagons. Trilim worked at one unpacking his cooking gear. "Could you please show this young man where he might fetch a spare tent?"

Trilim looked up from his pans and over at the wagons. Gazing at each in turn, he finally pointed to one. "There! Nestled in with the sacks of grain on the third wagon, see?" He glanced at Jintrill.

The young shaper walked in the direction Trilim pointed and put his hand on a burlap sack. "This?"

"Nix, lad! That *is* the grain!" Clytus knew Trilim would have never spoken to a Shaper that way, even one so young, if he had not seen Clytus do it on their first meeting.

*I will need to correct that. Even a young Shaper has more power than most. The Gods forbid if this one holds a grudge. That could mean trouble later for a common man like Trilim.*

Clytus gave Trilim a warning glare and walked over to the wagon. He pulled out a cream canvas sack wedged between several bags of grain and pushed it into the hands of the Shaper. "Here, you may pitch this next to mine. I think it is time for us to converse about why you are here, lad. And, mayhaps, a few ways you might be able to survive this little adventure we are on." Without waiting to see if the boy would follow, Clytus headed back to his tent.



For more than half an aurn the young Shaper's struggle to put up the tent entertained Clytus. When it became apparent that he would miss lastmeal if he continued to do nothing, he helped the Sier finish the task.

With Jintrill's tent in place, Clytus led the way to the cook fire where Trilim stood stirring a large pot and ladling out its contents to any man who approached with a bowl in hand. This eve's lastmeal consisted of a hearty stew heavily laced with barley, dried jerky and hard rolls. "Enjoy the rolls while you can, lad." Trilim spoke to the scout he served who was there before Clytus. "They will be gone before the second tenday passes. Then it will be flat biscuits for the duration."

Once they had gathered their food, Clytus and Jintrill returned to their tents and sat down. Clytus ate in silence. He guessed that Jintrill was not in too great a hurry to begin the conversation. Setting his empty bowl down, he turned his attention to the young Sier. "So, why do you think you were sent with me?"

Stuffing the last of his bread into his mouth, Jintrill took a moment to chew and swallow. "The Council only said that an expedition was leaving on the morrow and it was in need of a Shaper who held the gift of healing."

"On the morrow? They gave you only one day to prepare?"

*I have long believed the Council to be idiots, yet this?*

"One eve, actually." Jintrill set his bowl down next to Clytus'. "I was summoned to the Council just before sundown."

Clytus studied the boy for a long moment. "Tell me of that meeting."

"Well…"

Raising a hand to forestall Jintrill's answer, Clytus kept his voice low so no one passing would accidentally overhear him speak down to a Shaper. "And I do mean for you to tell me all that was said. Do not be the fool and have a false tongue with me now."



"Aye, then." Jintrill paused, seeming to collect his thoughts. "A message boy came to my room at dusk. He informed me that the Grand Elders had summoned me to the Ques'lian to appear before them. Except when I arrived, only Grand Elder Blanch sat in attendance. He told me that I was to meet a caravan led by you at the main gates first thing in the morn. When I asked where the caravan was headed he told me that you were heading into the Nektine hunting a Drakon for a need the Council has."

"Did he not inform you as to what to bring nor how long you would be gone?"

"Nix. I tried to ask a few more questions yet he simply said that it was Council business and for me to do as I was told for once." Jintrill shrugged his shoulders.

"It sounds as if you and the Grand Elder do not get along."

Clytus could not stop the smile that grew on his face.

*Mayhaps this young lad is not so bad after all.*

Jintrill wore a sheepish look. "Well, to be honest, I had several run-ins with a few of the Elders during my days as an Initiate."

Understanding crept into Clytus as to why Sier Blanch had sent this particular boy. "How long since you were given the blue robes?"

"The better part of two moons past."

"And you were still living at the Academy?"

"Aye. I am not posted yet."

Jintrill's puzzled look told Clytus the Shaper did not follow the events that bound him on this quest. Clytus felt sorry for the young man. "The Grand Elder, in all his pompous wisdom, sent you with me to get you out of his hair."

The boy stared off into the distance, his face a blank mask.

*It would be a hard line to swallow for any man. More so for a newly raised Shaper.*



"Be that as it may." Clytus clapped a hand to the young Sier's shoulder. "You are here and we will have need of more healing before this journey is finished. I promise that."

Jintrill's face took on a look of gratitude. "My thanks to you, Mir'am Rillion. I will do my part."

Clytus rose and gathered the dirty bowls. "Just so we understand each other. This will be no picnic. You are not in the protection of a city any longer. Stay sharp and do as you are told. If things fall apart, keep your head down and try to stay close to me. If I am not here, find Alimia. She will keep you as safe as she can."

"My thanks to you, sir." The Shaper's spirit seemed higher.

*And spirit may be all this boy will have to keep him alive out here.*

"Now, get some sleep. It will only get rougher as the days go on." Clytus turned and headed back to the cook fire.

# Chapter 30

Alant Cor watched the last sliver of sun bubble down into the ocean's depths and darkness fall over the whitecaps that stretched off into the endless distance. Stars came out to dot the sky like glittering jewels spreading out over a black cloth. Long ago, what little he could put down during lastmeal had abandoned him into the wake that trailed behind the *Mistbreeze Trader*. With the ship's gentle rise and fall subsiding, so did Alant's queasiness. Try as he might, he had found nowhere on this accursed boat to hide from the relentless rocking. Yet here, sitting with his feet dangling over the back edge of what he now knew to be called the quarterdeck, he at least did not feel so retched. He had spent most of the last tenday sitting here.



*At dusk, looking back at the sun as it sets, I could almost call it beautiful.*

Yet he could not think of much that had been pleasant on this journey. It would take them the better part of three tendays to reach Hath'oolan. With more than half that time behind them, Alant's only hope was not to starve to death before they reached land.

"I did think I would find you here, Sier." The now familiar squeaky voice of Krin sounded behind him and lifted Alant's spirits a bit. The boy waddled up, slid his almost jet-black legs under the railing, and plopped down next to Alant. "Tis be beautiful this part of day, huh?"

"Aye, one of the few moments I find peace on this miserable boat."

"Do no be so glum, Sier. You did keep your lastmeal for near three aurns this eve. You be improving." The boy giggled. "I do bet that by the time we do reach Elmorr'eth, you will done made a fine addition to this here crew."

"Oh, aye! Laugh it up! It surely did not feel much of an improvement when it went over the side, even if it did stay in my belly for three aurns." Alant did not begrudge the boy the jest. Despite their age difference, Krin had become a friend. He reminded Alant of a young Arderi, so full of life and happiness, eager to see the Plane and all its wonders. Unfortunately, this always reminded him of how much he missed his home and family.

Alant cut his eyes to the cabin boy whose room he shared. The sea breeze tussled the curly black hair that sat on Krin's head and threatened to drape it over his large, innocent eyes as they stared out to sea.



*So full of wonder. I wish I could take life with such ease.*

"Krin, you say you have been to Hath'oolan?"

Without taking his brown eyes from the distant horizon, the dark-skinned boy nodded. "Aye, Sier. About every turn of the seasons."

"Tell me of it." Alant's voice had an airy sound to it.

The cabin boy hrumphed and shook his head slightly. "No much to tell, truth be told. The Elmorians be a private race and do guard the secrets of their city well."

"What do you mean?"

"They do let no one past the harbor gates except them and their Gralets."

"Gralets? What are those?"

Krin took his eyes off the horizon to look at Alant with a serious manner Alant had never seen on the boy. "I be unsure myself, Sier. I asked the Captain about them once, except, he had no answers neither." His normal, wide friendly smile sprang back to his lips. "Have you ever seen an Elmorian, Sier?"

When Alant shook his head indicating he had not, the boy's smile broadened. "I have on occasion. Elmorians be dainty little creatures. Tall and thin like a mast, they do no pose much in the way of a physical threat, you might say."

"Aye, yet they are very powerful with the Essence."

The boy's smile faded and his face grew somber. "Oh, aye, that be true enough, Sier. Most times when one do take notice and really looks at me, I do feel...well, exposed for lack of a better way to say it. Like they be no looking at me so much as inside of me. Yet, still...having one or two of their monstrous Gralet'nars beside them—each built like a blacksmith's anvil—will set any man on the path of what be right and true."

Alant nodded his head. "So, the Gralets—Gralet'nars?—are some type of guard for the Elmorians?"

"Aye, Sier. Big and powerful they be. Like a walking tree that has a sword at its hip. Tis said they can no be killed by any natural means. They handle any labor the Elmorians needs be done—hauling cargo and the like."



Waving the boy to stop, Alant shook his head. "Aye, very well and good. Yet the city! Tell me of that! You must have seen *some* of it."

Eyes twinkling, the easy smile returned to Krin. "Tis be called the White City for a reason. Yet, as I did say, Sier, they no allow outsiders to enter the city proper. The only sight to see be those that do top the outer wall…" Krin let out a low, long whistle. "Tis a sight worthy to see though. Beautiful spires and towers that do stretch up to the sky, unbelievably thin, and they be so white that if the sun do catch them just so, your eyes water. It be said that the White City be no built by hand, rather it did be pulled from the very ground by the power the Elmorians have over the Essence." Krin looked back to the horizon and let a long, slow breath escape his lips. "Mere words do no give it justice. I would give much to walk its streets proper. No matter the cost the Elmorians may take from my hide."

Joining the cabin boy in staring off into the distance, the two fell silent. The last of Krin's words brought to mind the last thing Sier Sarlimac had said before Alant boarded the *Mistbreeze Trader*.

*I am going inside, into the very heart of the city itself. I wonder what price I will be forced to pay?*

# Chapter 31

The tall grasses of the field bent slightly in the warm breeze that danced past him from the east. Holding out a hand, he stroked the floret of their tips and smiled. He loved the tranquility of being in a field, surrounded by an ocean of grain. He gazed at the gentle rolling hills that spread off into the distance in every direction. Spinning in a slow circle, he filled his very core with the sights that surrounded him. A splash of white on the greenish-brown landscape unfolded before him and his heart leaped as his eyes fell upon the sight of a boy, sitting on a blanket, nibbling at some cheese. The boy giggled at something his mother said to him. Clytus Rillion stood there watching his family, his heart aching with affection.



They had tried for so long to have children—Lilaith came from a large family and had wished to populate the entire Plane. As the winters rolled by with no offspring, his wife would say it was the will of the Gods and they must not feel the time right to bless them with children.

Clytus snorted.

*The will of the Gods! More like simple old bad fortune.*

They sought out Shapers, drank enough Oolant Drought to choke a mule—not to mention pauper a rich man. Clytus had even allowed his beloved to drag him down to her priests, all for not. They gave up more than a decade ago. Still, Sindian had been born, late in the autumn, near six winters past. So small. So innocent. Clytus could almost have believed in the Gods with such a perfect gift cradled in his arms.

*Now, when I stand off and look upon him, I realize what the true meaning of immortality is.*

The snap of a twig drew his attention from his family, causing him to glance to his left. The entire field remained a steady swaying motion in the light breeze. A wisp of movement and the grasses parted like water before the prow of a ship some hundred paces away. Fur, perfectly colored to match its surrounding, sliced through the stalks as the hunter crept forward.

Clytus tried to call out warning, yet his voice failed him. The creature dropped to the ground, flicking its tail. In an explosion of power, it lunged, propelling itself forward at an incredible speed, directly toward his family…

*My son.*

Forcing himself into action, he tore across the field, heading for a spot that would intersect the prairie lion before it reached its destination. He hefted the short hunting spear he carried in his right hand and reached out for the Essence. The Sight of the Essence—all motion and energy—dropped on the field like a thin blanket of translucent fog, He saw its swirling Strands all around, interacting with the wind, the edges of the grass, the space between him and the lion sprinting across the field. As fast as he had ever done, he tied together the Strands as he ran, binding the spear to the lion. When he felt the connection complete, he hurled the weapon. His form powerful yet perfect, his aim true yet enhanced by the power he wielded through the Essence. The steel oak-leaf tip glinted in the sunlight as the missile arched, streaking across the sky. Alas, even willing the Essence to guide his throw, he felt it slip from him. The Strands unraveled and the spear spun sideways, tumbling in the air end over end. It landed well short of its target, swallowed up by the sea of tall grass.



Lion and man continued their pace, each focused on their own goal. Neither willing to give quarter. Clytus let his hand fall across his body to draw his sword, Dorochi, and almost stumbled when he grabbed the top of an empty scabbard. Whipping his hand to the other side of his belt, he found his dirk scabbard also sat empty. Clinching his jaw, he continued to race across the field preparing to fling his body at the beast.

*I will pay what needs be paid!*

He put his head down and quickened his pace. An icy chill

gripped his heart when he realized his path would not intersect the creature in time. With every fiber of his being he willed himself on, yet the harder he pushed, the less ground he covered. He had started his run just a few paces from his family, yet now they sat, oblivious to the doom approaching, well over twenty paces away.

*This cannot be!*

Again, he tried in vain to scream out warning, still struggling in his pointless flight to intersect the lion. His foot snagged something on the ground and he fell to hands and knees. Tearing through the grass on all fours like the beast he could not hope to catch, he regained his footing and sprinted onward.

Time slowed and the air around him turned thick as honey. His breathing labored and the pounding of his heart thundered in his ears. It pumped blood through his body, blood he would gladly spill to save those that mattered most. Slower and slower he moved, until he stopped, frozen. Frozen like a discarded statue from some long dead civilization.

He looked on in horror as the prairie lion took a loping gait in preparation for its final attack. With hind muscles bunched into tight knots, it sprang forward. Claws glinted in the eerie light that had settled over the land. 

Sindian continued to giggle. His mother reached out and brushed a stray bit of sandy-blond hair from the boy's face.

Maw opened. Fangs gnashing. The huge cat, biggest that ever existed, flew through the air, landing on his son like a hammer striking an anvil.

Jolting upright, the wool blanket slid off Clytus to puddle at his waist. He flung it off and dashed out of his tent on all fours. Firelight burned in his eyes as he sucked in the chilly, late evening air. The land stood silent save for the snoring of the men surrounding him. The smell of fresh fallen rain filled his nose. He breathed hard, as if he had actually run through the field of grass that now faded from his memory. Willing himself to relax, he reached back into his tent and snatched up his sword. He noted with satisfaction that Dorochi rested in its scabbard. Standing, he strapped it to his waist and nodded to a third watchman who approached.

"Sir? I heard someone cry out." Concern was apparent on the man's face.

"Nature calls, Hartin. Continue your vigil." Clytus waved Hartin away and strode out of the camp.

He did not have far to travel to gain the solitude he sought, for the campsite had been setup small and tight. The large outcrop of rock jutting from the small cliff overhead resembled a giant's hand descending to crush his men like ants. Finding a large rock far enough from camp to insure his privacy, he sat down and cradled his face in his hands.

*I will pay what needs be paid!*

Letting out a long, shuttered breath, he lowered himself to the ground and laid his head back against the boulder. It was still cold and damp from the rain that had raged over the past few aurns. Looking up to the heavens, he was gladdened by the sight of the stars shining high in the sky. Tracing the constellations, he found Argillian, the archer, and followed his arrow to Crysineis, the northron most star. The Bear stood just to the far side of Crysineis, roaring defiantly at the archer and preparing to charge. His mind wandered back to the times his own father would sit with him out in the garden behind their home. How his father spent aurns telling him the tales of those who resided on the canvas of the dark sky, forever frozen for all to see.



*What will Sindian remember of our moments together? Moments that were all too few. Please forgive me, my son.*

He sat up as something pricked his mind. Fear shot along his spine.

Silence enveloped the land.

*Even the crickets are hushed!*

In one smooth motion, he sprang to his feet and drew his blade. He welcomed the worn leather grip to his hand like an old lover. Standing motionless, he closed his eyes, focusing all his attention on his sense of hearing. All around him, the quiet became deeper—colder than a crypt. Even the wind had ceased.

A long, low note howled through the darkness, echoing off the cliffs of the Nektine. Its haunting wail cut through the darkness and bit into his very core. He sprinted toward the camp with only one image imprinted in his mind.

*O'Arkins!*

# Chapter 32

The trip had not turned out to be the adventure Arderi Cor had imagined when he buried himself into the supply wagon. After he awoke on the first day, the reality of hunger and the basic need to relieve himself had haunted him relentlessly. The crossing of the mighty Artoc river had left his stomach in knots—the swaying and jerking of whatever craft they had used to cross by had been horrible—and on more than one occasion during his time on the water he feared he would vomit, although he was unsure what would have come from his empty belly.



*By the sounds the horses made, I am sure they did not enjoy the crossing either.*

He had taken advantage of his time on the water to relieve himself, however, through a gap in the boards of the wagon bed. At one point, water doused the craft they were on and he was sure no one had noticed anything he had done. Later, he had found a sack of dried beef and used that to sedate his hunger. He could do nothing for his thirst, however. By the time the caravan made camp for the eve, he was parched. Luck smiled on him, for that evening he was able to sneak away from the camp, picking up a skin of water on his way. He spent only enough time away to relieve himself once more, then crept back and into his hidey-hole inside the supply wagon.

The next day, with a good stock of food and water to keep him from the discomfort of the previous one, Arderi stayed in much higher spirits. The boredom of nothing to see or do combined with the gentle rolling of the wagon—up one hill and down the next—kept him napping for much of the journey. Once the troop set up camp for the eve, and the men had gone to sleep, he itched to get out and explore his surroundings.

When he moved the sack of grain that served as the door to his traveling home, it shocked him to see so many men awake and walking the perimeter of the small campsite. A dozen men, all armed and alert, paced about, never leaving eyesight of each other.

*It will be impossible to sneak out! And I can, forget about returning!*

Due to all of the activity, he was forced to stay in the shadows of the wagons. Again he smiled at his luck, however, as the wagons had been placed against a cliff wall in a clump, only a short distance from the main fires. Due to the placement of the wagons, the men guarding had no reason to come near, giving him a dark pocket to move about freely. The eve remained chilly with a strong wind blowing. Soon Arderi longed for the warmth that lay just outside his reach. The overcast sky, with its low hanging clouds, covered the land like an ominous blanket—dark and unfriendly. Although the fire crackled too far away to provide him comfort, it did cast enough light to make him blind to whatever lay beyond its glowing reach. He could see that the area the troop had chosen for their camp was no longer covered in the tall grasses that surrounded his homeland. Instead, the ground lay hard and rocky.



*That explains the rough ride that jostled me about for the last several aurns of the trip.*

The part of the area he could see held small, barbed plants and an abundance of trees, though these seemed misshapen little things with large thorns. A light drizzle of rain cascaded down. One glance at the sky and Arderi was glad the wagons had been parked under an outcropping of rock. He crept from wagon to wagon foraging for food. Being cautious to make no sound when he shifted an item, he never lost track of the men who patrolled the edges of the camp. Within moments, the sky released its full fury and a torrential rain fell. Arderi ducked into the shadow of a wheel as a few of the guarders took cover next to the wagons. Large drops of water pelted the tents that lay scattered about the camp. The wind, constant most of the eve, lashed out with heavy gusts that uprooted anything left in the open and flung them away into the darkness.

The worst of the storm subsided within half an aurn. Arderi relaxed seeing the last of the third watchmen move out from under the rock and return to their rounds. Continuing to forage, he came upon a sack of bread. After eating nothing except the same dried meat for two days, he welcomed the change of diet. Wolfing down one, he jammed a second into his pocket. A find of a box of cheese added to his delight and he placed a lump of that in his pocket as well. The waterskin he had acquired on the first eve was half-empty, even with his careful rationing. He wished he could refill it, except the rain barrels were too far out in the open to afford him the opportunity.



Returning to the cheese box, he pinched off a second lump, sat down in a dark shadow against the rock wall, and nibbled on his prize. He watched the guarders wander about the fringe of the camp, and knew he could never slip past them.

*Yet with all the water on the ground, it should not matter where I relieve myself. No one will see a difference.*

He sat gnawing on his food and gazing at the drenched campsite. The rain eventually drizzled out and the fresh clean smell that comes only after a storm penetrated his senses. The place became so peaceful, he almost forgot he was in hiding. The guarders, still alert and vigil at their posts, reminded him of the fact. Arderi sat content to be out of his hiding spot and in the open—albeit an open hidden by darkness.

*Eventually, I will have to show myself. They cannot send me back now that we are this far out. Wherever* this *is.*

A sharp cry burst from amongst the tents jerking Arderi upright. He lunged for the cover of a wagon. Crawling to the edge of its shadow, he waited to see what caused the alarm.

On a small rise across from him, a tent flap whipped open and a man exploded from it. The man stood, breathing hard and looking around as if he meant to kill something. Leaning back into the tent, the man emerged with a sword and scabbard in hand. He buckled it on and stormed away into the darkness. One of the guards made a half attempt to stop him and the angry man brushed on by.

Arderi sat there staring at the empty tent, wondering if anyone else was in it that may have caused the man's agitation. Several moments passed without further event so Arderi slipped back to his resting spot against the rocks. Picking up the chunk of cheese he had dropped in his haste to look at the camp, he brushed it off and resumed eating. His mind drifted through several imagined scenarios as he tried to figure out a way to introduce himself to the group.

*I cannot just let them find me here amongst the wagons. They will take me for a thief!*



Looking down at the hunk of cheese in his hands, a pang of guilt ripped through him and he let out a long-winded sigh. A long, low horn off in the distance ripped his thoughts from his stolen food. It sounded like the wail of some injured beast. He wondered if it had anything to do with the man who left the protection of the camp. Stuffing the last piece of cheese into his mouth, he reached over to retrieve his waterskin. As he brought it lazily to his lips, his eyes landed on a peculiar sight.

*That tent is on fire!*

A flaming arrow stuck halfway through the thick canvas of a tent some ten paces from him. The fire licked its way up the shaft to the fletching yet failed to ignite the wet material it had penetrated.

All at once, shouts and screams broke the silence. Arderi lurched to his feet. Guarders ran in every direction. Half-dressed men poured from their tents, each held a weapon in hand. Something huge smashed into his shoulder and drove him against the rock wall. Pain shot through his head as it struck stone, filling his sight with a burst of light. With a groan, Arderi crumpled to the ground, blinded. When his vision cleared, he glanced up at a giant, shadowy form rummaging through one of the wagons. Arderi closed his eyes and flung up an arm when something was tossed his way. A pot clanged on the ground and skidded past him.

The thing at the wagon growled and lunged at Arderi. The loud thwack of steel striking wood echoed off the cliff. As the thing drew near, Arderi noticed that whatever the thing was doing, it was not lunging at him.

*The thing is backpedaling toward me!*

Huge and hairy, the creature's stench threatened to overwhelm Arderi as he lay cringing on the ground.

A second thwack and now Arderi saw the slim shape of a woman, sword and shield in hand, forcing the creature back, closer to where he huddled on the ground. Thwack. Agony ripped through Arderi as a large foot smashed into his ribs. The beast twisted and tripped. Something sharp dug deep into Arderi's side and he yelped in pain. Blood drenched his side. Moonlight glinted off the woman's blade as it snaked out like a silver tongue. A thick, goopy liquid poured over Arderi's face and he gagged as the vile substance washed into his mouth and nostrils. As the creature crushed down on him, it forced the air from his lungs under its tremendous weight. A thick pool of mud wrapped itself around Arderi's face, muffling all sound as his head sunk into the ground. Struggling to turn his head, his lungs burning for a taste of air, Arderi shoved his arms underneath his body. The mass of the creature on his back thwarted his escape. Reaching in and drawing on an untapped bit of strength, Arderi shoved at the rock wall beside him. The creature shifted and slid off. Pushing himself to his elbows, he gulped in air. Sucking a glob of muck into his mouth, it spattered against the back of his throat and he gagged. Vomit poured from him and he choked on the residue. When he was able to breathe freely, he struggled to his feet. Staggering around the body of the still creature laying next to him in the dark, he sought the edge of the wagons. Leaning on one for support, still trying to clean the mud and gunk from his eyes and nose, he marveled at the sight before him.

The campsite heaved with turmoil.

The clouds had dissipated enough for moonlight to bathe the scene in an unworldly glow—much of the camp lay trampled and destroyed. Tents lay askew—their poles broken and jutting out at odd angles. The logs from the fire had been kicked about—water-soaked coals and half-burnt wood scattered in a wide area around its original location. The sounds of metal ringing on metal resounded in every direction.

A man not five paces from Arderi let out a scream that turned into a gurgle as an axe struck him on top of his left shoulder. Blood sprayed out in a crimson arc. Crumpling to the ground, his lifeless eyes reached out to Arderi.

The creature who had delivered the deathblow stood over the man, howling and yelling in some guttural tongue. Arderi had never seen a creature so massive. The thing must have stood almost three paces tall. Its broad shoulders, covered in strips of leather and hide, rippled with strength. Although Arderi could not make out the creature's face in the darkness, large, pointed ears jutted from either side of its huge bald head. Its axe—so large a strong man would need two hands to swing it—seemed light in the things hand. It spun the weapon around its head and pointed, a string of grunting gibberish spilled from its mouth. Two other creatures ran off in the direction the one with the axe had indicated.



With a flash of steel and a high-pitched yell, the woman whom Arderi had seen earlier flung herself at the beast with the axe. Her sword came away wet and the large beast let out a sound that sent shivers slicing through Arderi. The great axe shot down at an angle to cleave the woman's head in twain. With feline-like speed, she stepped to the side and lunged with her own counterattack. Her small form jerked forward as the creature snagged her sword arm and lifted her off the ground in one swift motion. A sickening crunch sounded and her limp form tumbled through the air. She crashed a few paces from

Arderi, her body sliding across the mud-slick ground before coming to a stop at his feet.

The large man-like creature picked up the axe it had abandoned and stalked over to its victim. Arderi saw its face clearly now and his legs turned to jelly. A more hideous sight he could not imagine. Bore-like tusks sprouted out either side of its mouth to rise up and surround a flat, pug-like nose. Large, black eyes, set low and far apart, rested below an over-extended brow. The wrinkled skin covering its face, blotchy and pale, hung loose down his cheeks and jowl.

It paused when it saw Arderi hovering in the shadows. Opening its maw, it growled. Arderi recoiled, too frightened to move further. Grunting in what sounded like laughter, it looked down at the woman lying helpless between them. Rubbing a spot on its left shoulder, its hairy hand came away wet with a thick, dark substance. Taking the axe in both hands, it raised it high overhead.

And then, it stopped.



All was silent.

The noise and chaos simply ended.

The creature, its face scrunched up as it looked down at the woman with malice, stood like a statue. Glancing into the rest of the camp, Arderi saw man and beast locked in the struggles of life and death all around, yet everything stood still as if he looked now at a painting. In all the commotion, Arderi had not noticed that a man had been running toward them. Toward the creature with the axe. He too stood frozen in mid stride, a blood soaked sword gripped tightly in his hand, his face a mask of concentration.

*He looks like the man from the tent, the one who left earlier in a rage.*

Then the man moved. So slightly, Arderi thought he imagined it. He looked back to the thing with the axe and was certain it had not moved at all. Returning his attention to the running man, he…

*He* is *closer. Aye!*

The running man had taken a step, closing the gap between him and the creature. As Arderi watched, he saw that the man moved at a steady pace, albeit in slow motion. Arderi stood in awe of what he saw. Looking back to the thing in front of him, Arderi was startled to see that its axe had started to descend, yet only by the slightest amount. He concentrated on the axe and could tell that it moved as well, except much slower than the running man moved. The man made his way behind the beast at his creeping pace. Arderi tried to step to the side, to get out of harms way and get a better view, yet found himself unable to move.

*I am frozen as well!*

While his mind raced to understand what was happening, a blade appeared next to the creature. Inch by inch it moved into a position that would intercept the beast's arm holding the axe. Arderi glanced at the man's face. Their eyes locked and in that instance, Arderi felt the man's very being. Fear rippled through him anew and he slammed his eyes shut trying to break the unholy connection. Yet when he opened them again, the other man still had him locked in his sight.



The Plane snapped forward.

Sound slammed back into his ears with a crash. Arderi lurched back, as if someone had been holding him and suddenly let go. The creature with the axe howled in agony and waved the bloody stump of its arm through the air. The rest of the arm still grasped the axe that now lay embedded into the ground a hairsbreadth from the woman's head. The running man spun, his sword skimming through the air like a shaft of moonlight. The beast's scream of pain silenced as the blade sliced cleanly through its neck. The severed head rolled off its shoulders to splat in the churned up muck below. The body toppled over like a felled tree.

The running man spun on Arderi with inhuman speed. The tip of his sword hovered in front of Arderi's face. Arderi jerked back out of reflex, crumpling into a ball on the ground and covering his head with his arms. The image of his head rolling from his shoulders the way the creature's did a moment before permeated his mind and froze him with fear.

"I do not have time for this!"

By the man's tone, Arderi did not think he meant to kill him. Looking up, Arderi saw that the man had lowered his blade. "I know not who you are. Stay here and do nothing!" He jabbed his finger at the ground. The movement made him pause as he noticed the prone woman at his feet. "Nix! Drag her under a wagon and out of harm's way. Take care of her." The running man turned and melted off into the darkness. A darkness still filled with clangs and screams, and monsters come to life.

Reaching out, hand shaking like a leaf in the wind, Arderi grabbed the collar of the woman's thick leather jerkin. He pulled her through the mud and under a wagon. Blood flowed freely from her nose and her jaw jutted out at an odd angle, both broken. A bit of bone protruded through her right cheek. Ripping off his sleeve, he held it to her nose, squeezing it shut to stem the bleeding. A light moan escaped her lips.



"Shhh. You are safe now." He kept his voice calm.

*She may well be, yet what of me?*

# Chapter 33

Halfmeal had consisted of hard bread, cheese, and pieces of dried fruit that Alant Cor did not recognize. So far, it sat well in his stomach. Leaning against the front railing, he watched while the land stretching out over the horizon took shape. The sun had just passed its zenith and a gentle breeze blew across the bow of the *Mistbreeze Trader* as she cut a path to his final destination.



*Hath'oolan!*

Over the last tenday, life—and his stomach—had settled down. The voyage, at least from his perspective as a passenger, had become restful and uneventful. Without the constant urge to void himself over the side, he had adopted a more productive routine. He filled his days with reading and studying the various tomes and books his Sier, Sarlimac, had bade him to master prior to reaching Elmorr'eth. He even relished the eves he spent with the crew, listening to their wild tales of sea-monsters or pirate raids or all manner of things that could happen to one while at sea.

*For all their superstitions, they sure do enjoy hashing over gruesome tales and bad omens.*

Yet the trip was almost over. The port of Hath'oolan, the capital city on the Isle of Elmorr'eth, lay just out of sight and he had been told it would be visible within the aurn. The ship became a hive of activity while her crew made ready to pull into port. With nothing to do except watch, Alant drank in the sights, still trying to learn the meaning to all the words used on the boat. Captain Garson took personal pleasure in yelling at his crew—as a whole or individually. Before Alant knew it, a gleaming white dot materialized into a massive wall. Upon its appearance, men ran, ropes were pulled, and the sails rose and were secured to the masts. The *Mistbreeze Trader* rounded a bend in the land and a massive harbor, much like the one in Mocley, burst into view. Hundreds of boats and ships cluttered the area. Some sailing into the harbor, some from it, and others simply sat as if not knowing where to head. The massive, white wall, the guardian of the city proper, stretched from shore to shore and Alant knew that it would wrap around behind what he could not see of the city. The only things visible beyond the wall were towers and spires that extended into the cloud-streaked blue sky.

*Krin was correct—it is beautiful!*

The shoreline itself, beyond the multitude of stone docks that jutted out into the bay, was covered by low buildings in neat rows that seemed to huddle between the sea and the wall of Hath'oolan.



A tiny boat, no larger than a one-man dingy, left the mouth of the harbor and darted directly toward the *Mistbreeze Trader*. The craft carried a single occupant—a thin, gray being standing in its center. Alant saw nothing propelling the boat, yet it was moving at such a rapid clip that he feared it would not stop before slamming into the side of the *Mistbreeze Trader*. At the last moment, the small dingy curved around the back of the large barquentine, slid alongside her, and stopped. Its abrupt halt did not disturb the water around it. Jumping down from the fo'c'sle—Alant had learned this was the name for the front of the large ocean-going vessel—where he had spent much of the day in anticipation of their arrival, he raced over to Captain Garson. The big black man stood by a rope ladder that dangled over the side of his ship above where the little craft had stopped.

The Captain nodded to Alant as he approached. "Sier."

"Good day, Captain. May I?" Alant indicated a spot next to the big man.

A smile split the big man's face and he nodded. "Oh, aye! I do have to declare you to the Guide Master anyhow, so you might as well be present when he arrives."

"Declare me?"

"Oh, aye. Any Shaper that be aboard a vessel wanting to port on Elmorr'eth must be presented to the Guide Master. Tis their law and I will no break it. Elmorr'Antiens do have long memories and I will no have my trade interrupted."

Alant stepped next to the Captain just as a small, thin gray-blue hand reached up and over the side, taking hold of the railing. A gasp escaped the young Initiates lips.

*A hand that only has three fingers!*

He watched in awe while a blue-gray being pulled itself up onto the deck and stood in front of them. Towering well over two paces tall, the being looked so impossibly thin, it seemed as if it should not be able to stand at all, much less manage to climb the side of a ship. A thin, light-blue robe covered much of its body, yet cut to accentuate the oddness of the beings slender structure more than hide it. The hem of the garment stopped just above its knees leaving the majority of its willowy legs exposed. Slim, emaciated arms jutted out from the sleeveless top. A golden colored sash wrapped around its waist—a waist no thicker than one of the Captain's legs. Laced sandals completed its attire, yet even these managed to emphasize how skinny its calves were. The disparity of its head in proportion to the rest of its body increased the comical look of the being. It was large, smooth, and covered with the same grayish-blue skin as the rest of its body. Large, black eyes floated above two slits Alant assumed was a nose. Long, flowing white hair poured up and over its brow to cascade off the back of its head like a frozen waterfall—never touching the being's back.



To Alant's surprise, Captain Garson made a formal bow to the being on his deck. "Good day, Guide Master, please be welcome on the *Mistbreeze Trader.*"

*An Elmorian?*

"Captain Garson, so pleased to see you safely back, yes?" The voice of the Elmorian floated soft and light on the sea air, yet it resounded over the deck with authority. "What have you to declare, Hmm?"

The Captain held out a Silrith'tar. "Cargo manifest, merchants who be selling, and their intended purchasers, Guide Master."

The Elmorian waved a boney hand over the Crystal without actually touching it. "Anything to declare that is not listed, hmm?"

"There be one item we did pick up prior to setting sail out of Mocley that no be on the manifest." The Captain placed a meaty hand on Alant's shoulder. "This boy here be from the Shaper's Academy. I did be told that someone would be expecting him."

For the first time the Elmorian turned its attention to Alant, its huge black eyes engulfing him to completion. Pain laced Alant and he let out a gasp, shooting a hand to his chest. Something cold had struck him and now bored into his flesh. He pawed at the front of his tunic, his fingers encasing the Tarsith that had hung forgotten around his neck for much of the journey. When he returned his attention back to the Guide Master, he noticed the Elmorian's expression appeared different.



*He seems almost puzzled.*

Semi-transparent sheets, like smoked glass, slid down and up his huge globe-like eyes as the creature blinked. After a silence that stretched on for long moments, the Guide Master cocked his head to one side. "I assume you have an invitation, yes?"

The abruptness of the question shattered the silence and took Alant aback. "Aye, Guide Master." Alant became aware that the Tarsith no longer radiated cold. "I have a Silrith'tar from your Chandril'elian inviting me to study here in Hath'oolan." Removing his hand from the Tarsith, he fished into his pouch and produced the Crystal. The Elmorian waved a hand over it, again without touching it.

*He can draw upon a Memory Crystal without placing it upon his forehead! That is amazing.*

The Guide Master strode past him, heading for the bow of the ship. Without slowing or looking back, he spoke with an air of authority that brooked no argument. "Captain Garson, I will inform the Dock Master to fetch someone to receive the Human Initiate once we dock. Insure that he has his things ready so as not to detain those who come for him, yes? The guide boat is in position, have your men tie it off so we may proceed."

Alant did not wish to miss anything, so he hurried below deck to throw the last of his belongings into his bag. When he climbed back onto the main deck, the *Mistbreeze Trader* lurched forward without warning and he almost lost his grip on the ladder. After ascending the last few rungs, he stowed his bag next to the mainmast and rushed to the bow of the ship where the Elmorian leaned against the railing, its eyes transfixed upon the distance harbor.

*He is holding the Sight of the Essence.*

Looking down to the water, Alant saw the small dingy that had bore the Guide Master out to the *Mistbreeze Trader* was now tied to the front of the large barquentine. It pulled her toward the shore at a pace she could not have reached on her own.



*That burst of speed! It came from the guide boat!*

Waving his three-fingered hands in smooth, graceful motions, the Guide Master directed the *Mistbreeze Trader* into the heavy traffic of Hath'oolan's harbor. Once they rounded a natural outcrop of rock, more of the city burst into view. Massive stone piers, white as freshly fallen snow, jutted out into the water. A swarm of boats, both large and small—many times more than docked in Mocley—sat either moored, or being pulled in from, or out to, sea. On each boat, a thin Elmorian Guide Master stood on its bow. Squat, square buildings of varying sizes littered the shore, all made from the same white stone as the piers. They stretched off into the distance for at least a league or more. Behind the buildings rose the colossal wall at least twice the height of the great outer wall of Mocley. Smooth as glass, without a blemish to be seen—dazzlingly bright, it made the buildings below it look dark.

"Breathtaking to behold, yes?" Alant gave a start at the Elmorian's words.

"A...Aye, Guide Master." Alant could not keep the stammer from his voice. He longed to ask the Elmorian how the guide boat worked, yet something about the being disturbed him. He cut his eyes and studied its profile, watching the Guide Master wave his hands.

*I am actually looking at an Elmorr'Antien!*

The history and glory that surrounded their race was inspiring. Yet, standing next to one felt wrong somehow. As if the Elmorian was out of place compared to the stories he had read.

*Or, mayhaps it is I who is out of place.*

Alant returned his attention to the docks. The tiny specks, which seemed no more than ants while they were still out to sea, took on form now and he saw them scurrying about their tasks. One facet of what he saw shocked him most. "Those are Humans!"



"The Dasha'alan is mostly populated by Humans, yes?" The Elmorian spoke without pausing in his duties.

"Dasha'alan?"

"The town of the docks. Have you not learned the Old tongue, boy, hmm?" Disgust laced the Guide Master's voice—the first bit of emotion Alant had seen from him. "It seems one would apply themselves a great deal more in light of the great honor of learning here, yes?"

Not knowing how to respond, Alant remained silent. He watched the hustle and bustle of the port with interest as the *Mistbreeze Trader* slid into position alongside one of the stone piers.

Once the mooring lines were secure and the gangplank put in place, the Guide Master spent a moment speaking with Captain Garson who handed him a small bag, presumably containing coin, and left without ever looking back to where Alant stood.

Unsure of what he should do, Alant went up to the Captain.

"Where do I go from here, sir?"

"Well, now, young Sier, sir. Of that, I no be certain." The big man looked around uncomfortably. "The Guide Master did say you would be met at the docks, so I suppose it would be prudent for you to stay aboard the *Mistbreeze* for awhile. If you will pardon, Sier, I do have cargo to attend to."

When the big man disappeared below deck, a feeling of loneliness swept over Alant. It filled him more complete than he had felt since leaving his home stead of Hild'alan. With nothing to do, he sat down on his bag of belongings, rested his back against the main-sail mast, and watched the crew pull crates, bags, and boxes from the ship's hold. As the aurns slipped by, the sun continued its westronly trek to the distant horizon lengthening the shadows across the docks and the ships they held. The business of the port never slowed, and it became a soothing rhythm to Alant as he rested his head against the mast. This, added to the now relative calmness of the ship, helped boredom overcome him and he dozed off despite himself.

# Chapter 34

Master Gartin trotted up. "That is the last of them, sir." Breathing hard, the weapon's master hitched his sword belt. "Not sure, though I think it was a small scouting party, no more than a dozen I should say." They both looked around at the ruined camp. Clytus Rillion knew his weapon's master was thinking the same as he. Still, the old man voiced it first. "What was the butcher's bill?"



"Only two dead so far, both from Ras' crew." Clytus ran his hand through his sandy-brown hair in disgust. "I should have been more prepared. I just did not think the O'Arkin would hit us so fast. We are not even in the Nektine yet!"

"Tracks indicate they just wandered onto us, sir. I do not think they knew we were here until they saw our fires. Beside, it is not like they will be telling anyone about us." Gartin poked Clytus in the shoulder and pointed to the fire that Trilim had set up again. "Who is the boy?"

Clytus looked over at the young farmer huddled next to the flames.

*Like a wet puppy, far from home.*

"That is a good question, Gartin. One I mean to have an answer to." He dismissed Gartin with a nod and headed for the fire.

The boy raised his head at the sound of his footsteps with a look of fear in his eyes that Clytus knew stemmed from their shared Melding.

*Yet how did a boy with the power of Sujen end up here? As if my life is not complicated enough, I have to deal with this as well!*

He stood over the terrified kid in silence, mulling over the implications of the event. "What is your name, lad?"

The boy flinched as if Clytus had struck him. "What...what are you?"

Casting a quick look around to insure their privacy, Clytus crouched next to him. "I will explain everything to you in time, lad." He attempted to keep his voice low and calm. "I know what you saw earlier left you a little shaken. Still, I need some answers from you before we may continue. As of now, you are safe. Do you understand?"

The boy sat eyeing him. Then, as if reluctant to move, he nodded his head.

"Good. Now, unless you wish for me to continue to call you lad, you should tell me your name."

"Arderi, sir. Arderi Cor."



Clytus gave what he hoped was a fatherly smile. "A good start. I am Clytus Rillion, Commander of this mercenary troop." He reached out and fingered a bloody rip in the boy's shirt. "Are you injured?"

Looking down, the boy shook his head. "Not bad. One of the beasts stepped on me during the fight is all. It is not deep." Turning his head, Arderi looked over the fire to Alimia who lay wrapped in a blanket. The Shaper, Jintrill, knelt by her side and stared at her with the unseeing eyes of one embracing Sight of the Essence. "How is the woman?"

"Alimia? She will be fine. Tough as worn leather that one. The Shaper seems to know what he is doing." He stood up. "Come. Dawn is upon us. Let us take a walk."

Arderi returned his gaze for a time, then stood.

Taking the boy in tow, Clytus picked his way past men working to reclaim the scattered remains of their camp. Trilim had already erected the frame that held his large pot over the cooking fire and stood over it, stirring its contents. The man pulled out a spoonful of what appeared to be grits and took a testing nibble. A group of four men wrestled the corpse of an

O'Arkin onto a makeshift litter strapped behind a horse. Looking back at the boy, he motioned to the pot. "You hungry?"

With a grimace on his pale face, Arderi shook his head.

Approaching the campfire, Clytus retrieved two bowls and held them out as Trilim filled each. The cook questioned him with a look that Clytus could only answer with a shrug of his shoulders. With bowls in hand, he led the way out of the camp. Cresting a small hill, they arrived at the boulder Clytus had sat against prior to the attack.

*Has it really only been a few aurns since I sat here?*

Motioning for the boy to sit, Clytus lowered himself onto the large rock. Once comfortable, he held out the bowl of grits for Arderi, who hesitated before he took it. "So. Tell me your tale, Arderi Cor."

"What do you mean, sir?" The boy did not take his eyes from his bowl.

"Well...let us start with where you come from."

Arderi glared up at him. "I have no wish to return."



"Look, lad. This is not a contest nor am I interrogating you. We are a hundred leagues from civilization. Even if I wanted to send you somewhere, there is nowhere for you to go." Snorting, Clytus glanced back in the direction of the camp. "I certainly cannot afford to spare anyone to see you back. I need you to trust me if we are to accomplish anything here." He stared at the boy with a look he used on Sindian when his son would not admit to something he had done.

*Mayhaps I will give him over to the Shaper's care. Kill two fowl with one arrow.*

"I am from the Hild'alan stead." Arderi spoke the words in a rush before shoveling a spoonful of grits into his mouth.

*That is another good start.*

Nodding, a small smile coming to him, Clytus kept his voice at an even level. "So, the eve we camped in that stead, you hid in one of my wagons?"

"Aye, sir."

"Why?" The image of a boy slipping into his wagons late in the eve amused him. Still, Clytus could not quell the frustration that crept into the word.

"I want to join your troop. I want to be a mercenary."

Laughing aloud, Clytus shook his head and set his bowl down. "Most join a merc troop through the recommendation of another, you are the first one I know of who joined by hitching a ride. Do you even know what we do?" He gestured around the area. "Do you even know where you are?"

"I thought you were on your way to Mocley."

"Nix, lad! Far from it." Clytus stopped and took a bite of his grits.

*As if this trip has not been wrought with enough disasters—like some force is against me. Now I have some farm whelp that has gotten it into his head that he…*

"Tell me, Arderi. When you saw me during the fight with the O'Arkin, what *exactly* did you see?"

The boy's face went pale and he stared at Clytus like a rabbit facing a wolf. "It was...I was frozen, yet I could look around. Everything was frozen, yet my mind seemed free—as if I lay trapped inside my own body."



"Aye, as I suspected when I saw your eyes looking at me." Clytus put his empty bowl on the ground and sat looking off at the horizon. The sun broke over the far hills displaying a marvelous rainbow arching off into the distance.

*Everything moves on. The boy has the gift, that is for certain. Yet what am I to do about it? I have not the time to take him anywhere for training and this trip is hardly the place for a farmboy.*

"Sir?" The boy's voice drew Clytus back to where he was. "What did you do?"

He looked at Arderi for several long moments thinking, hoping to come up with a viable option.

*By all Nine Hells,* any *option! I cannot train a boy now. Yet I cannot allow one with the talent to be lost to the Order, either!*

"What you have seen we will not discuss at this time. Nor are you to mention anything you saw to anyone. I will choose the time we shall discuss it. Do not temp my anger in this, I am deadly serious. Know that if you do not do as I say in this matter, I will cast you out and you will have to find your own way home." He gave the boy a stern eye. "Do we have an understanding about this?"

Swallowing hard, Arderi bobbed his head. "Aye, sir." He glanced around. "What of me, sir? I am handy with a bow and I have always done well during the monthly militia drills at home. Though, I am afraid I have no weapons with me."

Clytus laughed out load. "The only weapons you will need shall be a scrub brush, lad. During your time here, you will remain under the watch of Mir'am Grith, the camp's cook." The farmboy looked abashed yet resigned to his fate. "If you do well by him, mayhaps I can have one of the men spar with you if there is a chance." He stood, scooping up the two empty bowls. "Come, there is nothing more that can be done about this by either of us."

Clytus led the way back to camp and was pleased to see much of it packed up and returned to the wagons. He led Arderi toward Trilim who watched them approach.

The old man grunted and shook his head. "Now why did I figure that a rogue boy, found wandering the camp one eve, leagues from nowhere, would end up as my responsibility, huh?"



Smiling at the look on the old man's face, Clytus dropped his head. "Aye, still, what else am I to do with him? Besides, I figured an old man like you could use someone to help lug things around."

Trilim gawfed. "Mayhaps so. Mayhaps so." He turned to the boy. "Well, you ever worked around a kitchen before?"

"My Ma leads our public house kitchen. She has shown me a thing or two." Arderi cut his eyes to Clytus.

"Hmm." Trilim made it sound as if he was truly impressed. "And what is your name, son?"

"Arderi Cor, sir."

Reaching out, Clytus plucked at the rip in the boy's shirt. "Before you start working the boy to death, Mir'am Grith, have Sier Deln take a look at his side. Arderi will do you no good if his wound becomes infected."

"So it is Sier Deln now, is it?" The look of amusement upon

Trilim's face did little to improve Clytus' mood.

"Oh, aye. Enjoy your merriment, yet the young Shaper does have the knack for healing. And this little trip of ours will have much need for such." Turning, Clytus headed toward the center of camp, then paused. Looking back to Trilim, he wagged a finger threateningly at the cook. "If you tell the Shaper I complimented him, you and I shall have words about it." With a grin, he continued on his way.

When he spied his scoutmaster picking through the remains of a shattered tent, he headed his way. "Master Hindar, what are your plans for finding me my basecamp?"

Hindar looked up, the scar running down his left cheek stretched taunt by the scowl he wore. "I had me a look at this area before you arrived last eve, and I can tell you, this range runs like a wall for many leagues east and west. I do not think I could get our horses very deep into the Nektine from here, much less the wagons." He spat on the ground.



Rubbing his chin and gazing up at the cliff they were camped against, Clytus' mood darkened. "Well, this is unmapped territory. Still, I know it has been traversed. To the west it gets worse, of that I am certain, and beyond that there is only the sea. It has been my plan all along to travel in an eastronly direction, so that is what I suggest you do. Have your scouts head out and start searching every valley and hollow. The troop will follow, staying to the foothills. When a suitable location is found, come find me."

The grizzly old scout bobbed his head. "Aye, sounds like the best we can do for now." He started to turn away when Clytus caught his arm and spun him back.

"I expect you and your men to report back every eve, these mountains are not to be taken lightly." They locked eyes for a moment before both men gave a nod.

Turning again, Hindar's yell sounded loud and clear as it echoed off the cliff's face. "Scouts to me!" He walked off toward the line of picketed horses.

# Chapter 35

"You heard the Commander." Master Grith nodded toward the Shaper who was still tending to the injured woman.

"Aye, sir." Arderi Cor crossed the camp to the makeshift infirmary. A handful of men sat around a small fire, each with a bandage covering different parts of their bodies.



A squat little man came up to Arderi when he approached the group. "Aye, lad. Sit here and let me have a look." He motioned for Arderi to take a seat on a stool. Arderi sat and the man helped Arderi to remove his shirt. Raising his arm over his head caused Arderi to wince. Probing the injury, the man spoke without looking up. "I have not seen you around. How is it you come by us?" With the shirt removed, blood flowed again from Arderi's side. The man spread the wound, pulling out bits of torn cloth and clotted blood, increasing the blood flow in doing so.

Arderi clenched his teeth from the pain. "I hid in one of the wagons, sir." He managed to say this once the man finally stopped his ministrations.

"Is that so?" The man looked genuinely shocked. Covering the wound with a clean cloth bandage, he reached to the side and picked up a strip of cloth. "Hold this here. I do not think anything is broken, yet there is a large patch of skin torn. The Shaper should mend this so as to protect against infection." He tied the strip of cloth around Arderi's chest to hold the bandage in place, then stood. "Fighting O'Arkins at your age? You may do all right with us, lad."

"I was stepped on, sir."

"What?"

Arderi felt his face flush. "I was not in the fight, sir. One of the—O'Arkins stepped on me. That is how I was injured, sir."

Laughter burst forth from the little man. "Ah, well then, lad, it is still a worthy tale. Many a man did not live through their first bout with the nasty beasties. Count yourself lucky." He held out his hand to Arderi. "I am known as Sarnet, the troop's medic...well, at least I was before we got us a Shaper."

Arderi took the offered hand and shook it. "Arderi Cor, sir. Well met."

"Well met, indeed. Your injury is not too bad. The Shaper still has a few aurns of Melding to do on others who need it more than you. Go, do what you need to for now—yet nothing overly taxing mind. Return after halfmeal, the Shaper should be free by then." The medic went to attend someone else.



Returning to the cook fire, Arderi spent the rest of the afternoon busy with the work set forth by Master Grith. He was thankful the cook kept his assignments light since his side burned and throbbed anytime he tried to use his right arm too rigorously. Once they finished serving halfmeal, the camp had regained some semblance of order.

Helping Master Grith gather the last of the wooden bowls, Arderi followed the old man to the edge of camp where a small brook ran. "How long have you been with the Commander, sir?"

"Master Rillion? Hmm, must be near twenty seasons by now." The old man kneeled down and placed the dirty bowls on the ground. "Why?"

"No reason, sir. He seems…" Arderi could not think of a way to proceed and still keep his vow.

Trilim laughed. "Aye, he is at that. And more." He stood up and held Arderi in his gaze. "I will guarantee you this, lad. Master Rillion will always do right by those who do likewise. A man could travel his whole life, span the entire Plane from one edge to the other, and not find anyone as honest nor good as

Clytus Rillion." He wore a grandfatherly smile. "Now, when you finish washing these bowls bring them back so they can be put away. Then you may go see the Shaper about your side."

"Aye, Master Grith." Arderi bent down, picked up a bowl, and dunked it into the freezing water.

When he finished and returned the dishes to the crate Master Grith kept them in, Arderi walked over to the makeshift infirmary area. The injured that had been there earlier were all gone and so was the medic, Sarnet. The Shaper, Sier Deln, lay on his back in the center of the area, staring into the sky. "Sier, sir?"

The young Sier sat up. The haggard look on his face made Arderi stop in his tracks. Letting out a deep breath, the Shaper bowed his head then struggled to his feet. "What is your name?"

"Arderi Cor, Sier." Wringing his hands together, he was in no hurry to have a Shaper work on him after the incident with the Test.



"Well, come on, Mir'am Cor. Let us have a look at you, shall we?" The Shaper kneaded the small of his back with a fist and walked over to a small group of stools sitting in a circle. "My duties may then allow me to have some rest. I am Jintrill Deln. You may call me Sier if you are more comfortable with that. Most here seem to be." Sier Deln sat on a stool and pointed to a second. "Pull that over here and show me your grievous battle wounds."

Retrieving the stool, Arderi sat down next to the Shaper and removed his shirt. Blood had soaked through and dried into the bandage. When they removed it, the wound bled freely once more.

"This is not too awful, only the skin is damaged. It should not take more than half an aurn to Meld it. The Shaper placed one hand onto Arderi's chest and stared at his side. A vacant, far off look fell into the Sier's eyes. The same look Arderi had seen in the Grand Master Shaper's the day of his Testing. Sitting there, staring at someone who gazed through him, made Arderi feel uncomfortable. He shifted on the stool to ease the numbness creeping over his backside.

"Be still, boy!" Arderi jumped at the words of the Shaper. "This will go quicker if you sit still."

"I did not know you could speak when you were...were... doing this."

"Of course I can speak." The monotone way in which Sier Deln spoke dampened any harshness of his words. "I am not in a trance you country fool. I am simply Melding the Essence that is in you so I may return your side to the state it was in before you were injured."

A mild tingle radiated from Arderi's side. If the open wound did not pain him so, it would feel like being tickled. Looking down, he saw no change to his side. Blood still seeped out and the torn skin looked ghastly. A stray thought took Arderi back to the strange event he had witnessed during the fight. "I know you can use the Essence to heal, can you also use it to stop time?"



"Ha! The Essence is in *things*, boy, things. You, me, the stool on which you sit are real. Time is not a *thing*. It is like the air between us—they exist, just not in a manner we can touch. How can you Meld with something that is not there?" Jintrill shook his head in disgust. "Working with the Essence is not like some fairytale magic, you know. It may seem so to a country lout, yet it is real—tangible. It is slow and methodical work. Just mending your little cut here will take the better part of an aurn." He let out a grunt. "Why am I even trying to explain this to you?" After a moment, he reached out and pulled the torn skin closed causing Arderi to gasp. "Sorry, this may hurt a bit." He held the flap of skin in place with his hand. "Where are you from?"

With the pressure Sier Deln applied to his side, the pain intensified forcing Arderi to speak through clenched teeth. "Hild'alan stead, Sier."

"Hild'alan. Why is that name familiar to me?" The Shaper paused, tilting his un-seeing eyes to the sky. "I think I schooled with a boy from there." He returned to his work on Arderi. "Yes, Alant was from there. He was an underling Initiate, yet quite the talk of the Chandril'elian over the past few turns of the seasons."

"Aye, he is my brother, Sier."

Sier Deln shifted and locked eyes with Arderi. Raw pain flooded back into his side as the tingling fled. Arderi yelped in agony.

"Sorry." The Shaper's eyes resumed their distant visage and in only moments, the tingle returned, chasing the worst of the pain from Arderi's side. "That should not have happened."

"What should not have happened?" Arderi felt himself relax as the tingling grew more intense.

"I lost the Sight of the Essence. You shocked me by, well, by being who you are."

A flood of emotions washed through Arderi. "Who I am, Sier? What do you mean?"

A half smile crept across Jintrill's face. "Well, let us just say that until your brother arrived, I was the star student. And now, here I sit, out in this Gods forsaken land, doing menial healing on the new star's little brother."



"You sound as if he wronged you in some way." Arderi flinched as a bolt of pain shot up his side. When Jintrill did not answer, he felt it best to keep silent.

Arderi's mind wandered while he sat there with nothing to do. Near an aurn later, the Shaper sat up and stretched. Examining his side, Arderi was pleased to find no trace of the injury remained. He rubbed his hand over the area, his fingers passed over smooth skin.

*Not even a scar.*

"Have you been Tested yet?" the Shaper asked rubbing the back of his neck.

Arderi's face paled and his pulse quickened. Without taking his eyes from his healed side, he heard himself mumble. "Nix, Sier."

"Well you should. I think you may have the gift."

Glancing up into Sier Deln's eyes, Arderi could not tell if the man knew something more. "Why do you say that? I thought that no one could tell except by way of the Test."

The Shaper's face contorted into a puzzled look. "I am not

sure. When I Melded to your Essence to heal you, I just felt... something. It was very odd. As if the Essence in you is—"

"Might I borrow the lad from you, Jintrill?" Both young men jumped back when they realized Clytus had appeared in between them. Without waiting on an answer, he snagged Arderi by the arm and hauled him to his feet. "Get your shirt! I have a task for you." His voice was as gruff as his actions. Releasing Arderi's arm, the man stormed away.

Giving a shrug to the Shaper, Arderi leaned over and swiped his shirt from the ground. Jogging to catch up with the Commander, Arderi fell in step behind and pulled his shirt on, tying the front lacing. The blood-soaked tear in the side dangled at an odd angle.

*This shirt is ruined! Yet, I have no way to replace it.*

He followed Clytus out of the camp, past the small brook where he had washed the day's dishes, and up onto a small, steep hill that overlooked much of the surrounding land. The sun hung low in the west and dusk would soon settle upon the land. Without warning, the Commander spun and grabbed Arderi by the shoulders with a ferocity that made his heart jump and stick in his throat.



"What in the Nine Hells were you discussing with that *Shaper*?" Clytus' voice stayed low and quiet, yet dripped with malice.

In the face of the man's wrath, Arderi's voice fled. Standing there with his mouth gaping, he had never been so afraid of any one man in his entire life.

Clytus shoved him back a step and turned toward the setting sun. The man stood there for a span with—to Arderi's terror—his hand resting on the hilt of his sword. When he turned back, his face was once again calm. "I am sorry, yet I need to know. What did you say to Sier Deln?"

Arderi glanced down at the man's sword. "Nothing, Master Rillion, sir. Well...nothing of what you forbade me to speak of."

"Then why was he explaining the workings of Melding the Essence to you?"

"I am not sure why. He schooled with my brother at the

Academy in Mocley. He also said he felt—" Arderi's voice caught.

Cocking an eyebrow, Clytus put his hands on his hips. "Aye... He felt?"

Arderi was trapped.

*Stupid! I asked, and he knows. I am going to die here!*

Reaching out a hand, Clytus placed it on Arderi's shoulder. The man bent over a little to look into the boy's eyes. "He felt the Essence in you. Is that what he said?" Letting out a sigh, he ran a hand through his hair. "You are forcing my hand, boy! With that damnable Shaper here, I have no options." The Commander was no longer looking at Arderi as he paced in a small circle. Arderi was not even sure the man was speaking to him either. "I cannot let you continue like this. Yet, my only option is unthinkable! I do not know if it has ever been done."

Without warning, tears flowed freely from Arderi. All of his emotions released in a torrential flood, washing over him in waves of agony. The failed Test, the grief his folks must now be feeling with his sudden disappearance, the fear of this place and the creatures from last eve, and now the knowledge that he was going to be abandoned—or worse. All this slammed down on him. His knees buckled at the weight of it all. Collapsing to the ground, he buried his face in his hands and cried.



Clytus knelt down next to him. "Tell me, please, so I may help." The compassion in the man's voice cut off Arderi's tears. He looked up into the man's face and told him everything. Of the Test and his failure. About his brother and his message in which he spoke of the power Alant had felt within Arderi. Of Jintrill's comments to the same effect. And last, he told him of his shame as to what he had done to his parents. How worried they must be, losing their son with no knowledge of what has happened. Through it all Clytus listened, asking simple questions occasionally which helped Arderi keep on track.

When Arderi finished, Clytus was slowly nodding his head. "Son, there is nothing we can do at the present to fix that which you have done to your parents. I only hope you get the opportunity to do so. Still, I can help you with the rest, I think."

He sat down next to the boy.

"What I am about to tell you can never be repeated. Not to your friends or family—especially not to your brother, the Shaper. And, especially not to the Shaper down in our camp. Do you understand?" He waited for Arderi to nod his head before he continued.

"I also grieve for what I am about to tell you. You should not be given this information at your age nor in this manner. What I am about to tell you may cost you your life before you are even given the chance to embrace what it means. Yet I feel I have no options left to me."

"I will, at least, give you this. I have the answers you seek. I will tell them to you if you wish. I need you to understand that once I tell you, there is no going back. Your path will be set and only death will release you from it. I will ask you only once. Do you wish me to give you answers?" He raised a hand to forestall any response. "Do not answer this question lightly, son, for it is more important than you can possibly know."



The sincerity with which the Commander spoke frightened Arderi. The memory of last eve during the fight, the man's ghostly eyes peering into his very soul. The only answer he knew beyond doubt was that this man could kill him. He felt that in his very bones. Gazing out over the horizon, the words of the old priestess he had met in the chapel of Saphanthia came back to him.

*We could choose a path and be led to ruin or be thrust into something that may lead us to greatness.*

Master Rillion looked at him with a puzzled look. "What?"

Arderi had not realized he had said the words aloud. Yet, in saying the words, an odd sense of tranquility fell over him and he nodded slowly. "Something an old priestess once told me. It did not make sense to me then and I am not so sure it does now." He reached up and wiped the last tear from his eye.

*If I am to be the Plane's fool, so be it. I must know.*

"Aye." He was happy to hear that his voice sounded strong.

Master Rillion stared into his eyes. When Arderi did not avert from his gaze he nodded once. "Aye, I think you may be stronger than I gave you credit." Getting to his feet, Clytus drew his sword. It was a slim gleaming piece of steel about a pace in length with a slight curve to it. Arderi saw no adornment on the blade nor its worn leather-wrapped hilt. "The name of this blade is Dorochi. I have carried it for over thirty winters. It was a gift, as all Tur'ganas must be."

Motioning for Arderi to stand, Clytus unwrapped the leather from the sword's hilt. A gleam of red spilled from the handle as its covering was removed. Nestled in the center of the hilt, imbedded in the steel that continued unbroken from pommel to tip, sat a red Crystal. Sharp, jagged angles of red light slashed out to gleam upon the surrounding terrain. Instantly Arderi recognized the similarity the Crystal had to the Ka'ilyth that the Grand Master Shaper had used during the Test, and took a step away.

*It is exactly like the lights from the Test! Only red instead of blue.*

"You failed the Test for the same reason a Shaper can feel power within you." Clytus' tone remained level. "Because you do have the power within you to manipulate the Essence. It is simply different from that the Shapers use."



A chill passed over Arderi. "Aye, yet what kind of power. Sier Deln said that the Essence was in things, yet I saw you freeze everything! You stopped time itself!"

"Nix, lad." A smile crossed Clytus' lips. "What you saw was me slowing down the reality of the Essence." He held the sword between them, horizontal to the ground. "There will be time for your questions. First, we cannot continue until you have been bound."

The Crystal embedded in the hilt pulsed. The violent flashes of red light dazzled Arderi. The brightness of the beams stabbed through his eyes, forcing him to raise a hand to block some of its intensity. His heart pounded in time with the pulsing. He felt it pumping in his chest. The throbbing seeped through him, saturating every fiber until he could feel himself oscillating in rhythm to the Crystal. Reality dissolved around him. Sky, mountains—the very ground he stood on—all washed away by the red glow that enveloped him. He floated in it's void. Mesmerized by it's life, it's being, it's…

*It is pure Essence!*

A voice spoke. Far off in a distant realm. A disembodied being attempting to pull his attention from the only thing that existed—the only thing that mattered. Arderi ignored it. He lost himself in the warm red glow of reality. Nothing else could compare to this.

Yet he heard and understood. Knew what the voice said even as he disregarded it. Its meaning burned in his mind. He heard a monotone voice speak and recognized it as his own. Knew what he said for he had said it for all of the eons that the Plane had existed. Knew that he would say the words forevermore. He listened to his words. "I shall never utter an untrue word. I shall protect the secrets of the Tat'Sujen Order. I shall be faithful to my duties and never waiver. A vow, which passes my lips, shall be broken only by death. To these I allow my Essence to be bound by the Melding of my very being to that of Ka'gana."



Existence snapped back and he slumped to the ground at Clytus' feet. Arderi, covered in sweat, gulped in air as if he had run a league. Raising his arm to wipe his brow, he found he did not have enough strength to complete the task.

"It is done." Clytus knelt down. "I have never heard of any of our Order being bound without understanding the full meaning of what they did. My heart grieves to know that I may have condemned you to death by my actions." Reaching out, he helped Arderi sit enough to be propped against the nearby boulder.

The weakness that filled Arderi soon fled and after a quarter aurn, he felt merely tired.

*I could sleep for a full tenday, I think.*

The cool breeze wafting over the land helped him regain some of his vigor. Raising a hand, Arderi brushed his hair from his face and looked up at Clytus. "What just happened?"

A look of pain cascaded over Clytus' face and, taking a deep breath, the man turned his face up to the sky. "I am sure at some fair or festival you heard tales spun by some bard of the Tat'Sujen?" He smiled at the boy's reaction. "Not all of them are tales, son, for the Order does exist. Having told you this I should now have to kill you." At the startled look from Arderi, Clytus raised a hand. "Settle. I will explain."

"Your brother and the Shaper are both correct. You do have a power within you. We call it the Sujen. It is much like what the Shapers use, yet in the manner that men are like women. Two sides of the same coin as it were. Except, where the gift to Meld the Essence is rare, the gift of Sujen is down right unheard of. Mayhaps four or five in a generation will have it."

"So I am a Tat'Sujen?" Arderi's head spun.

Clytus let out a small laugh. "Nix, boy. You have the power of Sujen, this is true. Alas, that does not make you a Tat'Sujen. Call it a prerequisite if you must."

"Normally, when one is found with the gift of Sujen, they are taken away to be trained in secret. If, during their training, they are found to be unworthy to join our Order, well...knowledge of the Sujen is not allowed to get out."

"Unworthy?" Arderi did not like the sound of that. "Then why do you tell me this, sir?"



"You have pushed me into a corner, lad! I had hoped to leave you washing pans until I could find some way to spirit you off to be apprenticed by our Order. Alas, the Shaper puts a kink in that plan. I could kill you, yet that would weaken our Order by your loss." Again, it seemed as if Clytus smiled at the discomfort his words caused Arderi. "And how would I be able to explain killing a farmer boy to my troop?" He laughed. "Nix, my only real option is to start your training myself." Clytus grinned. "Besides, I can always kill you later if the need arises."

Arderi shuffled his feet on the rocky ground. His mind raced as this new information seeped into him.

*This is what Alant felt! The odd feelings I have had my whole life, the Test, it all makes sense now.*

"Do I now need to hide from Sier Deln?"

The red streaks of light vanished as Clytus wrapped the hilt of his sword, Dorochi, once more in its leather housing. "Nix, lad. That is one of the benefits of being bound to Ka'gana. A Shaper will no longer be able to sense anything from you."

Still too weak to stand, Arderi rested his head on the boulder. "Ka'gana. I have heard that from somewhere. Yet, I do not recall where."

For some reason, this seemed to amuse Clytus. "Ka'gana is the true name of the Essence. The Essence is much greater than the Shapers of this Plane think it is. They see it more as a science. A way to Meld with physical items and change them. Yet Ka'gana is so much more. You have many things to master prior to learning of such things, however."

"So what happens now, sir?"

"Now?" Standing, Clytus reached out a hand and helped Arderi to his feet. "Now you go help Master Grith prepare lastmeal for the men. Then, I would suspect that you will have more dishes to wash."

Looking at Clytus with a puzzled expression, Arderi could not tell if the man made a jest. "I do not understand. How is that training, sir?"



Clapping a hand upon Arderi's shoulder, Clytus looked into his eyes. "Every action we make in life has consequences. You are a stowaway, lad, and you will be treated as such until the time comes when you earn a place among us. I have come here for a purpose, and that purpose is my top priority. Training you will happen when it happens." Turning, Clytus strode back toward camp leaving Arderi standing alone on the hillside.

*Why is it I feel the only one who received any satisfaction from our talk was him?*

# Chapter 36

Alant Cor awoke to a gentle shaking on his shoulder. For a moment, he was unsure where he was. Looking up, he stared into what, in his groggy state, seemed to be the face of a goddess. Brilliant, jade-green eyes, like the clearest emeralds ever shaped by a master jeweler, held him in their embrace. A smile, formed from lips as lush and dark as the finest chocolate, bathed him in their warm caress. Dark black hair, seeming softer than the finest silk, tumbled around the edges of her dark-skinned face, framing it in a radiance of shimmering light. He did not move for fear of breaking the spell.



Gracefully she stretched out her thin, supple hand. It floated across his field of vision like a gentle breeze. Pain shot through his chest as she poked him hard with a finger. "Do you be ill?"

Startled into action, Alant rose hastily, only to stumble backwards over the bag on which he had been sleeping. Embarrassment flooded through him as the fog of sleep lifted from his mind.

"Aie!" The girl hurried forward to help him up off the deck of the *Mistbreeze Trader.* "I do be sorry if I did frighten you."

"Frighten!? Um...N-no, I just…" Alant glanced around the boat trying to give his brain time to catch up to what was happening. Giving her a weak smile, he shrugged his shoulders and shook his head sheepishly. Reaching up, he pushed at a lock of brown hair that fell across his eye. "You did kind of sneak up on me, I guess."

The girl put a hand over her mouth to stifle a giggle. Her

green eyes sparkled at him and Alant experienced an odd tingling sensation deep in his chest. She stood tall for a girl, only a hand or so shorter than himself. A plain, yet elegant white robe covered her slim frame, accentuated only by the golden rope tied about her waist. Soft gold-colored slippers covered her feet. "I be looking for someone who traveled on this ship. A Shaper Initiate from Ro'Arith by the name Alant Cor?"

Her accent was strange and she spoke so fast he had trouble understanding her fully, yet he felt he grasped the majority of what she said. Looking down at his dingy woolen shirt and pants, he realized he looked more a part of the crew than a passenger. Swallowing hard, he tried to answer yet found his heart stuck in his throat. He stood in silence, gaping at the girl, feeling his face grow hot and red.

Smiling knowingly at him, she giggled once more. "That be alright. Someone else can help me."

She turned, as if to search for another crewmember, and he reached out to touch her arm. "Nix! I...I am Alant Cor."



"Oh! Well…" Her knowing smile turned into one of amusement as she looked him over.

*She looks at me like I was a mouse, and her the fastest cat in the stead!*

"If that be the case, I be Shaith Ku'rin, Initiate at the Chandril'elian here in Hath'oolan. I came to escort you." Shaith pointed to the bag he had tripped over. "Do those be your belongings?"

"Aye, well…" His stammering caused his face to grow even hotter. Mentally, he kicked himself, then bent down and plucked the bag from the deck, staggering slightly under its weight. When he stood, he gave the girl another weak smile and motioned for her to lead the way.

*Not a good start to my great adventure!*

Even though it was just past midday when the *Mistbreeze Trader* arrived at the docks of Hath'oolan, dusk now settled over the Island casting deep shadows over everything. The two wound their way through the congestion of the dock area and Alant still marveled that he saw nothing except Humans. "Why do I not see any Elmorians?"

Shaith spun around to face Alant so fast he almost ran into her. "Do no let the Elmorr'Antiens hear you refer to them by that name, they do find it degrading."

"Degrading? Why?"

"They be very sensitive to the Human tongue. They do know, in our tongue, we have a tendency to call a person by the land of their birth. You be Ro'Arthian and I, Silawaian."

Her retort puzzled Alant. "Aye, yet in the Old tongue, Elmorr'Antiens translates to the ancient people of Elmorr'eth. Is not that the same thing?"

"I did hear the Chandril'elian of Mocley be lax in its teachings, yet I was no aware how bad it truly be!" She gave him a sad look and shook her head. "Nay, no to the Elmorr'Antiens. Calling them the ancient people of a land be more respectful than calling them by a variation of the name of the land." The raven-haired girl turned and hurried on. Alant stood for a moment staring after her.

*She may be arrogant. Still, she is correct on one point, I am ill prepared if I do not even know what to call my new teachers.*



Noticing the distance between him and Shaith, he launched into a jog to catch her up. Falling in step next to her, he slowed to match her pace and catch his breath before speaking. "That still does not answer my question. Why do I see nothing except Humans here?"

She continued her brisk pace without looking over at him. "The Dasha'alan be populated exclusively by Humans. It be the only part of the Island where they be allowed, except us few Initiates, of course. The Elmorr'Antiens come here only if there be a need. Even then, they do send a Gralet'nar when they can."

*Gralet'nars! The henchmen of the Elmorr'Antiens.*

"I have heard of these Gralet'nars. Where do they come from?"

"They did always be as far as I do know. I think they be distant cousins to the Elmorr'Antiens. Gralet'nar be Old Tongue for Warrior Servant. They do serve their name and purpose well for they be big and strong, and fiercely loyal. I do find them no the brightest of races, yet we Initiates have very little contact with them on the whole." His heart skipped when she reached out and, in a gentle grasp, took him by the hand. "Come, we must hurry. Tardiness no be a trait the Elmorr'Antiens do tolerate." She quickened her pace to a fast walk, dragging him along after her.

*They leave me all day sitting on the dock and now* I *must hurry!*

They soon left the maze of low warehouses with its streets and alleyways of stacked crates and barrels to race along a smooth, white-stoned pathway, some four paces wide. It snaked along next to the massive wall that separated the dock area from the city proper. Towering over their heads by some two hundred paces or more, looking up at it from its base gave Alant a sickening feeling in his gut. Now that he was next to the white wall, he noticed that it was indeed smooth as glass. Even this close he saw no cracks or fissures upon its surface. Dragging his free hand down it as they ran alongside, it felt like frozen water, only not cold, slipping under his fingers.

*No mason could produce a stone this smooth! It is as flawless as if it is carved from one single piece!*



Movement ahead caught his eye and he realized they were approaching a small gate. Shaith slowed their frantic dash to a walk. When he saw what guarded the gate, Alant swallowed hard, despite himself. On either side of the opening stood two enormous creatures, each close to three paces tall. They dwarfed any living being he had ever seen. They had the same blue-gray skin and long wispy white hair as the Elmorian Guide Master from the harbor, yet all similarity between the two ended there. Legs as thick as a young hardwood tree supported their muscular frame. Arms that made the *Mistbreeze Trader's* Captain's look dainty were capped by hands easily the size of a man's head. The guards wore a strange, leathery looking armor that served as pants and sleeveless shirt. Their clothing appeared to be made from something resembling the skin of some giant reptile. By the look of their shoulders, each could rip a horse in half with their bare hands.

*I cannot imagine what need they have for the sickle-like blades hanging from their belts!*

Yet, of all the things about these creatures, it was their eyes—or rather, what should have been their eyes—that sent a wave of terror cascading over him. Hollow sockets, lost in deep shadows, sat high on their forehead. They gazed out—seeming to take in everything and nothing all at once—as they moved their heads back and forth, scanning the area in front of the gate without pause.

Shaith continued in losing her hold on Alant's hand when he stopped, rooted in place, several paces from the entrance. Turning, she flashed him a mischievous smile. "Do no be freighted, Alant. They will no harm you. You be expected." She let out a giggle at the horrified look he knew plastered his face.

"Aye, mayhaps. Yet...What are they?" The last words he said in a hushed whisper.

"They be Gralet'nars. Warrior Servants of the Elmorr'Antiens." She reached back and took his hand in both of hers. Despite the presence of the Gralet'nars, he could not keep his mind from how smooth and flawless her dark skin was. "Come! They will no trouble us." She tugged gently on his arm until his feet reluctantly moved forward. Without taking his eyes from the towering sentries, he let her pull him into the city of Hath'oolan. Just prior to crossing the gate, he thought he would lose his nerve, and almost ran back to the safety of the docks when one of them turned its haunting, blind gaze upon him. Yet, a moment later, the Gralet'nars lay behind him and he was on the other side of the massive white wall.



*Into the city proper!*

The road they followed curved around a large building and dumped them onto a wide, grand street, a boulevard larger than any he had seen in Mocley. The beauty of the sight that sprang up in front of Alant caused him to pause so he could take it all in.

The great boulevard they now stood upon was immeasurably wide—hundreds of paces across. Two pristine cobblestone lanes flanked a row of lush trees, colorful flowers, and leafy shrubbery that ran the breadth between them. Intermixed at intervals, fountains bubbled and shot streams of water high into the air. Ornate statues and large pieces of art carved into intricate designs stood scattered about, filling every empty area large enough to hold them. Many of these pieces sat between the enormous buildings that rose in elegance from the sides of the street. So high were these structures, the tops were lost against the now dark sky. Thin archways, their graceful lines accentuating the architecture, laced their way from building to building forming bridges and walkways, some so high it made Alant queasy just looking at them. A myriad of lights spackled the scene, casting dancing spots of color like the countless stars in the very heavens.

Everything he saw—the buildings, arches, fountains and artworks, planters housing the fauna, even the cobblestones making up the street, everything—was formed from the same, flawless white stone the outer wall had been made of. Even with darkness full upon the land, the brightness of the area gave the appearance of early dusk to him. The contrast of the brilliant stone set against the vibrant greens, reds, browns, and yellows of the many plants placed at strategic locations, made them stand out in vivid splendor.

"It is so beautiful!"

"Aye. It do take your breath away, at that." The boulevard stretched off both left and right far into the distance. "Come." Shaith, pulling Alant into motion once more, headed away from the outer wall and deeper into the city of Hath'oolan.



As they made their way, Alant could not help except to stare at the inhabitants. All around them, he saw Elmorians. Elmorr'Antiens he reminded himself. Hundreds of them meandered about, busy with whatever tasks had them out at this late aurn. Some accompanied by one of the horrible Gralet'nars, most of those burdened with large bundles or bags. A few gave the two Humans in their midst a casual glance, yet most ignored them entirely.

Once the two reached their destination, Alant felt close to collapse.

*We must have walked for near a league!*

The moon-long voyage, not to mention being unable to keep food down for the first half of the trip, had done nothing for his stamina and he found it difficult to keep up with the energetic young lady.

The last part of the boulevard ended in a circle that connected one side of the paved street to the other forming a large loop. On the far side of the loop stood a massive three-story building. A grand stairway, lined with columns, led up to a set of intricately carved doors. Large, stained glass windows lines the walls on either side of the doors. He did not know how, yet he felt certain this building was the Chandril'elian.

Still, the building was not what held Alant's attention. In the center of the circle created by the looping boulevard, directly across from the stairs leading to the entrance of the Chandril'elian, stood a huge tree unlike any Alant had ever seen. Blood-red leaves, broad and flat, dressed branches cloaked in a bark so black they made Shaith's skin look pale. The bark itself looked more like burnt flesh than wood. It did not stand proud and straight like a normal tree. Instead, it reached into the sky as if in great agony and begging the Gods to release it from its turmoil. At the base of the tree, a fine, red sand covered the ground filling in the circumference of the circle. Designs and patterns traced their way through the sand as if put there by some half-crazed deity. The entire area gave off an ominous, unholy vibe that sent a shiver running through Alant.

Shaith seemed to be gazing at the tree as well. "That be called the Chandril'chi tree. They be extremely rare,—this be the only one I do know exists, and it be said they do feed directly from the stream of the Essence itself. It do give me chills."



*The stream of the Essence?*

Before he could pose another question to Shaith about it, she darted into a side alley that ran next to the Chandril'elian, pulling him along in her wake.

Halfway down the alley, Shaith slipped into a side door and Alant found them inside a small anti-chamber. "Wait here for a moment while I do fetch you some proper attire. You can no meet the Hon'Vanria dressed like a common ship's rat."

Once Shaith left, Alant dropped his bag and sat down hard on one of the padded benches that lined the walls.

*Events are threatening to overwhelm me. Everything is happening too quickly.*

The room in which his lovely guide had deposited him into looked humble compared to the beauty of the city outside. Opposite the door they had entered, stood the small archway Shaith had disappeared through. Including the one on which he sat, four benches lined the walls, this being the total furniture the room had to offer. A wall hanging depicting an aerial view of the city hung on the wall across from him. Standing, he walked over to inspect it closer. The detail of it astounded him.

*I do not see any brush strokes in the paint!*

"That be a Fessio'tar. It be a fabric that be produced here on the Island and works much the same as a Silrith'tar—'err, that be a Memory Crystal." Shaith stood outlined by the archway.

Alant turned on her with a look of disgust. "I know what a Silrith'tar is!" He immediately regretted the hostility in his voice. "Sorry, the voyage here has put me on edge." When she favored him with a small smile, he swallowed hard. "You were saying about this Fessio'tar?"

"Aye. Just like a Silrith'tar, you can imprint a vision from your mind onto it. That be the view looking out from a balcony of the tallest spire here in Hath'oolan."

Turning back to the hanging, Alant gazed into its perfection.

*It does seem as if I am looking out a window instead of at a picture.*

"I have a robe for you. It should serve until you are settled in and they provide you with your own." She held out a folded white robe that looked much like hers. A golden rope sat in a coil on top.



He reached out, took the bundle from her, and busied himself with it. When she made no motion to leave, he felt his face grow hot once more. "Is there a place I may change?"

This seemed to startle her. "Aye! Of course, I…" She glanced down at one of the benches as if she meant to sit, then stared at him, a wicked smirk on her face. Finally, with a laugh that was deep and throaty, she pointed over her shoulder at the archway leading deeper into the building. "I shall wait within."

He stifled a groan. Once she was gone, he quickly stripped and donned the robe. It was a bit baggy on his now thinner frame, yet the rope-belt held it in place enough that he did not think he would trip over the hem. She had not provided him with any footwear, so he put his soft-soled shoes back on. They looked dingy and out of place next to the cleanliness of his new robes.

*Yet, as Papa always said, "it is not the quality of a man's shoes yet the quality of the man's walk that matters most." I hope my walk is good enough for what lies ahead.*

Stepping to the archway that led deeper into the building, he saw that it led to a long hall lined with doors. Shaith was occupying herself by looking at a tapestry hanging on the wall between two doors.

Upon noticing him, she glided over. "That be much better." She wrinkled her nose. "Well, if you no count the shoes."

Lifting the hem of the robe, Alant wiggled his toes in his plain fielders shoes. The faded brown of the leather looked about as worn as he had ever seen on a pair of shoes. "My Ma would have a fit."

Giggling, Shaith reached out and took his hand. His heart fluttered. "Come, I need to take you to the Hon'Vanria." At the blank look on his face, she sniffed and shook her head. "You really do know little of the Old tongue." She started leading him down the hallway. "What do you call your instructors back home?"

"Their title? We call them Sier."

"Strange. Sier do mean 'to Meld.' Why do they use that honorific? Vanria would be translating to 'teacher.' The Hon'Vanria be what you would call the 'head teacher.' Or, more accurately, 'honored teacher.'" She cut her jade-green eyes at him as they walked down the hall. "Alas, this may be the only time you see him. I did be here near two full turns of the seasons, yet this be only my second trip to his office."



"Does he not teach anyone?"

Shrugging, Shaith rounded a corner and headed up a wide flight of stairs. "As to that, I no be knowing. We Humans do no train with the Elmorr'Antiens."

Her statement shocked Alant to the core. "I will not be learning from an Elmorr'Antien! Then why have I come all this way?"

"Do no be silly! I said you no train with Elmorr'Antiens. We do have an Elmorr'Antien Vanria. Vanria Delmith be as fine an instructor as I have ever had, and I did have many in my life."

"Just one? Vanria Delmith is the only Elmorr'Antien who instructs us?"

"Aye. I have no ever seen another Elmorr'Antien look at one of us Human Initiates, much less teach us."

The winding stairs let out in a small receiving room. Cushioned benches and plush chairs lined one wall opposite a large, paned-glassed window that looked out into darkness. A set of elaborately inscribed double-doors rested in the center of the far wall. Strange runes, reminding Alant of those he saw carved into the blood-red sand that surrounded the Chandril'chi tree out front, were worked into the door in silver and gold. As the pair stepped onto the landing, the doors swung silently open. Alant started to pause, yet Shaith urged him forward.

A large, highly polished wooden desk occupied much of the room they entered. Papers, scrolls, and books littered much of its top. A pane-glassed window, twin to the one in the waiting area, filled the left side of the room. Bookshelves, each holding an assortment of items, lined the right.

Alant, however, gave the room no more than a cursory glance as, in his nervousness, he could not take his eyes from the white-haired Elmorian sitting behind the desk, writing in a book with a flowing script. His long flowing white hair spilled over his red silk covered shoulders to dangle down almost to the desktop. The two Initiates stood before the desk for long moments, the only sound the scratching of quill upon paper, until finally the Elmorian placed his quill into an ink jar and looked up, taking the pair in with its liquid looking eyes. As it had done on the deck of the *Mistbreeze Trader*, the Tarsith again radiated cold that momentarily shocked Alant. Flinching, he fought the urge to grab for the front of his robes. A puzzled look fell over the Elmorian and the Tarsith seemed to slip from cold to freezing. Alant clinched his jaws tight to keep from gasping out in pain, yet the Elmorian simply stared at him. When Alant knew he could take no more and was about to reach up to snatch the Tarsith from his skin, the cold was gone, and with it, all traces of the pain that had been in his chest.



"You are the Initiate sent to us from Mocley, the one named Alant Cor, yes?"

Not being able to stop himself, Alant reached up and rubbed his chest through his robe. "Aye, Sier—Vanria!"

Alant added the honorific instantly upon noticing his mistake, yet a small scowl twisted the Elmorians thin dark-gray lips. "The correct title you will use to address me by is Hon'Vanria, yes? I am Hon'Vanria here at the Chandril'elian. If you do not know enough of the Old tongue to know how to address your superiors, I will provide you with books so that you may educate yourself, hmm?" He turned his head and regarded Shaith. "Good eve, Princess, you have my thanks for retrieving our newest Initiate from the Dasha'alan."

*Princess?*

Alant cut his eyes to the dark skinned girl standing next to him.

Shaith made a formal curtsy. "It did be my pleasure, Hon'Vanria."

The Hon'Vanria retrieved his quill from its resting spot. "Please see that Initiate Cor finds his room, yes? I believe it has been prepared for his arrival." With that, he returned to his writing without so much as a glance at them.

Curtsying once more—Alant adding a hasty and clumsy bow—Shaith took Alant's hand, pulled him from the room, and headed for the stairwell in silence.

Alant was dimly aware of the doors to the Hon'Vanria's study closing behind them as they left. "That did not go well."



With her jade eyes twinkling, Shaith giggled and shook her head. "It did be a bore around here this past turn of the season since Plint did leave. It will be nice to have someone around who will entertain me."

Despite himself, Alant smiled. "Who is Plint?"

The smile slipped from her lips. "A boy from my homeland who did be an Initiate here. He be gone now." Dropping her eyes to the floor, she walked on in silence as if she had no interest in talking about it.

At the bottom of the stairway—Alant was not really paying attention to where they were going, yet he thought they were once again on the ground floor—Shaith turned down a hall and led him deeper into the building. The small hallway they were in, filled with closed doors on either side, let out into a larger one. This new hall, twice as high and three times as wide as the one they entered by, had the same white tiled floor except a plush, red carpet with swirls of blue ran its length. Looking off to his right, Alant saw an ornate pair of double-doors almost entirely made from paned-glass. Through the doors, he noticed the large boulevard that had brought him here and could just make out the black tree with the blood-red leaves in the darkness beyond. He gave a shudder. To his relief, Shaith led him to his right, toward the back of the Chandril'elian. The hall continued on, carpet covering its center, past arches and doors, to end at a second set of double-doors much like the ones at the front. Through the windows of these, Alant saw a lush garden, muted in the darkness.

Within a few steps, the familiar smells of a kitchen wafted over him. "Mmm. Either I am going mad or that is fresh bread baking."

"Oh aye! Still, you will no enjoy that smell for long. The Human quarters be in a small hallway behind those ovens that do bake that bread." She let out a sniff. "It be nice and warm in the winter...and miserably hot in the summer."

Opening his mouth to ask a question that had been plaguing him since the two were in front of the Hon'Vanria, Alant shut it with a click as an Elmorian stepped from a small doorway just ahead. Taking an additional step before realizing that Shaith had stopped, Alant quickly backed up and stood next to her. The Elmorian approaching them looked much the same as any he had seen so far in Hath'oolan. About a hand taller than Alant himself, gray-blue skin stretched tight over emaciated-looking arms and legs. A light-blue silk robe—more of a long shirt since it stopped well above his knees—did little to hide the thinness of the torso beneath. If anything, the robe accentuated it. Without pause, the Elmorian glided down the corridor toward the two of them.



Alant thought he should bow, yet since Shaith was simply waiting, he decided he would follow her lead. The Elmorian tilted its tear-dropped shaped head slightly and Shaith immediately dropped into a curtsy. "Good eve, Vanria Delmith." Awkwardly, Alant joined her by adding his bow.

"It is a good eve at that, yes?" Turning his large, black-liquid eyes upon Alant, the Vanria smiled thinly. "And you must be our newest, hmm?"

"Aye, Vanria. I am Alant Cor. Newly arrived from the Chandril'elian of Mocley." Reaching into the pockets of his robe, he realized he had left the Silrith'tar in the pockets of his old shirt. "I have a Silrith'tar here somewhere, Vanria." He started to unwrap the bundle of clothes he had carried forgotten under his arm and stopped with a wave from Vanria Delmith.

"You would not have made it to the Chandril'elian had you not had the authority to do so, yes?" Vanria Delmith tilted his head once more. "It is late, younglings, and the morrow promises to be taxing for young Cor here. I will see you formally in the morn, yes?"

"Good eve to you, Vanria Delmith." This time Alant was more prepared and bowed in unison with Shaith's curtsy.

Looking over his shoulder at the Vanria gliding away from them, Alant's spirits rose. "He is the first of the Elmorr'Antiens I have met that made me feel welcome."

*And the first the Tarsith did not grow cold from.*

A sheepish grin popped to his reddening face at Shaith's giggle.

"Well, at least the first that did not make me feel unwelcome."

Continuing down the hall, Shaith turned into a small archway that led into a hall thinner than any he had yet seen in the building.  Tiny doors, much the same size as his bedroom door back at his home stead, lined the walls five deep. Shaith made a gracious flurry with her arm. "Welcome to the Human Quarters, Alant."

"There are only ten rooms?" He was shocked. Hath'oolan was the center of Essence learning. How could there be so few Humans.

"Alas, that be double what we need. Though the last two doors be the lavatories." She eyed him sternly. "The one on the left be mine alone! You boys use the one that be on the right." Stopping at the second to the last door on the right, she lifted the latch and walked in. "Till you arrived, we did only have three in residence here this last turn of the seasons."

*Only three other Humans!*

The room was tiny, yet no smaller than the room he had occupied in Mocley. Light from a small stone set against the far wall sprang to life as they entered. A skinny bed was built against one wall and a small, mirrored stand with washbasin stood next to the door. Pegs lining the other wall for hanging belongings on rounded out the accommodations. Several white robes hung on the pegs, each with a golden rope dangling over them and two pairs of golden slippers rested beneath them on the white tiled floor.

Shaith took the two paces to cross the room and plopped down upon his bed. "It be small, yet it be all they do give us."

Glancing around the room, Alant did not feel cheated. His room at the Chandril'elian in Mocley was the same size. The disappointment in Shaith's voice about the room sparked his memory. "When we were in the Hon'Vanria's office, he called you Princess. What did he mean?"

A sassy grin and a twinkle in her eye said she was up to no good. "Just what he said. I be Shaith Ku'rin, High Princess of Mu'shadar, Keeper of the Chalice, Reader of the Scrolls, and Hand of the King's Justice." Rising gracefully, she strode past him and stopped in the doorway. "Only now you can add Initiate of the Elmorr'Antiens to that list." She did not sound happy to add that last title.

Feeling his mouth drop wider as her title grew, Alant felt dizzy. "So you are royalty or something?"



Looking up to him with her large, jade eyes, she smiled. Yet the smile was not a happy one. "I did be, and may be again. Never did one of the Family be found with the gift to Meld before." She twisted the word 'gift' into something akin to a curse. "I do hope things will return to normal upon my return." Her wicked grin slipped back in place. "My room be the first on the left, just so you know." With that, she bade him good eve and shut his door as she left.

Dropping his bundle of old clothes in one corner, he sat upon the bed and looked around once more at the small room.

*Well, I have arrived!*

A pang of homesickness washed over him and he forced it away. Rising, he started preparing for bed.

# Chapter 37

Clytus Rillion's patience was taxed further over the next tenday as the scouts searched for a suitable basecamp site. Skirting the edge of the mountainous range, the group inched its way northeast in the foothills of the Nektine. On many occasions, they were forced to backtrack to go around a gorge or other natural obstacle the wagon train could not circumvent.



*Thankfully, other than the one eve, rain has not hounded us. That, at least, is something!*

Riding ahead of the wagons, as he had done of late, Clytus guided his brown destrier, Starborn, past a scraggly tree. Its thorny branches, gnarled like the hand of a crippled beggar, reached into the sky. The sky itself had taken on a bleached, overcast hue, which did little to restrain Clytus' foul mood.

A clack of stone brought him out of his self-deprecating solace. Whipping a hand to the hilt of his sword, he reined in his mount and scrutinized the terrain ahead. Within moments, Hindar rounded a bend—his scoutmaster's mare sending a tiny avalanche of slate cascading down the steep slope as it descended.

Relaxing, Clytus nudged his warhorse forward. "A tenday, Hindar! A full tenday and we still wander eastward seeking a passage into these accursed mountains!" It pleased him that his shout startled the scoutmaster.

*At least I can still sneak up on folks.*

"Aye! These blasted cliffs offer no admittance!" Master Hindar reined in his skinny roan at the bottom of the slope and waited for Clytus to approach. "Every crack we penetrate seems to end before we traverse a half-league." A smile sprang to his lips. "Still, I do think I have found your campsite."

Reining in his horse, Clytus reached out and shook Hindar's offered hand. "Aye? That is good news." Leaning back in his saddle, he eyed the mountain range ahead. Sunlight barely penetrated the haze to glint off the snow-bound peaks. "And where might this location be?"

Leaning over the side of his mount, Hindar spit. "It will take the wagons the better part of two days to get to the gorge opening, though you cannot miss it. Jam'ees and his crew found it. Says they traveled into it for several leagues without seeing its end. I stationed Jam'ees at its mouth to rest up and wait on you. The rest of my scouts I sent on in to see how far it goes and find a suitable site for your basecamp. They should be reporting back by the time you drag all your wagons up to the gorge."

Peering over his shoulder, Clytus tried to catch a glimpse of his troop behind him, yet could find no trace of them.



*I must have wandered off further than I thought!*

"And what of your plans?" Clytus returned his attention to his scoutmaster.

A grin split the man's face. "A good hot meal and a bedroll thicker than a blanket will sure be welcome after near a tenday in these mountains."

Clytus chuckled. Spinning his mount back toward the west, the two men rode in silence back to the struggling wagon train.

Hindar was correct; it took two full days for the troop to reach the entrance of the pass. The gorge itself was some thousand paces wide. Steep, cliff-like walls wound away into the distance, the center of it panning out into a shallow V with a small creek trickling over slate rocks that had slid from the sides. The small shrubs and weed-like grass that found a foothold between the rocks would be no trouble for the wagons and only an occasional, gnarled tree dotted the area.

*Yet the incline and loose, flat rocks may be a different story.*

Hindar and Tylin came strolling up to Clytus, lost in thought. He felt their presence while they waited for him to turn and acknowledge them. "Aye, report."

"Tylin here feels he has secured us a basecamp site. Tell him."

Clytus noticed the young scout was not overly eager to speak. He nodded for Tylin to begin.

"This gorge stretches on for leagues, Master Rillion, with many a branch off or side trail. We searched as many as we could and thus far we see no end to the main route nor any access to the ranges above."

Letting this news wash over him, Clytus nodded. "It is as to be expected. As this is the only break we have found that will allow the wagons admittance, this is the path we shall take." Walking between the two men, he headed down to the waiting wagons, then paused. "Good job, both of you and all the scouts. We will take the wagons as far in as they will go, if no path is found to ride the horses into the mountains, I will go on foot if needs be."

Continuing on his way, Clytus called for the wagons to head up the gorge.

A tenday more—and several broken wagon wheels and other setbacks—and the troop emerged into a vast valley. The lake that took up much of the center of the area was bright blue and crystal clear. Large, lush evergreen trees fanned out from its banks and rose partway up the surrounding mountainside. The scouts had already camped here for many days and Clytus was happy to see they had not been idle in waiting. A large cleared area stood awaiting the wagons and the placement of a permanent camp.



As soon as the wagons rolled to a stop, Alimia directed the setting up of camp. Clytus stood on a small rise, watching to insure the new leftenant paid attention to placing the camp in a precise, defensible manner. Within an aurns passing, Trilim had a large cooking fire blazing, Hindar had tethered the mounts in a secure area behind the wagons, and tents dotted the area as each man staked out a spot to call home for a while.

*All in all, I do not think I could have done a better job.*

"Alimia, Hindar, Gartin, Trilim," Clytus yelled out. "To me!"

The four dropped what they were doing and headed off to join Clytus who stood gazing out over the slopes ascending into the peaks beyond.

Turning to his people once they all arrived, Clytus looked them each in the eye. "So it begins. Hindar, have your scouts ready to head out at first light. Tell them to keep to groups of four. If they catch sight or sound of our quarry, have them report back immediately and wait here for my return."

A puzzled look crossed Hindar's face. "Your return, sir?"

"Aye, I plan to be hunting as well. Alone. A large group may encourage the creatures to keep their distance."

Alimia responded first. "And you find this course of action wise, sir?"

"I would not have suggested it if I did not." Looking back at his scoutmaster, Clytus raised a questioning eyebrow.

Hindar cleared his throat and nodded once. "Aye, sir."

"Trilim, I know you have gotten used to having the boy, Arderi, to do much of your work for you, yet I have a second task that the boy needs to have time for. Gartin, I would very much appreciate it if you would spend a few aurns each day instructing the boy. He has no skill with a blade, and little with a bow. I would like this to improve if the boy has any talent whatsoever."

Both men accepted their tasks with nods and verbal acknowledgments.



"Alimia, I need not remind you of the dangers that lie in these mountains." Clytus reached out one arm and placed in upon her shoulder. "You are the one I am entrusting to keep the basecamp in order as well as defended. You have the skills. Do not lose your confidence."

The leftenant nodded.

Clytus flicked a finger over Trilim's shoulder. "What is the status of our supplies?"

The old man rubbed his chin and paused for a moment. "Losing the one wagon to the Artoc was not a tremendous loss since we split all of the supplies equally between each wagon. I know the days spent finding this camp has frustrated you. Still, if you will recall, we planned on twice that many days, so we are ahead of schedule. I would reckon we have at least four moons worth of supplies before we are to the point where we will need to head back to civilization."

"Very good." Looking them each in turn, Clytus stood in silence for long moments. "So it begins." Nodding, he walked past the four and headed back to camp.

# PART THREE

## The Journey Home

*A person can spend their entire life*
*searching for something.*

*Another might spend their time waiting*
*for something to search for.*

*Yet, no matter how long it takes to find it,*
*once you find your true niche in life, you*
*will realize that all of your life's teachings*
*have brought you full circle*
*to that one thing.*

MAD

# Chapter 38

Arderi Cor collapsed on his sleeping mat. His arms burned and it amazed him that he had once again found muscles that had never been used. These were stretched and tormented by the events of the last few tendays. His head throbbed from a sharp blow Master Gartin had delivered with the practice sword.

*I think the man gets pleasure from smacking me around.*

For the most part, the aurns Arderi spent at the basecamp had been uneventful. The majority of Arderi's duties centered on his work with Mir'am Trilim and the preparation of meals for the troop. Commander Rillion only came into camp every tenday or so, and never for more than one eve at a time. The first morn after his arrival, the man would set off again into the surrounding mountains. This frustrated Arderi. He still yearned to understand what had happened during the fight with the O'Arkins. The glowing Crystal hidden inside the man's sword pommel was another mystery, as well as how any of it connected to him. They had been at this basecamp site for over a moon, and all he knew for certain was that the group was in the Nektine Mountains, far to the north of his home stead of Hild'alan.

*The stories of the Nektine are deeply interwoven with death or doom whenever mentioned in any bard's tale I have ever heard.*

He also pieced together that, for a reason he had not as of yet discovered, Commander Rillion was in search of a Drakon.

A large, winged beast of legend that was said to have once ruled much of this land. Arderi had never heard of anyone actually seeing one of the creatures, and did not know if he really believed they existed at all. As far as he knew, they only existed in bard's tales.

Still, despite the bruises and hard work, Arderi found that he enjoyed his time now that he was no longer afraid Master Rillion would kill him nor throw him out of the troop to find his own way home.

Each day, Mir'am Trilim would wake Arderi before dawn so he could help with firstmeal. This would be followed by cleanup and storage of all the gear. He then would have an aurn or so of free time, which he spent mostly in the company of the young Shaper, Jintrill. Arderi enjoyed the Sier's company immensely and loved the stories the Sier told of Mocley and what his brother, Alant, was experiencing as an Initiate. Later, halfmeal would need to be attended to. These meals only consisted of dried fruit or beef served with flatbread and cheese, which required little in the way of preparation.



Arderi had thought the entire trip would be spent helping Master Trilim with his cooking and cleaning. However, life changed the day prior to Commander Rillion leaving for his first hunting excursion. The Commander took Arderi to see Master Gartin, the troop's weaponsmaster, for what he referred to as essential training for anyone wishing to become a mercenary. For three aurns each afternoon since that day, Arderi worked under the tutelage of the grizzly old fighter, who instructed him in the various methods of swordplay. First, he tested Arderi on the knowledge he had gained from the mandatory militia training every able-bodied man was required to take back home. Arderi had always imagined that the monthly trainings would serve him well if the need ever came and he would be required to fight. However, he soon realized how wrong he was.

*Master Gartin is a marvelous swordsman! Superior by far than anyone back home.*

Arderi sat enthralled listening to the weapons master

explain that fighting with a large group, like what he would do if his home stead were attacked, was much different from single, man-to-man combat. They spent their time together divided between discussions and practicing. Practice included both wooden weapons of various types as well as fighting with no weapons at all. Arderi found the strategic aspects and problems Master Gartin threw at him as exhausting as the physical ones.

Yet, no matter the pain nor weariness, lastmeal would be upon them and with it, his duties to Mir'am Trilim and the cook fires.

And now, as Arderi lay on his mat staring up at the canvas roof of his small tent, he felt a contentment he had never before known. "Riln, this is the life we dreamed of so many times. Here I am living it while you are back home, tilling dirt." Although the feelings of guilt and loss from running away still plagued him, with the passing of each day it diminished a little. Instead of dwelling on the bad feelings, he dozed off with various scenarios of valor playing out in his head.



All too soon, he felt a hand grasp his foot and shake him awake. Rolling over, he pushed himself out of the small tent and a damp chill cut through his light sleeping clothes. Mir'am Trilim knelt next to him when he emerged. Bobbing his head and stifling a yawn, Arderi motioned for the man to go and that he would follow. The old man smiled down at him, stood, and walked toward the cook fire's dim glow in the pre-dawn gloom. Reaching over, Arderi grabbed his boots and checked for creepy-crawlers in each. When he found that none had taken residence in them during the evening, he pulled them on.

By the time Arderi arrived at the fire, Trilim had it stoked back to a respectable blaze. He helped the cook lift the large pot onto the spit. Grabbing a bucket, he trudged down to the small stream that babbled nearby. Thus the day started, as each before it since the troop had set up the permanent basecamp. The remainder of the day passed like the rest—free time spent with Sier Deln, serving and cleaning up halfmeal, weapons training with Master Gartin.

Later that eve, after lastmeal, Arderi busied himself cleaning the dishes in the same small stream from which he fetched their water. A commotion back at camp caught his attention and, leaving the dishes in a pile next to the brook, he hurried to investigate.

The sun sank below the mountains casting the valley into a muffled darkness as a group of scouts rode into the camp. One of the shabby mountain horses they rode pulled a crude litter made of sticks strung between two large branches. A large black lump rested in the middle of the litter. At first, Arderi thought it might be a man's body.

*It is the right size for a man, yet not the correct shape.*

A small crowd of men had gathered around the newly arrived scouts and Arderi had to shove his way between more than a few of them to get up close enough for a good look. The black lump resting on the litter looked like a pile of broken, shredded leather thrown into a rumpled pile.



"All right! Make room you maggots!" The men parted as Alimia shoved her way through the crowd. "Tylin, what in all the Nine Hells is going on here?"

Tylin was one of Master Hindar's scouts. Thin and wiry, he held an easy grin on his face. Vaulting down from his mount, a shabby gray mare like the one pulling the litter, he sauntered over to the leftenant. "Me and my crew snagged us a Drakon!"

"This little pathetic lump of meat?" Alimia poked at the pile with a toe.

"Aye, it fits the tales, and that is so!" The put-off scout scowled at the leftenant.

Arderi worked his way to the front of the crowd and now stood next to the makeshift litter. The pile of leather did seem to fit the pictures painted by the bard's tales. Stab wounds covered the cat-like body of the creature. Two large leathery wings sprouted from its shoulders—one slit near in half lay draped over the edge of the litter. A long, serpentine neck extended out to a boney head adorned with tiny spikes. A black tongue flopped out of its maw between rows of tiny, razor-sharp teeth.

*It is just like a bard's tale...except...*

"Except it is much too small!" Arderi's face flushed with the realization that the crowd had turned to look at him.

"Oh, look everyone, the stowaway is a master huntsman now!"

Arderi dropped his head and took a step back as a ripple of laughter resounded through the troop.

Leaning over the body of the creature, Alimia peered into its dead eyes. "Nix, the boy is correct, Tylin. It seems to me you have bravely killed a baby Drakon." This time the laughter that resounded through the men lifted Arderi's spirits and he found himself giggling as well. "No matter, Tylin. Master Rillion will still be pleased. Mayhaps this will serve his purpose and we can leave these accursed mountains. If not, you can show him where you found this. Its mother should be close at hand."

A shrill shriek pierced the air causing everyone to flinch. The horse pulling the litter started to prance nervously and one of the men reached out and grabbed its reins to settle it.



"What in all the Nine Hells was that?" Blade in hand, Alimia spun half around to gaze out at the now dark forest.

As if it had materialized out of thin air, a large black creature slammed down onto the back of the horse pulling the litter. The mare shrieked as the force of the blow crumpled its legs and sent it slamming to the ground. Men scattered and chaos seized hold of the camp. The massive creature, easily twice the size of the dead mare it now stood upon, flexed the bat-like wings that sprouted from its shoulders. A long, serpentine neck stretched out, ending in an immense, spike-lined head.

The creature opened its maw, rows of shimmering teeth lined the dark chasm of its mouth, and bathed the area with another piercing shriek. The noise bore into Arderi's skull and forced him to his knees. He covered his ears with both hands trying to block out the sound. When the noise subsided, Arderi opened his eyes. The creature was gone, the horse it had perched on lay still, blood oozing from large tears in its side and neck. Someone grabbed his arm and yanked him roughly to his feet.

"Get out of here!" Alimia pushed him toward the wagons. "Take cover under a—" A blur of shadow passed before his eyes and Arderi stood alone. A sickeningly wet thump sounded behind him and he spun. There, at his feet, lay the remains of the leftenant's body. The woman's head, left arm, and shoulder—gone. Blood and bits of flesh splattered the dirt and in the fading light of dusk, it shimmered crimson before turning black.

Without thought, Arderi backed away, spun, and ran. His foot caught the edge of the litter and he fell to the ground hard, forcing the wind from his lungs.

Arderi could do nothing except lay there, staring at the thing on the pallet behind the dead horse. Finally, revulsion of the dead creature overpowered his mind-numbing fear to move and he pushed himself off the litter. Standing over it, he saw it was a carbon-copy of the larger one that now terrorized the camp. With a heavy thump, a large black mass landed on the other side of the litter so hard the ground beneath Arderi vibrated. In the darkness he could make out little detail save for a row of gleaming teeth under two eyes that caught the light of the campfire and reflected it back at Arderi. The creature opened its maw and an ear-wrenching screech blasted forth, slamming Arderi to the ground. Scrambling up, he launched himself into the darkness. Fleeing blindly, his heart pounding to escape the confines of his chest, he cared not where he ran so long as it took him away from the horror of a bard's tale come to life. A flash of light lit his vision, a burst of stars not of the sky, yet of his eyes, and Arderi fell. Fell into nothingness.

# Chapter 39

Dawn crept upon the land before Clytus Rillion crested the small hill that separated him from a hot meal and a warm sleeping mat. He had been out for well over a tenday, and the days spent alone amongst the peaks of the Nektine had taken their toll on him. His back ached, his limbs felt like lead, and the chill of the high mountains had seeped into his very bones.



*And all this time I have still not gotten any closer to finding one of those damnable beasts! At least I will have a decent eve's rest in camp…*

Looking down at the camp below, his mind reeled. Digging his heels into Starborn's side, he galloped down the small slope, reining hard at the edge of a smashed tent. Numbness fell over him like water. Starborn jerked to one side, becoming skittish of a dead body, blood pooling below a large gash in the man's side. Without thought, Clytus slipped from his saddle.

Everywhere his eyes fell, death surrounded him.

Men and horses, or the remains of them, lay strewn amongst the shattered remnants of tents and wagons. Black carrion birds had already found their morning meal. They feasted upon the bloating corpses of man and beast alike. Walking aimlessly through the carnage, Clytus thought he recognized the clothing of Alimia on one such body. Thin of waist and hip he knew of no other it could be. The body was missing much of its upper half, however, and he would need to roll her over to be sure. He did not think he could stomach the task. Pulling his eyes from the corpse, a clump of broken wood, barely recognizable as the remains of several wagons, drew his attention. In the center of the rubble, he found the body of Master Gartin, sword still in hand, upon a heap of a dozen men.

*At least you had your last stand, my old friend. I hope you made it count.*

Not far from the pile, the body of Trilim Grith lay crumpled next to the scattered remains of his cook fire. Clytus fell to his knees next to his old friend. A tear traced its way down his cheeks. The old cook's lifeless eyes bore into Clytus. Whatever had caused the man's death had torn through flesh and bone alike. Reaching out, he gently closed the lids.

*Sleep well, old friend, your travels have been long. I will miss you.*

Clytus remained on his knees as a rage swept into him like the waters of an icy-cold river. He let the current of pain and loss, of anguish and grief, fill him till it overflowed the banks of his mind. His grief turned to tears that spilled from his eyes and poured down his cheeks.



*They all trusted me, and I have led them to ruin!*

"I led them *all* to ruin!" His scream snapped the silence of the valley, echoing off the high mountain walls and causing several of the carrion birds to take wing. His words resounded back, mocking his pain and slicing through his very core.

Bowing his head, he ran callused fingers through his hair and grasped a handful in his fist. Clearing his mind, he concentrated on the slight pain he caused to his scalp—felt how each hair hung onto his head and how, collectively, they rooted themselves firmly in place. The more he tightened his grip, the more he focused on the pain, clearing his mind of all else—trying to wipe away the image of his men who lay all around him—yet knowing he never would.

When a snap of a twig penetrated his mental shield, Clytus launched to his feet, sword in hand. Facing in the direction of the noise, he stood there, unsure if he hoped to kill whatever had done this to his people, or to allow it to kill him and release him from his guilt. There, some thirty paces away, amongst the tree line, the young Shaper, Jintrill Deln, stood leaning heavily on a branch. Blood caked the side of his head—his brownish hair matted over that ear. A look of horror filled the young man's face.

Rushing to the Shaper, Clytus took his full weight from the tree and helped him toward the lakeshore, away from the destroyed campsite. A small rise separated the lake from the camp and shame filled him even as the relief of not being able to see his dead troop eased his mind.

Setting the young man down on a log, Clytus dipped a rag into the cold water and began cleaning Jintrill's head wound, trying to determine how serious it was. The young man did not flinch under his ministrations. The Shaper simply sat there, his eyes staring far off into the distance.

"The wound it not deep, yet this lump will take many a day before it fully heals."



At the sound of Clytus' voice, Jintrill looked at him for the first time since the boy emerged from the forest. "My thanks to you."

"What happened here, Sier? I saw no discernable tracks."

Looking over his shoulder, Jintrill stared in the direction of the basecamp for long moments. "Black death—it came from the sky…" The young Sier's words came flat, without inflection. "…as if the darkness itself had grown fangs."

Laying a hand on the Shaper's cheek, Clytus eased the young man's head to face him. "This was no boogieman, Sier. Something attacked this camp. I need to know what it was."

A voice sounded from behind Clytus. "I think it was your Drakon." Further up the beach, Clytus saw the boy, Arderi, clothes soaking wet, limping toward them. The boy's left arm hung limp to his side. Arderi winced as Clytus took his right arm and helped him over to the log where the young Shaper sat. "The Sier is correct, sir. The thing came out of the dark like a horror."

"Why do you think it was a Drakon?"

With another wince of pain, Arderi carefully pulled his injured arm into his lap. Clytus could see the break just below the shoulder and marveled at the inner strength of the lad. "It fit the descriptions of the bard's tales I have heard, sir. Cat-like body, serpentine neck, large wings from its shoulders." The boy shivered in the cool mid-morning mountain air.

Rising to his feet, Clytus pointed to Jintrill. "Stay with the Shaper. I will only be gone a moment." He headed over the small hill that led to the basecamp and was assailed once more by the visage of carnage that he beheld. Focusing on finding what he needed, it took him only moments to rummage through the wreckage of the wagons to find what he sought. Returning to the two young men, Clytus first wrapped a blanket around Arderi, then Jintrill, who's glossy eyes continued to gaze off into the distance. With a little coaxing, Clytus pulled the Shaper off the log and laid him next to it. The Sier's eyes never so much as blinked.



Hefting his waterskin, Clytus handed it to Arderi who gulped down the water. Some spilled out from between the boy's lips to wet the blanket tucked around his shoulders.

"My thanks, sir."

Taking the skin back, Clytus pushed it's stopper into the mouth and re-hung it at his hip. "I can clearly see you have been through a lot, yet I must know, boy, what happened here?"

"It all happened so fast, and I was so frightened." Arderi's voice trailed off.

"Easy, lad." Clytus reached out and patted the young boy's shoulder yet stopped when a gasp of pain escaped Arderi's lips. "Start at the beginning."

"One of the scout teams, Tylin's group, I think they found and killed a baby Drakon. They brought it in on a litter behind one of their horses. Its parent must have followed, for as soon as they made camp, it struck." Arderi looked into Clytus' eyes for the first time since the boy had appeared on the beach. "I am sorry, sir, Alimia is dead."

Clytus nodded, knowing the boy spoke true, and not just about Alimia. "I know, lad. I know. They are all dead" Standing, he turned to look out over the vast, beautiful lake—a shimmering glass pool, almost a league wide. The far bank, skirted by a thick layer of evergreen trees, created a shaggy green coating up much of the mountain slope. These gave way to a silky, snow-white blanket that followed the majestic peaks up to the very sky. A crystal-clear sky, without a single cloud to mar its beauty, so blue it seemed to have been created by a master artist.

*There are far worse places to have as one's final resting place.*

Reaching out to the young Sier, Arderi hesitated, then dropped his hand back to his lap. "Do you think the Sier will be all right?"

Jintrill still stared off into nothing, yet Clytus had seen people in worse shape. "Sometimes what a man sees can be as hard on them as a physical wound. Still, I think he will be fine soon enough. When he is up to it, we will see if he can tend to that arm of yours."



Pushing himself into action, Clytus busied himself by creating a small, mini-camp on the sandy shore. He built a fire, set up two tents, and helped both young men into resting spots near the warming blaze. Turning his attention to food, he built a make-shift spit and hung a pot of water to boil for stew. While rummaging for ingredients amongst the destroyed basecamp, he was delighted to find his small store of Oolant drought still intact. The wooden case holding them lay battered under a wagon bed, yet not a bottle of the drought was broken.

Returning to their new campsite, Clytus knelt down next to Arderi. "Here." He helped the boy into a sitting position. "This will mend your arm." Removing the stopper from the small, clay vial, he held it out for Arderi.

A convulsive look racked the boy's face as the odor of whatever lay inside assailed his nostrils. "What is that, sir?"

"It is Oolant. An Essence enhanced liquid that will mend the break in your arm in much the same way the Shaper would—if he were awake and able-minded." Clytus pushed the vial closer to the boy.

Reaching out with his good hand, Arderi took the vial and brought it to his nose. He shot his arm out to push the foul smelling container away, and eyed it with a look of disgust.

"Aye, lad. I know it smells. It is a single dose. Drink it down all at once, it is easier that way."

A warm feeling filled Clytus as he watched the boy force the thick, bitter liquid down.

*My little Sindian hates that stuff as well.*

Pain entwined itself through the dredged up memory of his son and Clytus' face hardened. "Now rest, boy. The Oolant is no faster at mending wounds than a Shaper is. It will be several aurns at least until that break mends." Standing, he turned to walk away.

"Commander Rillion, sir? Are you leaving us?"

The fear in the boy's voice reminded Clytus how young Arderi really was. Turning back to him, he calmed his features and forced a smile. "Nix, lad. Those men were my responsibility. I will not let them spend eternity under the open sky. I recommend that you rest now. The Oolant will help you fall to sleep, and when you awake, it will have finished its job of mending your arm."



Cresting the small rise that separated the destroyed basecamp from the makeshift one he created on the lakeshore, he steeled himself for the task at hand and kept walking, knowing that if he stopped, he may not start again.

*I will pay what needs be paid.*

# Chapter 40

Days rolled into tendays that had almost reached a moon's turn and Alant Cor had achieved a kind of rhythm to his life. Being schooled at the Hath'oolan Chandril'elian was not exactly what he had envisioned in his daydreams during the boat trip over the Great Ocean. Although the work was grueling, he had become more adept at Melding the Essence during this short span than he had in both turns of the seasons he had spent at the Mocley Chandril'elian.



*The Elmorr'Antiens push relentlessly! It is no wonder there are so few Humans allowed here. The pace they set would crush most of the Initiates back in Mocley.*

The Human Quarters of the Chandril'elian at Hath'oolan consisted of a small hallway of adjacent rooms crammed into an area behind the kitchens. The hallway was narrow, the rooms were small, and for most of the day, the air was hot and dry from the ovens located on the other side of the wall. These rooms were everything that the rooms the Elmorian students occupied were not. Not that Alant, nor any Human student for that matter, had ever been allowed to enter the Elmorian Quarters, which sat in the upper floors of the school. The rooms, however, were still a hot topic of conversation amongst the Humans when they were alone and out of earshot of any Elmorr'Antien.

Still, the small room assigned to Alant was little different from the room he had occupied in the Chandril'elian at Mocley, and he was unaffected by its bare furnishings and cramped living space. He spent little enough time there anyhow, much preferring to use his free time in the garden area at the center of the school building with its lush foliage, billowing fountains, and huge, winding hedge-maze.

The weather on the Isle of Elmorr'eth was a treat. The entire time Alant had been on the Island, he had seen nothing except blue skies. The climate, always warm and wonderful with a cooling breeze, remained pleasant even in the late hours of dusk. When he first arrived at the school, he assumed that the lushness of the gardens must have been Essence enhanced—something that was regularly done at the Chandril'elian of Mocley—yet, the more he visited the gardens, the more he realized that the weather of the area was simply conducive to plant life.

"I did hear the Elmorr'Antien students have private bath areas in each of their rooms and tubs lined with gold." Jerith De'thane, a skinny, ebony-skinned young man about the same age as Alant sat on the edge of a stone bench bouncing a small silver coin from his homeland of Silaway on one palm. Alant still found the thick accent of the Silawaians hard to follow.



"Oh, Jerith, you do have money on your mind at all times." Shaith Ku'rin reached out, snatched the coin from mid-air just as it left Jerith's hand, and slapped in onto the bench next to him. The jade-green eyed girl—by her claim a Princess to some kingdom in Silaway Alant had never heard of—had a mischievous streak that Alant found added to her allure. "They be Initiates just as we, if their quarters be a bit larger than ours, well, they be Elmorr'Antiens after all."

All of the Human students at the Chandril'elian—there were only four—had gotten into the habit of taking halfmeal together at one of the larger entrances to the hedge-maze. Here, several stone benches—ornately carved and formed from the same smooth, white stone like all the other structures on the Isle—as well as a small, matching table sat under the shade of a large, broad-leafed tree that Alant did not recognize.

"Aye, mayhaps. Thou I know when I am unwanted." Quiln Garfer hailed from Ro'Arith, like Alant. Yet their similarities ended there. Alant felt little affinity with the boy and not just because he was several winters younger than himself.

*He is about the same age as my little brother, Arderi.*

The thought brought on a pang of homesickness, which Alant ruthlessly pushed away, yet a wariness lingered.

*Arderi should have been Tested by now. I* felt *the power in him. Sier Sarlimac said he would notify me once my brother arrived in Mocley. I hope he has not gone and done something foolish!*

The main thing that bothered Alant about Quiln was the fact that the boy was not very skilled with the Essence.

*There is no doubt the boy can Meld the Essence. He will even make a fine Shaper one day. Yet why he was summoned to Hath'oolan remains a mystery. I was more skilled than he when I arrived. Yet, he has been here near a turn of the seasons already and is by far less skilled than the rest.*



Never knowing his parents, Quiln had grown up an urchin on the streets of Orlis. When the Siers discovered his ability to manipulate the Essence, they whisked him away to the Chandril'elian of Mocley. Alant did not know of what events had led the boy here.

"Tis because even your own whore mother did no want you." Jerith scooped up his coin from the bench and shot a hard look at Shaith before he slipped the coin into the side pocket of his robe.

The dark-skinned girl rolled her eyes and glanced back to Quiln with a mother's look of concern. "Do no pay any attention to him, Quiln. The Hek'kie say they do hate that we Mu'shadar look down on them like inferiors, yet it be they who be quick to cut down any they see as beneath them."

"Nix. Jerith is right." The orphan never sounded confident no matter the situation, yet whenever the subject of his parents arose, he was even more self-deprecating than usual. "I know my Ma was probably of a profession that most find repulsive."

Alant had no misunderstandings about the other two's right to be here. They matched his learning turn for turn, even though the two from Silaway had been in Hath'oolan for several turns of the seasons. Jerith had the same dark-chocolate colored skin as Shaith, and they were both about twenty winters, yet they were as different from each other as he was from Quiln. Jerith came from a small village he called Kasu'yama, deep in the heart of his homeland of Silaway. His father, some type of soldier, fought in a civil war both he and Shaith referred to as the Great War. His home village was supposed to be famous for it's warriors and supported a side referred to as the Hek'kie, which Jerith claimed meant 'Of the People.' Shaith said she belonged to a group called the Mu'shadar, or 'Shelterers of Life'—a disapproving snort came from Jerith when he heard her give the translation. Both he and Shaith agreed that the Great War had been raging for generations, although it was apparent that each had very different views on the reasons for the war itself. It was a topic Alant quickly learned should not be discussed when both were present.



Pulling the conversation away from the Great War, Alant returned to the one topic everybody loved to complain about. "I still say our rooms are not that bad." Ripping his eyes from Shaith's mesmerizing smile, Alant turned his attention back to his meal and plucked a grape from the basket. "They are much the same as I had in Mocley. Besides, I am here to learn how to Meld the Essence, not for the accommodations."

Adjusting her position on the short-trimmed grass, Shaith held Alant within her emerald gaze, reached out, and took a grape from his food basket. Rolling it between her long, dark fingers, she smiled a smile that had Alant blushing. "Oh, aye! A country bumpkin like you mayhaps knows no different. I, however, be used to a finer stature of life!" If her words held any sting, she washed it away with the twinkle in her eye and the smirk upon her lips.

Feeling his cheeks redden, the way they always did when she picked on him about his fielder upbringing, Alant studied the grape he held with more intensity than it warranted. When he thought his emotions were once again under his control, he popped the grape into his mouth and looked up. Shaith was rotating the grape between her thumb and finger and that wicked grin still marked her lips.

*My Gods, she is beautiful!*

A laugh broke out from Jerith. "Do leave Alant alone! No everyone have the chance to be raised in a palace, *your highness.*" Even though Jerith displayed a graceful bow when he used her title, he always made the honorific seem more an insult than compliment. The two Silawaians had never shown any physical aggressiveness toward each other—they both said violence here in Hath'oolan would betray something they called 'The Code' and hurt their honor, as well as the honor of their families. Still, Alant suspected it would not take much to have them go to blows.

Without even looking at her black-skinned countryman, Shaith waved a dismissive hand over her shoulder. "This be between me and Alant, Jerith. Go and seek the statue of the Chandril'chi tree that be in the center of the hedge-maze. If you can no find it, at the least you can get yourself lost in there! Mayhaps then Alant and I can have some peace together."



Jerith barked a laugh catching Alant's attention. "I do think it be your creamy white skin she finds most attractive. Very few of your kind make their way across the Great Ocean, fewer still travel inland when they do. Yet, I will bet five gold draughts to copper, her father would be burning mad if he found out she had eyes for you."

Looking back into her eyes, Alant melted under the girl's piercing gaze. Alant racked his brain for something to free himself from her stare.

*She has not stopped pursuing me since my first day here. Her forcefulness borders on the point of being obscene! Not a girl I could take home to Ma. Though, not due to the color of her skin, the girl's look is almost obscene!*

"I have always wondered about something, though." Alant

flinched inside when his words squeaked out, forcing him to clear his throat.

Continuing to look at Alant like a falcon eyeing a field mouse, Shaith held the wicked grin that raised one side of her lips in place. "Aye?"

Feeling the redness spring once more unbidden to his cheeks, Alant rushed his words. "Why have we never been instructed by anyone other than Vanria Delmith?" He forced himself to settle and slow his words. "In Mocley I had nearly half a score of Siers instructing me."

"None except Vanria Delmith did ever instruct us since I did be here, and that be longer than any of you." It was not the first time Jerith had made the claim about being here before Shaith. The subject was another irritation between the two and one that usually sent Shaith to fuming. This time, however, she let the insult slip from the conversation unnoticed.

"Aye, yet for what reason?" Alant had never received an answer that satisfied him as to why only Vanria Delmith instructed them.



*Why would they not spread us around more? Why always the same instructor?*

Shaith finally ate the grape she had taken from his food basket. "Do you feel that he no teaches us enough?"

"It is not that." Alant really had no objections to the Elmorian's teachings.

*I feel that I have gained much and will gain even more under Vanria Delmith.*

"It simply seems odd that we have such limited contact with the Elmorr'Antiens—though we live in the middle of their largest city." Setting his food basket down on the grass beside him, Alant fiddled with the golden rope belt tied around his waist. "We Humans are relegated to staying only on the first floor. Our living quarters, classrooms, even the small room we use to take meals—all on the ground floor. I have yet to have a conversation with one of the other students here. When the odd chance happens that I pass one in the hall, they do not even glance my way! The only circumstance that allowed me upstairs was my arrival when you took me to see the Hon'Vanria, and I have yet to see him again!"

Reaching out, Shaith patted his hand in a way Alant thought was meant to be comforting. Yet it only managed to bring his thoughts back to the softness of her skin. "They do treat all of us such, and I be sure the Hon'Vanria be busy."

Jerith snickered. "Oh, Aye. They be too busy for the likes of us."

Shaith continued as if she did not hear Jerith's interruption. "This be my third winter here, and I have rarely spoke to any except Vanria Delmith. Still, he seems nice and all of us learn more here than we would from our home Chandril'elian."

"Aye, you three have." Head hung low so he seemed to be speaking to the stone tabletop, Quiln sounded more depressed than normal. "I can barely keep pace. I do not understand why they even keep me around. You three outpace me by leaps and bounds. Even Alant! And he has just arrived. I was not even considered at the top of my class back in Mocley. It shocked all the Siers when I was invited to study here."

*The boy is correct. Half my fellow students there had more ability with the Essence.*

Alant tried to keep any pity from his voice. "Yet you are here. There must be a reason. Mayhaps Vanria Delmith knows. Have you spoken with him?"

The boy looked horrified. "Nix! I do not wish to bring more attention to myself. Mayhaps he just has not noticed me. If I open my mouth, they might figure out that I do not belong here and whisk me back to Mocley."

Letting out a giggle, Shaith turned to stare at him. "I be sure Vanria Delmith has no missed you in a class of four! I do agree with Alant, you be here for a reason. Mayhaps they think your ability will grow. Vanria Delmith always be kind to us, even if no others share his attitude."

As if on cue, their instructor, Vanria Delmith, came striding around a copse of squat fruit trees. The snow-white silk robe draped over his shoulders swallowed his too-thin limbs and lithe, blue-gray body. His sandaled feet whisked across the crushed stone path without making a sound. A second Elmorian walked by his side wearing a silk robe in much the same cut. As with all the clothing Alant had seen the Elmorr'Antiens wear, the pale blue robe accentuated the thinness of this one's body rather than hiding it. What surprised Alant was the red-laced trim at collar and sleeve covered with gold embroidery throughout and the large gold ring, the center of which held a red stone that glinted in the noonday sunlight, perched on the finger of his right hand.

*I have never seen any of the Elmorr'Antiens wear neither trimmed robes nor jewelry before now.*

Alant let out an involuntary gasp and bent forward as a ting of pain bore into his chest.

*"Yes, my Prince. I do feel that the Humans are advancing. So are the younglings. We have quite a skilled group."* Delmith's words sounded strange to Alant as he fumbled with the front of his robes to find the source of his discomfort. The first syllable his instructor spoke sounded as if the Elmorian sang in a flighty, musical tones—nothing Alant recognized as a tongue. He assumed they spoke in the Elmorian tongue. Yet, before the first word slipped from the Elmorr'Antien's lips, Alant knew its meaning. Now he could not tell if the Elmorian spoke in the Human tongue or if the weird speech coming from the being simply sounded like words he recognized. Still, Alant was certain he understood. His hand closed around the Tarsith that dangled from his neck hidden behind his plain white robe. Frigid cold radiated through the thick cloth. The coldness of it numbed his fingers. *"I must agree, my Prince, you are correct about the Essence, it is on a steady increase in power."*



*I should not understand the words escaping his mouth, yet somehow I do.*

The Tarsith pulsed with cold now. Adjusting his grasp to hold its chain between his fingers, he let the amulet dangle by the loop, being careful to keep it from touching his chest.

The Elmorians approached and all four Humans rose to their feet. The students stood with arms at their sides, except for Alant who clutched the front of his robe to keep the cold Tarsith from his skin, waiting patiently to be addressed.

*It is weird the Elmorr'Antiens feel it is proper for the superior to address the subordinate first. Back home it is the other way round.*

"Greetings, young Initiates." Vanria Delmith was the only Elmorian who, as far as Alant knew, had ever spoken directly to any of the Humans in a conversational way. This nagged at the back of his mind. Still, Alant had grown fond of Delmith.

"Greetings, Vanria Delmith." The four Initiate's voices rang together, their answer echoing loud in the normally tranquil garden area.

"Greetings, Prince Aritian." The other's added greeting shocked Alant and he gaped open mouthed at the Elmorian with the ring. Shaith dropped into a curtsy as the two other young men bent over at the waist in unison. Alant regained his composure and bowed a fraction behind the others. He hoped his awkward bow imitated the others well enough to keep him from looking like a country lout.



*Prince!*

The Elmorian with the ring on his hand, the one the other Initiates had called Prince Aritian, cast a cold gaze over the small group of Humans. The pair came to a stop in the small entranceway that led into the hedge-maze. A shiver ran through Alant that had nothing to do with the Tarsith's frostiness. The gray being's face showed no more emotion than any Elmorian's face Alant had seen while on the Isle, yet somehow it radiated…

*What? Distain? Hate?*

*"I still fail to understand why you try so hard with these…"* The Prince let a gasp escape his lips. *"They are not worth the time."*

Bowing his tear-dropped shaped head in deference to the Elmorian at his side, Delmith looked over his students. *"I find Humans to be interesting. Full of emotions, ambitions, desires."* His voice took on an airy cadence. *"They live such short lives and have much to off—"* The Vanria cut his words off as if just realizing to whom he spoke. Turning back to Prince Aritian, who held an obvious look of disgust on his face, Delmith inclined his head once more. *"It is only my curiosity, my Prince, of which I speak."*

*"Mayhaps, be that as it may."* The Prince looked back at Alant's group standing in the green grass, their food baskets forgotten at their feet. Alant thought he saw the beings lips tighten into what he could only describe as a sneer. *"Do not lose sight of why they are here, Delmith. Becoming attached to any of them will cause you nothing except grief."* The two headed toward the entrance to the hedge-maze, yet the Prince never took his eyes from Alant. *"You will need to pick one for the Melding, the Chi'utlan is nearly full. Mayhaps the new one?"* A thin, bony finger pointed at Alant. *"You said he shows promise and I do not like the way he looks at me."*

Quickly, Alant diverted his gaze, catching Delmith's eye as he did. The Vanria had a look that almost seemed mournful painted on it. Seeing this caused Alant to drop his gaze to the ground. *"He has just arrived, my Prince, and has not yet reached his full potential. It would be difficult to explain if anything happened to him so soon after his arrival. Besides, I feel if we wait with this one, he may have the greatest chance for success."*

*"Any skill they have with the Essence is moot! A Mah'Sukai will not be created until the Essence wills it. We simply need to keep attempting to Meld the Humans with it until we succeed. Then we will know it is ready."* The Prince stopped abruptly and turned on the teacher. *"Or would you prefer I sacrifice members of our own race? Mayhaps you are willing to undergo the Melding yourself in their stead? Become the first Elmorr'Antien Mah'Sukai ever in the history of the Plane? Alas, if the Essence is not ready..."*

Taking a step back, Delmith looked on the brink of fleeing. *"No, my Prince. I was suggesting no such course!"* The Vanria looked over his small group of students and did not look happy.

*It is as if he regrets something he has done or is about to do.*

Delmith's gaze came to rest on Quiln. *"Mayhaps the other Ro'Arthian would be a better choice."*

Waving a dismissive hand, the Prince turned and walked into the hedge-maze. *"A whore's son will not be missed should the worst happen, that is why we decided to bring him here. I will leave the details to you and we will attempt the Meld upon my return within the tenday."* The Prince's voice trailed off as the two Elmorians withdrew deeper into the hedge-maze and Delmith's response was too faint for Alant to hear.

"Why do you hold your chest?" Shaith's words gave Alant a start and he cut his eyes at her.

The Tarsith, no longer cold, fell back against Alant's skin when he released it. "Did you hear that?" He made no attempt to keep the fear from his voice.

"The Elmorr'Antiens? Aye." Quiln sat back down on the bench and started eating once more.



Looking at the boy as if he were mad, Alant thought he might never eat again. "Are you not worried? What is the Melding they spoke of?"

Shaith cocked her head to the side. "What do you speak of, Alant?"

Alant stared back at her, puzzled. "The Melding they just spoke of." He waved his arm in the direction the Elmorians had gone. "It sounded like nothing I would want to try! Even Vanria Delmith looked frightened!"

"Have you no heard them speak before in their own tongue?"

"Own tongue? They were speaking in the Human tongue."

She giggled. "Mayhaps you be sick, Alant. Their tongue flows like the script of the finest calligrapher, more akin to music than words. And it do have a way of tickling the mind, yet that be no Human tongue they did speak." Cocking her head again, her jade-green eyes twinkling, she reached out, took his hand and pulled him down onto the grass next to her. "You need to finish your food. Class starts soon and I no want to hear your stomach growling."

Casting a quizzical look over all three of them, he retrieved his food basket from the ground yet did not eat.

*The others, they did not understand. Yet I did!*

Reaching a hand to his chest, he placed his palm over the now warm Tarsith. Sier Sarlimac's words flooded back to him.

*Few have returned from the training unscathed. Some have even perished.*

*What have I been thrust into?*

# Chapter 41

Arderi Cor awoke with a start. A bright glow filled much of the dark sky. The crackling of a massive fire drowned out all other sounds and a sickly-sweet smell penetrated his nostrils. Sitting up in the small tent, he was pleased to note that he felt no pain in his arm. Reaching out a hand, he flexed his fingers and experimentally rotated his shoulder.



*The break is healed! Whatever was in that Oolant drought is amazing!*

Sliding out of the tent, Arderi stood and took in his surroundings. Through the hazy, pain-filled memory of the past day, he realized he was still on the lakeshore. The small fire Master Rillion had started earlier that morn had smoldered out and now lay cold and forgotten. Cresting the small rise, Arderi saw that a large fire took up much of the center area that was once the site of the basecamp. Its flames licked high into the air and burning embers raced over even the tallest trees standing nearby. The silhouette of two men stood some distance off from the fire itself and Arderi recognized the outline of Jintrill next to Clytus. Heading over to them, it shocked him that neither turned at his approach. A sudden understanding of the situation broke over him and, with no wish to break the silence, he quietly joined them in their vigil by the fire.

*This is a funeral pyre. All those men, gone.*

For long moments, the three stood in reverence, watching

the blaze. The wood crackled and popped as it bore the essence of those who had fallen here to the aftermore.

"We must be on our way." Clytus broke from the group and headed toward the lake. "This large a fire shall attract attention that I do not think we can handle."

Looking at the Shaper, Arderi saw that the young man seemed different, older. The grim look now set into the Sier's jaw had not been there before. Noticing Arderi's stare, Jintrill nodded to Arderi, then followed after Clytus. Arderi took another few moments to watch the pyre before he joined them.

Away from the rubble that used to be the basecamp, several packs lay in a pile. Clytus shrugged one over his shoulders as Arderi arrived. "Each of you lads grab a pack. I salvaged what I could while I cleared the dead from the debris. We have enough food to last us at least a moon's span. Now that I know a Drakon is nearby, that should give us enough time."

"Enough time?" The Shaper's voice carried an edge. "Enough time for what?"



Master Rillion looked hard at the Sier for several moments. "Enough time to finish what I came here for."

"You cannot be serious! You intend to continue? Surely, you must see that all is lost! The only choice left to us—"

Grabbing the young Shaper's robe and choking off his words, Clytus lifted him by the neckline. "All is not lost!" Master Rillion's growl came out ferocious, like that of a wild beast. Arderi stepped back, grateful he was not the object of the man's anger. "The only choice left to me is to finish what I came for!" The Commander shoved Jintrill away, causing the Sier to stumble and land hard on his back. "Go if you wish! I never wanted either of you along to begin with!"

Arderi quickly stepped between the two. "Master Rillion, sir. We will not survive out here alone. Neither of us have the skill. Do not blame the Sier for his fear, the Gods know I am afraid as well."

Bowing his head, Clytus ran a hand through his hair. "Nix, I do not blame you, lad." Raising his head, he looked directly into

Arderi's eyes and Arderi saw death within their depths.

*It is not what is out there that I need be frightened of, it is here in front of me.*

"I have paid much, too much. Yet I will pay more if needs be. My son, Sindian, will die unless we succeed here." Pulling out a small pouch, Clytus produced a strange metallic object. "This is a collector. We are here to collect the blood of a Drakon. Within the creature's blood is the Essence needed to cure my son." He wrapped the device and returned it to its pouch. "Only my death will stop me from continuing. Neither of you have to join me, there is food enough in the packs for you both to return home. Yet I will not leave these mountains unless I have what I came for. The choice is yours as to what you will do." Brushing past Arderi, Clytus headed up the slope that led deeper into the jagged peaks of the Nektine.

Arderi watched the man for a moment before turning his attention to the Shaper. Leaning over, he offered a hand to Jintrill and helped him stand. "We will never survive without him. I am not sure the man is still sane, however. I do not mind admitting he scares me as much as being in these Gods forsaken mountains alone." With that, Arderi bent over and picked up one of the packs. Under it sat a sword that he recognized at once.



*Master Gartin's blade!*

Kneeling, Arderi brushed a hand over the worn leather of the scabbard. He stared off in the direction Master Clytus walked and did not think the man had even looked to see if they were following him. Dropping his eyes to the sword once more, thoughts of the grizzled old weapon's master flooded into him.

*This sword has seen so much, I do not feel I would be worthy to hold it if I left the Commander alone out here on his own. Master Gartin surely would not!*

Rising to his full height, he glared at the Shaper. "If it is your intention to head toward home, Sier, you will be doing so alone. I will not abandon Master Rillion." Spinning on a heel,

Arderi started off at a brisk pace up the slope.

"Wait!"

Arderi heard the rustle of a pack and the swish of the Shaper's robes.

"Wait on me, Arderi. I am coming as well."

A grim smile came to him. Arderi did not stop his steps, yet he cut his pace to a walk.

# Chapter 42

Sweat ran in rivulets under Klain's thick fur as he raced over the land. Traveling on all fours, he easily kept pace with the mare galloping next to him. It had taken a long time for the horse to get over its natural fear of the Kithian. Even now, tearing over the open field, the creature stank of fear and would roll the occasional wild, wide-eyed glance in his direction.

His sword, resting in its odd shaped scabbard and belt, slapped against his side with every stride he made. It still humbled him that the Honored One, Sarshia, had bestowed such a gift upon him. 

*The sheath of this sword allows me to run unhindered on hindpaws or on all four with equal ease.*

The sword, made from some type of metal with black veins winding through it, held an edge better than anything he had ever seen.

*It is razor sharp, and I have yet to hone its edge!*

Glancing at Charver, riding high in his mare's saddle, Klain saw the elation of the young boy-cub as he spurned his mount on.

*It excites him to think he can win this race.*

Breaking from the line of fruit trees, Klain slowed his pace just a bit once the buildings in the back of the Vimith villa came into view, allowing the horse a step or two lead. The pair tore onto the dirt road leading to the stables, Klain trailing, and slowed only after passing the edge of the furthest building.

Dust billowed into the air as Charver pulled hard on the reins and the horse's hooves dug into dirt, sliding to a stop. "Ha! I have beaten you!"

Rising onto his hindpaws into a more Human-like stance, Klain jogged to a stop and swiped a paw at the air in front of him. "Aye, Young Master. Yet you have a fresh mount, and I have run all morn. Still, you ride the animal with skill."

Slipping from the saddle, the boy-cub landed lightly upon the ground. "I have had my own horse since I was four."

"Young Master Vimith!" Although Klain knew the voice of the Human who yelled at his charge, he still could not stop his hand from straying to the hilt of his sword. Nor did he soften the glare he gave to the man striding out of the stables toward them. "You will not treat my horses so if you wish to keep riding them."

Taking hold of the reins, Charver walked the animal to the stable master. "I am sorry, Mir'am Rist, I was caught up in the race."

The old stable master hobbled over and snatched the reins from the boy. "Be that as it may, you cannot go forcing a horse to slide to a halt without a good reason! Have you forgotten all the lessons I gave you? What if she broke a leg, or worse, threw you and broke your fool neck." At the sound of the growl, he spun and glared at Klain. "And you keep your fangs to yourself! I have tended this lad since he wore swaddling clothes." Tugging on the reins, Rist led the horse into the stables.



"Race you inside!"

Charver dashed for the back door of the villa. Reaching out, Klain snagged the boy's arm, halting his progress. "I think we have had enough racing for one day. Let us walk for a time."

"Oh, very well." The boy led the way into the patio area. "It is about time for halfmeal. You hungry?"

Smiling down at the boy, Klain wondered which of the two of them ate more. "Aye, Young Master, I could eat."

"Wait for me on the patio and I will have the servants bring us something."

Watching the boy jog off, Klain continued into the shaded sitting area and sat on one of the comfortable chairs arranged around the large stone table. Charver returned, trailed by a serving girl, and before long, both sat munching on trays of food.

Wiping a sleeve across his mouth, Charver took a long drink of water from his mug. "You run really fast. I wish I could run that fast."

"You are not built to cover ground like me, Young Master. It is not your fault for being Human."

"That is true, yet I still would love to be able to outrun a horse!"

Klain's hackles rose when he caught a smell floating on the wind. The scent let him know who was approaching long before he heard the booted steps upon the tiled floor of the patio. "Well, well. I am glad I found you, *beast*."

Jumping up before Klain could react, Charver shot Satner Timms a defiant look. "My father has already told you not to call Master Klain that!"

Grunting, Satner propped a foot on an empty chair. "Oh, aye! Alas, Master Vimith left this morn for Diamond Point. Will not be back for at least a tenday."

Charver looked shocked. "Really! How is it you are still here then?"

Raising a hand, Satner coughed into his fist—not a very convincing cough at that. "I seem to be a little ill. Master Vimith thought it better I stay behind." Turning to Klain, he snapped his fingers as if just remembering something. "Oh, *Master* Klain." Shooting a glance at the boy, Satner rolled his eyes. "Master Vimith left word that he wanted you to go into town with one of my men and pick up a particularly valuable item from the Merchantillian this day. Said it was might important and he wanted his best protecting it."



From the corner of his eye, Klain noticed Charver trying to catch his attention. He chose to ignore the boy-cub. "What is this item?"

"Well," Satner drug out the word and waved a hand in a mock show of disinterest. "It is not for the likes of us to know the details of our Masters, now is it *beast*!" Shooting a look at Charver, he grinned.

Moving his hindpaws with a deliberate slowness, Klain rose to his full height and looked down on Satner. Even though Satner would be considered big for a Human, his head stopped just below Klain's shoulders. "With Master Vimith away, I could not possibly leave young Master Vimith alone."

"Pah." Satner reached over and ruffled the boy's hair. "I will look after the lad. Tis no bother at all."

Reaching up, Charver took hold of the man's hand and pushed it off. Looking back at Klain, he shook his head and mouthed for him not to go.

After a moments pause, Satner pulled his foot from the chair and started to walk away. "Fine by me, beast. Still, it was an order of Master Vimith's that you go."

Looking down to the boy, Klain knew he had no escape. He also knew the boy-cub would be safe here at the villa, no matter what Satner's plan. "When am I supposed to leave?"

Stopping, the bodyguard turned and smiled, wiping a hand across his bald head. "Narn is saddling up his horse as we speak. He will be leaving within a quarter aurn."

"Tell him I will meet him out front."

Nodding, Satner turned and slipped between the plants that kept the patio area well shaded. After he left, Charver reached over and put his small hand on Klain's paw. "Do not go!" His whisper dripped with fear. "I have never heard of father requesting such a thing."



Sitting back down, Klain indicated that the boy do the same. "Neither you nor I know that for certain. If I go, and find that it is a waste of my time, I will see that Satner regrets the ruse."

"Please, Master Klain, you do not know these men as I!" The boy bowed his head and stared into his lap. "I have told you how sorry I am for helping them gang up on you your first day." Looking back up, Klain saw tears in his eyes. "You are more than a guard to me. You are my friend."

"Each of us has duties. If I have learned anything during my time with you Humans, it is that. Your father, Master Vimith, has been more than kind to me over the past tendays. I will not dishonor him by neglecting his request." Raising a paw, he stopped Charver's interruption. "Even if I think it is not a real request." Standing, he adjusted his sword belt. "You will be fine while I am away. Of that, I am certain. What happens to me is of no concern."

"Yet, if this is a trap?"

Raising his upper lip, Klain exposed his front fangs. "If it is, I will deal with it."

# Chapter 43

A piercing screech cut through the air and sent a shiver slicing through Arderi Cor. The high-pitched sound ricocheted off the cliff wall that rose on their right to disappear into the clouds above. The screech sounded much closer than before. Arderi felt the tension in the young Shaper, Jintrill Deln, who stood next to him holding Master Rillion's sword, Dorochi, in a tight grip. His head swiveled about as he tried to catch a glimpse of the creature they pursued.

*Or that pursues us.*

They had ascended the side of the mountain for nearly the entire day, following narrow goat paths where they could—climbing where they could not. Even though they had climbed for aurns, and Arderi was certain they walked higher than any man had the right to be, the top of the rocky peak was lost from his view overhead. Master Rillion was a man obsessed. Since they had abandoned the destroyed basecamp three eves prior, he had not paused in his hunt of the Drakon. He did not force Arderi nor Sier Deln to follow, yet what choice did they have?

*We would not survive out here on our own, that is for certain.*

Arderi and Jintrill stood in a small, thin copse of pine trees that had somehow found root on the rocky ledge. Both of the young men leaned heavily upon a tree, gasping for breath that evaded them for some reason. Arderi looked at Clytus who had stepped onto a small outcrop some ten paces away to survey the open sky and valley below.

Before he had stepped away, stating in a gruff voice for the two of them to remain within the trees, he had unbuckled Dorochi from his waist and thrust the sword, scabbard and all, into the Sier's hands. "Take this. You may have need of it."

Now the late dusk light glinted off his tarnished breastplate. He cast a striking image standing on the edge of the cliff. Beyond his silhouette, spackled here and there by a few thinly stretched clouds, a vast expanse of blue nothingness extended. He scanned the skyline, holding a crossbow with a poison tipped bolt at his hip. A bolt the Commander claimed would kill a Drakon with a single shot. Arderi knew that once Master Rillion acquired his target, it would take only a heartbeat for him to raise the weapon, take aim, and fire.

*If I have such faith in him then why is this fear in me so deep?*

Another shrill scream ricocheted off the peaks. Sounding mere paces away, it echoed off the rocks behind Clytus and Arderi flinched. Clenching his fists tight, Arderi focused on Clytus trying in vein to reign in his anxiety. He could not help except admire the Commander's confidence standing upon the rock. Strong, fast, skilled. Arderi hoped he would one day be that type of man. A crackle of stone on stone and Arderi moved his attention to the cliff face behind Master Rillion. The man must have heard the same for he spun and raised his crossbow at the same instant. Small stones and loose dirt slid down the face of the cliff not five paces behind Clytus, yet nothing was there. Staring at it for a moment longer, crossbow held against his shoulder at the ready, Clytus returned his attention back to the open sky. Still, Arderi could not take his eyes from the area where dirt and loose stones still slid down to pool at the base of the outcropping next to the Commander. Something odd held his attention.

*What are you doing, you foolish boy! Stop being a scared little tit hiding in the trees and staring at the dirt. Pay attention!*

Yet even with the self-scolding, Arderi could not move his eyes from the side of the cliff. His throat tightened and he sucked in a sharp breath.

*There* is *something there!*

A shimmering—the wisp of an outline, nothing more—yet he knew. He began to cry out a warning even as the form took shape within his gaze. The beast was massive, at least the size of a horse, if not bigger. Its bat-like wings nearly twice that in width. He could make out the entire Drakon now—whatever force had concealed it having dissipated completely. It clung to the side of the rock just a few paces behind Clytus' shoulder. Blackish-brown in color, its body built like that of a large, hairless cat. Lean muscles rippled beneath its leathery skin. Its hind legs, strong and powerful, obviously made for jumping, sat bunched in a tight curl, wound taut in anticipation of a leap. Its forelegs ended in hand-like paws that sprouted long, razor-sharp claws, which now dug into the rock face of the cliff, holding it steady. Its broad flat head, resembling the head of a shovel, hovered motionless as it stared focused on Clytus. Small, spiny bits of bone jutted out in two distinct lines starting on either side of its nostrils and extending up its head past its ears, which lay flat against its long, thin neck that snaked out at least a pace from its body like the branch of a tree. Its maw gaped open exposing rows of fangs and teeth. Yet, its eyes were what held Arderi—deep, black slits of fluid hate.

The creature's long tail slithered up the cliff face and the muscles in its hind legs rippled as it prepared to launch itself toward its target. Unwinding from its coiled perch against the cliff, it sprang forward releasing another ear-splitting wail. Its wings pumped one powerful stroke as it jumped, sending it racing at Clytus in a blur of black.

# Chapter 44

Hearing Arderi cry out, Clytus Rillion spun around. He watched as a shimmering pool of light coalesced, forming a Drakon perched on the cliff face behind him.

*This is how the creature has evaded me for so long! Somehow, it can bend light.*



Raising his crossbow, he reached for the Essence surrounding him and the familiar veil fell over him like a silken blanket. He stretched out his mind and began to bind the Strands of Essence around the beast even as it launched itself at him. Instantly, he knew something was wrong. The Essence Strands he tried to Meld stiffened, then were yanked away from his control. He felt the presence of Arderi, and knew the boy was caught up in the Melding…

*Yet it is nothing he is doing. There is another presence Melding the Essence as well!*

Fear laced into Clytus' thoughts and he looked closer at the Drakon. Alert eyes stared back at him and he understood. The beast was caught in the Melding as well. It reached out with its own Melding, thwarting Clytus' attempts to gain the upper hand.

*This creature is of the Sujen! That is why the Shapers need its blood to heal my son!*

# Chapter 45

A strange tingle congealed around Arderi Cor—one he had felt before. One of reality slowing. Stopping. A feeling of the bonds that held his mind to his body snapping free to wander in the corporeal realm. Arderi could not remember when he started, yet he knew he was yelling. His scream sounded low and distant, as if it came from the other side of a field.



Clytus slowly spun and stepped to one side. Raising his crossbow in line with the advancing creature, he looked like a man stuck in a thick pool of clear honey. The Drakon hung suspended in mid air as well, in a pose as graceful as that of a dancer, a mere pace from him. Arderi could have been looking at a painting—all stood still. Even the wind brushing through the trees seemed frozen.

Looking sideways, Arderi saw Jintrill—terror plastered across the young Sier's face. He stood frozen like the rest, a living statue. The Shaper's eyes remained locked onto the scene before him, yet Arderi could see no hint of life within them.

Something in the back of his mind nagged at him. Then memory struck like a gong.

*The Drakon's eyes!*

Turning his mind back to the creature, horror filled him as he stared into black eyes that focused on him. Large black eyes, vivid and clear…

*And alive! As are Master Rillion's.*

For the first time, Arderi saw the creature advance through the air. Its speed matched Master Rillion's own movement.

*Unlike the eve of the O'Arkin attack, the Commander has no advantage this time!*

# Chapter 46

*One shot.*

That was all Clytus Rillion had the opportunity to think before instinct took over and he released his hold on the Essence. Launching himself from the path of death, Clytus would worry about how the creature could Meld the Essence another time. The fight is all he cared for now, and it needed his full attention.



*Win, or die. I will pay what needs be paid!*

He felt the wind from the beast whip past him, saw—too late to make an adjustment—its claw whip out and rake his shoulder. Pain wrenched through him as razor sharp talons tore his armor to rip open his flesh below. Yet this was nothing compared to the impact of the creature's tail. Slamming square into his chest, the air whooshed from his lungs as his steel breastplate caved. The force of the blow lifted him from his feet and sent him sailing through empty air.

# Chapter 47

Arderi Cor saw a distinct look of fear pass over Clytus' face and he realized the man knew something was not right as well.

Reality slammed forward once more. Clytus dove to the side as the Drakon bore past him. It howled with rage at the failure of its surprise attack. Yet, even while it streaked through the spot where Clytus had just stood, it whipped out one front claw and caught him in the left shoulder. Blood sprayed from the wound, splattering the ground. Within the same movement, the creature whipped its thick tail around its body and smacked Clytus hard in the chest.



Arderi watched stunned as the force of the blow launched Clytus from his feet, smashing him to the ground. Commander Rillion slid across the narrow path toward the cliff's edge. If he did not stop, the drop would end his life as surely as if the beast had ripped into him with its fangs. Clytus' limp body stopped just short of the edge, yet his crossbow was not so lucky. It skated over the side of the cliff, taking with it a few loose stones and dirt.

# Chapter 48

Agony racked Clytus Rillion anew as he crashed into the ground with more force than a battering ram smashing into a keep's wall. He knew he was going to be launched over the cliff's edge from the hard impact. For some reason he did not. He found himself out of breath, his sight dimmed and filled with specks of light, and amazed that he still lay on solid ground.



Kicking himself into action, he rolled onto his back and struggled to rise to his feet—only his body would not comply. His chest, compressed by his smashed breastplate, sent a cough racking through his body. A spray of blood spewed from his lips—thick drops of gore mixed with a fine mist. Hundreds of dagger-like pains stabbing him all at once. Several of his ribs felt broken and a mangle of bone jutted out of his flesh from under the massive dent that covered the entire width of his ruined breastplate.

The sun felt hot on his face. The wind cool over his skin. He stared up into the clear blue sky and gazed into its clarity. The pain in him withdrew. When a shadow slipped across his body, he saw the beauty of the Drakon for the first time. How the majestic beast soared over the cliff face, caught an updraft of wind—its thin, membrane-like wings filling and stretching—it danced with the clouds in a graceful loop. Hovering at the pinnacle of Clytus' vision for a moment, the creature looked like a wondrously designed kite, hovering at the end of a child's string.

It crashed down upon him like an avalanche.

White-hot pain slashed through his left shoulder as claws ripped into his mail hauberk and sank deep into his flesh. He heard himself scream and his eyes drew of their own accord to his mangled shoulder. Hot breath rippled over his face. The stench of death a week old penetrated his senses. Agony filled him as he turned his head to face his killer. The Drakon stared down at him. He forced himself to gaze deep into its black liquid eyes.

There, in its eyes, he saw...nothing.

No anger, nor pity. No remorse, nor hatred. It was just a beast, and he knew he was nothing more than prey to it. Its nostrils flared out as it looked down at him, tasting him by smell. He watched its lips slowly retreat, exposing endless rows of yellowish teeth. It swiftly raised its head and then snapped it forward, mouth fully extended for the final killing bite. Instinctively, Clytus brought his right arm up to cover his face. The arm took the full brunt of the blow. He screamed again as the fangs crushed down, snapping bone as if it were straw. He felt his body rise up—held down only by the beast's great weight upon his chest. All at once, the flesh and tendons of his arm ripped away, leaving only a mangled stump were his arm had just been. Oddly, he felt no great amount of pain. It was as if he watched the events happen to another. The blood spewed from the stump below his shoulder, splashing across his chest and face. Even more poured from his body, spilling his life onto the ground.

# Chapter 49

Arderi Cor stood motionless. His breath caught in his throat as Clytus came to a stop just short of the cliff's edge. He exhaled only after the Commander rolled over.

*Aye! He lives! Get up! Why does he not get up?*

Yet Clytus simply lay there as the Drakon flew out over the cliff, making a tight circle high in the air. Swooping back around, the cat-like creature smashed down onto Clytus causing the man to release a scream that bit deep into Arderi's core.



The beast squatted atop Clytus for what seemed like an eternity.

Something grabbed Arderi by the arm and shook him. "We have to run!" Fear plastered the young Shaper's face. "We will be next!" Jintrill pulled Arderi, yet he shook free of the Sier's grasp and did not follow as Jintrill took a step deeper into the thin copse of trees they stood in.

Arderi looked after him backing away and almost laughed. Jintrill's white face—void of any blood—would have been comical in another place, another instance. Looking down, Arderi noticed the sword Jintrill still clutched in his hands, knuckles as white as his face.

*Clytus' sword. Dorochi.*

Grasping the hilt, Arderi pushed Jintrill away as he drew it from its sheath. Stumbling back, barely keeping his feet, the Sier slammed into the tree behind him. "What are you doing?!

You cannot kill that thing!"

Breaking from the cover of the tree line, Arderi burst from their hiding place and screamed as he raced at the Drakon, Clytus' sword raised high, point down. He did not falter in his stride when the beast ripped off Clytus' arm like a dog ripping meat from a discarded bone. He did not pause when blood, Clytus' blood, spewed forth like a fountain to strike Arderi across his face. He did not hesitate as he ran at the Drakon, sword held in both hands above his head like a spear, and stabbed down with all his strength. He drove the point of Dorochi into the creatures shoulder.

The sword struck bone, slid to the side, and twisted from his grasp.

Arderi's vision went black.

# Chapter 50

Clytus Rillion felt the pain seep from his body along with his life's blood. He saw the boy slam into the Drakon, saw his sword flash in the sunlight. He had always loved how his sword shone in bright light. The beast's neck lashed around, its shovel shaped head crashing into the boy with a punishing blow. Arderi sailed several paces to smash into the side of the rocky cliff face. His limp body slipped to the ground, landing in a heap. 

Clytus saw all this...yet felt nothing. No pain, no fear. Not even concern for the boy. He floated on the edge of consciousness.

*You are dying you old fool. And you are going to let them die as well.*

He pulled the hurt back into his mind. Forced the pain to seize him once more.

*I will not bow out! I will not!*

He focused on the pain. That was easy. When the Drakon spun to face his new attacker, it had ground him hard into the rocky outcrop with its claws, ripping open more of Clytus' chest, and releasing a torrent of new agony. The blackness threatened to take hold once more, and he saw nothing for a moment.

*The pain...live the pain!*

The Drakon still stood on top of Clytus. Waiting. Studying Arderi. As it had done before it had attacked him.

*Calculating its risk.*

Forcing his body to obey, he moved his remaining arm. Pain

sliced through him as if someone had shoved a red-hot iron into his chest.

*Yes, live in the pain!*

Running his hand down his leg, he felt the feathered tips of the bolts resting in the quiver strapped to his hip. He drew out a bolt and clutched it in his fist. Again, the blackness reared its head. The pain, the loss of blood—all of it stole his strength and he felt his hand slacken.

*I will pay what needs be paid!*

The bolt slipped from his fingers.

# Chapter 51

Light seeped into the slits of Arderi Cor's eyelids as he struggled to regain his footing, leaning hard against the rocky face of the cliff. All the breath had left him and he gasped for air. He could not believe the thing had hit him so hard with just its head.

The Drakon had snaked its long neck around and it now studied him. Watching. Waiting. For what, he had no clue. Glancing down at Clytus laying below the beast, his heart sank. The man was dead. Arderi saw that now.

*And I will soon join him.*

The adrenaline that had only moments ago flowed through his veins abandoned him, and his body shook with the realization of what he now faced.

Clytus' sword still stuck out from the shoulder of the creature. The Drakon reached up with its hindleg—like a dog scratching an itch—and flicked the blade from its resting place in its hide.

Still gasping for breath, Arderi fumbled with the hilt of his own sword.

The beast crouched, preparing to leap, and then rose as if changing its mind. It let out its screech again and took a step toward him. Its maw opening and closing like a many-teethed vise. It took another half step. Black foam filled its mouth and started to leak from its lips.

*Its salivating! I am going to be eaten alive!*

Arderi raised his blade in a semblance of the stance he had learned from Master Gartin. The blade shook violently and Arderi realized he could not move, much less fight. The Drakon took one step, swallowing the gap between them. The black saliva covered the Drakon's entire maw and hung down in a frothy beard that dripped to the ground. Bits of it flicked into Arderi's face as the thing let out a long, raspy breath. The stench made Arderi's eyes water. Black eyes held him. Arderi watched as tiny slits of white appeared at the bottom of each eye—like twin slivers of the moon. The slits grew in size and he realized that the Drakon's eyes were rolling in their sockets. It let out a racked, wheezing screech that covered Arderi with more of the black foam that was now flowing freely from the beast's mouth. As if some Gods hand reached out and cut the strings holding the Drakon up, the creature dropped to the ground, crashing at Arderi's feet with a meaty thump.



Pressing against the rocks behind him, Arderi skirted around the creature and stepped to the middle of the ledge. A feathery bolt protruded out from under the Drakon's right foreleg.

A weak, racking cough pulled his attention to Clytus' body. Limping over to the Commander, Arderi knelt down and placed his hand on the concaved breastplate.

Clytus' eyes fluttered open and a weak smile graced his lips. "I see…you yet live. That…is good."

"Do not try to speak, Master Rillion." Raising his head, Arderi looked back to the tree line. "Sier! Please come! Master Rillion needs help!"

The Shaper emerged from the shadows, took a tentative step, then cast a worried glance at the Drakon. Hurrying over to join Arderi at Clytus' side, Jintrill immediately closed his eyes and placed his hands upon Master Rillion's chest.

"Stop you young fool." The command was no more than a mere whisper soaked in blood, yet the Shaper ceased his ministrations.

"What are you doing?" Arderi could not keep the fear nor

anger from his voice. "Heal him! You must, you are a Shaper!"

Shaking his head, Jintrill averted his gaze from Arderi. "He is correct. His injuries are too extensive. He will be dead long before I could begin to Meld the Essence that would save his life."

A shuttered breath racked Clytus. "Leave us, Shaper."

Tears flowed freely down Arderi's cheeks. "There must be something you can do."

Jintrill stood and placed a hand upon Arderi's shoulder. "I am sorry."

With blurry vision, Arderi watched helpless as the young Shaper wandered over to where the Drakon had kicked Clytus' sword.

"Boy." Clytus' words were weak. "A drink of water." Arderi pulled his waterskin from his side, cradled the man's head in his lap, and dripped water into Clytus' waiting mouth. Most of it ran down the side of his cheek, washing away some of the blood. The Commander nodded, a look of genuine gratitude upon his face. "You must...not let...my quest die here...My son…must not…" His eyelids slid closed and his head lolled for a moment. He seemed to be waging some type of internal war. "In my pouch...with the coin...you will find a Silrith'tar... Give it my wife..." A surge of strength ran through Clytus and he reached up with his remaining arm and grabbed Arderi's shoulder pulling them closer together, his eyes wide, a look of determination on his face. "Swear you will finish what I have started! Swear to me you will not let my Sindian die!"



Under Clytus' grip, pain laced through Arderi's shoulder, yet he did not try to remove it. "I swear, if there is still breath in my body, I will return to Mocley and finish what you have started. I vow it shall be done."

A weak smile touched Clytus' lips and his head bobbled as his eyes closed. "Good."

"Master Rillion…" Fear raced to overpower the sense of loss inside Arderi. How would he survive to fulfill his vow if this man died?

At his words, Clytus jerked like a man who had almost fallen asleep and his eyes fluttered back open. "Take my coin purse. There is enough there...to see you to Mocley…" A weak cough came from him. Flopping his head to the side, he eyed the Shaper. "Dorochi...my sword… Take that as well… Ragnor, you must see Ragnor…"

The grip on Arderi's shoulder slackened and Clytus' hand slipped off onto the hard stone ground. The Commander's neck went limp, and Arderi heard the last of the man's breath leave his body.

# Chapter 52

The days rolled away and Alant Cor's unease continued to grow. His fellow students acted as if nothing was amiss. Even when he attempted to broach the subject of what he had overheard, they denied his story. Yet he could not get past what the Elmorian, Prince Aritian, said that afternoon in the gardens.

*What did he mean by the Chi'utlan being nearly full? Chi, in the Old tongue means 'of the Essence.' Yet combined with 'utlan—meaning pool or pond—the combination makes no sense. A pool of Essence? Essence is* in *things. How can there be a pool of something that is not tangible?* 

*And how can Melding with this Chi'utlan create a Mah'Sukai? Whatever a Mah'Sukai is. I have not been able to locate a meaning for either word in any book on the Old tongue I brought with me from Mocley.*

He tried once to ask about it. A few days after the meeting in the garden, Alant had approached his instructor, Vanria Delmith, and asked after the meaning of Mah'Sukai. He had never seen a reaction so severe from an Elmorian. The Vanria snatched him by the elbow, and a bone-biting cold bore into Alant's flesh at the Elmorian's touch. The strength in that thin gray arm surprised Alant as much as the cold—he still had a yellowish bruise where the three-fingered hand had gripped him. The Vanria practically dragged him into an empty room, demanding to know where he had heard the word. The Tarsith around Alant's neck had gone frigid several times during that little episode. Each time it went cold, Alant gained a look of frustration from Vanria Delmith.

Yet Alant had made a concerted effort not to grasp the pendant under his robes and he did not think the Elmorian knew of the Tarsith. Delmith finally let Alant leave once Alant admitted to the instructor that he had found the word in a small passage of an old book back at the Chandril'elian of Mocley. Even though the Elmorian let Alant go, he did not seem convinced.

*Since that day, Vanria Delmith has been distant in class.*

"As you feel you can stare out the window, Alant, please come here and show me how this is done, yes?" Vanria Delmith's tone shook Alant from his thoughts.

Glancing around the room, Alant realized with a start that he had no clue what the class had been discussing. "I am...uh..." The unblinking stare of the deep black eyes of the Elmorian broke no argument. Reluctantly, Alant stood and made his way to the front of the small room the Humans used for all their lessons. Bare of furniture except for the essentials—four ladder-backed chairs for him and his fellow students, and a large plush leather seat for Vanria Delmith, a wooden table sitting to the side. Glancing over to Shaith with a pleading look, his heart sank at the quirky grin that sprang to her dark-skinned face.



*She knows! She knows I have no clue what they were discussing and she will do nothing to help me.*

Not that he knew of any way in which the girl could help him now.

At his hesitation, Vanria Delmith waved a hand indicating for Alant to stand next to his chair. The instructor, tall even for an Elmorian, looked Alant straight in the eyes even though he sat and Alant stood. Approaching his teacher with trepidation, Alant bowed his head in proper form. He had learned much in his short stay. "As you say, Vanria Delmith." Shoulders slumping, Alant took the spot indicated and turned to stare back at the others.

"You may begin, Alant, yes?" Vanria Delmith's voice carried a knowing, accusing tone that added to Alant's anxiety.

He had paid attention at the beginning of the class—Alant pushed himself harder than his instructor did, if not so mercilessly. They started this lesson on changing the temperature of items. More specifically, the creation of cold food storage boxes. Except, once Quiln had asked one of his annoyingly redundant questions, forcing Vanria Delmith to go over items that the orphan should know by heart, Alant had tuned them out and let his mind wander. The small iron box they were using as a practice tool still rested on the small table beside the Elmorian. Alant did not think he had blanked out long enough for the class to have changed topics.

*And the little box* is *still there!*

Focusing his mind, the Sight of the Essence slipped upon him like a second skin. The Spectals he saw fell into place and the room took shape around him with a quickness he could never have achieved before coming to train under the Elmorr'Antiens.

*Less than two moons ago, simply gaining the Sight of the Essence would have taken me several moments! Now it comes almost naturally. I have learned so much in such a short period.*

Probing out with his mind toward the small, egg-sized iron box, Alant reached into the iron itself. Collectively gathering the Spectals that represented the temperature of the metal on the inside surfaces, he focused the pattern of what they should look like with an altered state of temperature. Concentrating on the Spectals that formed the inside walls of the box, he began his manipulations. The Spectals flashed into the pattern he willed them to be, then back to their original structure. He then flashed the configuration back and forth several more times before he decided on a final configuration.



*Aye, tis correct.*

Beginning the slow, meticulous process of Melding the Spectals to their final pattern, reality seemed to slow.

*There is no reality for a Shaper who is Melding the Essence. Only the Meld itself.*

Alant knew he would be working on the box for at least half an aurn. It was not his goal to create a full-fledged coldbox—even one the size of this small box would have taken him most, if not all the day. He merely needed to lower the box's internal temperature some. It was a simple enough task, one he had done on many occasions during the long periods of study the Elmorians gave him.

Letting his mind wander, he continued with the monotonous task, and found himself once again musing over the fact that only one Elmorian, Vanria Delmith, ever taught the Human students.

The school housed a half dozen or more teachers.

*And Vanria Delmith spends short enough periods with us Humans as it is, even if it is well spent. Still, I cannot complain. I am far superior now with the Essence.*

Only a handful of Elmorian students were in residence as well. No more than half a score, and these seemed very young to Alant.

*Vanria Delmith refers to them as younglings. Each as young as little Rik, and he has not even seen his sixth winter yet!*

Thoughts of his youngest sibling brought on a pang of homesickness that threatened to break his concentration. Pushing the image away, Alant held onto the Sight of the Essence firmly until he was sure he was secure in it, then continued his manipulation of the tiny box.

*Quiln is the only one who should not be here. He fails at most every task.*

Alant knew it was wrong to think this. Quiln had grown up one of the unwanted children on the streets of Orlis, forced to scrounge for every meal. Still—



"It is beyond me, Delmith, why you try so hard with these Humans!"

A piercing coldness laced through Alant's chest as the Elmorian words washed over him. Letting out a gasp at the unexpectedness of it, the Sight of the Essence slipped from him like water through a sieve. The room flooded back, its lines and angles muted compared to seeing it with the Sight of the Essence. As it left, he saw the Spectals of the box snap back to the state they were in prior to him beginning his Meld of it—all work he had done, lost.

His normal sight returned—the room seemed dull and colorless. Alant looked over his shoulder at Prince Aritian and his heart jumped to lodge itself in his throat.

Though the Elmorian Prince's face changed little from his weird, blank visage, Alant thought the Prince looked disgusted.

"My Prince!"

Vanria Delmith had obviously just risen to his feet and chairs scraped across the floor as the other Human students sprang to their feet as well, hands to their sides, waiting to be addressed as was the Elmorr'Antien custom.

At a slight nod from the Prince, Alant joined the other students in their greetings and their curtsy and bows. Alant still felt the Prince wore a look of contempt as he cast his eyes over the Humans. *"They are such a pathetic race. Might as well call them Ju'nar! The boy has been here near two turns of the moon and still has not learned how to hold the Sight."*

Stretching out a long, thin finger, Vanria Delmith pointed to Alant. *"This one here promises to be the strongest Human I have yet met."*

A sneer crossed Prince Aritian's lips. *"As may be. He still lost the Sight in the middle of his Meld. A youngling could do better! And he still seems to have no manners—eyeing me so."*

Delmith cut his large, black eyes to Alant. *"Yes. I have noticed that he reacts strangely whenever he hears our tongue. It is...curious."*

With his heart still in his throat, Alant dropped his gaze to the floor. He fought the urge to reach up and take hold of the Tarsith, and almost sighed with relief when his instructor continued. 

*"I had not expected you for a few more days at least, my Prince."* It was plain that Delmith was just as uncomfortable at being taken by surprise as the rest.

*"It is time, Delmith, the Chi'utlan is full to the brim."* The Prince had a look of urgency and kept his gaze long upon Alant. *"If you think this Alant creature so strong, I think we should use him next."*

*Use me next? Use me for what?*

*"I would like to instruct the boy a little longer, if it pleases my Prince."*

*"Instruct him longer?"* Prince Aritian's voice sounded strained. *"It sounds as if you are becoming attached to these creatures, Delmith."*

*"I will admit I find their race curious, yet do not accuse me of becoming attached, my Prince, you know whom I serve!"* Alant thought that an Elmorian could not rise to anger, yet Vanria Delmith's voice was as close as he had ever heard. *"Alas, I would request we not use the Alant boy. He is progressing nicely with each passing day."*

*"Why does this matter?"* Prince Aritian paced across Alant's

field of vision as he continued to stare at the floor. *"Why would you request this?"*

*"I feel the longer the Humans are allowed to progress in the Essence, the more chance they will have to survive the Melding with the Chi'utlan."*

*Survive the Chi'utlan? I still do not know what that is. Mayhaps this Chi'utlan is what gives the Elmorr'Antiens their power beyond those of the Human Shapers. Are they trying to increase our strength? I find this unlikely, considering their distain for us.*

*"Fine then! I will use the Quiln creature. He has no family to miss him , should things go badly."*

Vanria Delmith's head twitched as if he wanted to look over at Quiln. Instead, he bowed. *"As you say, my Prince, it shall be done."* Vanria Delmith sounded as if he would argue, yet did not. *"Never has the Chi'utlan replenished itself so quickly. Are you anticipating success?"*

As the Elmorians continued to talk, the iciness from the Tarsith subsided. It remained cold, just not painfully so.

*"I have known success was on the horizon my entire life."* Prince Aritian crossed the small classroom and stared out into the gardens through the only small window in the room. *"As a youngling, when I learned of the Chi'utlan in the caverns below the great Chandril'chi tree, I knew there was a reason. Even so young, I knew I was linked to it."* His voice took on a far away tone. *"I could feel the pull of it, as if the Essence itself tied me to it. You have read the stories, Delmith. You leaned as I did—as all younglings must—of the last Cycle! You have read the chronicles of the coming of the Age of Power, the Age of Conquest."*

Turning, Prince Aritian's eyes bore into Delmith's as he walked back to where the Vanria stood, reciting as if he were reading from a book. *"'And yet, as we Elmorr'Antiens retreated to the safety of our homeland, the races of Talic'Nauth ravaged the Plane of Talic'Nauth. Nations unto nations, led by those who could wield the Essence directly—the Mah'Sukai—to destroy cities with none other than thought. The mighty Mah'Sukai who no longer have to Meld the Essence—they bind the Essence to their will!'"*

Drawing in a deep breath, the Prince waved a hand of dismissal through the air. *"Yet it never spoke of how these Mah'Sukai came upon their power. That was most frustrating to me.*

*No matter what tombs I read, no matter who I questioned, not one of our race knew how or why the Mah'Sukai got their power—just that in each Cycle they did."*

*"I still remember the elation when my father sat me down, told me the truth of the Chi'utlan. The fervor in his voice that it 'must be kept safe!' Kept secret at all cost! That only our rulers and a few choice among the Circle know the truth."* The Elmorian's mouth twisted into a grimace. *"Yet our Chi'utlan is not the only one on Talic'Nauth. The old books say there are others. Lost now to us, yet still out there! They wait to be found—and the other races will find them! They have done so in each Cycle throughout history past. They will wield the power of the Essence once again. Become Mah'Sukai! Raining death and destruction down upon this Plane!"*

The Elmorian Prince now paced the classroom at a rapid clip, gesturing with his hands to emphasize his points. *"How can my father and the rest of the Circle be so blind? If we know how to seize that power for ourselves, why not do so?"* The Prince's gaze swept the room. *"Elmorr'Antiens are the supreme race upon this Plane! All others are like insects! Not even worthy of our notice. I will not wait for these... Humans "*—He twisted the word like a curse—*"to wield the full power of the Essence once more! I will not do nothing as my ancestors did. Let the rabble of Talic'Nauth sweep across the Plane and destroy everything around them. What if this time they do not leave our homeland alone as they have in past Cycles? I will not allow that to happen to my people! I will NOT!"*



Never had Alant seen an Elmorian so animated. The zeal in the Prince's voice sent a shiver down Alant's spine. Glancing around the small room, he saw that the other Humans stood looking at the two Elmorians as if nothing they said had any impact on their lives.

Visibly relaxing himself, the Prince walked to the door, placing a three-fingered hand upon the frame. He did not turn his head when he spoke. *"The time is close, Delmith. As soon as the Essence wills it, I will become the first of our kind to Meld with the Chi'utlan and wield the full power of the Essence as a Mah'Sukai. An Elmorr'Antien Mah'Sukai! Then our King and his precious Circle will see we no longer need to hide from the other races during the Age of Power. We can reach out our hands and insure peace—stability—for all. Have the whore's son ready this eve."*

Vanria Delmith stared at the door long after the Prince had departed. When he turned, he noticed that Alant still stood by his side and flinched. "You may return to your seat now, Alant, yes?"

The cold of the Tarsith left with the Prince. Before he realized it, Alant opened his mouth to speak. At the questioning look from Vanria Delmith, he shut it with a click of his teeth.

*Stupid boy! Hold you tongue. You heard nothing! Not that I understand half of what I did hear.*

Without thinking, Alant glanced at Quiln who stood with the others.

*What is it they mean to use you for?*

Realizing he had not moved as he had been instructed to, Alant looked back at Vanria Delmith. Bowing to cover the shocked look upon his face, he hurried to his seat.

Vanria Delmith continued with the class, yet he never lost the questioning look he kept for Alant.



*He knows something, yet how much is the question.*

# Chapter 53

"He is dead. As we shall be if we do not leave now." Jintrill Deln's voice came in a soft whisper, yet Arderi Cor heard fear imbedded within.

"Nix! We will bury him."

"That is madness! We must leave! Anything could have heard—"

Bolting to his feet, Arderi rounded on the Shaper. "NO! We will not leave until this man is buried and I have what we came for!"



Jintrill took a step back at the fury of Arderi's words. Looking down, Arderi noticed that the Shaper had retrieved Clytus' sword. Reaching out, he snatched if from the young Sier's hands. He pointed past Jintrill to the tree line the two had hid in. "In the pack I carried for Master Rillion you will find the collector. If you wish to help, use it on the Drakon. I am unsure of how it works. Yet, as a Shaper, you should be able to figure it out better than I. I will tend to Master Rillion."

Arderi knelt back next to the body and cradled Clytus' head in his hands. Hot tears streamed down his cheeks. Never had he felt so alone, so lost. How could this man have opened his eyes to a reality that Arderi could not even dream about, dangle it in front of him like food before a starving man, and then rip it all away? He had so many questions, so much he wanted to learn.

*It is not fair!*

He had no idea how long he stayed there. He was aware

of Sier Deln working, yet only at the fringes of his attention. When a hand squeezed him on the shoulder, he ignored it.

"We must leave! What if that creature had a mate?" Jintrill's voice, still laced with fear, shook as he spoke.

*What does he know of fear? He is a Shaper! He has a life. Respect, honor. What do I have except broken dreams?*

"We have to go. Now! I have the creature's blood in the device." Jintrill jerked him to his feet.

Flinging up an arm, Arderi shrugged him off and shoved him away. He stalked to the cliff's edge, crossed his arms, and stared across the snow-painted peaks that cut the azure horizon. The Shaper's shuffling feet slid on the loose stones behind him. The crackle of falling stone sounded faint in the distance. A chill in the air enveloped him. The stench of the Drakon's black blood still clung to his clothes, permeating his sense of smell. A thin trail of clouds, more like a bony tail, cut across the sky.

*Everything moves on. What is the point in trying to succeed in anything?*



Master Clytus' words echoed in his head and for the first time he understood how small he truly was. How momentous every action in life could be. He turned and looked down on the body of the man he had known for the briefest span of his life. The man he had grown to admire. As he did, shame rose in him and he hated himself.

*Here I stand, feeling sorry for myself, and this man died to save others. To save me, save his son…*

"I vow it shall be done." Arderi directed his harsh whisper at the entire Plane. "I vow it shall be done." A feeling of resolve washed over him. "I vow it shall be done!" His scream echoed off the far peaks, rebounding back in staggered waves—echoed off the vast canyon, repeating his assertion in the distance, as if the Nektine itself were adding its voice to his. He looked over at Jintrill who stood gaping at him. "You are correct, Sier. We must go. Help me attend him and his passage to the aftermore. We have a long journey ahead of us."

It took everything the two young men had left to withdraw

Clytus' limp form from under the great weight of the dead Drakon. Once free of his killer, Arderi bent and cleaned the dead man's face the best he could. They placed his body in a small, natural gully and set about collecting rocks. When they had piled the stones a little over a pace high, and Arderi felt certain that scavengers could not disturb the grave, they stepped back and surveyed their work.

An awkward silence fell. Arderi had little experience with death and his thoughts raced back to Ralin's funeral.

*Has it really been just a few moons since then?*

The two young men stood over the tomb they had constructed for the better part of a quarter aurn. Finally, Arderi bent down and scooped up the items Clytus had entrusted to him. Rising, he belted Master Rillion's sword to his waist then held out Master Gartin's to the Sier. Jintrill stood with his lips pursed tightly together until Arderi nodded once, then the young Shaper took the sword and belted it on. Without passing any words between them, they turned and headed down the thin goat trail and the direction of the old basecamp.



Darkness covered the land long before the two reached the valley floor. Uncomfortable with their surroundings, coupled with the fact that neither knew how to make a fire, they decided to continue through the darkness and try to find the abandoned camp in the hopes of replenishing their supplies. The thought of walking out of a dangerous and horrifying place like the Nektine left Arderi's mouth dry with fear, yet the thought of attempting the feat without enough provisions sounded down right suicidal.

*If we can find the camp, we can restock enough food for the walk home.*

Long into the eve, they tramped through the pine forest. The darkness of the enclosed valley was so oppressive that they dared not get out of reach of each other for fear of becoming separated. More times than not they stumbled over some root or loose rock and the close proximity of the other saved a fall that could have resulted in an injury. At one point, Jintrill offered to create a light by making one of their items glow, yet Arderi had declined as it might attract attention they needed to avoid.

Clytus' sword, Dorochi, hung heavy at Arderi's side. His own blade—Master Gartin's sword—Jintrill still wore, although the Shaper looked at the weapon as if afraid it would bite him. Arderi's back ached and he grew tired of tripping every few steps. The temperature had dropped into the frigid zone making his finger burn with pain. The hunger gnawing at his belly did nothing to improve his mood. He stopped to lean heavily against a tree. Reaching a hand out, he grabbed Jintrill by the arm. "I must rest. Besides, if we continue to wander these damnable woods one of us is bound to either break a leg... or worse." He slid down the trunk, unable to take one more step.

Jintrill bobbed his head, mouth hanging open as he gulped in air, and plopped down next to Arderi. "I fear we may have already walked past the old camp anyway. It seems as if we have gone too far to me. I cannot catch my breath in these accursed mountains!"



"Aye." Arderi was having a difficult time with his own breath. "Master Rillion said it had to do with the height of the ground. Though I do not understand how being high makes it harder to breath." By the blank stare Jintrill gave, Arderi concluded that he did not have an answer either. They sat huddled against the tree trunk, the cold seeping into every pore. Once they stopped laboring for air, an idea struck Arderi. "Back home we have stones that are warm and we keep them in our pockets. They are Essence enhanced somehow and never lose their heat. Can you not do the same?"

"Aye, that is easy enough. However, it would take too long. It would be midday before I could Meld the Essence to create enough heat to warm us sufficiently. I told you before, the Essence is not some type of magic. It is slow and methodical work."

Arderi let it drop. He was too cold to do anything about it and too tired to sleep. "Tell me of Mocley, then."

"Now that I can do." A hint of joy crept into the young Shaper's voice. "Mocley is a grand city. I was born there. My father is a perfumer and owns a shop in the Merchantillian. He sells the finest—"

A loud dull thwack popped next to Arderi's ear and he flinched. Jintrill slumped into Arderi's lap and a hulking shadow jumped from the side of the tree. Instinct took over and Arderi rolled to his side as something hard slammed into the trunk where his head had just been. The shadow let out a guttural bellow. In a panic, Arderi slid his legs out from under the Shaper and kicked the Sier's limp body toward his attacker. The thing lunged, its foot catching on the body, and fell entangled on its first victim. Arderi scrambled to his feet and ran blindly into the forest. Twigs and branches smacked him in the face, leaving whelps of pain, and several times, he fought to keep his footing. In an instant, the ground vanished from below his feet and he fell a short distance, landing in a heap. Stars burst in front of his eyes as his head struck something hard. Agony racked his entire body.



He laid there, heart slamming against his chest, straining to hear any sounds of pursuit. When the forest remained silent and he was convinced that there was no immediate danger of discovery, he tried to move. Looking around he found that he lay in a small, rocky gully.

*Mayhaps a streambed.*

He had only fallen a half pace or so, though he had not landed well. He tentatively moved each arm and leg, curling fingers and flexing ankles. He was sore and knew that by the morn he would look like someone had beaten him with a stick. Still, luckily, nothing seemed broken. He pulled himself off the stones and crawled over against the small bank he had fallen from, concealing himself in its darkness. Again, he listened for any signs of life or movement.

*I have to go back! Sier Deln could still be alive!*

Terror gripped him. Try as he might to stand, his body would not comply. Chastising himself for a coward, he placed a hand on Dorochi. His fingers wrapped around the worn leather hilt and he slowly drew the blade. Moonlight glinted off the polished steel. He liked the way it reflected the light. Without taking his eyes from the sword, he stood. Lowering the weapon to his side, he looked around the woods and knew what he must do.

Clambering over the bank, Arderi made his way back, careful not to make any noise in the process. He had gone only a few hundred paces when he heard the rustlings of something large ambling through the forest. Following the sound, he soon saw a shambling mound of a creature making its way through the underbrush, dragging something in its wake. The creature passed through a small clearing between some trees, and a sliver of light fell across its profile. Large pointed ears jutted out over the loose hanging skin that covered much of its head. A sharp tusk protruded from the side of the thing's jaw.

*O'Arkin! And it is dragging Sier Deln!*



Arderi lagged behind the beast as far as he dared so as not to lose track of it in the dense woodland. His mind raced as he tried to work out a solution to the problem. A distant horn howled off in the direction the O'Arkin traveled.

*There are more! It is taking Jintrill to its camp!*

Without further thought, he raced ahead, running headlong through tree branches and undergrowth, abandoning all concern for stealth. When he drew to within a few paces of the creature, it paused in its long strides, and Arderi knew he had been heard. It glanced over its shoulder just in time for Arderi to look deep into its dark, black eyes as he launched himself into the air. Hacking down with Dorochi as if it were a wood-axe, the tip of the blade slammed into the creature's left eye socket. The force of the attack made the blade slide sharply to one side. It clove the nose and mouth in twain and plunged out of the creature's head through its chin. A gurgle of a scream ripped from the O'Arkin as it covered its ruined face with a massive, clawed hand. Arderi's momentum carried him smashing into the beast's chest where he stopped as sure as if he had slammed into a wall. Black, goopy blood rained down on him, drenching his hair and face. Arderi gagged at the stench of it.

The O'Arkin blindly flung out a hand, and strong fingers wrapped around Arderi's throat. Immediately, his lungs were cut off from all air and his feet left the ground. Still holding its torn face together with one hand, the creature gazed at its captive from its one, un-ruined eye—hate and malice dripped from deep within its inkiness. Arderi felt his windpipe start to collapse under the ever-tightening grip of the creature. In a mad, desperate motion, Arderi jabbed Dorochi at the O'Arkin. The sword stopped when it struck the creature's chest, the ting of metal on metal resounded. Again, he tried to spear the creature, and again the blade did not find its mark. The forest, as dark as it was, began to fade before Arderi's eyes. His lungs burned for air. His neck was bent so far to the side he feared it would snap any moment.

With his strength leaving him, he struck once more in desperation, hoping to force his blade into some piece of the creature's flesh. The blade struck, yet something wrenched it from his numbing fingers. The ground rushed up and slammed into him and his lungs greedily sucked in air. Crumbling to his knees, he gagged and coughed while rubbing his throat. His body shook from head to toe.



It did not take long to see that the O'Arkin had fallen away from him, Dorochi's slender blade buried to its hilt in the O'Arkin's thick neck. Scrambling over to the creature, he yanked the sword from its gruesome sheath.

With blade in hand, he crawled over to the still form of Jintrill. In the moonlight, he saw that blood covered half the young Sier's face.

*Please be alive! Please be alive!*

Gently, he shook the Shaper. Arderi's heart leaped when a groan emanated from Jintrill's lips. Pulling out his water skin, he sprinkled some over the Shaper's face.

*Come on, Sier Deln. I cannot carry you by myself!*

He worked on the Shaper, all the while listening to the

sounds of creatures moving somewhere off in the distance. After half an aurn had passed, and the ruckus from what he assumed were other O'Arkins in the distance grew no closer, Jintrill regained consciousness. The young man did not seem to recognize any of his surroundings, though. His jaw hung limp, open to the side, and he could not focus his eyes. Waiting another quarter aurn, Arderi finally decided to wrestle the Shaper into a standing position. Jintrill leaned heavily on him, yet Arderi was glad that he at least stayed on his feet. "Alright, Sier Deln." Arderi kept his voice to a harsh whisper. "We need to move!" Taking a step forward, he pulled the Shaper along. Thankfully, the Sier took an unsteady step with him.

Half supporting and half hauling, Arderi managed to get the two of them into a steady clip. Down hill took them away from the sounds of the O'Arkins. Since down was the easiest direction to walk while burdened so, down was the direction he took. On more than one occasion over the next few aurns, they lost their footing and tumbled to the ground in a heap. After each fall, once they had slid to a stop, Arderi would force them back to their feet and start them moving once more. Once dawn broke, Jintrill could walk on his own, more or less. Exhaustion clung to Arderi like a ragged cloak. Fear became his main motivator as he forced one foot in front of the other.



At some point late in the morn, they collapsed onto a sandy bank beside a small stream they had followed for much of the morn. Arderi's entire body ached. He had pushed his muscles harder than ever before. Tiny cuts covered his hands and face. Bruises from his fall last eve forced him to hobble like an old man. Bolts of pain cascaded through him if he moved just wrong. He looked over at Jintrill who slumped with his back resting on an old log, his eyes closed. Dried blood and matted hair still covered much of the Shaper's face. They had not spoken since the attack—each had been too intent on simply remaining on the move.

"How is your head?"

A single eye opened and peered out toward Arderi and a

weak smile formed on the Shaper's lips. "My head feels like an O'Arkin tried to bash it in with a club."

A laugh escaped Arderi and he regretted it immediately when several parts of his body simultaneously complained. "Can you not heal yourself?"

Shaking his head slightly, Jintrill frowned. "Nix. I cannot Meld with my own Essence." He paused and flexed one hand, the look of pain raced across his face. "I could try and heal you."

"Nix, I know how drained you are after you heal someone. You need your strength for what is ahead. Here,"—Arderi held out a hand—"let me fill your water skin." He crawled over and submerged first one, then the other of the water skins into the stream. Once both were full, he tossed one over to the Shaper who sat up and drank from it with zeal.

"What now?" Jintrill wiped water from his chin with the sleeve of his tattered robe. "I think we have missed the basecamp."



"Aye, I was thinking on that. And a bit of luck it was as well. I figure the rest of the O'Arkins were rummaging through the camp. I think that is why they did not pursue us. I shutter to think what would have happened had we blundered into the camp to face an entire group of the creatures."

"Be that as it may, that still does not answer the question of what we are to do now." Jintrill resumed his reclined position on the log and closed his eyes.

The weariness lurking inside Arderi overtook him and he stretched out on the sun-warmed sand. "For now, I think we should rest." No reply answered him and his mind unfocused. Sleep fell upon him within moments.

# Chapter 54

Loping along at a leisurely pace, Klain took in the sights and smells flowing past him. He especially enjoyed the sight of dusk falling over the land. When the Honored One had taken Klain out to the Vimith villa, they had gone in a closed carriage. Now, keeping pace with the horse trotting along carrying Narn in its saddle, Klain could really enjoy himself.



The countryside surrounding the grand city of Mocley was mostly farmland, plowed flat by the generations upon generations of Humans who fed off plants. The occasional copse of trees dotted the land as well and these held wonderful smells that wafted through the warm, summer air.

His Human companion rode in silence. Skinny, even by Human standards, Narn had smelled of fear since they left the villa. Now that the walls of Mocley appeared off in the distance, the man down right stank of it.

*He should be afraid. If this is some trick...well—my claws are no longer covered!*

Flexing his claws in and out as he ran, Klain's mind drifted back to the villa, and young Charver.

*The boy-child is a handful! Yet, he has a good heart, like his sire. He will make a good Human one day. And the Gods know that race needs all the good ones it can get!*

As the two drew closer to the walled city, the road they traveled became more and more crowded. Almost to a person, everyone stopped in their activities to gawk or even gasp at the large Kithian. They even encountered an occasional scream from some woman or another. Yet the two traveled on, without pause.

By the time they reached the main gates, darkness had fallen across the land, muting all color in shadow. Even at this late in the eve, however, the large cobblestone entranceway bustled with activity. Carts and wagons, people and livestock, guards and carriages, all jostling each other for position and passage. Most headed out of the city, though.

Several guards, dressed in matching uniforms of yellow and blue, rushed forward upon seeing Klain. Narn threw his hands up as halberds were lowered in front them.

"What is the meaning of this?!" A man wearing much the same dress as the others strode forward, hand resting on the hilt of his sword. He brushed between the men with the halberds until he spied Klain. "By all Twelve Gods!" Taking a deep breath, the man visibly relaxed. "My apologies, Kith. Gave me a bit of a fright you did." Turning, he pushed the nearest poleaxe into the air. "Back to your posts! Have you lot never seen a Kith before?" He waved a hand gesturing for them to proceed into the city. "Until the Magistrate declares otherwise, Mocley is still a free city to all races! He has just as much right to enter the city as anyone else!" Falling in beside Klain, the man held out a hand. "I am Brue, Hinden Brue. Captain of the Third Watch here at Mocley."



Klain stared at the Human for several more steps. When it became apparent the man was not going to lower his arm, Klain placed his paw in it and let the man shake it.

"I assume, unless we are getting a migration of Kiths that no one informed me about, that you are the Kith from the Games a few moons back."

Keeping a steady pace, the trio walked into the tunnel that led into the city. The torchlight played off Hinden's breastplate. Finally, Klain grunted and nodded once.

"How wonderful! I am so pleased to meet you. I was there the day you competed. It was glorious. I made double this moons wage on you!" The man skipped a little as he said this, tripped, and barely kept his feet.

Letting out a snort, Klain shook his head. "I am happy for you, Human. Is there a reason you are following me like a dog in heat?"

Stopping in his tracks, the guard looked dumbstruck. "Following? Nix, I was..." His face turned a bright shade of red. Spinning on his heel, he hurried back to the front gate.

Glancing over at Narn who now led his horse by its reins, the two chuckled. It was the first bit of communication the two had shared the entire trip.

*He does not seem bad for a Human. Yet why does he stink of fear so? Surely, after two aurns together, he should be used to my presence by now! I may never understand Humans.*

Seeming almost embarrassed by the sharing, Narn concentrated on where they were headed and did not look at Klain again.

Trying to keep track of where they had been, and attempting to ignore the stares of those around him, Klain soon admitted to himself that he was lost. If not for his guide, he would not even have a direction to travel. Narn led his horse and Klain followed. Turn after twist, street after alley, shop after house. Everything passed by in a repetitious blur. More than an aurn passed while the two threaded their way through Mocley. At first, they passed huge stone structures, elegantly constructed and adorned with statues or fountains. Now, as the evening grew chilly, the streets became almost deserted. The smell of salt hung strong in the air and they traversed narrow streets littered with garbage. Some of the buildings they passed were little more than shanties. On a few occasions, Klain picked up what sounded like water slapping wood.



*Reminds me of my time aboard that Gods forsaken ship!*

"Where in this accursed city are we going?" Klain let all the malice he felt about this waste of a trip seep into his voice. "Is there no end to this?"

At his sudden break from silence, Narn jumped. With his thumb, the man pointed up the street they were traveling. "It is just up ahead. At the end of that alley." Giving an apologetic glance to Klain, he stepped to the side of his horse and mounted. Nudging the animal into a slow walk, Narn moved ahead of Klain and then turned the mare down the almost pitch-black alleyway. The narrow space ran between what looked like two warehouses and was so thin, both of the Human's knees brushed either side as he rode down it.

When they made the turn, something putrid assaulted Klain's nostrils.

*The ground is covered in filth and reeks of dead fish! That is why that damnable Human is mounted!*

Looking down the alley, his excellent vision allowing him to see much of the area even in the darkness, Klain grimaced as gunk from the ground squished between his toeclaws. He noticed that Narn had spurned his mount into a trot and had put a fair amount of distance between the two of them. Careful not to slip in the slime covering the ground, Klain sped to a loping gait, trying to close the distance. Upon reaching the end of the warehouses, the area expanded a bit. Narn, well out in front now, moved along at nearly a full gallop.

Klain opened his mouth to call Narn back when a large, heavy rope net slammed down upon him. It shot forward, scooping him from his hindpaws and bundling him into a tight ball. One of his hindpaws poked through the net to stick out at an odd angle. Once the swinging settled, Klain found that he dangled about a pace from the ground. A mouthful of rotten teeth materialized out of the gloom of a doorway and a fat, baldheaded black-skinned man slowly walked up tisking. It was a face Klain had seen for more than two turns of the seasons of his life, and one he had hoped never to see again. "I do think you have had enough free time, *beastie.* Your true profession calls."



His old Keeper carried a long, black painstick. Agony lanced Klain's body as the Keeper jabbed it into his side. Howling out, as much from frustration as pain, his roar echoed through the streets like a sonic tidal wave. His stomach emptied and vomit covered his facial fur.

"That is well enough of that." Estular Jerts joined the Keeper. "There is no need to wake the entire city." He flicked a finger at the Keeper. "Set it to max foci and let us take our prize home."

Shoving a paw through one of the holes in the net, Klain lashed out. One of his paws snagged the back of Estular's shirt and he felt the familiar texture of claw rending flesh. His sight filled with a brilliant sea of colorful lights. Then, pain came crashing down upon him and darkness claimed him in full.

# Chapter 55

Darkness fell full upon the land before Arderi Cor awoke. The once warm sand he had fallen asleep on lay bitterly cold beneath him now. Crawling over to the Sier, Jintrill Deln, he shook the Shaper and let out a sigh of relief when the young man opened his eyes. After a short discussion, they decided to continue following the stream, hoping it would lead them back to the river Artoc.



The four-day forced march out of the Nektine and across the grasslands were grueling on both of them, yet Arderi suspected the Shaper had taken the worst of it. What little food they had left in their packs, they had exhausted by the end of the first day and the two had had nothing except water to sustain themselves on for the remaining three. Without the ability to create a fire, they had spent the chilly evenings huddled together for warmth, sleeping little.

*Yet we have finally made it!*

Before Arderi, the great expanse of the Artoc River rolled by. Spanning hundreds of paces across—the waters churned up into a frothy white barrier of death—the far bank may well have been hundreds of leagues away.

"Which way now?" Jintrill collapsed onto the grassy bank of the raging river.

Shading his eyes from the glare of the sun, Arderi estimated they had several aurns of daylight left to them. "We head up river."

"Why? Civilization could just as easily be downriver, and the walk will be easier."

"Nix. Stillwater is the last town on the Artoc before the rivers turns…" Arderi waved a hand out over the churning water. "…well, turns into this. No boat could navigate that! The town must be upriver."

After helping the Shaper struggle to his feet, the two headed off, following the raging river and away from the setting sun.

Not more than an aurn had passed when Arderi noticed that the river began to widen, and the water settled dramatically. Rounding a bend, he almost cried once a small house on the far bank came into view. New life welled up inside him as they both sprinted to the wooden dock that jutted out into the water.

The sun had passed halfway below the horizon before anyone noticed the two young men yelling from the far bank. Arderi now stood watching the slow progress of the barge as it made its way to retrieve them.



A short, plump, balding man stood on the front of the barge being pulled through the water by two larger young men. With a deftness that belied his girth, the old man leapt from the barge before it fully reached the shore and bustled up to them.

"Now, by all the Twelve, how is it that a couple of young men, looking like a pair of starved street thieves, come to be on this side of the Artoc?"

"Street thieves!" Jintrill ran his hands over his tattered robe, all the blue had long since faded and any embroidery that had been on the sleeves had vanished along with the sleeves. "I am a Sier of the Shaper Order of Mocley!"

A big grin split the man's face. "Oh Aye! And me mother is the Priestess of Fatint!" He let out a bark of a laugh.

"Please, sir. My friend speaks the truth. We have just escaped from the Nektine and have not eaten in days."

A look of horror sprang to the man's face. "The Nektine? Not with that fool troop that crossed some three moons past?"

Arderi bowed his head. "Aye, sir. We are all who survive." A strong hand grasped Arderi by the arm and he tried to break free, yet had not the strength.

"Easy, lad. Easy. Tis alright." Looking up, Arderi saw the compassion in the old Ferrier's eyes. "Come, let us get you inside. Warm you both up and get some food into you."

Once the three men helped Arderi and Jintrill to the barge, the two younger ones took on the arduous task of pulling them back to the far bank.

The Ferrier's home was roomy, though modest. A large, open room sat at the front of the house—heat emanated into the room from the fireplace set against one wall. The kitchen area adjoined this room as well, with a doorway that led deeper into the house. A plump woman, a bit past her prime, greeted them and immediately began fussing over the two weary travelers.

She produced fresh clothing, which hung loosely from their shoulders, as well as thick wool blankets to wrap around themselves. Arderi sat bundled up before the fire, a steamy bowl of stew in his lap.

*I know it is just the hunger, yet this stew tastes better than any I have ever had before!*



Sier Deln sat next to him holding his own bowl and shoveling soup into his mouth with a flat wooden spoon.

"This is the best stew I have ever eaten!" Jintrill's outburst echoed Arderi's thoughts and Arderi smiled as the young Sier turned to face the Ferrier and his wife who hovered behind the pair. "May I have some more, please?"

The woman bustled forward and took the bowl from the Shaper's outstretched hand. "It would be my pleasure, Sier."

Placing his hand upon the woman's shoulder, the Ferrier stopped her from departing. "With the greatest of respect, Sier. I do not think that wise. Having not eaten in the last few days, if you rush into food it could cause you more grief than good."

Jintrill nodded to the Ferrier. Arderi did not think the Sier agreed, yet the young Shaper wrapped himself back in his blanket without complaint.

*The Sier has changed much since I met him. I wonder how my family will view me.*

With the sudden thought of his family, a pang of guilt slipped between Arderi's ribs and sliced deep into his heart. "My thanks to you both, again, Mir'am and Mis'am Riel, for all you have done." Reaching to his side, he started to fish his fingers into Clytus' coin pouch.

The Ferrier waved a hand to stop him. "Ah, lad, think nothing of it. The story you have told of your time in the Nektine is more than enough payment for the likes of us. I only grieve for the loss of your companions."

"And for that, Mir'am Riel, my thanks to you. However, our task is not yet finished. We must make all haste back to Mocley. A young boy's life hangs upon our return."

"Stillwater is a busy port. Trade goods from deeper within Ro'Arith make their way on a daily basis there. Most days a caravan of some sort is headed to Mocley. I will send one of my boys to see about getting you added to one. I would not think any wagon master will deny passage to a Shaper and his companion, so it should not be an issue."



"Again, my thanks to you, Mir'am Riel." Arderi turned back to the fire and lost himself amongst the flames, his meal, and his own troubled thoughts.

Not long after he finished his bowl of stew, the son the Ferrier had sent to check on passage with a wagon train to Mocley, returned from Stillwater. The son, one of the young men who had pulled them across the Artoc, inclined his head toward Jintrill before he turned to the Ferrier. "Father, there is a caravan leaving first thing on the morrow. I spoke to the wagon master and he would be honored to have a Sier along for the ride."

Mis'am Riel stepped forward. "These two are in no condition to travel. They need a few days of rest first."

"That would suit me fine as well." Jintrill smiled up at the plump woman. "I never thought I could be so weary."

"Nix!"

The sternness within Arderi's voice startled everyone. Shrugging out of his blanket, he rose. "We have no time to waste, Jintrill. We leave with that caravan!"

The scandalous looks on the faces of the Ferrier and his wife as they glanced from Arderi to Jintrill made Arderi realize what he said and to whom he said it.

*I* have *changed! I never would have spoken to a Sier that way before.*

"Aye." With a sigh, Jintrill stood and joined Arderi. "Arderi is correct. We carry something that we must take to the Shaper's Order in Mocley without delay. My thanks, Mir'am and Mis'am Riel, for your hospitality as well as your kindness." With that, the Shaper stood without glancing at Arderi. "Mis'am Riel, you mentioned something about a bed for the eve?"

The Ferrier's wife gave a start. "Aye. Aye, of course, Sier." She cast one last disapproving look to Arderi. "If you will follow me, please."

*We are back in civilization now. I must remember that. Whatever the two of us became out in the Nektine, that is behind us. Here he is a Shaper, and I am just a simple fielder.*



Nodding to the Ferrier once more, Arderi picked up his bundle, which included Master Gartin's blade the Shaper had returned as soon as they were back in civilization, and followed after the Shaper and Mir'am Riel.

# Chapter 56

Dreams plagued Alant Cor while he slept, causing him to toss and turn on his hard, thin mattress. Dreams of being taken, cast into a large, dark pit. After one such dream, he lay upon his back, only half-awake. A noise from the hall roused him fully, sending shivers running along his spine. Slipping from the warmth of his bed, ignoring the chill of the bare tile floor on his uncovered feet, he crept to the door. Careful not to make a sound, he lifted the small latch that held his door shut and cracked it open. The hallway sat empty except for the long shadows cast by a lone brazier flickering at the end of the hall. Straining his ears, he stood in the doorway holding his breath for long moments.

*You are jumping at shadows, you fool!*

Chastising himself, he pushed at the door to close it, just catching sight of a large shadow moving at the end of the hallway. He froze, door still ajar by the merest slit. The shadow detached itself from a wall and moved toward him. In the dim light, the shadow coalesced into a monstrous shape that nearly brushed the ceiling some four paces above. Blue-gray skin, glinting in the light cast by the brazier, stretched taunt over rippling muscles. The Gralet'nar lumbered into the Human quarters. Sightless eyes scanned the corridor stopping to look directly at Alant peeking out from his doorway. His breath caught and he felt, more than saw, the Warrior Servant pass his door, sending him reeling toward panic. An image of the large creature smashing into his room washed over him, and he could not stop his knees from going weak.

I could not stop it if it tried!

A click echoed through the silent hall followed by the quiet swish of a door opening. The hairs on Alant's head stood on end.

*Quiln's door! May the Twelve protect him!*

Risking discovery, Alant opened his door just enough to allow him to see the hall once more. He could not see further down the hall toward Quiln's room unless he stuck his head out, and he was not brave enough for that.

Straining his ears, hoping for some sound he could use as an excuse to step out of his room, knowing he would not even if it came, he stood rooted in his room. No noise came—no outcry, no sounds of struggle. Within moments, the large Gralet'nar's broad back and shoulders filled his vision again. The guard strode down the hall toward the exit of the Humans quarters with Quiln closely following. The boy plodded along, as unconcerned as if he walked the gardens under a noonday sun, fully clothed in his white Initiates robe. His golden slippered feet made a quiet rasping sound on the white-tiled floor as he passed. He followed the Gralet'nar as if he knew where they were headed, not looking to either side as he passed. Alant was about to step out, to ask if Quiln was all right, when a third form gave him pause. Vanria Delmith reached out a thin, gray-blue arm, pushed open the door, and stepped into his tiny room.

The Elmorian held his teardrop shaped head cocked to the side. He looked at Alant as if what he saw was a mystery. Cold laced the Tarsith and Alant fought the urge to grab at it. The Vanria's mouth twisted as if he tasted something disagreeable. "You, Alant, are an enigma, yes? I should be able to perform a Chi'tar upon you, yet, I cannot. And I have tried many times since you came here. Why is this, hmm?"

Thinking his pulse could not race any faster, Alant was shocked to find it could. "I—Chi'tar, Vanria Delmith?"

Delmith continued as if Alant had not even spoken. "You say

you read of the Mah'Sukai at the Chandril'elian of Mocley, yet you will claim to me now that you know nothing of the Chi'tar, hmm? To my knowledge, neither word is known outside of our tongue."

Alant could not think of anything to say. He had not heard of anything called a Chi'tar.

The Tarsith oscillated from cold to normal. At each instance the scowl upon Delmith's face deepened another notch. "I like a good mystery, yes? Yet this is not the time for it. Mayhaps you should return to your bed, hmm?" With that, the Elmorian pivoted and glided down the hall.

Swallowing hard, Alant closed the door to his small chamber and returned to his hard bed.

*This is insane! What is going on? I should have done something.*

He let out a sniff and shook his head. "You are a fool, Alant Cor! What can I do? Thousands of leagues from home—surrounded by the most powerful beings on the Plane of Talic'Nauth—what *can* I do?"



For many long aurns, he tossed under his thin blanket. Questions plagued him—questions he could find no answers to.

*What are they doing to Quiln? What power can he gain over the Essence? And if this Chi'utlan simply helps someone gain power, why all the secrecy?*

Scores of theories raced across his imagination, yet none seemed viable. Finally, exhaustion overtook him and he dropped into a restless sleep.

A knock sent him sitting bolt upright. "Alant?" Shaith's voice drifted in from outside his door. "Alant, do you be awake?"

"Aye." Alant scrambled from his bed, wiping sleep from his eyes, donning his robe and slippers before opening the door. "Where is Quiln?" He had not meant for it to sound like a command.

Shaith took a step back and shook her head. "He be at firstmeal where he do belong. It be you—hey!"

Not waiting on her to finish, Alant brushed past her and ran from the Human quarters. The small room where the Humans took their meals sat just across from the kitchens, so he only had a short distance to travel.

When he burst into the room, his golden slippers sliding upon the polished tile floors, Jerith looked up at him. "Well, you did drag yourself out of bed, finally."

Stopping, Alant glanced over at Quiln then back to Jerith. "Is he—Is he all right?"

Jerith looked puzzled. "Who?"

Stepping next to Quiln, Alant leaned over the table to see more of the boy's downturned face. "Are you all right?" Quiln did not stir. "Are you all right, Quiln?" The boy still did not move and Alant laid a hand gently upon his shoulder, causing the orphan to flinch away. Cupping a hand under the boy's chin, Alant forced Quiln to look at him. A gasp escaped Alant's lips and he took an involuntary step back.

*His eyes! By all the Gods, his eyes!*



Shaking uncontrollably, Alant covered his mouth with his hand. The orphan's eyes stared back at Alant, yet they held no recognition in them.

*They are...vacant!*

Yet it was not the blank stare that caused panic to rip through Alant to the point he wanted to flee. Slashes of red swirled through the whites of his eyes and lanced even into the dark brown centers.

The laugh that sprang from Jerith seemed so foreign and out of place, Alant looked at him as if he was some monster out of a wives' tale. "What do you be going on about? The boy did sleep poorly, that be all." When Alant's face did not change, Jerith pointed at Quiln. "Just look at his bloodshot eyes if you need more proof."

Gazing into Quiln's red streaked eyes, Alant swallowed hard and felt as if he might sick up. "You think his eyes are bloodshot? Are you mad?"

"Aye, he be mad." Standing behind Alant, Shaith peered around his shoulder. "Alant, what be the matter? You do look like you saw the dead rise."

"I—"

"Yes, Alant." Spinning around, Alant was shocked to see Vanria Delmith standing in the hallway behind Shaith. "Please, do tell us what is the matter, hmm?" His tall, thin frame looked even thinner by the presence of the huge Gralet'nar standing to his right.

Mouth going dry, Alant franticly looked for an escape route. His pulse quickened when he came to the realization that the tiny room in which he stood had only one exit. "I—"

"If you will kindly step aside, Alant, I need to collect Quiln." Without waiting on Alant to move, the Elmorian brushed past him. Slipping a gray, three-fingered hand under the orphan's arm, Delmith helped the boy stand and led him out of the room.

Shaith curtsied and slipped out of the Vanria's way when Delmith entered, yet as he left, she stretched out a hand and placed it tentatively upon his arm. Snatching it back quickly, she rubbed her fingers as if they hurt. "Where do you be taking him? If I may ask, Vanria."



Pausing in his stride, he tilted his head slightly and smiled at the girl before looking directly at Alant. "You may. A message came late last eve from Mocley. It seems that Quiln has been called back to study with his kinsmen, yes? I informed the boy as soon as I was notified. He did not take the news well it seems, and has only just stopped crying." A smile flicked over the Vanria's features as he caught Alant's eye. Turning, he led Quiln down the hall. The large Gralet'nar shambling along behind.

"That boy should have done been sent home." Jerith wrinkled his nose and sat back down before his plate of fruits and warm bread.

Rolling her eyes, Shaith turned to Alant. "You still no look well. What be the matter?"

Glancing from one dark-skinned youth to the other, Alant could not fathom why neither seemed affected by the events unfolding around them. "It—It is nothing. I do not think I slept well last eve myself." Brushing past her once more, he walked in a daze down the hall towards his room.

*Mayhaps I am imagining all this. Mayhaps Quiln's eyes were bloodshot. As my Papa always said, 'If you find yourself in a hole, stop digging.'*

*And mayhaps I have already let the Kruger out of the bag. I doubt it will be easy to put the beastie back in.*

# Chapter 57

For much of the ride, Arderi Cor sat in silence. The horrors of the Nektine, the death of Master Rillion, the intrusion of whatever the Tat'Sujen are and how it involved him, all weighed heavily upon his mind. The Shaper, Jintrill Deln, never struck up a conversation with Arderi, instead preferring the company of another of his kind who traveled with the caravan.



Just past midday, they arrived at the gates of Hild'alan. Sier Deln had convinced the wagon master of their need to spend the eve at the stead, which Arderi felt both grateful for and apprehensive about. The gold ta'narian Arderi had given to the man had also gone a long way to easing the burden of delaying their arrival to Mocley by a day. As the high walls of Arderi's home stead crept into view, he felt the full weight of his actions press down upon his shoulders. Hefting his pack, Clytus' sword, Dorochi, and the collector both wrapped tightly inside it, he caught the eye of the driver. "I would like to walk in, Mir'am Dorgnit."

Mir'am Dorgnit, the teamster on the reins of the wagon in which Arderi rode, nodded. "As you wish, young Master Cor. Just be sure to catch us up in the morn before we head out. Though you travel with the Shapers, the wagon master may still leave you behind if you are late."

Flinching inside at the honorific—Arderi had never corrected the old wagon driver in his assumption that Arderi was more than he really was—he knew the sword at his hip was as much a status symbol as it was a weapon.

*They see a young man with a well-worn sword on his hip and they assume I have earned it. Yet, more lies that I have buried myself under.*

Holding Master Gartin's sword so it would not hinder him, Arderi hopped from the wagon and stood to the side of the road until the caravan had passed by. Stepping onto the road as the dust settled, he walked heavy footed toward the gate. The walls looming over his head did nothing to relieve the strain of returning home.

"I seem to remember seeing a young fielder who resembled you leaving by this gate on many an occasion. Yet, the man walking in now, I do not think I recognize." Flinnok Nime stepped out of the guard shack and limped up to Arderi.

"You are hurt, Master Nime?" Arderi felt an odd sense of equality with the old Guarder Captain he had never felt before.



*Mayhaps it is not just the sword at my hip that is new.*

"Bah, just a small thing—a run in with a testy mare. I will be fine in a few days. It is why I am here on gate duty, however, and not out in the fields." Inclining his chin toward the boy's hip, Flinnok questioned the sword resting in its scabbard. "That seems a bit more than a fielder would normally carry."

"Aye, Master Nime." Arderi looked down at the blade and rested a hand on its worn leather. "It belonged to a great swordsman who instructed me for a while. It was given to me after the man's death."

A laugh escaped the guarder's lips. "You have been gone only a few moons time—a fact, by the way, that has caused your parents a great deal of grief." Flinnok rubbed his chin and stared at Arderi for a moment. "Yet you sound as if you have grown by winters. So, since we have all been mistaken and you are not dead, where have you been all these moons?"

Smiling, Arderi chuckled and shook his head. "I am unsure you would believe me if I told you. I will only be here one eve, however, and I would much like to see my folks. They will not take kindly to me after what I put them through, yet, it is not right for them to think me dead a moment longer than needed."

Master Nime slapped Arderi upon the shoulder. "Aye, in this I find you are wise. I do not envy you facing your Ma's wrath, for Mis'am Cor's temper is known well by many, yet I think you are right. They will be glad to know you have not passed into the aftermore. Plus, there is some trouble brewing with the fielders this day. I do think you may be in the center of it. It seems you have arrived when you were most needed." The old guarder stepped to the side and raised an arm. "Hurry along with you then."

Dipping his head to the guarder, Arderi strode through the main gates and into his home stead.

Arderi walked the cobblestone street toward the public house where his family lived. Every person he passed, be them known to him or not, stopped and gawked at his passing.

*Granted, a man wearing a sword on his hip who is not a guarder is odd, yet I would not think it should cause such stares!*

"By all Twelve Gods!" Instinctively, Arderi's hand fell to the hilt of his sword as he spun toward the shout behind him. Riln took a step back, his arms raised and his eyes wide with fear. "Take it easy, Arderi! By the Twelve, it is only me!"



Feeling like a heel, Arderi relaxed. "Riln. It is good to see you." Awkwardly, he held out a hand. Riln eyed it, yet did not take it. After a moments more hesitation, Arderi let his arm drop. "Have I changed so much?"

"No fielder I know of carries a sword and reaches for it without thought. Where have you been? Everyone is saying you are dead. That your body has just never been found."

"I joined a band of mercenaries who stopped here for the eve. They were headed—" A loud wail resounded through the street and Arderi's heart leapt into his throat. Spinning back toward his home, he saw his Ma rushing at him—her skirt and apron flapping out behind her in her haste.

Tears streamed down her cheeks. When she reached him, he started to speak yet was cutoff when she engulfed him in her arms. "My son has returned to me! The Twelve be praised, my boy is home!"

Arderi let his Ma hold him for several moments. Then, gently, he extracted himself from her embrace.

After wiping her eyes clear of tears, she gave him a stern look. "You have a lot of explaining to do, young man. Yet first, I am sure your father will be just as glad to see you in one piece as well."

They entered the public house, his Ma still smothering him under one arm as the elderfolk who sat on the front porch surrounded him and assailed him with questions. The small group entered the dining hall and Arderi was astonished to see the large room packed to the breaking. Not only did he see his whole family—his two sisters, Tary and Baith stood in a group of girls their own age at the edge of the crowd, and Siln held little Rik at his waist standing next to their father, Tanin—along with those who shared the public house with them in the hall. It seemed that every fielder from the entire stead was in attendance. When they entered, several men were shouting—Arderi did not know at whom or what—yet the room fell silent once they noticed Mis'am Cor leading her third eldest son into the crowd.



A lump welled up inside Arderi's throat once he caught his father's eye sitting on a bench next to Siln, and for a long moment, they just stared at each other across the silent room. Tanin Cor sat there, a look of grief, relief, anger, and disbelief all warring for dominance over his features. Finally, his lower lip started to quiver and he quickly crossed the room to embrace his son. The man let out an ear-piercing sob that rippled remorse through Arderi's heart with such pain as to be almost unbearable.

*There could be no greater punishment than hearing Papa cry like this!*

Tears streamed from Arderi's eyes as the two stood there holding each other. "Forgive me, Papa. Please, forgive me. I have failed you in so many ways."

Pulling Arderi from him, Tanin looked deep into his eyes. "Nix, lad! Nix! You are home. The Shapers have not taken both our sons! You have nothing to be forgiven for!"

Wiping the tears from his face, Arderi took a step back and stood at his full height. "Nix, Papa! I have wronged both you and

Ma. Yet, I have learned much over the past few moons. One lesson was not to run from the consequences of my own actions."

Mis'am Cor strode forward and put her arm around Arderi. "How can you be expected to take responsibility for what the Shaper's Order did to you?"

"The Shaper's Order?" At first, Arderi did not understand what she meant. Then, looking around the room at all the faces of the people gathered, it dawned on him. "You think the Shapers took me the day of my Testing? Is that why everyone is gathered?"

A stern look fell upon Tanin's face. "By the tone in you voice, I assume that we are not correct in this." He reached over, pulled out a chair, and motioned for Arderi to sit. "I think the time for speculation is at an end, at least in your case."

"What do you mean, my case?" Arderi sat.

Shaking his head, Tanin raised a negating hand. "More of that later, tell us your tale."

And so, Arderi poured out the events that had happened to him over the past several moons. His failure of the Test, stowing away on the wagon train, the journey into the Nektine—this received gasps even from the oldest in the room—the death of Master Rillion, and the flight home. It all flowed out of him as if a dam had burst, and the emotions that were released felt as sweet to him as a fresh rain.



When all was said, and those who asked questions were answered, Tanin leaned back in the chair he had procured for himself and let out a long whistle. "Well, my boy. It seems that you have had more adventure than everyone else in this room combined. Yet you are home now. Safe. And that is the way I mean to keep it."

"Nix, Father." Arderi stared at the spot on the floor he was grinding with the toe of his boot. "I will only be staying the eve. I leave at first light."

With a loud clack, the chair that Tanin sat in slammed to the floor as his father jumped to his feet. "You can put any thoughts of leaving out of your head right this instant, boy! I thought I had lost two sons. Now that I have one back, I am not about to give him up again!"

Slowly rising to his feet, Arderi looked directly into Tanin's eyes. Never before had he done so to his father. The fact that he did it with a sword hanging at his hip made him feel both foolish and cowardly.

*It is too late to remove it, yet damn the blade! I made a vow and I will never break one again, regardless of the consequences!*

"Nix, Father. I must travel to Mocley on the morrow and I will not allow anything to stop me."

Clinching his jaws, anger burned deep within his father's eyes. "If you think just because you wear a sword at your side I will stand here and let a child of mine speak to me thus—"

Putting a hand on his father's shoulder, Arderi shook his head. "Nix, Papa, that is not my intent. I do not wish to disrespect you further. Still, I have made a vow. If I do not go to Mocley, a young boy will die. Master Rillion's son, Sindian. I vowed, as he died in my arms, that I would complete his task."



Brushing between the two, his Ma took Arderi's outstretched hand in hers and cupped them to her breast. "Surely you have done enough? Let someone else take this collector back to Mocley, it is no longer your burden to bear."

Remaining silent, Arderi stared at his father.

Finally, Tanin reached out and placed his hand on his wife's arm. "Nix, Mel'Ona. This is not the same boy who disappeared a few moons ago. Still, Arderi is correct—he has a vow to keep. I did not raise any of my boys to break a vow. Besides, I do not think it is our place any longer to tell him what to do." He held out a hand to his son.

A warmness filled Arderi as he took his father's hand and shook it—not as a boy—as the man he saw reflected in his father's eyes. His face flushed and he fought back tears, yet the chaos of his mind reached out and grasped hold of a question. "Papa, what did you mean when you said you thought you had lost two sons to the Shaper's Order?"

Mis'am Cor brought a hand up to her mouth and Mir'am Cor's face went grave. "We received a Crystal from the Shaper's Order of Mocley. It arrived this morn. Alant is dead."

# Chapter 58

The strong smell of urine snapped Klain from a fog of semi-consciousness. A pounding reverberated through his skull and a swollen tongue filled his mouth. Flopping his head to the side, he pried his eyes open and glanced around. At first, his vision would not clear, nor could his brain discern anything distinct from the blurry images he saw.



*Shadows in motion.*

"All be in readiness, Master Jerts." The voice seemed distance.

"What did you tell the Captain of our cargo?" This voice was snide and curt. Klain tried to pull up a face in his mind and failed.

*Why can I not think?*

"I did tell the truth." A grunt of a laugh. "That we carry a wild beast and be bound for Silaway."

A silky blanket of soft blackness swept Klain's remaining thoughts away and he floated weightless, almost enjoying the sensation.

Once consciousness crept upon Klain again, darkness enveloped the room. His head still pounded, though not as severe. The strong smell of urine was still present and he realized that it was he that reeked so.

*My fur is coated in piss.*

Pushing himself into a sitting position, he looked around. He sat in a small, iron-barred cage. Beyond the bars, boxes stood in irregular stacks covering most of the large, open room. Cracks in the walls permitted light to seep in, yet Klain could not hope to know how long the sun had been up.

*Nor even how many days have passed since they put me here!*

The cage was not tall enough for him to stand, nor the bars wide enough for him to extend his limbs through, so he sat there, knees against his chest and his muscles cramping.

Watching the slivers of sunlight creep across the floor, Klain took advantage of being left alone to clear the cobwebs that still clung to his mind.

*I must still be in Mocley. The whole thing was a setup! I will kill Satner Timms if it is the last thing I do!*

"Master Klain." The whisper came out of the darkness sending a shiver down Klain's spine.

*No!*

"Young Master!" His words came out more of a croak than anything. "You cannot be here!" Twisting around in his cramped cage, Klain saw Charver slinking between some boxes not ten paces away. Even though Klain could see the boy clearly in the dim light, it was obvious Charver had not yet seen him. "Why are you here?"



Charver's eyes lit up when he spied Klain and he hurried to the side of the cage. "When you did not return last eve I worried. When Narn came back to the villa without you, I knew something was wrong. I overheard him tell Master Timms that everything had gone to plan and that some man had taken you."

Baring his fangs, Klain stifled a growl. "Aye! Alas, why are you here?"

"When Master Timms left this morn, I followed him. It was not easy out on the open road. Yet, it was not that difficult to keep pace with him unnoticed on the crowded streets of Mocley."

Klain could not stop the growl that came from him. Grasping the bars, he glared at Charver. "Boy! Why are you here?"

Charver looked taken aback. "Why? To rescue you, of

course!"

Letting out a snort, Klain shook his head. "You cannot be here! Go now! Putting yourself in danger to save me is not what your father hired me for!"

The dull sound of wood sliding over wood echoed throughout the building. A door creaked opened and for the first time in many moons, fear crept into Klain. "Shhh! Hide and say nothing. When you have the opportunity, you get out of here and back home."

The boy tried to say something and Klain cut him off with a wave of his paw. "Not a sound!" Slumping back into a sitting position, he rested his arms on his knees and hung his head low. Not so low, however, that he could not look out at the warehouse. There were too many boxes in the way for him to see exactly where the door sat or who had opened it, yet he easily heard the booted footsteps of four or so men walking his way.

"You have done me a great service, Master Timms."

Klain felt his hackles rise.



*Timms! And I clearly recognize the voice of Estular Jerts!*

Within moments, Estular Jerts, his old Keeper, another scruffy Human Klain did not recognize, and Satner Timms stepped into the small cleared area in front of Klain's cage. The painstick his old Keeper held did not go unnoticed. Upon seeing Klain, Satner halted and spun on the other men. "Why have you brought me here?"

Smiling his greasy grin, Estular waved his hand in a flourished, over exaggerated manner. "I assumed you might like to say goodbye to the beast."

Glaring at the cage, his jaws clinching and flexing, Satner looked almost remorseful.

*Remorseful he is not the one who will get to kill me, mayhaps.*

"What will become of him?"

"The beast? Oh, it is destined for great things. The Games are just becoming popular in my home country of Silaway. I should be able to turn quite a large profit before it is finally killed."

Ripping his eyes from Klain, Satner turned to Estular and held out a hand. "Just give me my coin and I will be gone!"

This made Estular laugh. "It seems you do not have the stomach for this, Master Timms."

When Satner did not lower his hand, Estular let out an exasperated sigh. "Oh, aye. Very well. Alas, you take all the fun out of this." Reaching to his belt, he unhooked a small leather pouch and handed it to Satner.

Klain's heart sank as Charver stood and darted around his cage. "I cannot believe you would stoop so low, *Master Timms*!" The boy stood defiant, hands upon his hips.

"Young Master! What are you doing here?" Satner sounded both enraged and horrified all at once.

"I came to rescue Master Klain! I—Hey, let me go!"

With a flick of the wrist, Estular had motioned the scruffy Human to grab Charver. The boy wiggled and kicked, yet the wiry man held tight. Klain growled and Satner lunged forward. "Hands off the boy!"



"My dear, Master Timms." Estular sauntered over to Charver and ran a hand through the boy's hair. "The boy has seen us. It is obvious we will not be able to buy his silence. He must hold some affection for the beast."

"That matters not! Our bargain was for the Kith. You will let the boy go now!" Letting his hand stray to the hilt of his sword, Satner fell into a defensive stance.

Snorting, Estular slowly shook his head. "It seems I was right. You really do not have the stomach for this. Mayhaps you should stick to bodyguarding. I cannot let the boy leave."

Drawing his sword from its scabbard, Satner screamed as the Keeper smacked him in the back with the painstick. The man, flung forward by the blow, slammed into a stack of boxes. He landed in a heap on the warehouse floor.

"Kill the boy. Then, kill that fool as well." Estular pointed to where Satner lay. "Then, get the beast ready to load on the ship. I want to be away from this accursed city!" Turning, Estular stormed away.

The metallic hiss of a small blade sounded. Realizing that the Human holding onto Charver had drawn forth a thin knife from his belt, Klain roared and viciously slammed himself against the cage door. The tiny cage shook and slid across the floor a little, causing the man holding Charver to recoil and drop his blade.

"That be enough out of you!" The Keeper strode over and jabbed the painstick between the bars.

When the black onyx rod touched him, Klain screamed out in pain and his stomach convulsed. If he had had any food in his gut, it would have come up. In a blind rage, Klain flung himself once more against the door. Bursting from its hinges, the iron door slammed against the Keeper, sending the man crashing to the ground. Spilling out onto the warehouse floor, Klain was momentarily stunned to find himself free. The scent of Charver wafted from his left and Klain spun. The scruffy Human still held the boy by one arm, a thick shortsword in his other.



*This one stinks of fear more than any Human I have ever smelled!*

Rising to his full height, Klain towered over the man by head and shoulders. Barely a pace separated the two. Exposing his fangs, a low growl rumbled from him and the man's sword began to quiver. The Human placed the tip of the blade against Charver's neck. "I swear by all Twelve, I will kill—"

Uncoiling his muscles like springs, Klain did not wait for the man to finish his words.

*His last words.*

Closing the distance between them in a blink, his sharp claws caught the man's throat, ripping flesh and tendons alike. A shower of blood sprayed into the dimness beyond. The force of Klain's blow lifted the man from his feet and sent his body flipping through the air. He landed with a dull thud, his sword clattering across the floor.

Rending pain slashed through Klain's spine and drove him to his knees in front of the boy. Reaching out, he pushed Charver away and spun on his attacker. The Keeper stood before him, painstick clutched in his meaty knuckles. Estular was at his side, a thin rapier in his hand.

"Aye, beastie. You do remember this painstick, do you no?" Reaching into a pouch at his side, the Keeper withdrew a small stone that matched the onyx of the staff. Placing the stone against the handle, he stroked it down the stick's length. A hiss, like the rasping of a sword against a sharpening stone, echoed through the warehouse. "And I do bet you remember what max foci feels like." The onyx staff crackled with energy as the Keeper waved it in the air in front of Klain. "Now, let us be a good little beasty and get back in your cage, alright?"

Anger boiled inside Klain. Hate, disgust, rage, and loathing. He allowed all of it to pour into himself—to fill him to the brim with raw, animalistic emotion. Feasting on its pureness. He lunged. The painstick caught him square in his chest. All vision left him and darkness filled his eyes. He knew he lay on the ground—knew he could not overcome the pain that gripped him in its tight embrace.



Forcing himself to his knees, he looked back at the two Humans and struggled to rise. The Keeper swung the staff in an arc aimed at Klain's head. Catching the painstick with his paw, pure agony of burning jolts shot down his arm and into his chest. His jaw slammed shut and a high-pitched screech echoed throughout the room.

Still, Klain did not let go—refused to let go. Sparks arced between his fingers and the smell of burning fur tickled his nostrils. Using the painstick as a support, he pulled himself to his hindpaws. The pain intensified by multitudes the longer he held it.

The Keeper's eyes bulged wide with fear at the sight.

Klain's wails of agony continued to ripple forth from his throat.

Striding forward, Estular stabbed Klain in the chest with his rapier. As the blade buried itself easily into his hide, Estular jerked violently and flew back as the power of the painstick flowed up his sword and into him.

With Estular's blade still in his chest, Klain knew he was already dead. Yet the pain from the onyx staff blotted out all other feelings. Drawing out one last pulse of strength, Klain jerked hard on the painstick, wrenching it toward him as he did. It tore from the Keepers hands, pulling the Human forward and to his knees at Klain's hindpaws. The worst of the pain dissipated, and Klain stood there, his body shaking uncontrollably, staring down at his old Keeper.

Lunging forward, the Keeper reached up and grabbed the hilt of Estular's sword that protruded from Klain and twisted it.

Klain roared at the new found pain. He spun the onyx staff he still held in his paw and rammed its tip with all his might into the Keepers face. The staff penetrated the man's eye and bore through and out the back of his skull. Sparks from the painstick arced up and away, trailed by a splatter of blood in their wake. The man jerked once and a few tendrils of smoke issued from the now inactive painstick. Klain let the Keeper's body slump to the floor.



Feet scuffed the floor behind him and Klain spun to see Charver emerge from the shadows. "Master Timms has fled."

Grunting, Klain looked down at the sword sticking from his chest. Gripping the hilt, he withdrew the blade from its resting place, his fur soaking up the blood that now flowed freely from the wound. He staggered.

A low moan caught Klain's attention. Limping over to Estular, he reached down and picked his former master up by the front of his brightly colored tunic. The man regained consciousness just as Klain raised him to eye level. Gazing into the Human's eyes, Klain looked for something, anything in them he could connect with. Estular simply let out a wail of despair.

"Do not kill him." Charver's voice rang out from behind them.

Klain did not take his eyes from Estular. "Why should I not?"

"That will make you just as bad as he. Do you not want to be better?"

"I am better than this piece of dung Human." Jerking his arm back, Klain rammed the rapier into Estular's chest, piercing his heart. Estular did not have the chance to scream. His body simply shuddered once as the blade struck home, then went limp in Klain's grasp. Letting the body fall to the floor, he turned and looked at Charver. "I am a Kithian."

# Chapter 59

That evening, after the crowd dispersed, Arderi Cor lay awake in his old bed long into the eve. He felt numb, empty.

*I cannot believe Alant is dead.*

Once the initial shock wore off, Arderi learned that the fielders had gathered that day out of anger and outrage over the events that had transpired since he left. They had forgone working the fields to meet at his parent's public house. 

*I have never heard of that happening before in living memory.*

When Arderi failed to return home on the eve of his Test, his parents had gone the next morn to the Magistra to inquire as to their son's wellbeing. Originally, they thought the Shapers had kept Arderi. His mother told him the public house was a-buzz with excitement, for never had the Shaper's Order kept a child the day of their Test.

"We assumed that you were even more gifted than your brother and they wanted to start working with you as soon as they could." His mother's words renewed his feelings of despair over his failure.

What his father added made the feeling twice as bad. "Yet when we arrived, we were told you had failed the Test and had left soon thereafter. They would not even let us see the Grand Master! After that, days passed and the Order remained silent. All requests for any information about you were met with sealed lips. Your Ma and I took our complaint to the Regent himself.

This too led to nothing except more frustration. It was if you had simply disappeared!"

Tanin took a deep breath. When he continued, Arderi could tell the memory of the events still haunted his father. "Later, with no other avenue to pursue, things slipped back to the normal day to day. Yet there was a hole inside me, like some infected wound that, instead of healing, grew larger with each passing day." When Tanin said this, Arderi knew he would never forgive himself for what he had done to his parents. "After receiving the Crystal from Mocley...Well, if you had not returned this day, things might have become ugly."

Arderi had already drawn upon the Crystal three times since he retired to his room, desperate for some glimmer of hope.

*A chance that something would change.*



The image imprinted upon the Crystal was that of an old man, his gray beard flowing down his blue Shaper's robes and ending near his waist. Golden starbursts adorned the cuffs of his sleeves marking him a Grand Master of the Order. The Sier looked genuinely sad. Several times during his message it seemed like the old Sier had fought back tears. He introduced himself as Sier Baroth Sarlimac, one of Alant's instructors in Mocley. The Sier said he had just received word that day from the Elmorian's who cared for Alant, and that due to the rigors of his training, Alant had succumbed and passed into the aftermore before his instructors could give him aid. The old Sier had gone to great length to convey his sympathy, informing the Cor family that not only was Alant one of the most gifted young men he had ever had the pleasure of meeting, he was one of the finest as well.

*I will never get the opportunity to tell Alant what it was he felt in me—not that I really know what it is. Still, I feel that many answers await me in Mocley.*

Sleep came to him only after many aurns and when it did

finally come, it was hardly restful since he tossed and turned through what little remained of the eve. He was up and dressed long before any sunlight had a chance to pour through his glazed window.

Rising, Arderi gave himself a swift cleaning in the washbasin and dressed quickly. When he finished, he reached over and picked up Master Gartin's sword. Cradling it in both hands, he took a moment to reflect.

*I have changed. People here think it is odd that I wear it, yet to me, it is just as odd not to wear it.*

Strapping the sword to his waist, he stepped back to the side of his bed and unwrapped his pack. It contained the collector and Dorochi, Clytus' blade. He rubbed his hand over Dorochi's hilt and it came alive at his touch. He felt the pulsing of the Crystal buried inside.

*It reaches out to me!*

Snatching his hand away, he rubbed his palm trying to rub away the alien feeling that had emanated from the sword's hilt. Insuring the padding around the collector still protected it, he re-wrapped the pack, tying it up so it formed a sling he could wear over one shoulder.



Quietly descending the stairs that led to the kitchen, Arderi hoped to scrounge up some food for his travel and be off before the house awoke.

To his surprise, when he arrived in the kitchens, his mother and Mag'Oella both stood in the kitchens waiting on him.

"You retired to your room so fast last eve, I did not have the chance to speak with you." Mag'Oella, her long, curly red hair bouncing on her shoulders, came walking up to him. Standing awkwardly in front of him, the girl twirled a lock of hair and fidgeted her feet.

"Hello, Mag. I was hoping to see you here."

The girl let out a giggle. "You never were much good at lying, Arderi, yet that is all for the better. You Ma says you are leaving again this morn."

"Aye. I have something I must do in Mocley."

With eyes sparkling, Mag'Oella reached out and placed a hand over Arderi's. "I have always wanted to go to a real city."

Extracting his hand from hers, Arderi reached out and took the girl by her shoulders. He felt uncomfortable talking to her in front of his mother, yet he knew he could not leave her this time without an explanation. "Look, Mag, I am truly sorry that I disappeared. I know we have all except been promised to each other." He shot a glance to his mother before returning to look at Mag. "Things have changed. I do not know where I will end up, yet I do not think it will be here."

Upon entering the kitchens and seeing her there, he had not known what he would say, nor what her reaction would be. The sharp sting her slap left upon his cheek had not even been on his list of possibilities.

"You leave without so much as a goodbye, letting everyone believe you dead or worse, and now you think you can simply brush me aside!" She flung up her hands. "Men!" Twirling around, she stormed from the room.



His mother greeted him with a wry smile, though thankfully said nothing about Mag. "Your Papa went back to our room to get something for you." She held out a sack. "There should be a good tenday worth of food here, if you can manage not to eat all of it in one sitting."

"My thanks, Ma." Taking the sack, he set it next to his own on the floor. "Ma, I—"

"Shhh!" She cut him off. "Do not make this harder for us than it needs be." She wiped her hands on her apron. "I want you to remember one thing for me, Arderi."

"Aye, Ma?"

"You have never fit in, we have always known this. You have always dreamed of being more than just a fielder. When your brother, Alant—" She paused and covered her mouth. It embarrassed Arderi to watch her fight off tears. "When he was...accepted into the Shaper Order, we saw how it affected you. How much you wanted to have that as well. Well, mayhaps that is not the life the Gods have planned for you. Mayhaps you will find something in Mocley. Yet always remember." She reached out and pulled him into a hug as she began to weep. "Never forget, if you do not...find what you are looking for...we will always be here for you. You are a man full grown now. Still, I do not want you to feel like you have to stay on your own." She held him out at arms length, tears flowing unchecked down her face. "You will always have a home here."

"I know, Ma." During the meeting on the past eve, Arderi told them most of what happened to him during his time in the Nektine. He had not, however, mentioned anything about the Tat'Sujen or any of the related subjects around the mysterious Commander Clytus Rillion other than the man's death. He wanted to say something more, something to make her understand, yet he did not know where to start.

*I do not even understand how it relates to me! What can I tell her?*

The door opened behind them and Tanin walked in. "It is almost sunrise, son."



Turning, he looked at his father and noted that the man first glanced to Arderi's hip before crossing the room. Tanin held out his hand, a stoic look upon his face.

Arderi reached out to take the offered hand, yet rushed in and embraced his father instead. "I love you and Ma so much, Papa. I am sorry for all the trouble I have caused."

Tanin embraced Arderi warmly, rubbing a hand up and down his back. "I know son. I know. I am not happy at the manner in which you started all this, yet I must say, I am proud of how you are handling it now."

Releasing his embrace, Arderi took a step back and looked into his father's eyes. "My thanks, Papa."

Biting his lower lip, Tanin reached out and placed his hands on Arderi's shoulders. "I only ask that you do me and your Ma one thing." Arderi nodded. "While you are in Mocley, you find out about Alant. There is only one thing that gnaws at the heart more than losing a son, and that is not knowing how or why."

Breaking eye contact, Arderi dropped his gaze to the floor.

"Aye, Papa. If it is within my power, I will do as you ask."

"Good." Tanin reached down, picked up Arderi's pack, and held it for him to take. "Now, you have a caravan to catch."

Taking the pack, Arderi turned to his mother. He knew she was fighting back tears once more and he wished he were not the instrument of that pain.

"Ma, I—" Arderi was once again cut off by his mother's crushing embrace. She cried fully now, and her quiet sobs shook her body. He returned her hug and let her continue crying until she broke from him on her own.

"I know you are doing what you feel you must, and I will not stop you. Yet keep in mind that I have already lost one son, do not make me bear the loss of a second."

The thought of reminding her that, until last eve, she had borne the loss of two sons crossed his mind, yet wisely, he held his tongue.

"Farwell, Ma. I will remember your words and, if it is in my power, do as you say."



They walked him to the front door and followed him out onto the porch. Arderi assumed they would walk with him all the way to the fair grounds where the caravan had stayed. When they did not follow him down the stairs onto the street, he paused and glanced back. "Are you not coming?"

"Nix, son. This is as far as we go." Taking a small pouch from his pocket, Tanin held it out toward Arderi. "It is not much, yet it is all that we have. It will serve you better than us."

Guilt swept over Arderi at the thought of the coins resting in his pack.

*In that one pouch alone, I have a lifetime's wage for a simple fielder like my father.*

Kneeling down, he opened his pack and withdrew two gold ta'narians. Standing, he walked back up the stairs, put one hand over his father's coin purse, and forced it down. "Nix, Papa. Let me lighten your burden for once."

Opening his father's hand, he set the two coins in Tanin's palm. Tanin stared at the money in disbelief. "Son, how could you have so much money?"

"Fear not, Papa, it is not ill gained. It was a final gift from Master Rillion. He instructed me to use it for any needs I may have. I have no greater need than caring for my family."

Speechless, Tanin nodded.

Not wanting to be drawn into more emotional embraces, Arderi quickly descended the stairs, re-slung his packs over his shoulder, and walked down the cobblestone street toward the fair grounds. He was about to round the corner of the last building on the row when he glanced over his shoulder. His parents still stood on the porch, clinging tightly to each other. He paused for a fraction of a moment to etch their image into his mind. Without looking away, Arderi took a few more steps and his parents disappeared from his view. A slow, burning ache crept into his heart and he stopped in the street.

*Do not make this harder than it needs be.*

Forcing himself forward, Arderi took a step, then another. Before he could stop himself, he raced along at a full run, thankful that the streets sat deserted at this early aurn.



Rounding a bend, the fair grounds burst into view. Many of the wagons were already hitched and waiting in a line upon the street that led out of the Hild'alan stead. Slowing to a walk, Arderi strode up to the front wagon.

Jintrill sat perched upon the bench looking uncomfortable as usual. "I wondered how I would go about locating you should you decide not to show this morn."

Taking the hand the Shaper offered, Arderi stepped up and plopped down beside him. "I could no more miss this caravan than I could stop taking breath."

Before long, the rest of the wagons joined those on the road and the caravan headed for Mocley. Heavy-hearted, Arderi sat and watched his home slip by. When they passed under the main gates, Arderi caught the eye of Guarder Captain Nime. The grizzly man stood with a hand resting upon the hilt of his sword and nodded once to Arderi as the wagon rolled passed. Nodding back, Arderi again realized how much he had changed since he stowed away inside Master Rillion's caravan. Thinking back to the day, his mind recalled the strange Priestess of Saphanthia he met during his time at the Palintium. If was unfortunate he had not thought of her sooner. He would have liked to speak with her once more.

*Well, Priestess, I am unsure of what road I now travel. Still, I think it has become a bit more narrow than it was before. My only hope is that it does not lead me to ruin.*

# Chapter 60

The crushed stone path crunched under the soft soles of Alant Cor's golden slippers. Though the weather had warmed and summer had fallen fully upon the Isle of Elmorr'eth, the foliage he walked among still bloomed in their vibrant greens, reds, yellows, and different hues of blue. Shaith Ku'rin, her dark silky skin radiating in the warm sunlight, strolled along beside him. Alant found he had grown to enjoy her company even more than the thrill of learning from the Elmorr'Antiens.



Almost two tendays had passed since Quiln had been sent home. Alant had nearly stamped out the fear that at any moment they would come for him, rip him from his room, and do whatever it was they had done to the orphan boy.

*Those red-slashed eyes, so vacant looking, still haunt my dreams.*

He shuddered, and Shaith cut her jade eyes at him. "You be cold? It be near as warm here as in my own land."

"Nix. I was just thinking."

"You do that a lot of late. There be a saying back home, 'Friendship be one mind in two bodies.'"

"And what is that supposed to mean?" He was never good at sayings.

She punched him in the arm. "It do mean that if you see us as friends, you should no keep secrets from me."

Rubbing at the spot where she struck him, Alant took a deep breath. "It is not that I am keeping secrets. It is just that when I try to talk with you or Jerith about what I have heard the

Elmorr'Antiens discussing, you do not believe me."

Letting out a sniff, Shaith reached out and plucked a small, light blue flower from a bush that rested along the side of the path. "You say this like it be hard to understand. You yourself said you no speak the Elmorr'Antien tongue, yet you say you know what they say." She brought the flower to her nose and smelled, while looking at him over the top of its thin pedals.

*I could drown in those green eyes.*

Not for the first time, he thought of telling her about the Tarsith.

*It has to be the Tarsith that lets me understand them. It is the only thing that makes sense!*

Yet, he did not dare break his word to Sier Sarlimac. And not just his vow to not tell anyone, also the old Sier's warning that people would die if an Elmorian found out about it. He could not bear the thought of anything bad happening to Shaith. Still, he wanted to tell her. "I wish I could explain, it is just—" The Tarsith radiated cold, jolting what he was about to say from his lips.



*"...full again? So soon!"* Vanria Delmith's voice came from just ahead of them, beyond the tall bushes that made up the outer wall of the hedge-maze. *"I had thought six moons was fast, yet this...It has not even been two tendays!"*

"What—" At Shaith's first word, Alant covered her mouth with his hand and pushed her off the path into a small thicket of plants.

*"I am just as surprised as you."* The snide voice of Prince Aritian floated from the same location. *"Yet I am sure. I went to the Chi'utlan as soon as I arrived. It is filled to the brim."*

*"I agree, my Prince, it must mean something."* Delmith's voice sounded both filled with excitement and dread all at once. *"Never before has the Chi'utlan filled faster than a full turn of the season, then, when the last filled in half that time, I thought mayhaps. Yet now..."*

*"Yes! That is why I want the strongest this time."*

A tingling cascaded down Alant's back.

*"Alant? It is too soon. The Shapers in Mocley may question—"*

The Prince cut off whatever Delmith was going to say.

*"I question why you would argue with me over this. I question whether you have forgotten who you owe so much to."* Vanria Delmith made a strangling sound that Prince Aritian continued speaking over. *"You seem to have an interest in this Alant creature that goes beyond a simple curiosity of their race. Tell me why."* Silence stretched between the two Elmorians and Alant was afraid they had walked deeper into the hedge-maze. *"Tell me why. Now!"*

*"As you say, my Prince, it shall be done."* Alant heard the strain in Delmith's tone. *"I am simply concerned that a second Ro'Arthian may lead to suspicion. Using the Silawaian, the boy from the warrior class, would raise less suspicion."*

*"Do not presume too much with me, Delmith."* The Elmorian Prince laughed. A sound like glass tinkling down rocks. This was something Alant did not know an Elmorian could do. *"That is not your reason. At least, not your only one."*

Long moments once again stretched out. Finally, in a lower voice that before, Delmith continued. *"I have some...concerns when it comes to the Alant boy."*

*"Concerns? How so?"*

*"Have you attempted to perform a Chi'tar upon him?"*

*"I have, and was unsuccessful. Yet, there are a rare few Humans whom it has been recorded that the Chi'tar cannot be preformed upon—all of them Shapers. It is an odd thing. I do not, however, see how it relates."*

*"As you say, my Prince. Yet, I also suspect that the boy speaks our tongue—or at least understands it."*

*"That is preposterous!"* Prince Aritian's voice made it clear that he truly had no doubt of this, yet Alant was more frightened now than ever. *"Never in the recorded history of our race has any outsider been able to speak our tongue!"*

*"As you say, my Prince. Alas, I do believe it may be so."*

*"Why? What cause have you?"*

*"Little things, my Prince. He seemed shocked the first time we spoke in front of him."*

*"Being shocked at hearing an unfamiliar tongue means nothing."*

*"No, not in and of itself. Yet he knew that we were coming for the Quiln boy. I found him watching from his room when we collected him."*

*"That is worse, yet still not incriminating."* The Prince laughed once more. *"I think you are—"*

*"He asked about the Mah'Sukai."* It was the first time Alant heard Delmith speak over Prince Aritian, and he held his breath as a long silence stretched between the two.

*"That is...a concern."* Long moments continued to pile up. *"It seems that decides it even more of a certain, then."*

A rustling told Alant that the two Elmorians were on the move. He strained his ears to catch anything else that might be said between them. He noticed that the Tarsith hanging around his neck had grown warm once more, and realized he would learn nothing else. Removing his hand from Shaith's plump lips, he stood, helping the girl up as he did.

Fire burned inside the green eyes of the dark skinned girl. "I do hope you have an explanation for this?"

Motioning her to be quiet—earning him another angry look—Alant took Shaith by the arm and headed back to the Chandril'elian at a brisk clip. He refused to say anything else to her until they were back in his room with the door shut.



With an exasperated sigh, she flopped onto his bed. "Either you be going crazy, or mayhaps I be for even asking, yet I will know what be going through that thick head of yours."

Sitting down hard next to her, he lowered his chin into his hands. "I am uncertain." Turning, he took her hands in his. "Look, I know you have trouble believing this. I understand what the Elmorr'Antiens are saying when they speak in their own tongue." He held up a hand to forestall her protests. "I know. We have gone over this many times. You do not have to believe me. Alas, I think this evening they are coming for me."

Her eyes grew large, then her mischievous grin popped to her lips. "You fool too much, I think." When Alant's facial features did not lose their worried state, Shaith's grin slipped. "Or you be paranoid!"

She adjusted herself on the bed so that she had one leg bent before her, the other draped over the edge, resting her foot on the floor. "Tell me what you did hear."

Blinking, Alant sat up straight. "So you believe me?"

"I never said I did no believe you." He gave her a wry look. "I just did say it be difficult to accept. I do have to admit, you do act strange every time the Elmorr'Antiens go to talking. So tell me."

"The first time—"

A loud click sounded through his tiny room and his door swung open, making both of them jump. Jerith stood in the doorway casting looks between the two with an odd expression on his face. "I thought I did hear your door, yet I no expected to find the *Princess* in here with you."

Alant felt his face go flush. "It is not what you think." Standing, he grabbed Jerith by the arm, pulled him into the room, and shut the door. With three now in the room there was no space for anything else. "Look, Jerith, you have been here longer than anyone." He glanced at Shaith and motioned for her not to be offended. "How many Human Initiates have you seen since you arrived?"

Crossing his dark skinned arms across his chest, Jerith leaned against the wall next to the door. "In the three turns of the seasons I did be here, there have been three others—no including you two."

"So two others, other than Quiln?"



The black boy nodded.

"And Quiln just left."

Snorting, Jerith dropped his head and shook it. "Aye, Quiln did be sent home. And that be good riddance. The boy had no the skill to train here with us."

Holding up his hands, Alant tried to halt what he knew would follow. "Just hear me out." He sat back down next to Shaith and looked into her eyes. "I agree that Quiln was not skilled in the Essence. That he should not have been here. Yet, even Jerith said he did not speak at all the morn he left."

"It did be apparent that the boy be upset." Jerith gave the same response whenever Alant broached the subject of Quiln's sudden departure.

"Be that as it may. The fact is he seemed…" Alant wanted to say stunned, yet he knew Jerith's response to that as well. "… different."

Shaith crossed her arms below her breasts. "Aye, he did seem more withdrawn that morn, yet…"

"And the others before him?" Alant looked back to Jerith.

"What happened to them?"

Shrugging his shoulders, Jerith pushed himself off the wall. "The last did be a golden-haired brat from someplace she said be eastron of here, yet she be crazy as there be nothing in that direction except ocean."

"I care not where she was from, what happened to her?"

"She did leave."

"How? When?" Alant tried to keep the exasperation from his tone, yet found he was failing.

Shrugging once more, Jerith made a non-committal sound.

Shaith let out a loud sigh. "Her name did be Srist, or some such. She did be here when I arrived. And she did be sent off before we even knew she no be here anymore."

"What were you told?"

"Nothing. She simply did be gone one morn."

Making an exasperated sniff, Jerith yanked open the door. "You both be making more of this than it is. That little chit did be sent home. That be that." Stepping into the hall, he slammed the door behind him.



"He just be jealous."

This shocked Alant almost as much as Jerith's anger. "What do you mean, jealous?"

She giggled and Alant's heart skipped a beat. "Of us, silly."

Finding his throat suddenly dry, Alant swallowed. "What do you mean, us?"

The dark-skinned girl laughed out loud. "Do no be so nervous. I simply did mean of us being friends. You may no see it, yet Jerith, he be Hek'kie. They be bred to fight, even if they no understand what they fight for." The grin that always said she was up to no good sprang to her lips. "Still, it be good to know you think there be more to us."

At the touch of her hand brushing his arm, Alant jumped from the bed. She followed him up and backed him against the wall, her wicked grin never leaving her mouth. "I still think you worry too much." Reaching under his arm, she lifted the latch to his door. It swung silently open. Striding into the hall, she glanced back at him. "I say you will be fine. Alas, if the gray-ones do come for you, there be no much we can do about it." Shutting the door behind her, she left him in the dimly lit room.

Looking around the tiny room, as if it were new to him, he found that he was at a loss as to what to do.

*I should be scared out of my wits. I have no idea what the Elmorr'Antiens plan for me. Alas, I am unsure if that is my biggest fear, or my feelings for Shaith.*

# Chapter 61

As the wagon crested a hill, Arderi Cor was met with a hauntingly familiar sight of the grand city of Mocley. Though this was the first instance his eyes had beheld the city, his mind knew it had been here before.

*Alant's Crystal!*

It looked exactly the same as he remembered. Mocley spread out over the land like a blanket covering hills and fields alike. It was as big as he remembered, and the outer walls ran like a great stone snake stretching off into the horizon. The vast, blue-green waters of the Glonlore Bay rolled off to the left of the city.



"It is so strange, returning somewhere you have never been."

The Shaper, Jintrill Deln, shot him an inquisitive look. "What?"

Letting out a forced laugh, Arderi shook his head. "It is nothing." Reaching under the seat, he withdrew the pack that contained the collector and Master Rillion's sword, Dorochi.

"Are you planning on wearing two swords in town?"

"Nix, Sier." Arderi carefully withdrew the collector. "I want to deliver this as soon as we enter the city."

"Aye, I will take us directly to the Chandril'elian. The Council of Elders will be expecting it."

"Nix!" Arderi had not meant for the word to come out as a command. Yet, the thought of appearing in front of a group of

Master Shapers troubled him. He still had no idea what *power* rested inside him. Until he knew, he intended on keeping a good distance from any Master Shaper. "We will deliver it to Master Rillion's widow. I owe him that much at least."

Nodding, Jintrill sat back onto the wagon bench. "Aye, as you say. It should be easy to find his villa. I understand he was well respected here in Mocley."

The wagons passed through Gatetown, its streets busy with activity, and toward the main gates. Even though Arderi had experienced the ride into Mocley through the Crystal Alant sent his family, the sheer oppressive weight of the massive walls of the city still bore down upon him like an avalanche. Guarders by the dozen, each garbed in yellow and blue tabards adorned with a talon clutching a wheat stalk, worn over a mail hauberk, milled around the entrance. For the most part the guarders ignored the hundreds of people and animals who filled the square going about their daily lives.



Pausing in the large, cobblestone-paved area just outside the tunnel that led into the city proper, Arderi lost himself in the commotion as the caravan master conversed with a guarder who approached. Without incident, the lead wagon lurched forward and disappeared into the maw of the city, followed by the rest of the caravan.

The wagon he rode entered the tunnel and all light from outside disappeared. A sense of apprehension gripped Arderi. The shadows created by the torches lining the walls bounced and danced as they rode deeper into the interior of the tunnel. He stared up at the vaulted ceiling and the massive, iron portcullises embedded in the center. As before, he could not fathom what mechanism could raise such a massive weight.

The smell of the Bazaar reached his nose long before the sight of it, and the sounds deafened Arderi. The wagons lurched back into the light and the surrounding sights overwhelmed him. People by the thousands milled around the entrance to the Bazaar. Men and women and animals, all mixed together in a swirl of motion and color. All fighting their way through what looked like an impenetrable mass of bodies.

Turning, Arderi focused on Jintrill in the hopes of regaining some semblance of sanity. A feeling of hopelessness threatened to overwhelm him. "How can we possibly get anywhere in this?" His voice strained as he yelled, attempting to be heard over the din of the place.

"This?" The Shaper waved a hand over the crowd and a broad smile sprang to his lips. "This is just market day. It is not hard. You just have to catch a current of people going in the general direction you wish to travel."

Looking back over the crowd, all Arderi saw was a chaotic sea of bodies slamming into one another. The wagons had made little progress since entering the city proper, even though the caravan master shouted at anyone in front of him while snapping his whip violently in the air above their heads.

"Come on." Jintrill tugged at Arderi. "We will make faster time on foot." Pulling Arderi along in his wake, the Shaper jumped off the wagon and threaded his way through the crowd.



Arderi was thankful that the Sier kept hold of his sleeve, for if they became separated, he doubted he would ever see him again.

*I am not certain I could even find the main gates again!*

Although, with one last pull from the Shaper, Arderi found that they were in a group of people heading in the same direction and their pace increased dramatically. Worming his way past an old woman with a large sack thrown over her shoulder, Arderi fell into pace beside Jintrill. "Do you have any idea where we are headed?"

Letting out a laugh, the Shaper clasped a hand on Arderi's shoulder. "Aye, my brave swordsman. I grew up here. We are headed to Old Town. That is probably the best place to look for our destination. The crowds will thin some the closer we get to Old Town as well. I will ask a Watchman of the Gate and see if anyone knows if Master Rillion has a villa there.

The stream of people surrounding the two young men

carried them through a smaller, interior gate and into a different part of the city. Stepping through the large arch, Arderi was awestruck by the sight of a massive, marble building. It was more than massive, taller by far than any building he had ever seen.

*Some if its spires stretch so high, they are lost in the clouds!*

Wide, open staircases ascended for dozens of paces, each bedecked with meticulously carved statues of the Twelve Gods of Man. The stairs led to a wide-open porch framed with low walls decorated with frescos carved into the stone.

"Welcome to New Town." Jintrill smiled at Arderi. "I have been told that our Palintium is the most beautiful temple to the Twelve anywhere on the Plane."

Swallowing hard, Arderi nodded. "Aye, I never dreamed a building could take my breath away."

Grabbing Arderi by the arm, Jintrill pulled him away from the Palintium and further into the city. The two walked down a wide, cobblestone-paved street winding their way through tides of people.



*How can so many live in one place?*

The splendor of the Palintium faded from Arderi's thoughts once they walked into the shadows of an even larger stone structure. This building's walls were as high and wide as those of his home stead. Arderi stopped in his tracks and had to crane his neck to see the top where colorful streamers wafted gently in the breeze. "Is that a stead inside the city walls?"

Letting out a laugh, Jintrill shook his head. "Nix. That is the Grand Coliseum, you country lout."

Pointing upwards, Arderi's jaw fell open. "That is a building? It is bigger than Hild'alan!"

"Aye, and nearly a quarter of all the people who live here in Mocley can find a seat inside during one of the events held here."

*This is where the Games are held! How many Bard's tales have I heard centered around this very building?*

They followed a road that skirted alongside the great

building. Arderi could not stop staring up at the Coliseum as they passed.

Finally, after walking inside the city walls for near an aurn, Jintrill strode up to a guarder who stood watch at yet another interior gate. "Hail, Watchman."

The guarder nodded briskly. "Hail, Sier. How may I assist?"

"I am hoping you have heard of a man who goes by the name Clytus Rillion. I am told he has a villa somewhere in Old Town."

"Aye, Sier. If you mean Clytus Rillion, Commander of the Rillion mercenary troop."

"Aye, that is the man I seek."

The guarder rubbed his chin. "I have not seen him for many a moon. He may be out of the city." The man threw a thumb over his shoulder, pointing deeper into the city. "His villa is not hard to find. Continue down Coliseum and head west on Cross. It is down in that section."



"My thanks to you." Jintrill stepped past the man and through the gate.

Raising a hand to wave at the guarder, Arderi hurried to catch up with the Shaper. After a few more inquiries, the two arrived at the gates of a small, walled villa.

The walls themselves were some four or five paces high of smooth, white granite. An iron-spiked fence adorned the top and followed the wall as it snaked from the entranceway and off in either direction, curving out of sight. Peering through the bars of the gate, Arderi saw a spacious, cobblestone courtyard. In the center, surrounded by blooming flowers, a large fountain gurgled. Beyond the fountain, he saw a flight of steps, which led to the main door. From his right a loud banging resounded as someone slammed the stable door shut.

A gruff looking shirtless man came striding up to the gate. Arderi had never seen a man with skin so dark, as if someone had painted him black. Sweat poured down the sides of his face and scarred chest. Pulling a dirty rag from his belt, he began wiping down his body. "Aye, Sier, What might I do for you?" Exasperation dripped from his voice.

The man's accent was thick and Arderi had a difficult time understanding him.

"Is this the home of Clytus Rillion?"

Tucking the rag back into his belt, a grim look passed over his features, and his words were no longer irritated, they were down right angry. "Aye, tis. I did already tell the Order I no have any news as of yet."

"You misunderstand, sir." Jintrill took a step back and waved an arm toward Arderi. "The one who needs to speak with you is this young man."

Arderi's face flushed. He had spent the time since Jintrill started inquiring about directions trying to decide what he would say once they arrived at their destination.

*Where do I begin?*

Kneeling down, Arderi un-slung his pack from his back, opened it, and withdrew Master Rillion's sword. Rising, he held the blade out before him.



The shirtless man's eyes went wide. Without looking away from the sword, he reached out for the latch on the gate and fumbled with it for many moments before he wrenched the gate open. Taking a step out onto the road, he simply stood, rooted. Finally, he raised his head and locked eyes with Arderi. "Then he be…"

Arderi saw the pain in the man's eyes. Not trusting himself to speak, Arderi bowed his head and held out his hands, offering up the sword.

Taking the weapon, the man turned and walked into the villa. "Come, you both look weary. I will see that you get refreshments."

The man led the way into the villa, and showed them to a small room directly off the entrance hall. They found several large chairs scattered around the room and each sank cautiously into one of them. They stared after their guide as he disappeared further into the villa.

Glancing nervously at Jintrill, Arderi opened his mouth to speak. He snapped his mouth shut when a loud, mournful wail of a woman sliced through the house. The cry viciously attacked anything that had ears with which to hear. It rolled out continuously, seemingly without end, and Arderi wondered how one person could have so much breath. When it finally did stop, a haunting silence filled the air.

Shifting in his seat, Arderi watched Jintrill's face go pale. For some reason this calmed him a bit.

Within moments, the man from the gate, now wearing a shirt, came in caring a tray of meats and fruits and a pitcher beaded with sweat. He poured two mugs of a golden colored liquid and handed one to each. "My name be Ragnor. I be the custodian here while Master Rillion be away." He had a formality to his tone, laced with a numbness Arderi himself felt. "The mistress of the house will join us when she be up to the task. For now, I would hear your tale."



Taking a quick sip from his cup, Arderi told his story the same way he had in the dining hall of his home. Here too, he refrained from telling anything that happened in private between Clytus and him. While he told of the events, Jintrill added things that the Shaper felt were important.

Once all was said, Ragnor rose to his feet and bowed low to each in turn. "Sier Deln, Mir'am Cor, my thanks to you both. For your friendship to Master Rillion, as well as your courage and loyalty to his cause." Reaching out, he picked up the collector that Arderi had removed from his pack during his tale. "I will see that this be used for the purpose it did be meant for."

Reaching out, Arderi grabbed onto Ragnor's arm as the man started to turn and leave. "One more thing, Mir'am—"

*I do not know his surname!*

"Please, do call me Ragnor."

"Aye, sir." Arderi reached into his pouch and withdrew the Crystal Master Rillion had given to him. "I was also instructed to pass this along to you by name. Master Rillion said you would know how to handle things from there."

A puzzled look crossed Ragnor's dark face as he reached out and took the Crystal. "It be getting late. Do you two have somewhere to stay for the eve?"

Jintrill rose. "I have rooms in the Chandril'elian and I think the Council of Elders would be cross with me if I delay my return much longer." He looked over to Arderi. "You may stay with me if you wish."

The thought of staying in the building that Alant had called home brought up a tang of pain.

*Yet the thought of being surrounded by Shapers is more unsettling for some reason.*

Arderi stood as well. "Nix, Sier. I am thankful for your offer. I am unsure of what I will do. Yet for now, I think our paths separate here."

"That is an easy question to answer, Mir'am Cor." All three men flinched as a woman, tall and dark, with a look that spoke of emptiness and pain, glided into the room. "You will stay with us for as long as you wish." She turned and gave an empty smile to Ragnor. "You will see to it, Ragnor?"



Bowing low, Ragnor inclined his head. "Of course, Mistress."

"I am to understand that you are the one who returned with the collector." The woman, whom Arderi took to be Clytus' widow, locked her haunting gaze onto Arderi, and all he could do was nod. "For that deed alone you have the gratitude of House Rillion. Whatever your need, you have only to ask and it shall be done."

Arderi mimicked Ragnor's bow. "My thanks to you, Mistress Rillion. And I am truly sorry for your loss."

At his words, her spine stiffened, though whatever pain she was feeling never touched her face. "I am grateful for what you have done." Turning, she drifted from the room without ever looking back, leaving an air of tension floating between all three men.

Clearing his throat, Jintrill broke the silence. "As you say, Master Ragnor, it is getting late. I will take my leave now." He moved and looked at Arderi. "Are you sure you do not wish to join me at the Chandril'elian?"

Glancing first to Ragnor, Arderi shook his head. "Nix, Sier. I am grateful for your offer. Yet I will stay here."

*And mayhaps I can glean some answers to my questions.*

"Very well then." Jintrill reached out, placed one hand upon Arderi's upper arm, and took his hand in his. "I have never thanked you properly. If not for your courage, I would have died up there in the Nektine. I will not soon forget that."

"I do not feel I would have survived without you either. I think we are even on that score."

The two young men exchanged a long look before Jintrill withdrew from the room.

Watching him leave, Ragnor let out a grunt once the Shaper passed through the main doors. He allowed the Shaper enough time to cross the courtyard before he turned back to Arderi. "It be unwise to forgive a debt that be owed to you by a Shaper, Mir'am Cor. Debts of that level be hard to come by, and be valuable when needed." He pointed back toward the chair Arderi had vacated. "Sit, we do have much to discuss."



Arderi sat, except instead of Ragnor joining him, the man looked at the Crystal still in his palm, then left the room heading in the direction Jintrill had taken. More than a few moments passed, and Arderi wondered if Ragnor meant to return.

When he did return, he carried Clytus' sword in his left hand. Kneeling down in front of Arderi, he drew the blade and rested its point upon the floor. Unwrapping the leather from the hilt, he allowed the red light from the Ka'gana stone to flood out into the small sitting room. He then bowed and rested his forehead upon the sword's pommel. "I, Ragnor De'haln, pledge to you, Arderi Cor, to uphold all that be Sujen. I shall protect you, always be faithful and no waiver in my vows neither to you nor to the Tat'Sujen Order. To these, I allow my Essence to be bound, once again, by the Melding of my very being to that of Ka'gana."

Arderi's eyes opened wide as the red glow from the Crystal

buried inside the hilt expanded to envelop both himself and Ragnor. "What—" Arderi's throat went dry and he coughed to clear it. "What has happened?"

Standing, Ragnor re-sheathed Dorochi and held it out across his palms, presenting it to Arderi. "All will be revealed soon. Take Dorochi, she be yours now. As of this day, your training as a Tat'Sujen begins."

# Chapter 62

The eve rolled on, yet Alant Cor never left his room. Shaith Ku'rin came by to ask him to lastmeal. He declined even her.

*I do not think I could keep any food down anyway.*

The events of the last few tendays, along with all that he had learned, rolled over in his mind like a whirlwind inside his skull. He could not puzzle out what the Elmorr'Antiens planned for him—what need they had of Humans at all. Mah'Sukai, Chi'utlan, the Chandril'chi with its black bark and blood-colored leaves—they were all tied in some way.



*Ha! They are all tied around my neck!*

Over and over he tried to recall all that he knew of the Elmorians. Things he had learned while in Mocley, bits of stories he had picked up at his home in Hild'alan. Though he had to admit, most of what he learned prior to going to Mocley was petty fielder superstition. No one from his home stead had ever actually seen an Elmorian.

*Alas, much of what I learned even in Mocley is of little help either. The Shapers do not really know the Elmorr'Antiens any better than my Ma or Papa.*

A knock sounded at the door and Alant rolled over on his hard bed to face the wall. "Go away, Shaith. I need time to think."

"Thinking is always good, yet I think we need to talk instead, yes?"

The silky-smooth voice of Vanria Delmith sent a shudder surging through Alant and he sat bolt upright. The Elmorian stood in the open doorway. Alant had not even heard the latch lift. "What—what do we need to talk about?"

Tilting his blue-gray tear-dropped shaped head to the side, his teacher stood for a long moment staring at Alant. "You are almost believable enough to have passed here unnoticed. Actually, had it not been for the fact that I alone work with the Human Initiates, no one may have noticed you, yes?"

"I…um…I do not understand, Vanria Delmith."

"Of course you do not." Thin black lips slipped into a razor sharp smile that did not touch the Elmorian's black liquid eyes. "Come." Raising a bone-skinny arm, he indicated the exit of the Human quarters.

Swallowing to moisten a throat gone dry, Alant rose to his feet, yet did not move. "Where?"

"You have been summoned to the Hon'Vanria's office. There is nothing to fear, provided you keep a true tongue, yes?"

Hesitating for another moment, Alant's mind raced.

*Like a rat trapped in a corner by a housecat! I have no hope of escape!*



Slowly, hesitantly, Alant nodded his head and walked into the hallway. It turned into a somber, quiet trip. The two wound their way through the halls that took them to the stairs leading to the Hon'Vanria's private office. It was only the second time Alant had ever been allowed onto any of the upper floors of the Chandril'elian—the first, being the eve he arrived on the Island of Hath'oolan when Shaith had taken him to this same office.

Reaching the top of the stairs, Alant noticed that the receiving room outside the office had not changed since his first visit. Benches and chairs sat opposite the large window looking out onto the end of the boulevard at the front of the school.

*The area that holds the Chandril'chi—that Gods awful tree!*

Without pausing, Delmith crossed the room to the double-doors leading to the inner office, with their strange carved runes of inlaid gold and silver. The doors swung open silently at his approach. The office too, looked the same. Bookshelves lined one wall stuffed with an assortment of items, and opposite these another large window, twin to the one in the waiting room, and the enormous desk that filled much of the space between.

Yet, like his first visit, Alant paid little mind to any of it. In fact, even though Prince Aritian and the Hon'Vanria stood on the other side of the desk, they held none of Alant's interest either. All his attention fell on the black-skinned boy who shared the Human quarters with him.

"Ahh!" Prince Aritian sounded as if he were greeting an old friend. "Young Initiate Cor has finally arrived." Turning to Jerith, he lifted a hand to the doors. "Initiate De'thane, you are excused, yes? We shall use your…"—the Prince cut his eyes across the desk to Alant—"…information."

With a hasty bow and a hurried glance at Alant, Jerith scampered out the doors.

*What has that fool done! How could he have betrayed me like this?*

Once the white carved doors shut, Prince Aritian glided around the desk and pulled one of the chairs from the side of the room. Sliding it in front of the desk, he rested both his hands on its topmost ladder-backed rung. "Please." He indicated to the chair. "Sit. I think we have much to discuss, yes?"

Alant took a step toward the chair, then paused. The thin Elmorians already stood a hand taller than he and the thought of reducing his height by sitting—having them looming over him even more—appalled him. "I think I will stand, if that is acceptable, Prince Arit…tian." He stuttered the last word as a bolt of cold from the Tarsith shot through him. It was all he could do to stop from grasping the amulet hanging around his neck.



Shock raced across the Hon'Vanria's face. His eyes opened wide and his mouth fell open. "He knew! The boy knew when I preformed the Chi'tar upon him! And you are correct, my Prince, I failed!" Anger replaced the shock upon the Elmorian's face. "How did you do this, hmm? Tak'ju'nar!"

Thoughts spun in Alant's head, things he might say to clear himself. Yet, fear clamped his mouth shut firmer than the gates of his home stead after dark. Unable to speak, he simply stood there looking from one blue-gray face to the next.

"Yes, you are an enigma, Initiate Cor. Yet, I think we all know what you are and why you are here, hmm?" The Prince paused as if he expected Alant to answer. "No? Very well. Silence may be your best defense now that we have found you out."

Anger finally breached the fear that held Alant silent. "Defense! What need do I have to defend myself?"

"Let us not play any games here, Initiate Cor, yes?" The Prince's words dripped with scorn. "You *Humans* think you are so…cleaver, just because you can see the Essence. You are like children to us! We know that fool Council of Elders has sent you here, yes? Sent you to spy on us, yes? A Tak'ju'nar in our very home. Spying and sneaking, trying to bore out our secrets. What is it they wanted you to discover, hmm?"

Even though the accusation appalled him, Alant felt a surge of relief.

*They do not know about the Tarsith! They are just worried that I am a Tak'ju'nar—a spy.*

His heart sank at the realization that being a Tak'ju'nar could be worse for him.

"I do not understand why you think I am a spy. I was invited here by the Elmorr'Antiens."

"Pah! We invited a promising young Initiate named Alant Cor. It is true you have skill—even Delmith agrees in that—yet there is no way you are a simple farmer boy from some backwoods stead, yes?" At Alant's silence, the Prince raised a hand and flicked up one finger into the air. "You speak our tongue, or at least understand it enough to know of what we speak." The Prince added a second blue-gray finger. "You know of the Mah'Sukai. A word that has not been uttered in over eighteen thousand turns of the seasons." The third and final finger joined the others. "And you ask too many questions about past Initiates who have studied here. How could all this be if you are nothing except a Tak'ju'nar sent to us by your so-called Council of Elders, hmm?"



Alant stood, stunned. He could explain it—or most of it anyway—by revealing the Tarsith he carried.

*Yet, my vow. Not to mention that people may die! Oh, Sarlimac, I do not think you foresaw this when you gave me that accursed amulet!*

Thinking of his old Sier brought back the old man's words of warning. Remembering the vacant eyes of Quiln—the slashes of red through them—added to his fury. Alant did not know what they planned, yet he knew for certain they were up to no good. "You accuse me! You stand there and see *me* as the villain! Yet what did you do to Quiln? I saw his eyes. They were not bloodshot from crying. Those jagged streaks of red slashed even the colored parts of his eyes! He was…changed, somehow. He looked at me as if he did not recognize who I was nor even where he was! What did you do to him!?" He breathed hard once he stopped his rant, yet he did not back down nor remove the anger from his eyes.

Prince Aritian's face had drawn into a sneer as Alant shouted. Now his face became a mask of rage. *"As if you do not know!"* The Prince's words screeched out, forcing Alant to cringe away in fear. The Tarsith grew cold while the Prince continued, and Alant did not think the Elmorian realized he had slipped into his native tongue. *"It is you Humans who destroy the Plane each Cycle! You Humans who misuse the Power of the Essence!"* Alant had seen an Elmorian angry before, at least *this* Elmorian. Yet even the Prince's own kinsmen gaped at him with shocked looks and shied away from his rant. *"My father and his Circle may sit by and let the time come again when you Humans rip the Plane asunder. I will not allow it! I will not!"* Jabbing an accusing finger into Alant's chest, very nearly striking the Tarsith, spittle sprayed from Prince Aritian's black lips. *"Your Council of Elders knows. I am sure of it! They know of the Mah'Sukai and covet the power they could wield. Your being here—being sent here to spy upon us—that is proof they do not know the secret!"* A wicked grin sprang to his lips, one that never touched his eyes, and he squinted at Alant. A high-pitched laugh filled the room, a laugh without mirth. *"Oh, I do think it is time that you accomplished what you came here for, Tak'ju'nar."* Turning, the Prince glanced at Delmith. *"Yes, yes. It is time the boy gets what he is seeking. Take him back to his room till I am ready. Have one of the Gralet'nars keep him company!"*

With a slight bow of his head, Delmith started toward Alant. *"As you say, my Prince, it shall be done."* Grasping Alant by the arm—bitter cold penetrated Alant's flesh where the Elmorian's gray fingers touched—he half-led, half-dragged Alant from the room.

A pair of the giant Gralet'nars waited for them at the bottom of the stairs and fell in behind the pair as they walked down the halls toward the Human quarters. Mulling over all that had transpired, Alant's mind still reeled with unanswered questions. His imagination rippled with the horrors that could be awaiting him.

It was a shock when Delmith broke the silence. "I do not feel the Prince is correct concerning you, yes?"

Lifting his eyes to his teacher, Alant glared at him.

Former *teacher. I will not be here much longer no matter what happens.*

Alant saw him for what felt like the first time. "I am no spy, no Tak'ju'nar!"

With the slightest bow of the head, Delmith smiled. "As I said, I am inclined to agree, yes? However, that does not explain why none of us can perform a Chi'tar upon you. Nor how it is you know our tongue." Alant could think of nothing to say, so he kept silent—a silence that forced Delmith to continue. "You are an enigma, Initiate Cor, yes? Unfortunately, there is nothing I can do for you now. Once the Prince has set a course of action, none can alter it, yes?"



"What is to happen to me?" A pit of anguish nestled deep inside Alant's core, yet the Elmorian strode along in silence without answering.

When Delmith did answer, he sounded as if he spoke more to himself than to Alant. "Mayhaps nothing. Though, I think not this time. Never before has the Chi'utlan filled so rapidly. It must mean something." Turning his gaze to Alant, Delmith jumped as if he only just realized Alant still walked by his side. "We shall see, Initiate Cor, yes? We shall see. It will be quite interesting, yes?"

Just before passing under the arch leading to the Human quarters, Delmith stopped short. When Alant stopped too, a Gralet'nar shoved him further down the hall toward his room. Turning from the hallway, Delmith disappeared back the way they had come, still talking to himself. "Quite interesting indeed."

Not wanting to be left alone in the hall with the hulking Warrior Servants, Alant opened his door and entered his room. Sitting on his hard little bed, his mind still a jumble of chaos, he lay down and covered his eyes with his arm.

*There is no way out. I am like a sheep waiting on the butcher. Only, I do not know what the butcher intends! Yet I am not a sheep! I am a man! I will not die sulking. Whatever they intend, I will not give them the satisfaction of seeing me afraid ever again!*

# Chapter 63

A warm glow still filled the tiny sitting room as Arderi Cor rose and took Dorochi, Master Clytus Rillion's sword, from Ragnor's outstretched palms.

*My sword.*

Looking up into the face of Ragnor, he saw a mixture of both joy and pain warring within the older man's eyes. "I am sorry. Master Rillion told me nothing of what I am supposed to do."



"Aye, lad. Imprinted upon the Silrith'tar that you did deliver, Master Rillion did tell me thus. His hope did be that eventually you would come to forgive him for what he did to you."

Fear laced through Arderi's heart. "What did he do to me?"

Ragnor's dark lips parted in a warm smile, softening the man's hard visage. "Please, Young Master, sit yourself down." They both sat and Ragnor stared out into the darkening corridor of the villa for a long moment before he spoke again. "You be familiar with the Shapers and how they Meld the Essence. Yet that no be all of the Essence. It be so much more."

Pulse racing, Arderi's mouth went dry. "What else is it?"

Ragnor shook his head. "Alas, Young Master, I do no have the gift. I be a servant of the Order only. I did earn an honored privilege that few do get. I be a keeper of secrets, a holder of knowledge. Yet I have no the ability that Master Rillion did possess." He turned and looked deep into Arderi's eyes. "That you possess."

Swallowing hard, Arderi rubbed his sweaty palm across his thighs. "And this is why I saw Master Rillion doing all those amazing things?"

"I, unfortunately, have no ever seen any of that, so I no have any knowledge of what you speak of. Yet, I do know who does." Ragnor adjusted himself upon his chair. "The Tat'Sujen be a group of people who have a special gift. They use the Essence in a way that be wholly different from how the Shapers Meld it. The gift be very rare. Where only a handful of people manifest the ability of a Shaper, this number be infinitely large compared with those who be touched with the Sujen."

"Yet, what power? I feel nothing." Fear and excitement battled for dominance deep inside Arderi. "Why do I need to forgive Master Rillion? I do not see how he has wronged me."

Raising his hands in surrender, Ragnor shook his head. "You ask what I can no give you. I be no Tat'Sujen. I do only pass along to you what Master Rillion did instruct me to."



Aggravation swept through Arderi. "So you give me nothing except more questions!" He slammed his fist onto his thigh in frustration.

Ragnor looked at him with a stern gaze. "Calm yourself, lad. I did be instructed to take you to a place where you will find the answers you seek." Ragnor stood. "Come."

Getting to his feet, Arderi glanced around the room. "Now? I have been on the road for more than three moons."

Nodding sadly, Ragnor placed a hand upon the boy's shoulder. "Aye. Master Rillion did be quite clear about this. I am to deliver you to Bin'Satsu on the first eve you arrive in Mocley." At Arderi's inquisitive look, he sighed. "Bin'Satsu be a place of refuge for all Tat'Sujen. There be forces at work within our Plane unseen by most that live here. Master Rillion did no wish to take the chance of you stumbling upon something you no be ready to deal with. There be no safe haven for you here in Mocley. So I must take you to Bin'Satsu. At least until you be trained."

Picking up his pack, Arderi paused. "What of the widow and the boy. Will they be alright?"

Arderi saw a sadness pass over Ragnor. The man's head drooped and his shoulders slumped as if a heavy burden had been placed upon them. Reaching out, he grabbed Arderi by the elbow and led him into the entrance hall. Instead of heading out of the villa as Arderi had assumed, Ragnor led him up a flight of stairs and out onto a balcony overlooking the back garden. In the far corner, almost completely hidden in the shadows of the late eve, a dark haired woman sat on a bench. With her arms wrapped around her waist, she rocked slightly back and forth as if pushed by a gentle breeze.

"Clytus did love Shaith. He did love her more than most men have the right to love. They both did love little Sindian doubly so. It shall no be easy for either of them, yet Clytus did be no fool. He always knew this day would arrive and did plan for it for many a turn of the seasons."

Watching the woman grieve in silence by herself in the garden, Arderi now understood why Master Rillion had been so bent on completing his task.



*Will I ever love so deeply?*

Pulling his attention from the woman, he turned to Ragnor. "May I see the boy?"

"Sindian? He be asleep. The illness he has robs him of his strength."

"I will not wake him. I would simply like to see him before I go."

Nodding his head, Ragnor led Arderi down the hall to a dark room. A cool breeze wafted through the room from two large windows on the opposite wall. Waiting for his eyes to adjust, Arderi crossed the floor like a shadow to the form buried in the covers of the bed. He bent down. All that was visible of Sindian was a mop of sandy blond hair covering the boy's head. With a gentle sigh, the boy rolled over exposing his round face. The urge to reach out and cup the boy's head in his palm bubbled up, almost overwhelming Arderi. He knelt there for many moments, studying the boy's features.

*I see much of your father in you, little one.*

Something warm and wet landed on the back of Arderi's hand causing him to start. Reaching up to his face, he wiped away tears from his cheeks that he had not known were there. A rustling from the doorway informed him that Ragnor was growing impatient. Reluctantly he stood and returned to Ragnor's side at the door.

Ragnor reached out and stopped Arderi by placing his hands upon his shoulders. He peered deeply into his eyes. "Once we leave, do no speak of the Tat'Sujen, nor ask me more questions. The wrong word heard by the wrong ear can be deadly. Do you understand me?" He kept his voice to a whisper, yet Arderi knew the man was deadly serious.

Arderi matched the man's volume. "Aye, I will hold my tongue."

With a heavy heart resting in his chest, Arderi strapped the sword, Dorochi, to his waist and followed Ragnor from the villa. Darkness had fallen in full and lit torches now filled the courtyard.



A stablehand brought out two horses, each saddled and ready for travel. Ragnor reached over and took the reins of one, placed his foot in the stirrup, and swung his leg over the animal. Sitting comfortably, he gave Arderi an exaggerated look. "Well, lad. Mount up."

Glancing from the horse to Ragnor, a sense of dread swept through Arderi. "I—" Swallowing hard, he chastised himself for being a country lout. "Master Ragnor, I do not know how to ride a horse."

"You have no ever ridden a horse?" Ragnor laughed. "Well then, it be lucky we no have far to travel." Dismounting, he handed the reins of both mounts back to the stablehand. "Let us be off, Young Master." He clapped a hand on Arderi's shoulder, and then walked out the main gate disappearing into the dark street beyond.

Arderi glanced over at the stablehand leading the animals

back to the stable and thought he saw the boy grinning. Breaking into a jog, he ran to catch up to Ragnor.

The late summer eve was a bit cool and Arderi rubbed his bare arms as they walked along the mostly deserted streets.

"It be the Bay."

Catching Arderi off guard, he looked over at his guide—the dark-skinned man barely visible in the low light. "What is the Bay?"

Raising an arm, Ragnor pointed off in the distance to his left. "The Glonlore Bay. It be the reason the eve be so chilly during this season."

Nodding, Arderi tried to quell the chaos in his mind.

*I have so many questions!*

Picking out a thought at random, Arderi spoke mostly just to fill some of the silence that had fallen between them. "How long did you know Master Rillion?"

Looking over at him, Ragnor stared at him without answering as they strolled along. When he did answer, his voice quivered with loss. "For more winters than you did be alive, lad. Yet, if it no be for Clytus, I would be dead long before you did be birthed." Gazing up at the sky, he ran a hand through his long hair. "I will miss him, make no mistake about that."



The other questions racing through Arderi's head were ones he promised not to ask, so he plodded along next to a man he barely knew heading for a place that both thrilled and terrified him.

They did not walk far and Arderi could not understand why Ragnor had wanted to ride such a short distance—barely a league. After about an aurn, the two entered a brightly lit hostel. The sign above the door bore a picture of a sword embedded in a large reddish-tinted Crystal. The main room was a well-cleaned eating area. A large bar ran across the back of the room and a score or so tables and chairs were scattered everywhere else. Although the place was not filled, many of the tables held people and several serving girls flitted about the room.

Ragnor caught the eye of the man behind the bar and

headed toward him. Kicking a foot onto the footrest, he slapped some coin onto the counter. "Barkeep! My friend and I require food and a comfortable room for the eve."

The barman nodded and scraped the coins from the bar. "Aye, sir. I have a room. If you will follow me." The man stepped from behind the bar and headed off down the hallway that led deeper into the hostel. At the end of the corridor, the barman stopped at the last door on the right and fished out a ring of keys. Unlocking the door, he ushered them both inside. Instead of leaving, the barman entered as well and locked the door behind him. "Ragnor! What is the meaning of this?"

Glass containers, much the same shape as lanterns, flared to life as they entered the room casting light that filled every corner, though Arderi could not say how they did so. The room the barman had locked them in reminded Arderi of the Dining Hall at his parent's public home—only much smaller. A large table took up most of the room, cushioned chairs lining its edges. Opposite the door sat a large, cold fireplace. Tapestries hanging around the room completed the furnishings.



Taking the barman's offered hand, Ragnor shook it with a smile. "Mort, it be good to see you after so long."

"Aye, aye, and you as well, Ragnor." Mort shot a glance at Arderi. "Yet, what brings you here?"

The smile slipped from Ragnor's face. "I do come with a heavy heart, friend. Clytus...he be dead."

Shock and horror filled the barman's face. The man staggered backward and fell into a chair. "What? How?"

Taking a seat across from the man, Ragnor indicated for Arderi to join them. "He did fall in his quest to the Nektine."

Mort covered his mouth with a hand. "Then young Sindian. He will not get what he needs?"

Shaking his head, Ragnor gestured at Arderi. "Nix. This young man did finish the task. Sindian shall live, the Gods willing."

Looking at Arderi in awe, the barman reached out and took the boy's hand. "My thanks to you, sir. You have done more than you will ever know."

"I have additional news as well."

A silence fell upon the room and the barman fidgeted. "Well, do not keep me in suspense!"

"There be another."

Renewed awe sprang up in the barkeep and he looked back at Arderi. "You mean—"

"Aye, friend. Clytus did find him and send him here to me."

Mort stood and paced the small chamber. "Are you certain? This is not something we can be wrong about. How I wish Master Rillion were here delivering the boy himself."

Pulling a Crystal from his pouch, Ragnor handed it to the man. "You can hear it from Clytus' own lips, if you must. Yet, the boy be of Sujen."

"Have you lost your sense! Do not mention that before someone who is not bound!"

Ragnor raised his hands. "Settle yourself, Mort. The boy did be bound by Clytus."



The man threw a hand to his head. "Before he was trained! What if he is found unworthy? Clytus has condemned this boy to death if he should fail."

*Condemned me to death if I fail!*

"I am no sure of all the details. Yet, I do know Clytus would no have done such a thing if he did have any other options."

Arderi had sat quietly, listening to the conversation as best he could. Yet he could not stay silent any longer. "I am here! Do not speak around me! *What* has happened to me?"

The barman turned and looked at Arderi as if seeing him for the first time. His look softened and a fatherly smile spread over his lips as he reached out and put an arm around Arderi's shoulder. "You are frightened—"

Shrugging off the man's arm, Arderi shoved him away. "I am not afraid! I just want answers!" Anger pulsed through his veins and he noticed that his hand now rested on the hilt of Dorochi.

"Calm yourself, lad!" Ragnor stepped between the two. "You

be here to find your answers. Do no belittle what you represent to us. We did no simply lose a friend. We did also lose one of the most powerful men of our Order. You must give us time to wrap our minds around what you do present to us."

Arderi forced himself to calm down, yet he did not remove his hand from his hilt.

"The boy is not a fair trade for Master Rillion!" Mort brushed himself off.

Ragnor shook his head and shot the barman a hard glance. "That be no up to you to determine. The Essence owns its will. We be merely servants. Clytus did send us this boy. Aye, he did bond him and that may cause this lad no end of trouble. Still, that be no for the likes of us to discuss." Pointing to the far wall, Ragnor stood to his full height. "You be the keeper of the way, of this I no challenge you. Yet, and do hold this well within you heart—Clytus bade me bond myself to this boy, which I did before we came here. If you no admit him, I can no abandon him."



"You say you do not challenge me, yet you force my hand all the same." Throwing his hands up in disgust, he walked to the far wall. "Oh, very well! The Essence owns its own and my feelings shall not deter it." Mort reached into his shirt, pulled out a necklace, and lifted it over his head. An amulet, made of a plain circle of iron, covered in rust and pocked on both sides, dangled from the man's fist by an old piece of string. It looked about as worthless as anything Arderi had ever seen. Why the man wore it, he could not fathom. Holding it out at arms length, the man stared at with an intensity Arderi found almost comical.

*Has he lost his mind? It is a worthless old trinket.*

Yet, as Arderi watched, the amulet began to glow. At first, Arderi thought the glow was simply a reflection from the strange lanterns hanging in the corners of the room. Soon, however, there could be no mistake. The reddish glow emanated from the medallion itself. The medallion started a slow spin upon its string and the intensity of the glow increased. A red, jagged light, bright as the midday sun, soon pierced Arderi's eyes and he was forced to throw up a hand to deflect some of the light. When the room began to dim, Arderi, to his amazement, saw that Mort no longer held a simple iron disk hanging from a string. A thin, silver chain now laced its way between the man's fingers. It cascaded down to thread through a golden loop embedded into the top of a blood red Crystal.

"Like the one in Dorochi's pommel."

Arderi's whispered comment received a grunt of a laugh from Ragnor. "Aye, lad, yet it no be the same. It be a Ka'gana Crystal, like the one that be in your sword, yet this one do no have the powers that yours do."

The barman nodded. "Aye, this is merely a key."

Still staring at the Ka'gana Crystal, Arderi loosened his grip upon the hilt of his sword. "A key to what."

Mort flashed a sharp look at Ragnor, who motioned for him to continue. Letting out a sigh, the barman strolled to the far side of the room and removed a tapestry depicting men on horseback hunting in a wooded area. He re-hung it overtop one on an adjacent wall. The uncovered wall held beauty of its own. A small, round fresco was etched into the wooden wall. Its intricate design of lines and curves all culminated into a carved circle at its center. Slipping the Ka'gana Crystal into the center hole, a loud click resounded through the chamber. The entire section of wall that contained the circular fresco snapped forward, then swung into the room like a door. It revealed a long stairwell descending into darkness.

Two unlit torches sat on either side of the entranceway, and Ragnor walked over and retrieved them. Picking up some flint and steel that sat on the fireplace's mantle, he first struck one, then the other, until both were lit. He held one out for Arderi to take. "Take this. You will need it for the rest of our journey."

Striding forward, Arderi peered down the steps. They curved away to his right and disappeared from view. A deep, musty smell filled his nostrils. "Where does this lead?"

"To your destiny." Ragnor thrust one of the torches into his hand and slipped past. Arderi watched as the man descended the stairs, disappearing around the bend. The light from his torch played off the stone walls as it followed the man down.

"Best get a move on, Young Master. The Undercity is a dark and confusing place. Not somewhere you can find your way out of alone." The barman stood somberly, looking at Arderi.

"What is the Undercity and where is Ragnor taking me?"

"He is taking you to Bin'Satsu. The only protected place that our Order has. You will be safe there and receive all the answers you seek."

Glancing again down the dark stairwell, a sense of foreboding crept into Arderi.

*We could choose a path and be led to ruin, or be thrust into something that may lead us to greatness.*

Swallowing hard, Arderi started down the stairs. Before he rounded the bend, he heard the door close behind him. A loud click ricocheted past him and echoed further off in the depths of the Undercity.



*My only hope is that this is not a path that leads me to ruin.*

# CHAPTER 64

Alant Cor lay on his bed wide-awake when a knock resounded throughout his tiny sleeping chamber. His door swung open and it astonished him to see so many standing in the hallway. Prince Aritian stepped into the small room followed closely by Vanria Delmith. Alant swallowed his anticipation and, with muscles complaining, rose from the hard, thin mattress that covered his stone-slab bed. Swinging his feet to the floor, he stood, trying not to let the shaking of his knees show.



*Calm down, I am not a boy anymore! I must keep my mind sharp for whatever they are planning for me.*

Alant did not even flinch when his Tarsith fell cold.

*"Good. You are ready."* Prince Aritian smiled down at him with his thin, dark-black lips.

*A smile that does not touch his eyes.*

*"Do you ever plan on enlightening us as to how you have come to understand our tongue?"* After a moments pause, he shrugged his bony shoulders. *"No? I did not think you would. The better for me, I guess. I absolutely detest speaking in the Human dialect. It is such a crude tongue."* The Prince gestured with a thin gray arm and Alant stepped out into the corridor.

Before he turned down the hall, Alant glanced up into the deep pools of Delmith's black eyes and found it rewarding when the Elmorian averted his gaze. Stepping past a host of waiting Elmorians, most of which he had never seen before, he headed out of the Human quarters.

The door to Shaith's room cracked open as Alant passed, and he saw a glint of ebony skin and one piercing green eye peek out. Tightening his lips, he closed his eyes and gave one slow shake of his head while he marched past her door. It eased shut and Alant felt a wave of resolution slide over his heart.

*If not for me, than to insure she will never have to go through this. Whatever I must do, this ends this very eve!*

Once he passed through the archway that separated the Human sleeping chambers from the main hall, a pair of Gralet'nars joined them. Each carried a massive crossbow at the ready along with their sickle-like blades strapped to their sides. They stood in his path, leaving no doubt as to which route he should take. Forcing Alant to turn down the main hall and deeper into the building, the two Warrior Servants fell in on either side of him. Their huge frames filled most of the wide hallway leaving just enough room for Alant to walk between them. One of them gazed down at the boy with its lifeless, empty eye sockets and Alant felt his air of confidence shatter like glass.



*They do not even care to continue the deception any longer. I am no longer a student. I am a prisoner.*

With the Gralet'nars in position, The Prince slipped forward and took the lead. *"I must commend you, Tak'ju'nar. Most Humans are not so willing to meet their fate. Yet, you seem almost eager."*

The now familiar coldness of the Tarsith bore into Alant's flesh as the amulet translated the Elmorian's words in his mind. He resisted the urge to reach out and snap the Prince's scrawny neck.

*It would be of little use. The Gralet'nars would cut me down before I could wrap my fingers around his skinny throat.*

Alant had no idea how late it was, yet the main hall sat deserted as the group left the Initiate quarters and headed for the rear of the Chandril'elian and he knew that dawn had not yet broke upon the land. With the Prince in the lead, the procession walked past empty classrooms and offices that lined the long passageway. The grandeur that adorned the walls—which had so enthralled Alant upon his arrival to the school—did nothing to lift his spirits now.

Reaching the rear exit, Prince Aritian thrust open the twin doors allowing the chilly, pre-dawn air to rush into the building. Gooseflesh ran the course of Alant's body under his thin robes and he felt the hairs on the back of his neck prickle. Low-lying clouds covered the sky and silvery moonlight played off their undersides bathing everything in haunting, silvery shadows. A light breeze blew across the garden sending a locket of Alant's bangs over one eye. He stepped down the stairs and onto the gravel path that splintered off to the various buildings surrounding this lush area he had enjoyed so much on past days.

Without pause, the Elmorian Prince continued on the path that led deeper into the gardens. A shove to the back sent Alant staggering forward informing him that he must follow.

The small party entered the hedge-maze and threaded their way without deviation to its center. Though darkness bathed everything, it did nothing to detract from the beauty of the place. The white of the Chandril'chi tree statue was subdued, yet its tormented branches were clearly visible. The broad, snow-white stone leaves—blood red on the real tree that sat in front of the school—glistened with dew, as did the benches that sat upon the lush grass surrounding the art piece.



Prince Aritian stepped up to the base of the statue. *"Delmith, I will give you the honor."* He took a step back to let the Vanria approach.

*Nix! Not Vanria! Not anymore. He is not my instructor, he is simply Delmith. I will not honor any of these creatures!*

Placing his hands on the upper corners of the base, Delmith bowed, his wispy white hair draping over to cover the sides of his teardrop shaped head. Almost immediately, Alant felt his former teacher Melding the Essence. It appeared as if a great weight had been placed onto his thin gray shoulders. Alant noticed his small ribcage expand and contract rapidly as the Elmorian gasped from the exertion.

Throwing his head back, Delmith took a step back with his arms still raised. The side of the base of the tree-statue started to shimmer. Then, as if made of ice, the rock melted away revealing a stairway descending into blackness below. Alant stood stunned.

*All the times I sat in this place, gazing at that statue, I never suspected!*

The Prince produced a glowing orb from his pocket and proceeded down the stairs. Delmith, giving one last pained looked in Alant's direction, followed.

Knowing the Gralet'nars would give him no choice, and not wanting them to push him down a flight of stairs he could not see the bottom of, Alant stepped forward, pausing only briefly before plunging down after the two Elmorians.

At the base of the stairway, a small, limestone tunnel curved around, heading back in the direction of the Chandril'elian's main building. The tunnel itself, with rough walls and an uneven floor, seemed to be a natural formation.

*As if it were carved by running water.*

It was wide enough for two or three people to walk abreast, yet the Gralet'nars had to stoop to avoid scraping their heads across the ceiling. The tunnel stretched off into the distance, and even though enough of the Elmorians who followed had produced light orbs to illuminate the surrounding area for several paces, the darkness seemed to stretch on forever.



The tunnel continued straight without curving one way or the other. The natural cut of the tunnel soon gave way to stone that had obviously been worked. The limestone walls flattened, the ceiling curved into a perfect arch, and large, square marble tiles now covered the floor. The look of it surprised Alant more than the place itself.

*This is not made from the white stone that everything else in this city is made of! This is much older. Someone's hands carved these walls. And the floor tiles are the first bit of granite I have seen since arriving here in Hath'oolan.*

Alant noticed intricate runes carved into the walls as well. He recognized several of them from the Old tongue. Yet, at the pace the Elmorian Prince set, he had no time to discern their meanings.

After another few moments of the brisk walk, they reached the end of the corridor. A massive set of double doors barred their way. Each door was intricately decorated with a picture of a Chandril'chi tree inlaid in gold and made of a smooth, black material that did not seem to be a metal nor a stone. Prince Aritian strode forward with an arrogant air, and Alant felt hatred mixed with fear pour over his body.

*Whatever they have in store for me, it waits on the other side of those doors.*

The Elmorian lifted his arms—his thin gray limbs slid out from the red folds of his gold embroidered silk sleeves exposing his tiny, three-fingered hands—and Alant once again felt the Essence being Melded. With a shutter that sent a thin layer of dirt floating to the floor, the doors slid apart.

Though the glowing orbs of the Elmorian's lit the hallway well, a brighter, shimmering-silver light spilled out through the opening doors and into the tunnel. The bright light forced Alant to raise a hand and shield his eyes. He stood squinting into the blinding light, searching for details of what awaited him past the entranceway. Finally, with a sharp gesture from the Prince, a Gralet'nar shoved Alant forward, forcing him into the chamber.

Alant tumbled down a small flight of stairs that lay just inside the doorway and slammed hard onto the sand-covered, limestone floor. Prince Aritian descended the stairs gracefully and stood over him. Struggling to his feet, Alant gazed around at his surroundings. He was in a massive chamber. The glare from the light was now bearable and the sight before him left him standing in awe.



The chamber—some sixty or seventy paces high and at least double that across—was as large as any public house back in the Hild'alan stead. The floors and walls were cut from the same rough limestone as the tunnel that led them here. Its reddish-brown hue gave a sharp contrast to the shimmering silver pool dominating the center of the room. The pool sat on a raised dais that looked naturally formed as well. Surrounding the dais, he saw pillars of joined stalactites and stalagmites, which created a ring around the dais' base making it look like a large, stone cage. Opposite the doorway sat a limestone ramp. The ramp ascended from the floor to the pool upon the dais.

The delegation of Elmorians spread out along the walls of the chamber. The Prince alone stayed at the foot of the stairs with Alant. The Prince stretched out an arm indicating the pool. "*Your destiny awaits,* Alant. *Do not fear it.*"

Looking up and into the deep black eyes of the blue-gray

creature, Alant realized how foreign and alien the Elmorian appeared to him.

*You are not the awe-inspiring beings I admired upon my arrival, and I shall not give you what you want. To this, I vow!*

He glared at Prince Aritian. "It is *you* who are the coward. You who fear me and *my* race! Think *not* that I go into this blind!"

The Prince dropped his arm and took a quick step back. Fear is not what Alant saw in the Prince's eyes…

*He is terrified!*

Prince Aritian made to reach out and grasp Alant, as if he would stop him from going to the dais. Forcing himself to smile as menacingly as he could, Alant turned and faced the center of the room. Steeling his nerves, he strode across the dusty floor and up the natural stone ramp to the pool as if it had been his choice to come here—as if the others had been his procession not his subjugators. Stopping at the top of the ramp, the edge of the silvery substance only a few inches from him, he was captivated by what he beheld.



The liquid did not form a pool as he assumed. It barely covered the dais with a thin sheen of a silvery substance. The reddish-brown limestone was visible through the surface now that Alant stood looking down at it. The bright silvery light emanated from it, however, and spread out to cast up and beyond, illuminating the entire chamber. Now that he stood directly over the pool, he saw that the surface looked more like a mirror—thin and delicate. Yet, it also seemed vibrant, alive in a way, as it covered the base of the dais. Leaning forward, he tried to catch his own reflection upon its surface. A gasp escaped his lips.

*A reflection of me, aye! Yet one seen through the Sight of the Essence.*

He marveled at the vision laid out before him. The swirls of colored Spectals spun around, filling all he gazed upon. They had a finality to them, a solidity. A reality he had never before experienced.

*This is the way things should look. I am now seeing things as they really are. How I saw things with my normal vision—or in using the Sight to view the Essence—those were all false! They were nothing except lies to what reality should look like!*

Removing his gaze from the pool, Alant scanned the room to see if he still held his regular vision or if somehow he had slipped into the Sight of the Essence without realizing it. All seemed normal. He glanced over his shoulder to the group of Elmorians milling about the doorway. None of the white-robed gray beings looked directly at him. They all looked in his general direction, yet their gaze slipped passed him as if they could no longer see him.

Returning his attention to the pool, he once again became mesmerized by the clarity of the Essence reflecting off the thin membrane of silver. It struck him then what he was seeing.

*I am not seeing the Essence inside of something! I am seeing the Essence itself! This is liquid Essence or, at least, Essence in its natural form. This is the Chi'utlan!*

Understanding flowed into him like wine filling a chalice.

*This is a place where the very Essence spills out and onto the Plane of Talic'Nauth! This is a source—what the Siers call an Essence Node, yet they all think they are myth!*

As he watched, his eyes were drawn to a spot at his feet some three paces inside the dais. A small bump had formed on the near perfect finish of the Essence pool. He watched the bump well up, forming a small bead of silver, the size of the tip of his little finger. It shimmered and danced upon the surface. It grew larger, swelling into an oblong shape about the size of his thumb. It shivered, as if from the exertion of holding up its own weight, then fell…up. His eyes followed the droplet with wonder as it streaked to the ceiling some fifty paces overhead. The droplet plopped into a huge pool that covered the roof closed in by the stalagmite-stalactite pillars lining the dais. He stood with his mouth open and watched as the ripples the droplet created on the surface of the pool above him radiated out to lap gently at the rim of an upside-down bowl. The pool of Essence above his head was certainly not a thin sheet like the one covering the floor. It had depth with a thickness that Alant's gaze could not penetrate.



*I was wrong. That is the Chi'utlan!*

He continued to stare up at the wonder clinging to the roof above him until a second droplet plunked up into the pool a short distance from the first. It added its own ripples to the now dissipating ones of the initial drop.

Glancing back down to the floor, he noticed yet another droplet forming no more than a pace from where he stood. Tentatively, he stretched out one foot and placed it on the surface of the Essence covering the floor. The silvery liquid squished out from under his golden slipper as if he had stepped into mud. He felt the firmness of the limestone beneath. Steeling himself, he added more of his weight until his trailing foot joined the first out on the shallow pool. Surrounded now by the Essence—both above and below—Alant was once again lost in the beauty and solidity of the Spectals reflected about him. He took a few more small steps into the center of the dais until he stood in front of a tiny, beadlike droplet forming on the ground.

It grew at the same steady pace as the first one Alant had witnessed, and looked much like water seeping through a cloth—only upside down. It broke away and fell up, past him. Reaching out a cupped palm, he caught the droplet as it streaked toward the ceiling. Cold was the first sensation he felt. Turing his hand over he was surprised to see that the liquid pooled in his palm instead of continuing to fall up. Moving his hand in a small circle, he swished the metallic looking liquid around, delighted to see that it remained whole, like a little ball.



It took a moment for the searing pain to penetrate the wonder he was feeling. The ball of Essence grew colder, freezing his palm to the point of burning. Instinctively he flicked his wrist to rid himself of it, yet to his horror, instead of flying off, the ball flattened out and covered more of his palm. Grasping his wrist with his other hand, he attempted to stem the intense feeling of pain from shooting up his arm. He glanced around, looking for help. The Elmorians still did not seem like they could see what was happening to him. They stood along the walls, staring at different parts of the dais. He let out an involuntary gasp of pain that made several of them glance in his direction, yet none made eye contact with him.

A wail escaped his lips as the liquid Essence burned through the soles of his shoes. He tried to turn and run back to the edge of the pool, yet his body would not obey. Fire shot up his legs and he felt the silvery substance pour into his slippers and under his robes. He heard the screams of a man off in the distance and felt sorry for him, until he realized through the haze of pain and turmoil that he heard his own screams echoing off the distant chamber walls.

Air rushed past him before Alant realized he was falling. Falling up toward the pool that hung over his head. He flung an arm up to protect his face before he slammed into the surface of the liquid Essence. He plunged deep into the substance, never hitting bottom. Agony racked his body from every direction. Burning cold liquid rushed into his mouth. Down his throat. Cutting off his screams—making him gag and wretch. He flailed against the pain, wishing only for release. For death to come quickly and end his suffering. He became dimly aware that he had finally struck the bottom—top—of the pool. His very flesh felt as if it had been scorched away. Muscles and bone smoldered and turned to ash. In his mind, he begged for death.

The gulp of fresh air came cool and sharp. It tasted sweeter than anything he had ever savored in his life. His hands brushed a hard, sandy surface and he realized he lay on the limestone floor. He forced lids as heavy as weights open and found himself in the center of the dais, curled into a fetal position. Bringing one hand to his face, he cautiously flexed his fingers. It amazed him to see that flesh still covered it. He felt none of the pain from moments before and pushed himself effortlessly to his feet. He became instantly aware that eyes now rested upon him. Glancing to the door and to the faces of the Elmorians standing next to it, he saw that each of them now looked directly at him. Each seemed to have a different look; from fear to curiosity. Yet when he looked at the Prince, he saw a thin, almost maniacal smile etched across the Elmorian's face.



Moving his attention back to the ceiling, he noticed that the pool overhead sat empty. A large, natural looking bowl, some three paces deep, hung above him covering the entire span. Thick, black vine-like roots penetrated the bowl in several locations, fanning out across much of the area. Alant recognized the flesh-like black bark that wrapped those roots.

*This chamber must lie directly below the Chandril'chi tree sitting in front of the school.*

While he scanned the empty shadows where the liquid Essence

had so recently filled, a small streak of light shot past him and he watched a drop of silvery Essence splat inside the dome and slide down—up—to the center of the bowl. Glancing around at his feet, he noticed other spots on the ground showing signs of liquid Essence seeping through the dais.

Without understanding why, Alant felt an urgency to remove himself from the platform. He did not have a desire to return to the Elmorians and their guards so he continued forward, crossing to the far side of the dais opposite the natural ramp he had entered from. Squeezing between two stalagmite-stalactite posts, he hopped down to the floor on the other side of the room. His spirits sank with the realization that the chamber held no alternate exits apart from the double doors he had used to enter the room.

Looking back, Alant saw the Prince grasp Delmith by the cuff of his robe with one hand, a look of euphoria passing over his inhuman face. *"Well, Delmith, it seems that our little rat has survived, would you agree?"* Though the words he spoke were not loud, they echoed throughout the chamber. *"It has worked! The Essence is ready! No more shall we have to fear the Age of Power!"* The Elmorian tongue still sounded odd as it translated inside Alant's mind. He was distantly aware of the fact that the Tarsith had not gone cold against his skin. Delmith stood staring in what Alant could only describe as stunned silence.



*"Gralets!"* Contempt dripped from Prince Aritian loud call. The two Gralet'nars who had escorted them had remained outside the chamber. They now rushed into the room at his call and the Prince pointed toward Alant. *"Kill the Human!"*

The Prince's command struck Alant to the core. Fear filled him as the Essence had moments before. Running to the far wall, he pressed his back against the cool limestone. Both Warrior Servants advanced, parting around the dais like huge gray boulders rolling down a hill, each coming to either side, cutting off all routes of escape. Stopping a few score paces from him, they raised their heavy crossbows and took aim. Never before having his life threatened, Alant stood frozen with fear. In almost perfect unison, the twang of two strings slapping against staves echoed through the chamber. Alant watched as the bolts, their pristine white fletching spinning them smoothly through the air, tore across the empty space separating them.

*Or is it empty?*

All of a sudden, Alant noticed that...something...hung in the air all around him. Wisps of lines flowed all about him, swirling and interacting with each other and all the things in the room. It reminded him of seeing Spectals from the Essence, yet not exactly the same. It was as if the Spectals had been stretched into string instead of their normal round dot shape.

*Still, it is an Essence gone mad! The air contains no Essence, the Essence is* inside *solid objects!*

Even as he chastised himself, knowing he could not see what he now saw, he knew he *did* see it. The swirls formed the very air—so very unlike the Spectals of the Essence—and danced before him. He reached out with his mind. Could he touch these...Strands? He was amazed to make contact. Experimentally he pulled on a strand. It moved to his will. He almost laughed and reached out further with his mind, connecting with every strand of...

*Of what? Not Spectals certainly! Still, made of the Essence, no less!*



He balled them up, unwrapped them, drew them forth, and sent them away. Lost in the revelry of this new experience, a spasm of panic racked him when he remembered the death that had been shot at him. Should have long since pierced his breast and left him bleeding—dying. He jerked his head up and his jaw dropped open. Two crossbow bolts hung in the air a few paces from him. He knew they still raced toward him, of that, he was certain. Though, he had no idea of how he knew. Still, he felt he could walk up to them and pluck them from their course. He looked past them and saw that everyone else in the room stood frozen as well. Like living statues, alive and unmoving.

*Reality has stopped! Is this what happens when you die?*

He started to move aside, to remove himself from the path of certain death, and found that his body would not cooperate. Glancing down he noticed that he stood frozen in place as well.

*It is not the Plane that has stopped. It is that my consciousness has sped!*

Looking back at the bolts, he noticed that they drew closer—still slicing through the air.

*They are moving! I am sure of it! Not frozen then, just slowed.*

Curious, he reached out with his mind. He could feel the Strands of Essence surrounding the bolts, see how the Strands followed the bolt, led it, almost understood how they twisted and slid away from the approaching projectiles. He took a Strand and wrapped it experimentally around one shaft. Without understanding what he was doing or how, he pulled the Strand tight, nudging it slightly to the side. The bolt continued on its painfully slow trajectory. Yet, with the Strand attached to it, he noticed that the bolt began to turn. It followed the new direction he had set using the weird Strand of Essence. Reaching out to the other bolt, he repeated what he had done to the first. Once finished, he stepped back and realized he had not been in his body.

*I am floating outside my physical form! How am I to return?*

Terror gripped him and he forced it down. Focusing, he slipped back into his mortal confines. He did not know how, he just did what seemed natural.

*As if any of this is natural!*



Two loud thunks slammed into his ears as the bolts embedded themselves into the soft limestone wall on either side of him. Snapping his head to the side, he felt his stomach lurch. One of the bolts rested no more than a hands width from his head.

*It would have pierced my eye!*

"*Fools! You missed!*" Prince Aritian's hiss echoed across the large chamber. "*Kill him! Kill him now before it is too late!*"

The Gralet'nars dropped their crossbows and drew their long, sickle-like swords. With only a moments hesitation they dashed across the room toward Alant.

Noticing that he no longer saw any of the Essence strings from before, Alant tried to reach out with his mind once more. Tried to regain the distorted Sight of the Essence he had achieved when reality had slowed. Yet he had no idea how he had done it in the first place. Lunging forward, thinking to dash across the dais, Alant was cut off as one of the Gralet'nars hopped in front of him forcing him back against the wall, once more trapped.

He had to get away, find some way out. Terror gripped him as he watched the Gralet'nars approach, their bulging arms rippling as they gripped their swords. They closed in for the kill. One stepped forward and raised his blade over a shoulder preparing to slash Alant in twain.

*It cannot end this way! I must escape!*

Snap!

Pain laced up Alant's arm and the Gralet'nar lowered its sword, befuddlement painted across his eyeless face. Alant looked down at his arm and was horrified to see that it had shattered, crumpled into a hideous awkward bend as it rolled up upon itself.

Crack! Crack!

A scream burst from his lungs and Alant slumped to the floor. Both his legs bent back and twisted upon themselves. Through the pain, he saw both Gralet'nars back away. One of them held an arm up to protect his face against what he saw.

*"What is happening?"* The Prince brushed past his Warrior Servants and hovered over Alant, staring down at the boy with a mixed look of anger and terror.

Alant heard himself scream again. A scream cut short when his chest caved in, squeezing out all the air from his lungs. His body thrust forward and his spine snapped with mind numbing agony. His head pounded as though caught in a vice. Even through the anguish, he knew he would not survive. Realized he did not want to survive. All that was left to him was pain and suffering that stripped all hope from him, leaving death as his only salvation. A fast succession of pops and cracks resounded through the chamber as the last of his bones snapped and broke. One last, loud crunch resonated in his ears and he was aware that his skull was caving in. He could not contemplate the horror of what that meant for him.

Everything went black.

# Chapter 65

An icy-cold droplet of water smacked into the back of Arderi Cor's head and snaked down his neck, sending a shiver cascading down his leg. Scowling, he held his torch high overhead and peered further along the dark stairwell descending into the bowels under Mocley. For near a quarter aurn the stairs had descended without end, taking him further and further into the Undercity. The air stank of death, and a thick coating of filth now covered his tongue. Rivulets of water ran down the walls at irregular intervals and large swaths of a greenish mold grew in the crevices between large stone blocks that formed the tunnel.



A shuffling sound—an image of a corpse being drug across the floor—echoed from below. "Ragnor?"

"Aye, lad. You be almost to me."

Rounding a final bend in the stairs, Arderi entered a small corridor. As he stepped from the final stair, his feet submerged into water. Throwing out a hand, he grab onto Ragnor's arm for balance when he slid on the thick, slimy substance covering the floor.

"Easy, lad. The floor under the water be slick as ice. It be easier to slide your feet across the bottom as opposed to walking."

Arderi regained his footing, then motioned for Ragnor to release his arm. "What is this place?"

Turning, Ragnor held his torch in front of him and

Arderi saw that the same mold-etched stone lined the walls. The corridor ran off to disappear beyond the circle of light provided by their torches. Gliding his feet through the water, his movement creating a thick ripple that lapped against the walls, Ragnor began moving down the corridor without lifting his feet. "This be the Undercity. Very few know of its existence, no one knows its true history."

On unsteady legs, Arderi mimicked the older man's gait. Within a few steps, he found that his feet slid easily over the floor and soon caught up with Ragnor, matching the older man stride for stride.

*I cannot tell if the floor here is stone like the stairs were. If it were not for the smell of the stagnate water, and the icky feel of it, this might well be enjoyable.*

"What do you know of it?"

"Mocley, which do sit above us now, be near two thousand seasons old."



Thinking back to Alant's first Crystal, Arderi remembered his brother's history lesson. The memory brought back the remorse of his brother's death and a sense of loss welled up again inside him.

*Brother, I have not even had the opportunity to mourn your passing into the aftermore.*

Pushing the feeling away, he concentrated on Ragnor's words.

"No one in living memory has any knowledge of a city at this location prior to Mocley's foundation by the Elmorian, Artimus Mocley. As far as it did ever be told, this area did be grassland. Home to the Asgarthian's who now roam the lands far to the east."

"Yet, many winters after Mocley did be built, the Undercity did be discovered. Whatever the name of this ancient city, and whoever did build it, that knowledge vanished long ago." Ragnor slid to a stop forcing Arderi to do likewise. Turning, he looked into Arderi's eyes. "Yet one thing be certain, whoever did build this place be far more powerful than any who do live now. There be…things down here."

The two men continued down the hall and an odd foreboding settle over Arderi. "Why do you say that?"

"You shall soon see. Suffice it to say that there be secrets to be found down here that no exist elsewhere that I know of."

Plodding along, torchlight flickering off slick stone walls, Arderi paid closer attention to his surroundings. They did not travel down one solid hall. Many doorways or intersecting passageways appeared at irregular intervals. Stone and rubble blocked many of these areas where whatever lay beyond had collapsed. Still, Ragnor continued at a steady pace, taking a turn here, or ducking into a thin passageway there, until Arderi lost all sense of direction.

*If we become separated, I will never find my way out!*

So Arderi followed as the older man jutted down one passage until he turned down another intersection that led them off on a new route. For nearly another aurn—Arderi was sure it was no more than an aurn, it was hard to tell in the cramp, dark tunnels of the Undercity—they slid along in silence.



Finally, when Arderi was about to ask for a respite, he noticed a glow emanating from somewhere in the distance. It lay well beyond the light cast by the torches they carried. The glow shone red and pulsed off the slime-coated walls in the way a campfire might.

*We are not alone down here!*

"What is that ahead?" His voice was nothing more than a whisper, yet it echoed off in every direction.

Turning to look at him, Ragnor pointed his torch ahead. "That, lad, be the reason we did risk entering the Undercity."

The corridor ended in a massive arch. Carved stones, each engraved with strange runes and glyphs, adorned the top of the archway. Stepping through, Arderi saw a massive round chamber. Its domed ceiling stretched high overhead and at regular intervals, five additional archways led out of the room. Yet, it was the center dais that captured his attention and held it firm.

Circular stairs, set in the center of the room, rose up from the brownish-green water to stand about a pace from the floor. Six large pillars, as smooth as silk and blacker than pitch, rose up from the edges of the platform and each arched in, like the fingers of a giant hand. At their tips, they held aloft a massive red Crystal about the size of a small child.

Unconsciously, Arderi dropped his hand to his sword's hilt. "It is also like the Ka'gana in Dorochi!"

"Aye, lad. It be, at that." Sliding up to the dais, Ragnor stepped out of the water. Stopping at the top step, he turned and motioned for Arderi to join him. "This be a Quay'ka'gana—a sending stone." The older man held out a hand to steady Arderi as he stepped from the water. "It did be discovered by our Order some thousand seasons past. This be the gateway to Bin'Satsu."

"You have mentioned Bin'Satsu before. What is it?" Arderi stared into the deep facets of the large, red Crystal suspended over his head by the thin, black pillars.



"It be a citadel, the only safe haven the Tat'Sujen have to call their own." A loud clack echoed from one of the other passageways and Ragnor snapped his head around. "Quick, now. Although our journey here did be uneventful, this be no the place to tarry. There be things down here that you no want to meet, if you can avoid it. Once you be safe in Bin'Satsu, all of your questions will be answered."

"Me? Are you not coming as well?" The thought of losing his newfound guide disturbed Arderi more than he wanted to admit.

*Ragnor is my one connection to whatever this new life is.*

The older man shook his head. "Nix, lad. My duties, for the now, be here taking care of Sindian Rillion. Yet, I did bond to you. If you do have any need of me, I will be at your disposal." Taking Arderi by the arm, Ragnor guided him into the center of the dais then stepped back onto the bottom stair. Extending his arm, he pointed to Arderi's hip. "Unsheathe your blade and unwrap the hilt."

Arderi did as instructed. As he freed the Ka'gana nestled within his hilt, a blinding flash of red light cascaded out and up, merging with the light radiating from the larger stone above. He gave a questioning look at Ragnor. "What do I do now?"

A look of remorse filled Ragnor's eyes. "Now you have nothing to do except wait. I be sorry. This will no be pleasant for you, lad."

Snap!

Dorochi slipped from Arderi's hand as pain shot up his arm. Gripping his wrist with his other hand, it horrified him to see that several of his fingers had bent backwards, the bones within them breaking.

Through the agony of his hand, fear reached out and gripped Arderi. He looked wild-eyed toward Ragnor who took another step away, a sad look upon his face.

*I have been betrayed!*

Crack! Crack!

His knees buckled and Arderi fell to the floor as both of his legs warped into a perverted, twisted shape. The agony of his broken bones caused him to writhe upon the floor. Unable to control himself, he screamed out in anguish until his chest caved in, crushing all the wind from his lungs. Crumpling into a ball, Arderi rolled over onto his back and stared up at the Quay'ka'gana. Streaks of red slashed across the room and bore into his eyes, blinding him to all else.



*All is red! There is nothing except the red! Like blood! I am covered in it! The entire Plane bleeds!*

A loud crunch reverberated in his ears and he knew his skull was caving in. One last scream escaped him as the pain and torment bore him into nothingness.

# Chapter 66

The trip out of the warehouse was a hazy blur. Klain remembered Charver leaving for a while as he lay against a box waiting for death.

*It would have been a welcome release.*

Yet the boy returned before death had taken him into the aftermore. Charver had half-helped, half-dragged Klain outside into the bright, noonday sun. Through begging and cajoling, Charver loaded Klain into a wagon that waited in front of the warehouse.



Lying in the back, watching the clouds play in the clear-blue sky, Klain had no other memories of their journey until he awoke here, in a small stone room. Charver sat slumped in an unpadded, ladder-backed chair at his bedside.

When the boy noticed Klain stir, he jumped up and ran to his side. "Master Klain! You are awake!" Slipping his tiny hand into Klain's paw, he gave it a squeeze.

A calm feeling of restfulness covered Klain like a warm blanket.

*I feel as if I have slept for days!*

Reaching up, Klain waved a paw over the spot Estular's sword had penetrated. Young Master Vimith smiled, a twinkle glinting in his eye. "There is not even a scar! The Shaper who mended you did a wonderful job."

Just then, the door cracked open and a balding Human poked his head inside. Seeing the two next to each other, the man smiled and stepped into the room. “I thought I heard voices.” The man was dressed in a plain brown robe. Thin, brown leather sandals and a rope belt finished his outfit. Shutting the door behind him, he looked down at Klain. “How do you feel?”

Klain propped himself up on his elbows. He felt neither aches nor pains. “I feel fine. Like waking from a restful sleep.”

The man in brown looked down and smiled. “You should. You have been asleep since the eve before last.” He pointed to Charver. “The boy has not left your side.”

Giving Klain a sheepish grin, Charver let go of his paw and stood. Reaching into a small pouch that hung from his waist, he fished out a fat, golden coin and held it awkwardly toward the man. “For your help.”

The man seemed genuinely shocked by the gesture.

*Or, the amount. I still do not understand the value of Human coin.*

Still, the man overcame his momentary astonishment, reached out, and plucked the coin from the boy’s fingers. Bowing his head slightly, he opened the door. “If you are ever in need of my services again, young Master Vimith, you have only to summon me. I wish you both well.”



The door closed behind the man and Klain sat up and swung his paws to the floor. “I stink!”

Giggling, Charver crossed the room and opened the door. “There is a bath down the hall. Be quick, however. I would like to make it home before sundown.”

Taking in the room once more, Klain cocked his head. “Where are we?”

“Still in Mocley. We are at one of my father’s shops in the Merchantillian. This is my father’s apartment. We stay here sometimes when we are in Mocley.”

“Does your father know we are here?”

“Nix, there are no servants here if we are not present.” Tapping his little foot on the floor, Charver pointed down the hall. “Now go! Daylight is wasting.”

After he cleaned the vomit and urine from his fur, Klain felt like the events of the past day had not happened, as if he had simply been told of them. Following Charver downstairs, they entered a small front room with a few plush chairs scattered about. Before they had reached the bottom stair, Klain's heart leapt into his throat. The blade the Honored One had given him, sheathed in its scabbard, lay on a small, round table in the center of the room. "My sword!"

The boy ran forward and snatched it up before Klain could reach it. "Oh, Aye! I found it outside the warehouse where they held you in that awful cage." The boy presented it with a flourish. "Are you happy to see it?"

Clinching his jaws, Klain fought back the urge to weep. "I thought it gone. Aye, I am happy to see it. I am grateful." He crossed the small room and picked the boy up into the air. "My thanks for this, and for coming to my rescue!"

He set the boy down and they left the shop. Klain was pleased to see the sun still lay closer to the dawn than midday. "We will easily reach the villa before this eve."

Closing the door behind them, the boy reached into a pouch and pulled out a small, purple stone. Pressing it flat against a silver plate just above the door handle, Klain heard the sound of a bolt clicking into place. "What is that?"



"This?" The boy rolled the stone over his palm for a moment before slipping it back into his pouch. "Have you never seen a lockingstone before?" Klain shook his head. "Most of the shops here in the Merchantillian have them." He patted the wall of the shop. "Shapers Meld the Essence of a building creating a sort of bubble around them. Once the stone activates it, nothing can enter."

Reaching out, Klain dragged a paw down the door. His claws stopped just short of touching the wood and did mar its white-painted surface. "That is amazing! Why do not more have this lockingstone?"

"My father says it is very expensive to have a Shaper create one. He told me it takes a team of them working day and eve for many moons just to get it ready."

The wagon they had used earlier stood waiting for them outside. Telling Klain to wait, Charver ran down the street.

When he returned a few moments later, he led a young Human pulling a horse behind him. Once the young man hitched the horse to the buggy, Charver handed him a coin and the two climbed into the front seat. Taking the reins, the boy drove the wagon out of the city.

Although it annoyed Klain to have people gawk and stare at them, which did not end until they were well out of the city and surrounding buildings as well, no one made any attempt to hinder their progress. For the most part, Klain traveled in silence. Much to his chagrin, Charver did not. The boy chatted away the aurn it took to reach the villa, speaking about Mocley and all of the places he had been while there. Klain was not happy to hear that the boy had gone alone into the city while he had been incapacitated. He spoke of his favorite bakery in Gatetown and all the wonderful sweets they carried. He talked of many other things that Klain let slip past his troubled thoughts without comment. Yet, when the boy's topic turned to Master Timms and what he thought should be done, Klain cut him off in mid-sentence.



"I have not yet decided."

The fact that Klain said more than a one-word answer or a grunt stunned Charver into silence. It did not last long, however. "What do you mean? He sold you into slavery!"

"Aye, he did. And for that I should feast on the marrow in his bones."

"Should!" Giving Klain an incredulous stare, Charver snorted.

A long moment passed between them with only the crunching of the wagon wheels grinding the crushed stone of the highway to fill the void.

"Well, I know what my father will do when he learns of it. He will—"

A vicious growl erupted and Charver jumped, nearly slipping from the wagon bench. Klain almost felt remorseful and sat trying to regain control of his emotions. "I said I have not yet decided."

It surprised Klain that the young boy rode the rest of the

way to the villa in relative silence. This was fine with him, for he found himself lost in his own troubled thoughts. The sun had passed its zenith in the sky by the time the horse-drawn wagon made the turn from the main road and headed down the skinnier, dirt path leading to the villa. Once the horse's hooves echoed off the paving stones covering the entrance courtyard, a large lump formed in the pit of Klain's stomach.

Ascending the stairs and passing through the double-doors of the manor, the two walked into a bee's nest of activity. Upon seeing them, one of the servant girls—Klain knew she worked in the kitchens and thought her name was Tisna—let out a scream and ran for the boy. Immediately, the staff of the household surrounded the two with a dozen questions flung at them all at once.

"What is the meaning—" Master Vimith burst into the room from his study and, noticing his son, ran over to scoop him into his arms. "I have been so worried!" Rohann glared at Klain. "Where have you been?" His words were harsh, yet Klain did not begrudge the man.



"Father!" Charver gave him a hug. "When did you return?"

"Only just, and found that no one had seen you since two days prior!" Rohann's smile dropped when he shot another glare at Klain. "Well, you have some explaining to do."

Squirming from his father's arms, Charver jumped down to the marble-tiled floor. "It all started with Master Timms!"

"Oh? What does he have to do with this?" Taking the boy by the hand, Rohann headed back into his study. Padding along behind, Klain saw several of the bodyguards who had stayed behind and probably knew what had transpired.

*Neither Timms nor Narn are anywhere to be seen!*

"He sent Klain into town!" Charver made that phrase sound as if it was a horrible punishment. "That is where—" The boy fell silent in mid sentence, prompting Klain to speed into the study.

Standing in the middle of the room, looking as if he would rather be anywhere else, stood Satner Timms.

Rohann stopped next to his son. "That is where what,

Charver?"

Satner stood with his feet slightly apart. Although his hand did not directly rest on the hilt of his sword, it lay close enough for it not to matter. He watched Klain with an intensity that the Kithian knew all too well. Charver seemed uncertain as to what to do. It was obvious the boy did not want to enter the room, yet with Klain in the doorway, he could not withdraw either. Klain simply stood fixated upon the other man's eyes.

*Now is the time having an Elmorian's power would serve me well.*

As if he did not notice the tension in the room, Rohann crossed the study to the small table that held a decanter of brandy. Picking up the crystal vial, he poured himself a small amount in a glass, turned, and held it up in offering. "Would anyone care to join me in a drink? I think there are explanations to be heard."

"Nix, Master Vimith." Satner did not take his eyes from Klain's.



Setting the decanter back on its silver tray, he sat down. "Master Timms? Master Klain? There seems to be an issue here."

Several moments elapsed as the two continued to stare at each other, waiting for the other to move first. It was Satner who finally broke eye contact and looked at the carpet. Shoulders slumping, he drew in a deep breath. "The Young Master is correct. I did send Master Klain into town. He was to be—"

"Enough!" Klain practically roared the word out. Turning to Master Vimith, Klain thrust a thumb to his chest. "I became lost in the city." Returning his attention to Satner, Klain was pleased to see the look of surprise on the man's face. "I am sorry, Master Timms, I was unable to retrieve that which you sent me for."

"Hey, wait!" Charver's voice, high pitched normally, rose several octaves.

Glaring at the boy, Klain exposed his front fangs for a split moment. "Aye. I will not forget you, Young Master." Focusing on Master Vimith once more, Klain laid a paw upon the boy's shoulder. "If it had not been for the Young Master here, I may never have found my way back."

Sipping his brandy, Rohann looked first at one, then the other of his two employees. He studied them for long moments, and whatever conclusion he reached, Klain was sure he had not believed the story. "Very well." He stood. "If there is nothing else to tell, it seems that all has worked itself out. Charver, go and find out what Cook is preparing for lastmeal. Mayhaps we can go riding if there is time before then."

"Aye, father." Eyeing both Klain and Satner with the same look of irritation, the boy scuttled off.

With Charver gone, Rohann set his glass onto his desk and turned to the men. "I understand then, there will be no more issues with this matter?"

"Aye, sir." Satner's answer was quick, causing Rohann to raise an eyebrow.

Satner cleared his throat. "There will be no more instances. By the Twelve, I do swear."

Turning his gaze to Klain, the merchant gave him a quizzical look. Nodding once, Klain spun on his hindpaw to stalk from the room, yet stopped when Rohann grabbed his arm.



"Master Klain, if you ever make a decision that puts Charver in danger again, *I do swear* that I will find a way to kill you."

Clinching his jaws, Klain knew the man spoke true. A smile exposed his front fangs and he turned his gaze to Satner. "Aye. And if I ever make such a poor judgment call again, I just might let you."

Crossing the entrance hall, he bounded up the stairs closest to him and headed down the hall to his room.

"Master Klain!" Klain had known Satner trailed him by the man's unique smell. "Wait a moment." Turning, Klain watched the bodyguard ascend the last few stairs and close the distance between them. "I do not see you as someone who forgives a debt so easily."

This caused Klain to laugh aloud. "Nix, I am not."

"Then why?"

"If you had not intervened, Charver would most likely be dead."

"Aye. Still, if not for me Charver would have never been in danger."

Shifting one hindpaw to the side, Klain took up what he knew Satner would recognize as a fighting stance. "Are you trying to change my mind? I have no issue with killing you if that is your desire."

Raising both hands before him, Satner took a few steps back. "Nix, that is not my intention."

"Regardless of how he got there, you were not willing to let harm come to the boy. You took the full brunt of the painstick allowing me a moment more to free myself. Had you not, Charver would be dead. That is payment enough for me." Stretching to his full height, Klain glared down at the man. "However, should you be foolish enough to repeat this incident, I will not be so kind." At the look on Satner's face, Klain grunted once then continued toward his room. He noted that Satner did not move from their meeting spot.



As Klain reached for the handle to his door, Satner whistled to catch his attention. "I can think of no better protection for the boy than you, Kithian. You will have no more issues from me nor any of mine."

Without looking back at the Human, Klain entered his room. Closing the door, he caught the whiff of Charver. "I know you are here, Young Master."

The boy slunk out from behind the large curtain that hid the only window in the room. "Master Klain, why did you let Master Timms get away with doing what he did?"

Crossing the room, Klain sat on the bed in front of Charver. "I do not know much of Humans. Truth be told, I do not know much of any race. I know only what is in here." He touched his chest. "In here, I feel that Timms was punished for his deed. That is enough for me."

# Chapter 67

A chill wind racked over his skin causing goose pimples to rise, yet he did not feel the cold. He felt nothing. Opening his eyes, the piercing blue vastness stretching off in every direction dazzled him. His attention lingered upon a stray cloud that sped across the sky.

"Ahh!" A voice, soft and airy like the expanse that dominated his vision, floated into his ears. "How do you feel?"



*How* do *I feel? I feel nothing. I should feel. I have felt before. I felt—*

Bolting upright, Arderi Cor looked down at his hands.

*I felt my bones breaking!*

Yet his hands seemed fine now. Rolling them over, he looked at each side. Reaching down, he rubbed his legs—kneading their muscles. The bones underneath felt intact.

*I really do feel fine!*

Arderi sat on a soft cot. Its cream-colored canvas easily supported his weight. Glancing around, he saw that he was in an opening between several white pillars, the tops of which were covered by a large, dome-shaped marble ceiling. Covering the ground below him were cut flagstone tiles that ended at the pillars. Beyond the tiles, vibrant green grass, neatly trimmed, covered the rest of the small hill. The grassy area stretched only a few paces wide then dropped out of sight. Majestic mountains surrounded him as far as he could see—their snow-capped peaks stabbed against the clear-blue sky.

*None are above me. I am on the highest peak!*

A hand gently rested on his arm. "Are you well, sir?"

Following the arm, Arderi gazed into a pair of liquid blue eyes. The eyes adorned a face so perfect that all breath left his lungs. Golden blond hair covered the girls head and framed skin so white, so smooth, he thought for a moment that she must be made from porcelain. A gentle smile lay on her ruby-red lips. She raised a hand to cover a giggle and Arderi realized that his mouth hung open.

*Curse you for a country lout!*

"Sir, are you well?" Breaking eye contact, she looked him over. "You do not seem to bear any wounds."

Not trusting himself to speak, Arderi shook his head.

Smiling again, the girl bowed her head. "Good, then. I am called Rinear."

She looked expectantly at Arderi for many moments before he realized that she was waiting on him to speak. "I…I am Arderi, Arderi Cor." Glancing around once more at the mountains surrounding them, he motioned to them. "Have I returned to the Nektine?"



"The Nektine?" The girl looked puzzled. "I have not heard of such a city."

Shaking his head, Arderi cupped both his hands to the sides of his temples. "It is not a city, it is a mountain range."

"I am sorry, I still have not heard of it."

Taken aback, Arderi cut his eyes at her. "How could you not have heard of the Nektine? They are the largest mountains in all of Ro'Arith!"

The girl looked somber, almost repentant, and Arderi felt bad for raising his voice. "I apologize. I have not heard of them and I have never been to the lands of Ro'Arith."

*Never been to Ro'Arith! This girl is either mad, or—*

He scanned the surrounding area once more. Then Arderi realized he saw nothing except the tops of mountains. The plateau he sat upon seemed alone amongst the clouds. His throat constricted with fear. "Where am I?" His words came out as a croaked whisper.

"Please, come." Gripping his elbow, she helped him stand.

As Arderi stood, the surrounding area came into view. The patio he stood on was like a stone gazebo, set high on a small plateau, only a score of paces across. On one side of the plateau, a flagstone walkway led away from the area, winding down a steep hill, its destination lost from his sight at this vantage point. On all of the other sides, a sheer drop over jagged rocks disappeared into the clouds below. As he peered over the nearest side, his stomach gave a queasy jerk and a feeling of vertigo swept over him.

*I am* above *the clouds!*

The girl reached out and stroked his hair. "The dizziness of your transportation will soon pass." Turning, she walked down the path, quickly disappearing over the lip of the steep slope.

Unsure of what to do, Arderi glanced around at the scattered cots and chairs resting on the patio around him. He gazed out over the distant mountain peaks jutting through the clouds, and gawked at the blanket of cloud tops forming a misty-looking lake far below him.



*By the Twelve, where am I?*

Walking toward the path, Arderi abruptly stopped on its summit. Spreading out below him, built on a plateau many times larger than the one the patio sat on, he saw a magnificent, pure-white citadel standing regal against the azure-blue of the distant horizon. Sunlight glinted off its pristine walls causing the building to glow and forcing Arderi to shield his eyes. From the roof, delicate spires shot up, so thin they looked like shards of glass reaching into the sky. Beautiful arches connected the higher towers, creating a cacophony of passageways high in the air. The flawless walls were marred only by the advent of colorful, stained-glass windows set at regular intervals. On each side of the citadel visible to Arderi, cliffs dropped away into nothingness.

*There seems to be no access to this place!*

The blond-haired girl walked down the path toward the

citadel. Arderi noticed that a tall man in white robes met her as she reached the main arch that led inside. Pausing next to him, she turned and looked back up the hill to where Arderi stood. Patiently the two waited, simply gazing up at Arderi until he felt the fool.

*You cannot stand up here all day!*

Forcing himself to action, Arderi headed down the flagstone path. Once he reached the archway, the tall man, long jet-black hair pulled into a tight braid behind him, bowed before him. "It is always an honor to welcome a new Brother. From where do you hail?"

"I was in the Undercity, below Mocley. Ragnor took me there. And then..." Arderi glanced around again.

"I recognize that blade!" Pointing to his sword, the man looked shocked. "How did you come by it?"

The harshness in the man's voice forced Arderi to step back. "It was gifted to me by its former owner, Master Rillion."



The dark-haired man studied the boy in silence, then relaxed. He bowed once more. "Forgive me, Brother, I meant no disrespect. I knew its former owner. He was a good man." The sound of loss in the man's voice reverberated through Arderi.

*He knows Master Clytus is dead!*

"Yet the Essence owns its will, and here before me stands one to take Brother Rillion's place." A weak smile crossed his lips. "Forgive an old man's rants. I have forgotten my manners." He held out a hand. "My name is Larith Rine."

Taking the offered hand, Arderi tried to mimic the old man's bow. "Master Rine, my name is Arderi Cor."

Covering Arderi's hand with his other, Larith's face became grave. "Well, Brother Cor, welcome to Bin'Satsu. It seems you have arrived just in time. Your training with our Order must proceed with all haste."

At Master Rine's words, questions flooded Arderi and he was at a loss as to which to ask first. "What training, sir? What is the Tat'Sujen Order? Where am I? How did I get here?"

Each questions brought an added look of surprise to Master

Rine's face. "Do you know nothing, Brother Cor? I sense that you have bonded to Ka'gana, you must have some of these answers!"

"Nix, Master Rine. There was no time during the expedition into the Nektine. Master Rillion…he…"

Letting out a sigh, a weariness filled the man's eyes. "Aye. No time. You are here like a babe in swaddling cloth and it has already begun."

"What has begun, sir?"

Master Rine shook his head. "The Tat'Sujen Order has waited diligently for thousands of winters. We have waited, watched, and guided. We are the keepers of history. The only ones who know—well, we suspect the Elmorr'Antiens know, yet they share little with the rest of the races. A time will come when things will change. Power will flow into the hands of men and the Plane of Talic'Nauth will be ripped apart. The Tat'Sujen Order stands ready to see this does not happen."

"And you, Arderi Cor, are now apart of us, a brother of the Tat'Sujen. Your tasks will not be easy—your burdens not light. The first Mah'Sukai of this Cycle has been created by the Essence. We of the Tat'Sujen must see them dead—or die ourselves in the attempt."

A grim look settled on the man. "The War of Power has begun."

# Chapter 68

A warm breeze blew gently over his face carrying with it the fresh scent of maple. How he missed the scent of the maple trees that surrounded his home stead in the summer. The scent of maple, the smell of fresh tilled earth, the warm smile of his Ma, the firm clasp of his Papa on his shoulder—so reassuring. He missed them all. They had protected him, guided him, loved him.



Floating inside nothingness, he felt weightless. He let his mind reach out toward the rest of his body, yet he did not have the energy to open his eyes. The warm breeze softly tickled his face once more. He was at peace.

Over time, sensations crept back into his awareness. He felt the gentle caress of grass on the back of his neck, the weight of his body pressed onto the ground, a pebble resting uncomfortably under his right elbow, and the gentle waft of the breeze ruffling the hem of his collar, its thin material grazing against one cheek.

Opening his eyes, he looked up into a bright blue sky. He followed the lazy gait of a cloud crossing overhead. His eyes closed and he bound his mind to that cloud. Joining it. They drifted together through the heavens. He reveled in the feeling of gliding away, and slipped off into a dream of flight.

Alant Cor awoke with a shiver. A thin sheen of dew covered him, soaking through his robes. The dampness gave the slight wind a colder feel than it deserved. A hoot from a small copse of trees in the distance announced to all that an owl had recently acquired its supper. Sitting up, he gazed out over a field of half-grown wheat stalks. A full moon hung low in the sky casting a silvery glow over everything.

*Wheat? There are no wheat fields on Elmorr'eth.*

Scanning his surroundings, Alant recognized the low, grassy hills that spread out into the distance. The stars overhead twinkled down upon a scene he thought he would never again see. Turning around, a smile crept over his face and a joy filled him to the brim. The tears that welled in his eyes blurred the distant glow emanating over the walls of the Hild'alan stead.

*I am home! How?*

Threading his way between the short rows of wheat, he stepped out onto the gravel road he knew all too well. Standing in the middle of the road, he spun in a circle, unable to accept what he saw. The place looked as if nothing had changed. The gravel road, rutted with wagon tracks, lined with fields, the low fences of the stock pastures just down the way. It was as if he had never left.



"Oiy!"

Alant jumped, catching the hem of his robe under the heel of a slipper. He fell hard, gravel skinning his palms as he reached out to catch himself.

"Begging pardon Sier, I did not expect to see anyone out and on the road this late in the eve."

Looking up, Alant saw a large man, dressed in the boiled leather of a guarder, standing in the road a few paces from him. The guarder held a torch high over his head.

The man rushed over and held out a hand. "Here, Sier. Let me—By all Twelve Gods!" Horror filled the man's face and he backed away. Dropping his torch to the road, he pawed at the hilt of the shortsword hanging from his side. Steel rasped over leather and the guarder held the sword out in front of him with hands that shook like a tree in a windstorm. "Mercy! Have mercy on me!" Spinning, the man flung his sword onto the road and sped back toward the main gate of Hild'alan.

Alant regained his footing and stood staring after the man running away. Reaching up a hand, he felt across his features expecting to find some horrid deformity.

*It feels normal.*

Striding up to the man's discarded sword, Alant bent and retrieved the blade. Using the flat side like a mirror, Alant gasped. Staring back at him was his own reflection, one he had seen his entire life.

*Yet, those eyes! They are not mine!*

The eyes that looked back at him were horrifying to behold. His pupils had stretched, like those of a reptile. Around his new pupils, in a sea of liquid velvet, a deep shade of red covered everything.

*They glow! My eyes glow red!*

# Pronunciation Guide

Aalholm – [ale-holm]
Aktita – [ack-tea-ta]
Alant – [a-lawn-t]
Arderi Cor – [are-dare-ee core]
Aritian Cor – [a-rid-ee-an core]
Asgarthian – [ass-garth-ee-an]
Baroth Sarlimac – [ba-roth sar-li-mack]
Baylain – [bay-lane]
Bin'Satsu – [been-sat-sue]
Chandril'chi – shan-drill-chee]
Chandril'elian – [shan-drill-el-ee-in]
Chi'utlan – [chee-oot-lawn]
Clytus Rillion – [cl-i-tuss rill-ee-on]
Dasha'alan – [dah-sha-a-lawn]
Delmith – [dell-mith]
Elmorian – [el-more-ee-an]
Elmorr'Antien – [el-more-ant-ee-an]
Elmorr'eth – [el-more-eth]
Felstar Lysentoc – [fell-star lie-sin-toc]
Gaylain – [gay-lane]
Gralet'nar – [gray-let-nar]
Hath'oolan – [hath-oo-lawn]
Hek'kie – [heck-kie]
Hezmire – [hez-me-er]
Hon'nar – [hon-nar]
Jam'ees – [jawm-ee-z]
Jerith De'thane – [jer-ith du-thane]
Jintrill Deln – [gin-trill deln]
Julitans – [jewl-ee-tans]
Kasu'yama – [ka-sue-ya-ma]
Katsujai – [Cat-sue-jie]

Kithian – [kith-ee-an]
Klain – [klay-n]
Komar Isle – [co-mar]
Magistra – [ma-gis-tra]
Mah'Sukai – [maw-sue-kie]
Maja'Kasta – [ma-ja-cawst-ah]
Mocley – [mock-lee]
Mu'shadar – [moo-sha-dar]
Nektine Mountains – [neck-tine]
Nithshilo – [nith-shy-low]
Oolant – [oo-lant]
Orlis – [or-liss]
Palintium – [pa-lint-ee-um]
Ragnor De'haln – [rag-nore d-hal-n]
Ro'Arith – [row-are-ith]
Salintine – [sal-in-tine]
Sarshia Mocley – [sar-she-ah mock-lee]
Sar'Xanthia – [sar-zan-thia]
Shaith Ku'rin – [sh-aith coo-rin]
Sier – [see-er]
Silaway – [sill-a-way]
Silawaian – [sill-a-way-ee-in]
Sindian Rillion – [sin-d-an rill-ee-on]
Spectals – [speck-talls]
Tak'ju'nar – [tack-jew-nar]
Tarsith – [tar-sith]
Tat'Sujen – [tat-sue-jen]
Vanria – [van-ree-a]
Velvithia – [vel-vee-thia]
Wartin'alan – [war'tin'a'lawn]

# About the Author

Maxwell Alexander Drake – or Drake as is known to friends and fans alike – has been writing fantasy for over 28 years. An avid role-player and game-master, the fantasy genre has always held a special place in his heart.
Currently, he lives in Las Vegas with his wife and two sons.

Find out more about him on his official website, www.maxwellalexanderdrake.com.

Bin'Satsu
Katsujai
Silaway
The Great Ocean
Nithshilo
Aktita
Hath'oolan
N
The Isle of Elmorr'eth